BLOOD SONG

Tor Books by Cat Adams

Magic's Design

BLOOD SINGER
Blood Song

Tor Books by C. T. Adams and Cathy Clamp

TALES OF THE SAZI
Hunter's Moon
Moon's Web
Captive Moon
Howling Moon
Moon's Fury
Timeless Moon
Cold Moon Rising
Serpent Moon

THE THRALL
Touch of Evil
Touch of Madness
Touch of Darkness

CAT ADAMS

BLOOD
SONG

A Tom Doherty Associates Book New York

This is a work of fiction. All of the characters, organizations, and events portrayed in this novel are either products of the author's imagination or are used fictitiously.

BLOOD SONG

A Tor Book
Published by Tom Doherty Associates, LLC
175 Fifth Avenue
New York, NY 10010

www.tor-forge.com

Tor® is a registered trademark of Tom Doherty Associates, LLC.

ISBN 978-0-7653-2494-8

First Edition: June 2010

Printed in the United States of America

0 9 8 7 6 5 4 3 2 1

DEDICATION AND ACKNOWLEDGMENTS

First and always, we would like to thank Cathy's husband, Don, and Cie's son, James, for unstinting support and believing in us. Also to our wonderful agent, Merrilee Heifetz; her able assistant; our editor; and the throng of other folks who help bring a book from the idea stage to actual, written words on the page. Special thanks to our friends and family, and the other writers who offer understanding when we need it.

Cie would like to specifically thank her brother, Tim, whose inexhaustible knowledge of baseball helped more than we can say. Even though we didn't get to put much of what he told us on the page, it was necessary to know for setting the scene. Special thanks go out to the folks at McAnally's Pub on Jim Butcher's forum, and particularly Lord Nedd for the use of the fez. For the record, there are a couple of instances of homage to Jim Butcher in this book. In this case, imitation really is meant as the sincerest form of flattery, as we find his books to be brilliant.

Last, but not least, thanks to you, the readers, for coming along for the ride. We hope you enjoy reading these books as much as we enjoy writing them.

A NOTE TO READERS

First, in my (Cie's) opinion, for the most part happy families do not make for interesting reading. I don't know why. They do, however, make for happy writers. Every time a writer creates a character with a particularly troubled background (or a kinky sexual bent), it seems that somebody out in the "real world" assumes that the writer is working from personal experience. So allow me to state for the record that Celia Graves's background and troubles are all her own. They do not reflect any personal experience on the part of either of the authors. Thank God!

Part of the fun of writing is research. In order to make the fantasy portions more believable, you have to be very careful to get the "real" portions right. Still, inevitably, some glitches slip in. The setting of this book is Southern California. We created a fictional city of Santa Maria de Luna and slapped it down on the coast between San Juan Capistrano and Oceanside, right on top of Camp Pendleton, which obviously doesn't exist in this reality (our apologies to the U.S. Marines). Just as we created our own city, we came up with a university and rehab facility. But there are scenes that take place in Anaheim Stadium and other actual locations. While those portions of the book were researched heavily, it is possible that errors slipped in. If so, please forgive us.

In this reality, the kingdom of Ruslund is located in the western half of the Ukraine, a few miles to the west of Kiev. It was formed about the time of the Union of Lublin, with a splinter section allying itself with the Cossacks to form the new country with one of the nobles becoming king. The religion was Eastern Orthodox (which pleased the Cossacks), and the people resisted the Polish conversion to Catholicism that actually caused rifts in the Ukraine in our version of history.

—C. T. Adams and Cathy Clamp

FAN INFORMATION

Fans who wish to sign up for our newsletter can contact us at catadamsfans@gmail.com. Our website is located at http://www.catadams.net.

BLOOD SONG

1

I pulled the Miata to the curb and checked the address one more time. I stared at the building and the neighborhood. It wasn't what I'd expected. The interview I'd had with the prince's retainer had taken place in a conference room at one of the very best Los Angeles hotels. In fact, at this moment I knew that the press and several royal bodyguards were stationed at that same hotel. This place was nice, palatial even, but it was far enough off the beaten path that I'd had to use MapQuest to find it.

I shut off the engine and looked down at the file sitting on the passenger seat. I thought about looking at it again, but I'd practically memorized the contents already. Prince Rezza of Rusland was in the United States with his father's blessing, meeting with private defense contractors. Publicly the prince was being the very image of a religious conservative. Ruslund was a small kingdom in eastern Europe, nestled primarily between the Ukraine and Poland, touching on the Czech Republic as well.

Rusland might be small in size, but it was gaining a whole new level of prominence politically thanks to the discovery of a huge supply of natural gas in the region. The Russians were practically apoplectic. Their control over Europe's natural gas supply was critical to their economy. Having a competitor next door wasn't making them happy.

Despite their common ancestors, the Russians hadn't been happy with the Ruslunders since . . . well, ever. Still, the little country managed to stubbornly exist as a monarchy in the face of socialism, communism, and rampant capitalism. How they'd managed not to be overrun by Germany during World War II, or absorbed into the Soviet Union afterward, was one of those burning political questions that nobody either could or would answer.

Traditionally the public religion of Rusland was Orthodox, but a fundamentalist regime was gaining power and influence. It was the kind of political turmoil that makes you worry about assassination. The prince had very publicly declared his anti-American sentiments and allied himself with the zealots— who would not necessarily be pleased with his private plans while in L.A. Which was why an impostor was taking his place for the evening, freeing the real prince up to do whatever it was he had in mind. The retainer had been fairly coy, but the prince's upcoming marriage had been made very public. So I was guessing this was the equivalent of sowing the last of his wild oats. Besides, using a stand-in is a fairly common ploy when people like royals are trying to ditch the paparazzi. It's difficult and expensive to find someone good enough at magic to do a long-term illusion, but they exist, and there's always the old-fashioned "body double."

Whatever. I wasn't about to judge, especially not given Vicki's situation. My job is to keep the protectee safe. Celia Graves, personal security consultant. At one point or another I've served as a bodyguard for movie stars, politicians, authors, celebrities, and, now, royalty. I protect them from the press, overzealous fans, and, when necessary, the monsters. I'm good at what I do, so I charge quite a lot and stay in business by myself, for myself. I'm *not* particularly good at the political and social sides of the job: too blunt, too sarcastic, not inclined to suck up and play nice. The "attitude" has cost me jobs, so I try to work on it . . . and generally fail miserably.

I was getting ready to grab my jacket and climb out of the vehicle when I caught sight of the brightly patterned photo envelope sticking out from beneath the folder. I checked my watch. I was early. I could spare a minute or two to look at the pictures from my best friend's birthday party this afternoon.

I grabbed the envelope, pulled it open, and began flipping through the photos. The ones I'd taken weren't great. I'm no photographer. But the others, taken by one of the staff members at Vicki's insistence, were really nice. There were shots of Vicki blowing out her candles. There were flowers from Vicki's girl-friend, Alex, and a balloon bouquet in the background. One or two really good shots of the two of us, and even more of Vicki standing in front of the present I'd bought her.

Her face was absolutely alight with joy, and I couldn't help but smile in satisfaction. Unlike Christmas, or her last birthday, this time I'd actually managed to find the perfect gift. Vicki's a level-nine clairvoyant. She uses a mirror to focus her gift. I'd found an antique mirror, backed with real silver, and had it put under multiple protection spells until it was well nigh un-breakable. That way she could have it in her room at Birch-woods.

I sighed. Vicki had been at Birchwoods, a high-end "treatment" facility, for almost five years now. She could probably move home. Then again, maybe not. A clairvoyant of her power could actually change the future if she got out of control. Right now she was stable, but I didn't doubt that the shielding and protected atmosphere of Birchwoods helped her. So it didn't surprise me that she showed no desire to leave, even though I knew Alex wanted the two of them to live together.

It was none of my business. Vicki might be sweet and quiet, but she had a will of iron. She would do what she was going to do, and that was the end of it.

I was still smiling as I stuffed the photos back in the envelope and tossed it back behind the passenger seat. It wouldn't do to have anyone spot them accidentally. As far as the world is concerned, Vicki is *not* at Birchwoods. Like the prince I was about to meet, she has a body double. Hired by her wealthy parents, the fake Vicki plays on the Riviera, vacations in the Hamptons, and skis the Swiss Alps—none of which the real Vicki has ever had the luxury to do.

Just thinking about that took away my smile, which was fine. It was time to get down to business. I climbed from the vehicle, grabbing my blazer from the passenger seat. I slid it on. It took a minute of shifting things around to get everything balanced comfortably. Despite the fact that it was practically a walking armory, the jacket didn't bulge. The tailoring and illusion spells cost a small fortune, but I consider it worth every penny. Hidden discreetly beneath that jacket I had not only the holster with my Colt but also a pair of "One Shot" brand squirt guns filled with holy water, a stake, and a very special pair of knives. Oh, and a garrote. Mustn't forget the garrote, although honestly, I've never used it and couldn't imagine drawing it quickly enough for use in a crisis. I was also wearing an ankle holster with a little Derringer, but if things got desperate enough for me to draw that I was in deep shit. Still, when it comes to weapons, better too much than too little. Some of the older bats are damned hard to kill, and on my best day I wouldn't want to take on a werewolf or ghoul without backup.

I glanced down at my watch: ten fifteen. I wasn't due on shift until eleven. I still had plenty of time to use the nifty new gadget I'd picked up at my favorite weapons shop. I reached behind the front seat and pulled out a black box not much larger than the wallet I carried in my back pocket. The lid was hinged, like a jewelry case, with the store's logo embossed on it in red foil. Very classy. Considering the price, it should be. I'd actually thought twice about whether or not to get it. But if it worked as well as advertised, it would be worth the money.

I grinned. I'm such a geek. I love gadgets, and this one was sweet. I could hardly wait to take it for a test drive.

Flipping open the lid revealed what looked like a Matchbox car and a small remote. Made primarily of silver, the little car gleamed in the light of the street lamp overhead. I set the tiny vehicle onto the pavement at my feet, facing the building where the prince was staying. I took out the remote, then closed the box and slid it into my front pocket. Pressing a small green button on the remote, I said, "Perimeter check," as clearly as I could. The little vehicle zipped forward with astonishing speed. It stopped just inside the driveway of the building and turned sharply right. I followed on foot, watching in pleasure as, with a soft whirring noise, it traced the invisible magical barrier that surrounded the building, protecting those inside from preternatural creatures. I followed it over well-lit lawns, around to the one-lane service road that ran along the back of the building. Abruptly the little car stopped, emitting a sharp, high-pitched whistle. A light on the remote in my hand began flashing red.

I looked from the remote to the car and back again. "Well, hell. This can't be good." I rummaged in my pocket to withdraw the box, where there'd no doubt be the instruction manual that I should've read ahead of time but hadn't. Oops. It took a minute, but I finally managed to retrieve the instruction booklet and flip to the appropriate page.

When encountering a perimeter break the unit will issue a warning in the form of a whistle.

No kidding. I never would've guessed. But that didn't explain the light show.

The type of energy causing the break will be indicated by color on the transmitter unit. Green indicates the presence of ghouls or other necromantic magics; amber, werewolves; blue, vampires. A red flashing light indicates non-vampiric demonic energy. A continuous red light indicates a current presence.

"A *demon*?" I stared at the remote in my hands in disbelief, my hand shaking the tiniest bit. Yes, the demonic exists. So does the angelic. But it's not like I run into either of them every day. In fact, unless a person works for one of the militant religious orders, they probably will go their entire *life* without running into either the angelic or the demonic—other than vampires. Real demons are *rare*. Which is good. Particularly if you don't have the clearest conscience in the world. How bad a problem this was depended on whether we were looking at a half-demon spawn, an imp, or a lesser or greater demon.

But even flipping desperately through the directions, I didn't see any way of telling which it might be.

Crap. I mean, good news, the light was flashing. Bad news, it was red; I was dealing with a freaking demon of one level or another, and the barrier was down.

I needed to fix this. Fast. I'm neither a mage nor a true believer. About the only thing I had on me right now that would hurt anything demonic was the holy water in my One Shots. One Shot being both the brand and a literal description. For a vampire, it would burn like acid, I hoped buying me enough time to kill it with one of my other weapons. But this wasn't a simple bat. It had taken something big and bad to break through a standing magical barrier like this. If I wound up facing whatever it was, my little squirt gun would probably just piss it off.

Think, girl . . . think. You need the barrier back up, at least long enough to call in a mage or a warrior priest.

If there was enough residual magic left from before the break I *might* be able to get the barrier partway back up if I could reseal the break. It wouldn't be as strong, but it would be better than nothing. Of course, if I sealed the barrier I *might* be sealing the demon *in.*

I debated the pros and cons for a few seconds, and decided it was better to get the barrier up. If I sealed the demon in, we'd have it in a contained area when the priests arrived. If I sealed it *out,* more the better.

I slid remote and manual into my jacket pocket and drew out one of my two little plastic squirt guns. I really didn't want to use both. I might wind up needing one if the demon was still around. Ever so carefully, I drew out the refilling plug and began dribbling holy water in a delicate line. As every drop hit the ground, the little scanner moved forward, the headache-inducing whistle giving a little hiccup before restarting. Still, when the last drop fell and my little gun was dry, the gap snapped shut. I knew this because the little silver car went silent and shot along the reraised barrier, around the corner, and out of sight.

I jogged after it, across the asphalt and sprinkler-soaked grass, all the while keeping alert for anything out of the ordinary. My head was throbbing from the combined effects of stress and that ear-piercing whistle.

I would like to say I was surprised that no one came to a window or door to check out the racket. Sadly, I wasn't. Alarms mean trouble. People don't *like* trouble. On the whole, most of them will cower behind charmed thresholds or inside power circles, hoping and praying that whatever's out there will pass them by.

I came around the corner just a few feet from where I'd started, to find a blocky man dressed in the kind of nice clothes that wouldn't look out of place in the better clubs but would still hide the same kind of arsenal I was carrying. He stood on the perimeter, holding the probe in his hand, examining it with a rapt expression on his face.

I came to a skidding halt in the wet grass. "Johnson?" I stared in disbelief. It was Bob. It really was. Seeing him standing there made me feel better. Because Bob Johnson is an experienced professional. Hell, he's the man who'd convinced me to go into the business when I first got out of college. Everyone else had told me that a "vanilla" mortal with no magic or psychic abilities had no business fighting the monsters. Bob said that *no* human was a match for the monsters, talent or no, that the two things that were most important were brains and good equipment. I'm not stupid, and I'm willing to pay for top-of-the-line weaponry.

I met Bob when Vicki's grandfather hired him to work up the security for her estate. It had been the old man's "house-warming gift." I'd watched Bob set everything up. He'd been patient enough to explain the how and why of everything he did—let me follow him around for days. It was obvious he knew his stuff. With an almost unlimited budget to play with, he'd done one hell of a job. I'd been impressed at the time. I still was.

His plain features lit up with a delighted smile. He brushed a hand over shaggy hair the color of warm honey. "Celia Graves, as I live and breathe. Don't tell me you're here to guard the prince?"

I nodded my affirmative, and Bob's grin widened. "Is this yours?" He held out his hand to me. The little scanner looked almost impossibly tiny balanced in his huge palm.

"Yup. Just bought it this afternoon. Works like a champ."

"I heard. But why didn't you put it on stealth mode? What good is the deluxe model if you don't use all the bells?"

"There's a stealth mode?" *Yow!* I couldn't help but grin—nearly identical to the one Bob had on his face.

He snorted and rolled his eyes but proceeded to flip the little car over and show me a switch I hadn't noticed before. "So what was with the alarm?"

I told him about the break in the perimeter. His expression sobered instantly. He handed me my car without any fuss and said, "Show me."

I showed him. He didn't have a lot of magical talent—

almost none really. But that didn't keep him from squatting down and using what little he did have to test the area around my little "fix it" job.

He looked up at me, his expression serious. "This isn't going to hold up for more than a few minutes. We need to get upstairs, warn the client, and call in the cavalry."

"Agreed."

I let him take lead. Neither of us had a weapon drawn, but our jackets were open, our hands loose, so that we could react in a hurry if need be. We moved deliberately toward the side entrance, eyes scanning the area for any sign of trouble.

Nothing. Not a damned thing. It should've reassured me. Instead, I felt the tension in my shoulders tighten another notch. Why would a demon break a barrier and then just *leave*?

I turned to the side, providing cover as Bob took the wallet from his back pocket and pulled out a key card. I'd been provided a similar card when I'd been hired. From the corner of my eye I saw him slide the card through the black security box. A series of small lights flashed green. When the last one lit, I heard the lock on the door click open.

We stepped inside and the door swung shut, locks and spells closing behind us. I waited as he repeated the process with the service elevator.

I blinked, trying hard not to stare as I caught sight of him in the polished stainless-steel door. His whole body language had changed. He looked like *hell*. Oh, he was still clean, and the clothes were pressed. But there was this sense of *defeat* about him. You could almost smell it, like a cheap cologne. It showed in the slight slump of his broad shoulders, the hesitation in his movements that had never been there before. He

was pale—but then he'd been living on the East Coast. Probably hadn't had a lot of beach time. Still, there's pale and there's
pale. I hesitated, trying to think what to say, and couldn't come
up with a damned thing that wasn't prying. So I reached forward to hit the intercom button.

"Celia Graves." I pronounced each syllable of my name
clearly as I held down the button to the intercom speaker.

"Bob Johnson."

The two of us turned to face the security camera, giving
them a good look. I didn't bother to glance up at the monitor
mounted near the ceiling in the corner.

"So," he said, while we waited for someone to answer. "You're
looking good—really good. The business must be agreeing with
you."

It was my turn to snort. "Hardly, but thanks." I unconsciously
smoothed fingers against my ash-blond hair. The hair is shoulder length at the moment, longer than I like to keep it. I've had
enough business that I haven't had a chance to get it cut. If I
hadn't been wearing it pulled back it'd be driving me crazy.

"No, really. You're closing in on beautiful tonight."

That made me stare at him with an open mouth. I am *not*
beautiful. Oh, sure, I have pretty good bone structure, but my
features are too harsh to be considered traditionally pretty. At
five ten, I'm too tall for my body type, and my skin goes beyond
"creamy" to nearly goth pale. My last boyfriend described my
eyes as the gray of storm clouds with chips of ice. A fair enough
description, and certainly more poetic than I would have expected.

"I'd better not look beautiful. Seriously, Bob. That's not
good for business. Be honest. Is this outfit too . . . much?" I

looked down at my clothes and then looked up at his face. He finally understood what I was talking about and my question made him look at me critically. I was wearing mostly black, from the comfortable flats on my feet to my jeans and blazer. The only contrast was the deep burgundy of my blouse. Well, that and the garnet earrings I was wearing that matched it. I'd put on makeup, but it was minimal. I was, after all, here on business. I'd noticed that if I look too good, male clients get the wrong impression—start treating it as a date—and the other bodyguards don't take me seriously. Better to keep things simple and avoid misunderstandings.

He'd just opened his mouth to reply when a voice came through the speaker above. "You're early." The tone made it sound like we'd done a bad thing, but I heard the whir of machinery as the private elevator descended toward us from the penthouse.

"We came early to check the perimeter for threats. There was a problem." Bob did his best bored, professional voice. "We'll need to report it to the authorities."

I could've sworn I heard swearing in the instant before the intercom was cut off. It surprised me a little. One of the first things I'd learned as a bodyguard was that you don't let the protectee know you're upset. Concerned is okay. But you stay calm. Emotions just get in the way, so you bury them deep. Don't get me wrong, you still feel them, but they're under control and they *don't* show.

Which meant somebody upstairs wasn't a professional. Terrific. I just love working with amateurs. (And if you believe that, there's this bridge . . .)

I cast a meaningful look at Bob, and he rolled his eyes. We

stood in silence for a few seconds. In the end he was the one who spoke first.

"The outfit is fine. Not overdone. Sorry. I understand how compliments can be a double-edged sword." He paused. "So, how's Vicki?"

I shrugged off the compliment. He'd meant well, but . . . well, it does always worry me. "Still in the hospital. She seems to like it there." She did. I'd have felt trapped, but she liked the safety of it. "How's Vanessa?"

He flinched, and I saw a flash of pain in his eyes before he was able to hide it. "We're divorced." He closed his eyes for a second. When he opened them again, his face was a pleasant mask. "Back on the market again." He smiled, but I knew him well enough to know he didn't mean it. "She got everything except the clothes on my back and my weapons. That's the main reason I took this job. I didn't really like the look of the guy they sent to talk to me, but I needed the money."

"Speaking of weapons, what have you got on you?"

He held open his jacket to show me his main gun, a Glock Safe Action 9mm in a custom leather holster. Loops in the lining of his jacket held a pair of throwing knives. I knew they had high silver content, and could tell from the engraving that he'd sprung for the throwing accuracy spells. But that was it. Which was so not like him that I was actually taken aback. I tried to hide my surprise, but it must've shown, because he answered me, his voice gruff with embarrassment.

"I had to pawn some of my stuff to pay for the ticket out."

Well, shit. I really didn't know what to say in response to that, so I kept my mouth shut. It just seemed safer.

"Well? I showed you mine—" He made a gesture that was

more a demand than an invitation. Which was fair, I suppose. But I was almost embarrassed to show him. Steeling myself, I held open the jacket and watched his eyes widen as he took inventory of my armament. "Damn, girl! And it doesn't even show."

"Special tailoring and spells on the jacket," I admitted. "And I had the sleeves made wide enough that I could draw my knives." I did just that, pulling one with a smooth, easy draw. I held it out to him hilt first. Anybody else, I wouldn't have shown the knives. They were a gift from Vicki and are valuable as hell. The spell work on them is such that they rank as major magical artifacts. People have killed to get their hands on that sort of thing. For me, though, they were a major part of my kit, because a single scratch from the blade will kill pretty much any of the monsters. I never wanted to get close enough to have to use them, but I damned well wanted to have them . . . just in case.

Bob let out a long, low whistle as he ran his hands over the polished wood handle. I was guessing he was testing the spell work as well but couldn't be sure. "Damn, girl, you get the *best* toys."

"Gift from Vicki," I admitted.

He shook his head and passed the knife back with what was almost reverence. "Keep those out of sight if you can. Don't want to invite trouble."

I just nodded my assent and thought about the possibility of trouble. Something about this job was bugging me. (Other than the obvious demon thing.) It wasn't obvious, just a pebble in your shoe kind of thing. Bob had said he didn't like the guy who'd interviewed him. I couldn't say I disagreed. The guy

I'd talked to had been vague about details of the job to the point of being coy. I don't *like* coy. He'd answered my questions in ways that really didn't tell me much of anything. I'd come damned close to rejecting the job.

And then there was the fact that I suspected I might have been chosen just because I was a woman, to force Rezza into toeing his father's progressive line.

Don't get me wrong, there are cases when a woman is specifically needed—you get a female client, she needs someone who can check out the ladies' room without problems, go into dressing rooms. But that wasn't what this was supposed to be.

"I feel better knowing you're here." Bob admitted quietly.

"Back atcha, big guy."

The elevator bell rang. We stepped inside the elegantly appointed cabin. Pressing the button for the top floor, I turned to face the front as the doors whooshed smoothly closed. When they reopened I stepped into an expansive living space. One entire wall was a bank of windows, open to show a panoramic view of the city lights sparkling below.

Stupid. Unless those windows were bulletproof, I could see three perfect spots for a sniper's roost, and that was without really trying. I thought about the demon again. What if he was in the room with us already? I needed to figure out a way to check each person. I couldn't do it openly for fear of a violent reaction with possible hostages. But leaking a little holy water onto my palm and then shaking hands with everyone would just make it look like I had sweaty palms.

"You're early." The retainer repeated his earlier complaint. In photographs in my research file, he was always just a pace

behind the king, always with the same dour expression. I turned
to face him, keeping my expression neutral. He stepped away
from a group of men standing by the bar. His voice was disapproving. I'd thought that the photos just made him look cranky,
but they'd only captured the real him. I immediately felt sorry
for whoever his significant other might be.

Standing at about five nine, he was a little bit shorter than
me. I could tell he didn't like it. He was apparently used to looking down that beakish nose and glaring with those beady
black eyes until the person opposing him backed down. If
that's what he wanted, he'd picked the wrong girl. I wouldn't
start trouble. Certainly not with a client. But I wouldn't grovel
or toady, either. Wouldn't be much use as a bodyguard if I
did. I gave him the pleasant, not-quite-blank expression I re-
serve for difficult clients. He didn't seem to like that, either.
Sometimes, you just can't win. I held out my water-soaked
hand. He looked at it like it was a distasteful bug.

Crap. Now what?

I lowered my hand after a few awkward moments. There
would be other opportunities before we left. "I came in a little
ahead of time to check the perimeter, meet up with the other
guards, find out who's going to be in charge, and iron out the
details." I sounded polite, professional, without even a hint of
irritation or sarcasm. My gran would be so proud.

"*I* will be in charge."

The man who glided away from the bar spoke with a hint of
an accent and more than a hint of condescension. I recognized
him from his pictures. The prince was six two and slender, he
moved with a sleek grace that should have been effeminate but
wasn't. He was wearing gray dress slacks with a cream-colored

silk shirt that had enough buttons left open to expose a lightly muscled but hairless chest. His light brown curls were artfully mussed; his dark eyes narrowed with appraisal as he looked me over from head to foot. He kept his hands clasped behind his back.

"Ultimately, of course" — I gave a respectful nod — "but generally with a multiperson team, there's a coordinator the other guards report to. I was wondering who that was going to be."

He stopped, barely two inches away from me. I think he expected me to react. He was obviously used to women reacting sexually and men backing down. I didn't do either. I simply stood my ground, pleasant and impassive, waiting for him to respond. I was pretty sure I knew what he was going to say. But maybe I was wrong. Surely he wasn't *that* much of an idiot—

"*I* will be in charge," he repeated.

Apparently he *was* that much of an idiot. Oh joy. I cringed inwardly but kept my mouth shut, counting to ten so that I wouldn't say anything stupid. I could walk away from the job, but the money was damned good and the connections were better. Any small business grows by word-of-mouth referrals. Tick him off and I could be going hungry for a long time. But it was tempting. Because his stupidity could get me killed. On the other hand, Bob was here. He'd have my back—and I'd have his. Risking my life is part of what I get paid for. And, again, I was going to be getting an almost obscene amount of money for this.

I glanced across the room to where the rest of the security team was standing. I mean, I couldn't actually be the only person worried about this, the only one to notice the prince's

glassy, bloodshot eyes, could I? Surely *somebody* else was bothered by the situation?

Two of the guards stared past me as if I were beneath their
notice. I felt my jaw clench, and had to force myself not to
grind my teeth. I didn't know either of them, which surprised
me. I'm fairly well connected in the industry. I've worked with
most of the independents at one time or another, and most of
them have come to respect my abilities and treat me as an
equal. I'd have bet half of what I was making that they were
pissed because I was a woman. I've dealt with the prejudice
before. You'd think I'd be used to it.

You'd be wrong.

Bob's soft cough drew everyone's attention while I was shaking hands with the third guard. He was clean . . . or at least
human.

"We checked the perimeter. There was evidence it had
been broken by a demonic presence. Ms. Graves put together
a temporary patch, but we need to contact the authorities."

He said my name as if he'd never met me before tonight. I
might have said something, but he gave me a quelling look. He
was probably right. The prince didn't seem the type to appreciate socializing among the staff, and it wouldn't do to have the
other guards pissed at *him*, too.

The prince's eyes narrowed, and he gave me a long, assessing
look. "My people contacted the authorities while you were on
your way up." He turned to one of the nearest retainers, a short,
square man with blunt features and small dark eyes. "Jean Paul,
take Josef downstairs and deal with Ms. Graves's 'patch.'"

The two men hustled off, not looking particularly happy.
Then again, they didn't seem the sort to be happy about much

of anything. Maybe they were paid to be surly. In which case, Josef deserved a bonus.

Prince Rezza stared at me, trying to judge my reaction. I tried to keep it neutral but failed. His expression darkened. "It's being dealt with. Satisfied?" His tone was challenging.

Not really. I'd be more satisfied when some of the militant religious were on scene. But saying that would just piss him off more. So would forcibly touching him. It might even create an international incident. We'd already started off on the wrong foot, so I kept my mouth shut and gave a curt nod.

"Good."

2

The prince hadn't wanted to get entangled with the authorities. So we left before they arrived. I didn't like it. Since I was the one who'd discovered the breach, I was pretty sure they'd want to talk to me, not Jean Paul. But it was made very clear that arguing would cost me the job. So I settled for leaving a business card with my cell number in case they wanted to call, along with an offer to give a statement the next day.

So, with minimal delay we had started the prince's night on the town. Now, at 3:00 A.M., my shift was half-over. Thus far there had been no signs of assassins, demons, or really much of anything. Good. Even better, I'd managed to stay professional. That had been harder than I'd thought. The prince was impeccably bred, ridiculously wealthy scum. I hadn't quite been reduced to counting the minutes till I could be away from him, but I was coming close.

We were settled in at our fourth "strip club." I'd thought we'd reached the bottom of the barrel hours ago. I'd been overly optimistic. Apparently things can always get worse. Even the dim lighting couldn't disguise that the place was filthy. The "dancers" had a desperation about them, the kind of fear you could almost smell in the air. Their bodies were scrawny, except for one or two who'd invested in the kind of plastic surgery that made Dolly Parton's figure seem positively understated. None of them could afford even the cheapest beauty charms to enhance their looks magically, so all they had to work with was their own assets, and most of them had been living hard for too long. They looked rough.

The theme of this place had something to do with "pussycats." I was able to deduce this not only because of the sign out front but also because the dancers wore cat ear headbands. The headbands were nearly their entire costumes, along with G-strings and jewelry. The G-strings were a formality so that liquor could be served. Pay enough for one of the private rooms and they could disappear just like magic. Illegal as hell, of course, but I suppose that was the point. The prince was slumming, and he seemed to be working at finding the skankiest spots in the area. Doing a damned fine job of it, too.

Honestly, were I him, I'd be worried about catching something antibiotic-resistant. Of course he was too far gone to think of that sort of thing. He'd been imbibing various substances to excess since before I came on shift and was blasted out of his frigging mind. Woe to his people if he wound up their king.

I'd thought hiring me had been for publicity. But we hadn't gone anywhere he was likely to meet paparazzi. So maybe I actually had been hired on the strength of my reputation. Whatever. If the opportunity came up to work for him again, I'd be saying no.

Bob was the only other guard who showed me any kind of

respect. The other two just ignored me. I could live with that, so long as they did their jobs. Unfortunately, only one was. So, three of us stood alert for danger, ignoring what was going on behind us. Bob was to my right. Beyond him was the biggest, blackest man I'd ever seen, with skin like polished ebony. He was built like a refrigerator—an *oversized*, industrial-style refrigerator. Huge and square as he was, you would've expected him to be slow. Instead, he could move with the sudden grace of a hunting cat. I'd seen it when one of the bouncers made a wrong move. Blinding speed and utter ruthlessness.

I didn't know his name. We'd finish tonight's job and I'd never see him again. Wouldn't break my heart, either.

The fourth "guard" was practically useless. At the prince's demand he was taking pictures with an expensive digital camera. He was young, and green enough that he'd acceded to the prince's wishes. Stupid. If anything went wrong, he'd be shit out of luck. The rest of us insisted on actually doing our job. At least as well as we could under the circumstances.

An attorney once told me that my business contract had more restrictive clauses than some major motion picture deals. I told him I'd learned from past experience.

If His Royal *Highness* died of a self-induced overdose, I wasn't liable. If he caught AIDS, herpes, or anything else, I wasn't liable. I protected him from violence. Period. End of story. My own morals would probably require me to haul his ass to the hospital if his stupidity made it necessary, but I didn't expect it to happen. He could function even after some pretty unique drug cocktails, so he must have years of self-abuse under his belt.

I heard something behind the door to the main room.

Almost in a single movement the three of us turned to face the possible threat. Bob shifted his weight, his hand hovering near the butt of his weapon.

The manager of the club stepped through the door with a bouncer at his heels. They came through at warp speed, slamming the door behind them with a level of controlled panic that made my neck hairs rise. The manager was a small man but tough looking. He had tiny, shrewd eyes and a sharp nose. But by far the most notable thing about him was his scars. A group of them ran from a mangled left ear down to and across his neck. It looked as if someone had tried to slit his throat with a beer bottle or claws.

He slid home the bolts and turned to face us. He didn't look alarmed or afraid, more *pissed*. At his nod the bouncer crossed the room to a second door and started to use keys on a number of locks. I assumed the door led outside.

"The cops are out front." The manager sounded disgusted. "It's a raid. You've got to get out of here."

A couple of the girls shrieked and I saw the flash of naked flesh in my peripheral vision as they scurried out from the pile of bodies to start dragging on the nearest discarded undies.

"I have diplomatic immunity." The prince's words were slurred, but there was no mistaking his condescending tone.

It occurred to me that the purpose of having a double had been to give the prince discretion—discretion that would be ruined if he got caught, immunity or no, but maybe he was just too stoned/drunk to care.

The manager was unimpressed. "Well, I don't, asshole. And I don't need the kind of media attention that will come with you being caught here," he snarled, "so get the fuck out." He pointed at the door. The bouncer opened it on cue. A dim beam of yellow light overhead revealed a narrow, filthy alley. A strong wind blew through the door, hard and cold. The stench it brought with it was horrific, even at this distance.

His Highness shrugged and seemed bored, as though this was a frequent occurrence. "Oh, very well." I saw him pulling together his clothing with uncoordinated movements. His eyes were unfocused, but his speech wasn't too bad. "You, and you—" He waved in the general direction of Bob and me. "Take the lead. We'll follow."

Someone had to take point. I would've done it, but Bob moved into place ahead of me. He brushed past the bouncer, deliberately giving the larger man a little shove on the way. The bouncer growled but didn't start anything. Probably a smart move, as Bob had pulled and worked the slide on his nine and was holding it with the kind of confidence that didn't bode well for anyone who posed a threat.

I moved two steps behind Bob. I'd pulled my gun as well, a 1911 Colt. There are other 1911s, but they're clones. The Colt is the classic design that was military issue in WW I and is hard to improve on. Other people have argued with me about modifying the barrel, but I like it just the way it is. It's my favorite gun, and completely reliable. It fits my hand well and has plenty of stopping power. If I shoot something, I want it to *stay* down long enough for me to stake or behead it. With that in mind, I keep my gun loaded with silver-plated bullets.

There were three steps leading down from the back door. To the immediate left was a Dumpster. Up close, it stank badly enough to make me want to vomit. In the background I could hear the manager's swearing and the prince's laconic response.

The only light was from the doorway behind us and the distant glow of a halogen streetlight past the alley entrance some twenty yards away. The odd lighting made the shadows deeper, so that every recessed doorway seemed sinister, every Dumpster perfect cover. I kept my eyes moving, scanning not only ground level but also the metal fire escape ladders and the tops of the flat-roofed buildings. The door we'd come out of was the fourth down in the row of buildings, giving us about twenty yards to traverse to the main street if we went right, almost a hundred yards if we turned left.

I stared down the alley, catching a glimpse of the front of the building reflected in the porn shop window display across the street. I didn't see flashing lights reflected in the glass or any sign of a police cruiser. Before I could piece together what that might mean, a sound made me turn.

A rat skittered. It was bigger than some of the more fashionable dogs, and had been startled by something. I didn't fire, but it distracted me, costing me a valuable second of concentration.

As I turned back there was a wet, tearing sound . . . then a grunt of pain. A shot rang out as a warm rain splattered my face and I smelled raw meat and fresh blood. Just that fast, Bob was down. I fired into the eye of his attacker that was visible above the throat where he was feeding. The entry wound was deceptively small, but blood, brain, and bone splattered against the wall behind him, sliding in runnels down the rough surface of the brick. The vampire dropped Bob, lunging for me with (literally) mindless rage. I fired two more shots directly into his chest until he went down for good and I was sure there wouldn't be enough heart left to stake.

"We've got bats!" I could barely hear my own voice shout the warning to the other guards as I turned on instinct to fire at a shape moving at me with blurring speed from beside a Dumpster. The vampire shrieked but kept coming, swinging a clawed hand at my head. I ducked the blow and waited for that split second when the momentum would swing his body around, then fired a pair of shots through the back at an angle intended to take out the heart.

He fell, like a puppet whose strings had been cut. I fired into his head. My last shot in the Colt.

My hearing was almost completely gone now, too much gunfire echoing off the metal of the Dumpsters and fire doors, but if there were more vamps, they were holding off. I called for the others to cover me, holstered the Colt, and grabbed Bob's body under the armpits. I started dragging him backward toward the light still coming from the door to the strip club. He was hurt badly enough that he was going to die in minutes without help. A pair of dark shapes were closing in from either end of the alley, moving with that eerie grace some of the older vampires have.

I was almost to the base of the stairs. Bob's body wasn't moving, but blood was still pumping, leaving a wet trail in our wake that was dark and all too visible as I backed into the light.

I risked a glance backward. There was a scuffle going on inside the door. I couldn't see the young bodyguard, but I caught a glimpse of the prince. As I watched, the royal body began to shimmer, features moving as if made of badly molded clay until another man stood where the prince had been. He and the manager were firing steadily into the doorway where the refrigerator was still upright, despite the explosions of flesh and blood from his back.

Time slowed to a crawl. I had all the time in the world to watch the huge black man fall backward in slow motion off the stairs to slam into the Dumpster. As his body bounced life-lessly to the floor of the alley, the fire door swung solidly closed with an echoing clang.

With the disappearance of the light and my escape route, the vamps grew bolder, two of them moving forward as a third dropped from the fire escape of a nearby building, landing soft and silent as a snowflake.

Fuck a duck.

There was no time for a stake, my remaining squirt gun was *literally* a one-shot, and my backup gun was a Derringer. Two shots. None of it was going to do me a damned bit of good against these numbers. Then Bob shifted, struggling against my attempt to keep him still. He grunted in pain from the effort, and while he couldn't talk, the movement showed me he had a backup gun he hadn't shown me earlier.

Bless you, Bob.

I set him onto the ground and drew his weapon. Stepping back, I settled into a shooting stance, my back against the fire door.

The vampires were moving in slowly. I didn't think it was from caution, although they knew what silver bullets can do. It was more to savor the moment, revel in the scent of my fear. Because in the end, even the toughest human is afraid of the monsters.

I fired, and the loads in his gun were hot enough that the

textured grip tore at the skin on my palm. Instead of a clean shot to the heart, the barrel pulled up and right, so that the bullet sliced through the vampire's neck. It took out his spine, and blood sprayed in a fountain from the severed arteries.

Too many deaths in too small a space. The smell of blood and meat filled the alley, overwhelming even the stench of rotting garbage.

It hadn't been intentional, but it was at least graphic enough to stop the other bats in their tracks for a second. I kept firing, adjusting for the pull from the loads, trying for heart shots in the hope of breaking the pack or at least slowing them down.

It didn't work. The tallest, a lanky male with red hair and freckles who looked like Opie, bared fangs. Apparently he was one of the leaders. One look from him and they moved, circling like a pack of animals on the hunt. He hissed, baring fangs at me a second time. It was an inhuman sound. Every hair on my body stood at attention. My pulse thundered in my ears. But I held my ground and fired again.

The first shot missed. He'd moved fast: too damned fast, launching himself at me with everything he had. I kept firing, even as his body slammed into mine, driving me into the door behind me with a force that drove the air from my lungs and fractured ribs. My head slammed into the heavy steel hard enough that for just a second I saw stars. The gun fell from my hand, but at least he was done. I'd taken his heart. Hell, I'd taken most of his damned *chest*. I was soaked with blood. I struggled to move, but I was pinned by the mass of his lifeless body. The others used that to their advantage. The ones who hadn't stopped to feast on Bob and the other guard closed in on me. There was no more time. I twisted and ducked, managing to break loose long enough to pull one of my knives from its wrist sheath. I slashed at random, cutting at anything and everything that came into range—praying all the while that the magic in the razor-sharp blades would work as advertised but knowing that the first time I used them would probably be the last.

As the vampires closed in and I went down in a flash of intense pain, I heard a scream and realized it was my own voice.

Dying was going to suck.

3

Voices floated over me from a distance. I could hear them, knew I should recognize them, but I couldn't make my eyes open, let alone focus my mind. Too much pain, from too many sources. I couldn't feel parts of my body that I knew I *should* be able to, and other parts that normally stayed in the background were front and center.

"We need to get her to the hospital." A woman's voice. I knew that voice. Dammit, who *was* she?

"No! They'd just stake her and take off her head." A man.

"Maybe they should." Cold, rational. A thought I'd have if I could think straight.

"She's not a bat. She's not going to *be* a bat." Such determination. He sounded positive and that made my cheeks feel warm. Or maybe it was just that everything else felt so cold.

A pause, and then a skeptical tone to her words. "You don't know that."

"Yeah, I do. I can tell."

"Because she's your *Vaso*?" Now the woman's voice practically dripped venom. Whoever she was, she didn't like me, that was for damned sure.

"I keep telling you. She's *not* my Vaso." The man's voice was growing desperate. "Look, I know somebody who can help her. Take her back to the lab. I'll make some calls."

I felt my body being lifted, and coherent thought was swallowed in a dark wave.

4

I **rose** to consciousness slowly, like floating back to the top of a deep pool filled with cold black water.

What the hell? What's happening to me?

I knew who I was. But I had no idea where I was or how I'd gotten there. The last thing I remembered clearly was wrestling the mirror I'd bought for Vicki's birthday into the Miata and heading for Birchwoods. The mirror hadn't wanted to fit. In fact, it'd been enough of a problem that I'd been seriously glad of the protection charms I'd had put onto it.

There had been no danger, no threat. It made no sense for me to have been unconscious.

Sounds and smells that were starting to filter through the fog in my brain: The whir and beeping of medical equipment I understood, but stale pizza, french fries, and Chopin's *Nocturnes?*

It took more will than was pretty to force my eyes open, but I managed.

I wasn't in the hospital. I was on a slab in a lab. A very familiar lab, as it turned out. I recognized the gleaming wall tiles with flecks of gold and black and the acoustical ceiling towering forty feet above my head. I'd stared at those tiles and that recessed lighting many times before, soaking in the words of one professor or another. While I couldn't actually see them, I knew that there were seats set up in an auditorium-style semicircle, with wide concrete steps leading up to the higher rows. Painted metal pipe bent so as not to have any sharp edges served as the handrails up the steps. They were painted glossy black to match the rubberized strips that served as trim and skid stops on the stairs themselves. This was the room where Warren Landingham gave his lectures on controlling zombies and ghouls.

It seemed a little strange that while I wasn't a zombie or ghoul, I'd been strapped onto the slab and put in restraints.

Oh, *shit*. I don't like restraints. I have *never* liked restraints. I have my reasons—reasons that I won't go into with anyone ever again if I have my say. Those memories were magically blunted, not erased, and I felt an instant wave of pure, high-octane terror.

I closed my eyes and forced myself to take slow, deep breaths the way I'd been taught. It helped a little. *I can do this. I'm alive. This isn't the past. This is now. I'm not in too much pain, which means I'm not in bad shape*. When I opened my eyes I wasn't calm, but I had managed to beat back the panic for the moment.

There were tubes running from my arm to the medical machinery clicking and beeping to my right. But I felt *fine*.

So why restraints? And why no injuries? I felt my stomach tighten as another wave of panic prepared to hit.

I let myself be distracted by the click of heels on linoleum just outside of my vision. The footsteps were louder than usual, but I recognized the rhythm of the footfalls. Emma Landingham. As ever, she was the personification of brisk efficiency. Her clothes didn't wrinkle or her hose run. Ever. They simply didn't dare, any more than her honey-colored hair would ever hope to escape from the tight confines of its bun. I vaguely re-membered hearing voices. Had one of them been Emma? I wasn't sure. But it would make sense.

"What's up?" I tried to speak. The croak I managed wasn't even close to coherent. I cleared my throat and tried again. "Emma, what's going on?"

She turned with a swift movement that was the essence of en-ergy contained. I've never seen anyone alive or dead move like that who wasn't a gymnast. No surprise there. She'd been one. Emma wasn't graceful but was capable of explosive movements: power, energy. And she was beautiful: petite golden blond per-fection, as opposed to Vicki's tall, dark elegance and Dawna's exotic beauty. I was definitely the duckling in our crowd.

"Who are you?" Emma snapped the question out sharply without even bothering to look up from the readout she was scanning. Gee, glad to see she was worried about me.

"Celia Graves." The "s" sound in "Celia" sounded . . . wrong, different from usual. It took me a second to realize why. I had acquired the barest touch of a lisp. I'd never had a speech impediment. I didn't even have an accent. Pure plain American English without any telltale anything. Not even the highly mocked but reasonably accurate "Valley girl" dialect.

I tried to lick my lips and found . . . fangs. *Oh shit, oh shit, oh shit, oh shit—*

The words ran through my brain over and over. I found my-self gulping in air and had to close my eyes and forced myself to go back to the breathing exercises. When I'd reached the point where I thought I could speak normally, I tried again. "What the *fuck* is going on, Emma?" I tried to sound tough. Pure bravado.

Fear produces biological reactions. Fight or flight. Neither was a viable option right now, but I wasn't going to convince my nervous system of that. Adrenaline rushed through my veins, clearing away the last of the cobwebs. My body tensed, poised for action. The metal restraints groaned in response. *The metal . . . groaned?* These restraints were built to withstand a raging zombie without strain. That simple sound implied a level of strength that sent another wave of panic coursing like ice water through my veins. A normal human couldn't put enough pressure against the restraints to do that. Which meant I wasn't human anymore.

"Tell me about your family."

She was testing me, making sure I had memories. Smart girl. If I had fangs I'd not only been bit by a bat, I'd also been at least partially changed. Which made no sense. Vampires generally just bite you and leave you. You either get treated and live, or you die. Once in a very great while a master vamp will do the whole bite and spell thing to bring someone over, but it's a rare bat with the power to do it. So, if I was a vampire, I should be feral and have no memories. But if I was human, I shouldn't have the fangs and superstrength.

Shit. How I answered would be incredibly important, not only to Emma but also to the authorities. If I was tied down, it was because someone was on the way—someone with an extermination kit. The sooner I proved to Emma I was still me, the sooner I could get the damned restraints released. So, calmly as I could manage, I stated the basics.

"I'm the only surviving daughter of Lana and Charles Graves. My sister Ivy died when she was just a kid. My mother . . ." I paused, not sure what to say about my mother that didn't sound seriously awful. She's a drunk with the moral sensibilities of a cat in heat? She'll do anything for a buck? I settled for, "My mother and I don't get along, and my father left us. We don't talk about him." There, that was diplomatic enough that even my gran couldn't object. "My grandmother is still alive. I love her, but she enables my mom and keeps trying to turn me into a true believer."

"Let her loose." The male voice came from inside the room but out of my line of vision. I didn't know who it was, but it wasn't "El Jefe"—Warren Landingham, Emma's father—or Kevin, Emma's brother. Come to think on it, nobody I knew had a voice like that. *If Warren isn't giving the orders, who is? And why?* Warren wouldn't defer to anybody willingly. Certainly not in his own territory, and not about *me*.

"My father—," Emma began to protest.

"Your *father* is still at his conference in Chicago. Your *brother* brought me into this as the best hope Ms. Graves has to survive with her sanity intact. If you don't care to follow my directions, however, I'll be glad to leave you on your own."

I could actually hear her teeth grinding. Emma doesn't take orders any better than Warren does, and she has considerably less of a sense of humor.

"It's daylight. It could hurt her," she argued.

The man's voice was smug. "Her waking early could mean that she is more human than vampire. Or it could mean that there will still be a stronger connection to her attempted sire. They will both have a *compulsion* to find each other. If so, it will give us a better chance of hunting him down before he finds Ms. Graves and either kills her or finishes bringing her over."

I didn't like either of those options, but the man was right.

I twisted to the right and strained my neck to get a look at the owner of the voice, but he'd moved away again. Frustrating.

"You'd best hurry, Ms. Landingham." The bastard's voice had a hint of amusement. "You'll want to be finished before your brother gets back."

"My brother would never hurt me." Emma spoke with cold certainty. And well she should. Kevin adored his baby sister. There was no way in hell he'd ever do anything to put her at risk.

"Are you sure? Werewolves can be so . . . unpredictable. Especially at the full moon." He sounded so sure, so reasonable. Probably exactly the same tone the snake had used with Eve when talking about that pesky apple.

"What an assssss." I muttered the words under my breath, but Emma heard. She glanced at me, and a flicker of something close to understanding cut through her rage. The main reason we've never been close is the fact that I am so very irreverent and rebellious: "stuck at thirteen developmentally." She hates that Warren and Kevin care so much about me. Now, probably for the first time, the poster child for repression was taking a hike in my shoes. Flying by the seat of her pants in a dangerous situation wasn't making her any cheerier than I usually am.

She hit the button to release the restraints. They made a screeching sound that made my ears hurt and halted about halfway down, apparently disliking the shape I'd bent them into. Normally they slid smoothly into the surface of the lab table. Dammit. El Jefe was probably going to make me pay for the repairs.

I sat up and tried to figure out how to remove all of the various electrodes and tubes. It takes a certain finesse to remove medical equipment without damaging either your body or the equipment. I'd heal, but if I ruined any more of Warren's stuff he'd be seriously pissed.

I turned and looked at the stranger. He met my gaze without flinching. Nor did his eyes wander, not even to the tattoo. I have a vine of ivy tattooed onto my left leg, winding around my calf and up my thigh. It's beautifully done and very eye-catching. People always comment on it when I wear shorts or a skirt. But he didn't say a word. My body was just that . . . a body.

He looked at me with cool appraisal, watching in amusement as I took his measure in return. He wasn't handsome, or ugly, or truly much of anything. You could look at him closely and five minutes later you'd have forgotten him. Pleasant features, hazel eyes, hair that color that hovers between blond and brown—cut so that it was neither short nor long. His charcoal-colored suit was the kind of mid-price off-the-rack but not cheap suit that your average businessman would wear. My guess was that he either was currently with or had once worked for a three-letter agency of one sort or another and would be introducing himself as "Mr. Smith."

The only thing that wasn't studiously ordinary about him

was the scars that peeked out from beneath his starched white collar. You had to look very closely to see them, but they were there.

"Hello, Ms. Graves. I'm John Jones."

Not "Smith," but close enough.

He extended his hand to shake. When I took it I got a jolt of psychic power that brought an involuntary gasp from my lips and a faint smile to his.

I could see in his eyes. He'd done it deliberately. He was testing me. I didn't like it, didn't like him. But I'd be careful. Because Mr. Jones wasn't just dangerous, he was deadly. I wasn't sure I wanted him on my side—but I sure as hell didn't want him working against me.

And Kevin knows him well enough to call in a favor. I'd always wondered about Kevin's past. Werewolves live several decades longer than humans. I didn't know exactly how old he was, just that he was the product of Warren's misspent youth and had decided to go to college later than most, so that he and Emma were just a grade apart. But he'd been around a while, because Warren is well past tenure. But Kevin doesn't talk about the past. Ever. I made the mistake of asking . . . once. I'm not stupid enough to repeat that error. Of course that didn't keep me from being curious as hell. But Kevin's my friend and Warren's son. I won't snoop. Still, based on Jones it appeared that Kevin might have lived an even more colorful life than I'd given him credit for in my wilder imaginings.

I glanced around the room, feeling suddenly very awkward. Clothes may not make the woman, but running around naked generally puts you at a disadvantage. You have to be very secure in your body to be nude in a group of fully dressed people and carry it off. I'm no prude, but I'm not that secure. So I was very glad when Emma pulled one of my duffel bags out of the lab's storage closet. Everything I needed was in there, neatly packed. And lying on top was something I didn't need but absolutely wanted—the holsters with my guns and the polished wooden case that held my knives when they weren't in use. A holsterless but cleaned and polished 9mm sat on top of my wallet and a stack of neatly folded clothes. It wasn't my gun, so why was it with my stuff? I felt a stab of something that wasn't quite a memory as I ran a finger over the grip. I tried to force it, but the more I tried to remember specifics, the further it slipped away from me.

Frustrating.

Growling under my breath, I shoved the gun aside and turned my attention to the knife case. I flipped open the lid and there they were, all cleaned, shiny, and oiled. The thorough care smacked of Kevin's work, but he couldn't have touched the blades. They're magical, and they were created specifically to kill monsters. Still, whoever had cleaned them had done a fine job.

"You sssstill haven't told me what's wrong with me." I kept my voice neutral as I asked Emma the question. But it was Jones who answered.

"You are an abomination."

"*Excusssse* me?" I raised my brows, my voice bordering on insulted. He laughed. From the expression on his face, it took him by surprise.

"I take it you don't laugh much."

"Not really, no," he admitted. The humor was gone as though wiped from a slate. He was talking directly to me, as if Emma weren't even there, but that didn't seem to bother her. I would've been pissed. "'Abomination' is the term used by the vampires for that small group of persons who *should* have died, or been turned, but instead survived with only partial physiological changes. They live, they have a soul and possess their own memories, but have been altered significantly. Each person's physiology changes differently. We're still determining that with you."

"I ssssee." I did. I didn't *like* it, but I definitely saw where he was going. I was now in possession of more strength than the average bear, a lisp, and a pair of really impressive fangs. What else had changed? Would I be able to go out in daylight? Could I eat real food, or had I developed a taste for blood? God, I hoped not. Even thinking about it was just *so* gross. "So you're going to follow me around and watch me? See what I do and what makes me tick? Is that a good idea?" I'd imagine that was a pretty dangerous way to operate.

He shrugged. "When we've worked with abominations in the past, we normally kept them under for a full month to weaken the tie to their sire."

I didn't ask who "we" were. I had a strong suspicion but didn't really want to know. Nor did I think he'd tell me. Or maybe he would. Which might be worse.

"Did it work, and if so, why am I awake?" Or had it *been* a month? I probably should ask what month and year it was. "How long have I been here, anyway?" I pulled on a pair of elegant powder blue lace panties and matching bra, then promptly covered them up with a serviceable navy sweat suit. I used a covered rubber band to pull my hair into a ponytail at the back of my head. It felt about the same length as it had this morning. Or whenever. I reminded myself, yet again, to find time for a haircut. Of course, it occurred to me that my hair might not grow back . . . ever. Man, I'd better find a *really* good stylist if it was going to wind up my last haircut.

"You've been here about six hours. It's around ten A.M. And a month didn't work perfectly. No."

He didn't elaborate, and his tone was absolutely neutral. Too neutral. Sometimes the absence of something tells me more than its presence. My guess would be that the mission he'd been referring to went very bad, very quickly. It might even be the source of the scarring on his neck. Or not. I wouldn't ask. It was rude. Yes, since I apparently *was* an abomination I should probably find out as much as I could; and I would . . . eventually. But right now I needed to find out what had happened in the hours I'd lost. Because I hadn't just lost six hours. The last I remembered was getting ready to visit Vicki.

"Can you sense your sire?" Jones's words brought me back to the situation at hand.

I thought about it. Nothing. There was no sorrow or rage or even happiness connected to the lack of a connection. Just bland neutralness. "No. Is there a trick to doing it?"

"No. Generally the connection's just there." He seemed genuinely puzzled and not particularly pleased.

"That's not terribly helpful, you know," Emma said coldly. She wasn't looking at him as she said it. Instead, she was very carefully cleaning and putting away every bit of equipment they'd used. In moments there would be no trace of my having been here at all. Except, of course, for the video camera.

"Make sure they keep the film of my being brought in."

"Why?" Emma sounded surprised.

I wanted to look at it, to see if the video prompted any memories. But that's not what I said. "The police may want proof that I didn't leave the crime scene under my own steam."

"No police." Jones sounded as though he were scolding a particularly dim-witted child.

"Look, it's fairly obvious I was attacked, and I wouldn't have gone down without at least a few shots having been fired. That gun on top isn't even mine, so weapons were used. The police have ballistics on most of my weapons from a couple of previous incidents. They're going to match up the pieces when they start digging through the scene. They know what I do for a living, so it isn't usually an issue. It isn't a crime to kill a vampire, but people are generally supposed to report that sort of thing."

Jones shrugged. "Ah. A good, law-abiding citizen." There was a hint of condescending amusement.

To my surprise, his tone didn't irritate me. Probably because he was trying too hard. I do have a short fuse, but I don't like playing into people's expectations. So I smiled and spoke sweetly. "It makes life easier. I like easy."

Emma gave me an odd look. She knows me well enough to have expected me to put up more of a fight. I saw her open her mouth as if to speak, then close it, compressing her lips tightly.

I looked from one of them to the other. "Here's what I

propose. I call the police, arrange to come in and make my statement." Not that I could say much, with no memories of whatever had happened. But I might be able to *get* some information. They might even do a memory enhancement for me. Or not. That sort of thing was only used as a last resort— too traumatic to the witness. Besides, the courts were split on whether or not the evidence obtained that way could be used because of proven cases of mental manipulation. Still, worth a shot.

"After that I go to Vicki, see what she knows, maybe see if she can help me track my sire's daytime hidey-hole. If that doesn't work, we go back to wherever you found me and see if we can find any clues." If my sire was going to be stalking me with death or undeath in mind, I wanted to get the jump on him. Preferably in full daylight with as much specialized weaponry as I could carry. I've fought vamps. I've killed them. But mostly they've been babies, new to the game. Vampires that are old enough to actually bring humans over are good. Scary good. They've got strength, magic, mind games, the works. I was going to need every advantage I could get to get close enough to kill the bastard, before he killed me. Vicki has a better than 99 percent accuracy rate. Odds are she either knew what was going on or could find out. And it certainly wouldn't hurt to try.

Emma nodded, which I expected since she knows Vicki nearly as well as I do. But I hadn't expected Jones to speak.

"I'd recommend that. But I'd suggest you see Vicki first. The police are open twenty-four/seven. Birchwoods isn't." *That* was interesting. How did Jones know about Vicki? While it was possible Emma or Kevin had told him, it didn't seem likely.

No, I was betting that Jones had found out the information on his own. If so, he'd been researching all of us. Maybe he'd done it after Kevin had called him. But I doubted it. He'd have had to work fast and be amazingly good. Because Birchwoods takes confidentiality very, *very* seriously. If a starlet or executive wants sympathy, they check into one of the other rehab facilities. If they want secrecy to the grave and beyond, they choose Birchwoods. It's pricey as hell, but for folks who value their privacy Birchwoods is worth every penny. And there was no way Vicki's parents would leak she was there. It would be too damaging to their lily-white reputations. Hell, they're so worried about their image that they hire a double to impersonate her for the press. So how had Jones known?

I turned toward him, my expression studiously blank. "Are you in this for the duration?"

He shrugged. "I owe Kevin Landingham a significant favor. Helping you will repay that."

"Fair enough."

I turned, giving Emma a long, hard look. What I was about to do was virtually guaranteed to annoy her, but it was necessary. If she came along, she'd get in the way. Besides, I didn't want to wait for Kevin, but I wanted him riding shotgun as soon as possible. Call me paranoid, but I didn't trust Jones with my back. I just didn't know him well enough. "When your brother gets back—"

"I'm going with you—," she interrupted, but I kept talking over her.

"—tell him where we're headed so that he can catch up."

"We can leave him a note. I'm going with you. I am *not* sitting here and waiting like a good little girl." She wasn't shouting, wasn't hysterical. In fact, there was a level of cold, hard determination I'd never seen in her before. It made no sense. Why now of all times, and about this?

"Em—"

"I'm *not.*"

"You're not what?" We turned in unison at the sound of Kevin's voice.

He stood outlined in the doorway, looking better than any man had a right to. My heart sped up at the sight of him. At the moment, his sandy blond hair was just a little long, so that it fell in front of eyes the color of a perfect summer sky. His T-shirt and jeans were faded and worn, and just tight enough to show off a body to die for. I never managed to look at him without my body reacting. It's not just his looks, either. He's the whole package, brains, body, *and* a sense of humor. His strong jaw is softened by the deepest dimples. He has a smile that could make the clothes melt right off my body. I've wanted him from the minute I first laid eyes on him. I wouldn't have done anything about it when I was with Bruno, but that's been over for a long time now. But Kevin's with Amy. I don't know if she's a werewolf or not, but it doesn't matter. I have ethics. Besides, that woman is scary.

"What are you doing up?" The words were directed at me. The *look,* however, was for Jones first, then Emma.

"I did it," Jones said. He gave Kevin a broad smile that didn't reach his eyes. "It's necessary. We have to find her sire. Doing so in daylight, when he's helpless, would be preferable, don't you think?"

"Not if it kills Celia in the process." Kevin snarled.

The smile grew, and Jones's eyes started to twinkle. "Well, you're in luck. She's not dead."

I let out a very unladylike snort of laughter. I couldn't help it. I'm a sucker for sarcasm. Besides, he was right.

All three of them turned to glare at me. I not only didn't wither, I didn't even flinch. Bully for me. I held up a placating hand. "There's no point in arguing. I'm up. No harm done. And I've got work to do."

Kevin's expression grew stubborn. He crossed his arms over his chest, his stance balanced and solid. "Tell me what you remember."

Shit. He would ask that. "Not a damned thing."

"The fourteenth," he said with significance. Should that mean something? I already knew I'd lost a full day.

Well, crap. Yesterday had been Vicki's birthday. I'd gotten ready to go, but had I even visited her? I didn't remember it. She'd be upset that I was injured. But she'd be hurt if I forgot her birthday. And I wanted her to have her gift. I mean, that present had taken *months* to find and get the spells worked. But she wouldn't know that if I hadn't made it out there to give it to her.

Kevin stared at me for a long moment, as though he were reading my mind. "You think you're fit to go out hunting your sire, when you can't even remember a birthday?" He didn't bother to hide his derision, which raised my hackles.

"I *think* I'm not going to have much choice, Kevin. Jones just told me I'm going to feel *compelled* to find him pretty soon. I'm not just going to sit around waiting for him to hunt me, and would rather go looking before I turn into a drooling idiot.

You don't go after a master vamp after dark, and if I don't find and kill him first, he's going to be stalking me just as soon as the sun goes down—unless your friend Jones over there was lying."

"He's not," Kevin admitted grudgingly. "But *you* don't have to be the one to hunt him."

"Did you have any luck tracking him back from where you found Celia?" Jones's tone was deceptively bland.

Kevin answered Jones's question with one of his own. "It's broad daylight. Celia. Do you even know if you *can* go outside?" Kevin's voice had softened just a hair, as if he sensed the distress I wasn't willing to show. Maybe he could smell it? I didn't know enough about werewolves to know one way or the other. I'd passed up on that class in favor of two semesters of history of magic.

I flinched involuntarily, just a little. I needed to keep my head in the game, but I really was having a hard time focusing. *Shit.* "Only one way to find out." I gave him my perkiest insincere smile and was rewarded by a dark flush creeping up his neck.

"You"—Jones looked from me to Kevin and back again— "are either very brave or very stupid."

"Both," Emma said drily.

"Gee, thanks." I was still lisping a little but was determined to ignore it. I rummaged around in the duffel for sweat socks and running shoes, then plopped down on the edge of the slab to pull them on, leaving the others to argue among themselves, which they proceeded to do. With vigor. I ignored it for the most part. I had other things on my mind. Like sunlight, spontaneous combustion, the fact that I would have a really,

really hard time explaining an aversion to holy objects to my gran.

The three of them were still arguing when I finished with the shoes and socks. I think that's why they didn't hear the commotion in the hallway. Emma might have missed it either way, but werewolves have excellent hearing and from the jolt I got when I touched him, Jones wasn't your average human, either. But I heard and, even more weird, *scented* it. Three men in hard-soled dress shoes were coming down the hall. They walked with the kind of confidence that comes with the weight of authority. I smelled gun oil and the tiniest hint of powder, as if the weapon hadn't been cleaned quite as well as it should have been after its last use.

They slowed to a stop outside the heavy steel of the main door. I heard the metal shift as someone began pulling it open, and a voice I recognized as belonging to Dr. Reynolds from the university health clinic, babbling nervously. I watched, alert, as their figures were silhouetted against the sunlight of the glass-walled outer hallway. The sunlight seemed too bright, like staring into a spotlight onstage. It made my skin itch even from a distance, and I felt my muscles cringe. That annoyed me.

From the corner of my eye I saw the argument between Emma and Kevin cease. Jones had simply disappeared. Like magic. Except that I know magic . . . and nobody I'd ever known or heard of was capable of that particular trick.

The man who held the door was familiar to me, and probably to every student who graced the halls of USC Bayview. University president Donald Lackley had movie star good looks, a permanent tan, and shoes that had once roamed free in the Florida swamplands. His designer suit was impeccable, perfectly tailored, and probably worth as much as the car I drive. He is a *presence*, and as such never misses a photo op or a chance to cadge donations for the campus. That said, he is still one *hell* of an able administrator. No detail is small enough to escape the notice of those sharp dark eyes. Most people would have been surprised that he'd choose to lead the charge down here himself. I wasn't. If he was here he could control the situation. Like most administrators, Lackley was *all* about control. If he hadn't already been married, I'd have said he was the perfect match for Emma Landingham.

"Good morning, Emma . . . Kevin." Lackley's voice was much cooler than usual when he spoke to them. He knew my name but didn't greet me. I wasn't surprised.

He looked at Emma. "Dr. Reynolds explained to me that there's been an . . . *incident* involving Ms. Graves."

Kevin glared at the good doctor, who flinched a little under the heat of his gaze.

"I did say you had the situation in hand," the doctor mumbled.

Lackley spared the doctor an eloquent *look*. The poor man shifted nervously from foot to foot. He was a small, mousy little man with a receding hairline and a slight paunch that didn't show when he was wearing a lab coat. He seemed to be a fairly good doctor but a poor politician. Today he just couldn't catch a break. No matter what he did, he'd be pissing somebody off.

"You did. But I'd be remiss if I didn't personally check to make sure that a potentially deadly monster hadn't been brought onto the campus."

I smiled and hoped the fangs didn't show. "I'm fine, President Lackley. But thank you for your *concern*." Unlike Kevin and the doc, I don't work for the university and am thus exempt from kissing administrative booty. So long as I paid my tuition on time, there wasn't much they could do to me. I could be as sarcastic as I wanted—provided I didn't appear to be a threat.

I saw the muscles in Lackley's jaw tighten, but he didn't say a word in response. So I turned my attention from him to the third man in their happy little group.

C. J. "Rocky" Rockford was the head of the campus security forces. We'd had occasion to run into each other, and while he knew he probably shouldn't like me, he did. We even went to the shooting range and worked out in the gym and weight room together occasionally. "Hey, Rock."

Rocky's a big guy, former boxer and tough as they come. His skin is deep brown with copper highlights. He keeps his hair cut short enough that you can see the scalp beneath it. He isn't a handsome man, but he is *impressive*. Which allows him to, in the immortal words of Patrick Swayze, "be nice, until it is time *not* to be nice." Rocky was always armed, but today he was carrying a plain black nylon satchel. I was betting I knew what was inside: holy items, a stake, a mallet, and a saw—your typical vampire kit.

"Graves. What happened?" His voice didn't sound particularly friendly this morning and he was rubbing his finger along a ridge of scar tissue at the bridge of his nose. He does that when he's nervous. I couldn't say as I blamed him. Never makes things easy when the ultimate boss takes a *personal* interest. Plus, I'd like to think Rocky hadn't been looking forward to staking and beheading a workout partner.

"I don't really remember much about it. I should be dead,

from what I've gathered. But I'm not and, despite the fangs, I remember who I am. I was out on the slab until just a few minutes ago."

He blinked a couple of times in surprise but finally managed to ask, "Hit? Here on campus?"

Kevin answered that one. "No."

"Then why is she here?" Lackley's gaze locked with Kevin's and neither of them seemed inclined to back down.

"It was my fault." Emma spoke quietly. "I'm a level-four clairvoyant. I knew Celia was in serious danger. I called my father and brother and told them what I saw. My brother went to get her. Dad's in Chicago on business, so he called Dr. Reynolds. Nobody wanted to risk what happened in that emergency room in Denver, so he brought her here and brought the equipment in. The restraints on this table are graded to hold an uncontrolled ghoul if need be. We figured they'd be strong enough to handle whatever she became."

I was surprised. Emma's gift is sporadic at best, and usually only works in connection with people she cares about. I wouldn't have put myself on that list. She'd saved my life. Of course, she'd turned around and risked it a couple hours later, but still. I turned to look her in the eye. "Thank you."

She blinked, obviously startled. "You're welcome."

"So, you admit to bringing a potentially dangerous monster onto campus and not reporting it."

Emma flushed at the implied criticism. "I did report it. To the local police, over the phone, while Dr. Reynolds was giving Celia the blood transfusion." She met Lackley's gaze head-on, her chin thrust up in defiance. "And if you check the voice mail for your office, you'll find an urgent message from me."

Lackley didn't rise to the bait. "What did the police say?"

"They said they'd look into it." She turned to me then. "When I called back they said there were no dead bodies at that address, or even in the area, monster, human, or otherwise."

I blinked. That made no sense. None. I blinked a few more times, trying to process what she'd just said, without much success.

"The officer I spoke to seemed to imply that I was being hysterical. He was polite. *Extremely* polite. But I got the impression he considered me a nutcase."

Whatever he'd implied, they were most likely working on it. She probably hadn't made a particularly good impression — she could be a raging bitch in heels, and they wouldn't take to it. But somebody was probably doing the legwork. They take talk of monsters and dead bodies very seriously.

"For the record." I turned and spoke directly to Lackley. I didn't want Warren and the others getting in trouble for saving my life. From the sound of it, they would. If not from the university, from the authorities. Endangering the public is a serious crime. I couldn't do much about that, but I could deal with the university brass. At least I *thought* I could. "I'm one of the students who signed up for the *full* alumni package."

"I know." Could Lackley have made those words any drier? Of course, I didn't really blame him. Bayview, like every institution of higher education, was always in need of donations. Someone had come up with a bright idea that would get alumni donors to fork over more cash. It was based on the same principle as gym memberships—and the same assumption of attrition. Offer a limited time deal. Donate a certain hefty amount and they reactivate you as if you were a student. You get full benefits—use of the athletic facilities, student discounts, *use of the student health facilities, and insurance*—as long as you enrolled in two classes per semester and remained in good standing.

Most people who could afford that level of donation really didn't need the benefits. The first time it became inconvenient, they'd stop signing up for classes, and that would be that—the university would have their money and no further obligation to them. I'm not most people. Considering how hard it is for a woman with my job description to get health insurance, the deal seemed like a steal at twice the price. I jumped at the chance, and have been working my way through every elective in the schedule. Hell, at some point I might even get serious about it and get my master's.

"What courses are you taking this semester?" I could hear the resignation in Lackley's voice.

"Music Appreciation and Ornamental Gardening."

Kevin snorted and I glared at him. "Don't laugh. David's been talking about making changes to the grounds and Vicki thought that at least one of us should know what he was talking about." David and Inez lived at the estate and ran the place for Vicki. I rented the guesthouse. It was an arrangement we'd worked out shortly before graduation and one that had worked well for us for several years.

"The ghoul-proof table means they took precautions not to

endanger the campus." Rocky's voice was a low, soothing rumble.

Lackley's eyes narrowed, but he gave Rocky a curt nod. It was obvious Lackley was very unhappy about the situation, but even he would hesitate to go up against El Jefe. The nickname might have started out as a joke, but it stuck because Warren *is* "the Chief" when it comes to the paranormal. He's internationally renowned and brings a lot of prestige and money to the university. Lackley might win this particular battle, but pissing off Warren would cost him dearly long term, and he was too astute a politician not to know it.

"Dr. Reynolds—since Ms. Graves appears to be alive and in full possession of her faculties and memory, is there any reason why she should remain here instead of recovering in the comfort of her own residence?"

"Well, sir . . . ," Reynolds stammered a little. I knew he was going to argue. As a doctor, he'd feel compelled to take a conservative course with regard to little things like, oh, sunlight, holy water. . . . But I knew it would go badly for him if he did. He didn't have the clout Warren did, so he'd be practically defenseless, and Lackley was in the mood to rip someone a new orifice.

I didn't want Dr. Reynolds to be punished for saving me, so I spoke up before he could argue. "It's all right, Doc. I was planning on leaving anyway."

"I hate this." Kevin glared at me when he said it, and I could feel the heat of his anger. "You shouldn't risk going out into the sunlight." I knew his beast was close. I could *feel* it. He usually has better control than that, and it made me nervous. I wasn't afraid of him. I was afraid *for* him. Because most people see werewolves as monsters and think they all should be either killed or locked up, which was why nobody at the university knew about his condition. If Kevin gave them an excuse, we'd have more and worse problems than we already did.

I tried to show him all that in a look, and he subsided a little.

"I need to know how bad this is going to be, Kev. If I *have* to stay in, I will. But if I can handle the sunlight, I'm going." I took a deep breath, gathering my nerve. If I was going to do this, I needed to get it over with.

President Lackley and the others stepped out of the way, Rocky even went so far as to open the door for me.

The hallway had an entire wall made of windows overlooking the campus quadrangle. Bright sunlight was streaming through the east-facing glass.

Everyone stared in hushed silence as I paused at the very last edge of shadows.

Taking a deep breath, I stepped into the light.

I didn't incinerate. *Yay!*

"I'm fine." All right, "fine" was an exaggeration. I could actually feel my skin heating: like a sunburn on fast forward.

I stepped back into the shadows wondering if my trusty SPF 30 would be helpful, and for how long. I've always had naturally pale skin, so I kept bottles of it pretty much everywhere. Of course I could go up to SPF 45, or even (ugh) sunblock. But if that didn't work, life was going to be damned inconvenient. We were, after all, living in sunny Southern California, next to the Pacific. It's my home and damn it, I *like* it here.

Kevin was at my elbow. His words were a bare breath of air meant only for my ears. "I can smell your skin burning, Celia."

He took a step back, but his eyes were glowing. I felt his power roll across my skin, raising the hairs on my body. No surprise there. What was . . . disturbing . . . was that *my* power rose in response, making my skin glow white enough to banish the shadows from the hallway. My eyes felt . . . odd, my vision shifting into a kind of hyperfocus that showed me every nick in the painted wall, every flaw in the glass. I could see the pulse beating in the throat of a student hurrying down the sidewalk outside a hundred yards away, and it made my stomach growl.

Oh, shit.

"Should she be able to do that?" Emma was obviously fascinated. I'd heard her use the same tone of voice when discussing research results with her father.

Kevin gave me a long, assessing look. "That, and more. She's not human anymore."

There was both fear and . . . *excitement* in his voice when he said it. If I'd been able to get my throat to respond enough to speak, mine would only have held fear.

5

Vampires look quite a lot like humans . . . well, except for the teeth, and the unnatural pallor. And of course there's that whole red/gold-eye thing. But vampires are purely nocturnal. They're dead when the sun is up. It was full daylight. So even though my reflection in the windows showed someone unnaturally pale, with a really impressive set of canines, I was pretty sure I wouldn't get mistaken for a vampire. Maybe. I hoped.

My "sunburn" subsided in a minute or two. I could actually see my skin heal. *Très* creepy. Useful, though. I wondered how it would work. What was the healing rate compared to that of a normal human? Were there any references I could use to find out? From what they were telling me, it didn't sound as if this was exactly a common problem. Which was probably why they hadn't covered it in any of my courses.

As we walked down the hallway, him being the gentleman and carrying my duffel and the umbrella I'd borrowed from Emma, Kevin lowered his voice until it was the barest whisper. Yet I could hear him *as clearly* as though he were screaming the words. "We're letting you go, and I've made Jones promise not to follow you. But I want you to check in every few hours. And if you feel *anything* odd, call immediately and I'll come get you. Okay?"

It occurred to me then that I was being given a rare gift—I was being *let go*. Warren's vamp lectures came back to tighten my chest and make my heart pound. Vampires are never let go once they're in any sort of custody. They're staked, imprisoned, or tested. But they're not *let go*. *Crap*. That could disappear in an instant if I wasn't careful.

"Thanks. I'll stay low-key. Mostly I want to do some research and catch up with people." That wasn't precisely true, but mostly. I would do the research, when I had time. Right now there were more important things I needed to be doing. So I grabbed my bag and the umbrella and walked with false confidence toward the sunlit entrance. Kevin started to come with me, but President Lackley stopped him with a gesture and a firm, "I have a few more questions for you, Mr. Landingham. *If* you don't mind."

He obviously did. But he didn't argue. He couldn't if he wanted to keep his job. Lackley was just in that foul of a mood. I could hear him trying to call Reynolds on the carpet, with minimal success. The doctor had more backbone than I'd given him credit for. Too, he knew his stuff. This was a campus, with hard-partying students. Mine was not the first vampire bite he'd treated. Most individual bites aren't fatal. A single vampire can't hold that much blood. Oh, they can deliberately open several wounds and let the victim bleed out, but they generally don't. Like all good parasites, they know the value of keeping the host alive and in the larder. Only when there's a group all draining a single victim, or a master vamp siring a baby, do they drain a victim dry. Since a bat seldom attacks the same person twice—which would imply more planning than most have—standard procedure is to replace the lost blood and put the victim under a four-hour sleeping charm in case of complications. Which was exactly what Reynolds had done, only with the added precaution of the restraints.

I could hear their voices, still arguing, all the way to the parking lot as I walked out to my car in the shade provided by the umbrella.

I knew I looked ridiculous, and it pissed me off. Not enough that I'd risk second- and third-degree burns, mind you—but enough to make me irritable. As promised, I got no hint—either scent or sight—that Jones was around, which was a concern of a different sort. There'd been some real tension between him and Kevin before Jones did his disappearing act, which made me wonder about their relationship. They obviously weren't friends. Former business associates most likely. And how the hell had Jones vanished like that? Experts have been working on invisibility spells for decades with no success. Illusion maybe? That sort of thing is difficult, but at least marginally possible for folks with enough talent.

I pondered it all the way through the parking lot as I searched for my vehicle. Kevin had used the spare key to fetch my car from wherever I'd left it parked. I juggled umbrella, duffel, and keys as I walked across the scorching asphalt to a spot in the very last row. There, tucked between two monster trucks, sat my gleaming midnight blue *convertible*.

Well, hell.

Yes, the top was up, but the thought that I might not be able to ride around during the day with the top down just pissed me off even more. But I was alive. And I had more important things to think about. I had a lot to do. First thing, I wanted to call Gran. I was supposed to have had dinner with her last night, so by now she'd probably contacted the authorities to make sure I hadn't been in an accident. Then again, maybe not. I do tend to work weird hours.

Second, I *definitely* needed to chat with the police. Something very weird was going on and I was right in the middle of it. I mean, *no bodies*? I wouldn't have gone out at night alone. I'd been scheduled for a job. If I/we'd been hit, there would've been more casualties than just me. I'm good enough not to go down without a fight. So, why no bodies? Who would move them? And *why*? Getting rid of that kind of evidence takes real work.

I put my duffel in the minuscule trunk. It fit, but there wasn't a lot of room to spare. I love my little sports car. It is a joy to drive and everything I've always wanted. But practical it isn't. I collapsed the umbrella and let myself into the car, dropping the umbrella onto the floorboard on the passenger side.

The car was an oven. In seconds, sweat started to trickle down my back, between my shoulder blades, and under my breasts. I started the ignition, put the air conditioner on full blast, and set about looking for clues.

The first and most obvious was the file folder sitting on the passenger seat. I knew what that was—my research on Prince Rezza. That it was here in the car instead of in my files at the office said that I'd actually made it as far as going out to the job. More interesting to me by far was the little multi-colored photo envelope peeking out from behind the seat.

I didn't remember celebrating Vicki's birthday, but apparently we'd done it. I flipped through the snapshots over and over, *trying* to remember. We'd obviously had a great time. From the expression on her face, she'd loved the mirror and the card. There were pictures of us laughing and hugging. But I didn't *remember*. I tried, but there was nothing. Not a damned thing. I felt a lump in my throat and a pain in my stomach. Memories lost were just that—lost. Sure, there would be more smiles, but I'd missed these and not even the pictures could give them back. They might as well be photos of two strangers.

I slid the photos back into the envelope and reached over to open the glove compartment. Normally I tuck my cell phone in there when I go out on a job. After all, no calls when you're on duty.

It wasn't there. I swore under my breath. If it wasn't in the glove box, it had probably been in my pocket. Which meant it was gone—along with who knew what all else.

Since I put the file in the car, I must have gone to the job, and I would have been wearing my jacket and carrying my new gadget—both of which were valuable and neither of which I had any longer. Dammit!

I thought about what to do as the car engine did its best to blast cooler air through the vents. I reached back into the glove compartment and grabbed a bottle of suntan lotion. SPF 30 would have to do. I could already feel my skin reacting where it was exposed to patches of sunlight. The smell of coconut, aloe, and chemicals filled the car as I slathered thick white liquid on my exposed flesh, hoping what I was about to do wasn't as stupid as I thought it was.

Pay phones aren't easy to find in the cellular age. The days when Superman could pop into the nearest phone booth have been gone longer still. About the only place you can find a usable public phone is at the occasional convenience store, and even then it's just as likely to be out of order.

Fortunately, I was on campus. I knew of at least three convenience stores that catered to students. Surely one of them would have a phone I could use. I left the parking lot with a particular 7-Eleven in mind.

The first store had a phone, but the cord had been severed. I struck pay dirt at the second shop. The phone was even in the shade. Yeah, there was graffiti on it, but the cords were all attached, it wasn't covered with anything sticky or awful, and when I picked it up I got a dial tone. I dropped a pair of the coins I'd rummaged from the ashtray of my car into the slot and dialed Gran's number from memory. I let it ring eight times. No answer. Since she didn't have voice mail or an answering machine, I hung up.

But I have voice mail. Maybe she left a message. I dropped the coins back in the slot and dialed the number of my mailbox. Unfortunately, the recording told me the service was *presently unavailable* and suggested I call back later.

Well, that was a waste of money, but I'd definitely be checking back frequently. It might be the key to my own past.

After scrounging around between the seats, I found more change. I dropped another pair of coins in the slot, dialing a different number.

The phone rang exactly once before a businesslike female voice answered. "Police, Detective Alexander speaking."

"Hey, Alex." I greeted the woman on the other line with breezy familiarity that was only a little bit forced. I like Vicki's lover. The three of us have had dinner a few times since they met, including, apparently, the birthday party. But I have to admit it's been a little bit awkward. Maybe Alex and I are just too much alike—both hard cases with a sarcastic bent. Whatever the problem, things between us have always been just a little *strained*. Still, we both love Vicki to pieces. She's my best friend and Alex's lover, so we all pretend everything's peachy.

"Graves. I just got the weirdest call about you." Alex's voice was gruff but not unfriendly. "A friend of mine from downstairs called, said there was a report of you getting bit by bats and being taken for medical treatment, but nobody could find you at any of the hospitals. Then, when they checked out the site of the supposed attack, there was no evidence of anything. The alley was clean. Which is just fucking weird."

"Well, I was attacked. I was damned near killed—apparently some time after Vicki's birthday. So there *should* be evidence if they look hard enough."

"Are you all right?"

I thought about how to answer that for a few seconds. The cops didn't like monsters. Would she consider me one? I hoped not. But what was the point in lying? First time she set eyes on me she'd know the truth. "Yes, and no. Ever heard of an abomination?"

"No. What's that?" Her voice was tired, resigned, like she didn't really want to know but knew she needed to.

I explained what had happened and as much of what it meant to me as Jones had had time to impart—not much, really.

"If that's true, then the master that bit you is going to be after you—and you're liable to wind up with bloodlust."

"I'm not a monster, Alex. I'm not going to *be* a monster. I'm just a human in need of a good dentist." My voice was cold, hard, and uncompromising.

"I hope you're right." Alex's voice was as hard as mine had been, maybe more so. Then again, she's a cop. "But let's get this real clear right up front. If you ever show signs of slipping over that edge I'll take you out. No hesitation. Vicki or no."

She would. I knew it. In fact, I was counting on it. "If I slip over that edge, I want you to."

There was a long moment of silence between us, each of us lost in thoughts that were best unshared. I didn't want to think about bloodlust, the urge to look at my fellow humans as snack food, but I needed to. I needed to think about that and so many other things. But if I did, I was liable to lose it, and that could get me killed. So, I forced the fear and worry down hard, knowing even as I did that I'd pay for it. Denial is a great short-term coping mechanism. Long-term it's pretty destructive, but hey, I just wanted to *get* to the long term.

I broke the silence before it got too uncomfortable. "Can you get me the address of the alley? I'm going to have to see if I can get a hunt sanctioned, then see if I can get any evidence and track the bastard down while it's still daylight."

"No, Celia. You don't understand. And I'm not allowed to explain some of it to you. Suffice it to say that the alley your friend sent us to is *clean*. Someone even hauled away all the trash. The rest of the neighborhood's a dive, but my friend swears you could eat off the pavement in that alley."

"What the—" I blinked a few times with shock. "That's just . . . bizarre."

Her tone said she agreed. "Like I said, weird. Somebody went to a *lot* of trouble to get rid of the evidence of something—presumably your vampire attack. My friend would like to know why."

"So would I."

"They're going to see if any of the shops in the area have video surveillance, but he's not particularly hopeful, considering the neighborhood. Obviously, he'll want to take your statement."

"How soon do I need to be there?"

"Sooner is better than later. Go to the front desk and ask for Gibson. I'll tell him to expect you."

I sighed. I didn't want to do this. But if I played nice with the cops, they were more likely to issue the warrant sanctioning my hunt and I might be able to keep my concealed-carry permit. If I didn't agree to the questioning . . . well, paperwork can be lost, delayed, misfiled, all kinds of things. They wouldn't do it to get me killed. In fact, they'd probably be hunting for the bastard who did this to me just as hard as I was. But they'd keep me out of it. I didn't *want* out of it.

She laughed, but not like it was funny. "You sound so martyred. It won't take that long. Besides, if you cooperate he may be willing to pass along what little information they've been able to gather. The master vampire that tried to turn you is going to try to either kill you or finish bringing you over. And someone went to a lot of trouble and expense covering this up. You're going to need all the help you can get."

"Yeah. Wish I knew what I needed help *with*." I said it for Alex's benefit, but it was the truth. Vamps frequently run in packs, but they're not *organized*. They don't generally clean up their messes, either. Something big was going down and, lucky me, I'd stepped right in the middle of it.

"Look, you're only about ten minutes away. Come straight over. I'll meet you in the lobby and bring you up. Otherwise people are liable to freak when they see you."

She wasn't wrong. Just on the short trip to the car from the lab I'd noticed a couple of people doing a double take and hurrying away from me. Daylight or no, something about me scared them, even with me carrying Emma's pretty floral umbrella.

Alex seemed to sense something in my silence. "Just get here. One step at a time."

"Right. See you in a few."

She hung up without saying good-bye, but then, she usually did. I set the handset back in its cradle and steeled myself to go inside. I wanted a replacement cell phone sooner than later. You can get a basic phone cheap and easy at pretty much any convenience store—such as the one I was standing in front of—and it only takes a couple of minutes to activate it and load up some minutes. Maybe I'd find my regular phone. If not, I could get it replaced for a small fee by the company that held my plan. But in the meantime, I needed something.

I took a deep breath, told myself that it was broad daylight. Everybody knew that bats were nocturnal. I'd be fine. I was still repeating it like a mantra when the clerk behind the counter let out an earsplitting shriek of abject terror, grabbed one of those huge multitank squirt guns, and began hosing me down with holy water.

It wasn't how I would've wanted to test whether or not I could handle holy water, but hey, I got lucky. It didn't burn.

Nor did the cross she held up glow, burn, or react to me in any way. I was grateful for that. But it embarrassed the hell out of me, and made me just a little bit pissed. Because everybody in the store was staring and muttering to each other under their breath, even as the clerk apologized and handed me paper towels to dry my face and hair.

I practically threw the money onto the counter for the phone, the minutes, and a large blessed cross set with enough rhinestones to blind the unwary, and ran from the store.

Sitting in my car, I fought not to cry. Stupid, really. I was alive. The water hadn't burned me, hadn't hurt me at all. For a brief moment, I was relieved beyond measure.

But I could still see the expression on that woman's face, the naked *fear* in her eyes, could see and hear the pulse pounding at her throat.

It made my mouth water.

I hate feeling helpless. Yeah, I know, pretty much everybody does. But I *hate* it. I've spent years in therapy, and more years doing just plain hard work, to gain as much control as I can over my life. I train my body, my mind. I run my own business so that no one can order me around. I make sure that each job is planned to the last detail, and that I have the absolute best equipment so that I can control everything as much as I can.

Her fear had made me *hungry*.

How the *hell* was I supposed to cope with that?

I thought about calling in to my office, but I had to charge the phone first and then load the minutes. A black and white police cruiser pulled into the lot and I decided against using the pay phone again. Apparently the clerk didn't like that I was still "lurking" outside. I said a couple of uncomplimentary things under my breath and started the engine. I even gave the cops a cheery little wave as I drove past. Bitchy? Possibly. But it made me feel just a teeny bit better. Today, I'd take every little bit that helped.

I'd stop by the office and check my messages after I finished talking to the police. I wouldn't stay long. I was already tired, and I had lots of things to do if I was going to get ready to hunt my sire.

I was distracted enough that I almost missed my turn. I managed to get onto the Loop, but I had to cut across two lanes of traffic to do it. Traffic was lighter than usual, so I made good time. Normally I'd have slipped in a CD, but I turned on the radio instead. I was listening for the news. If I'd made it to the job and the prince had gone down, it'd be a headline story at the top of the hour. If he hadn't, the politicos would probably sweep the whole thing under the carpet. Because while the press may love a scandal, royalty generally doesn't, particularly when the folks back home are fundamentalists.

The news came on just as I was pulling into the multilevel parking garage that serviced the Santa Maria de Luna PD. Nothing about the prince. In fact, other than the unrest in Pakistan and the peace talks going on in the former Soviet satellite nations, there didn't appear to be much going on at all.

I knew from past experience that if I parked in the garage attached to the police department I could take an elevator directly into the second-floor lobby of the building. No sunlight. Which, all things considered, was probably a good idea. Yes, if I had to, I could use the umbrella again, but I didn't want to. Maybe it was denial, or just plain stubbornness, but hiding from the sun just felt . . . wrong.

The parking garage was dim and cool enough to be almost welcoming after the car's heat. The soft sound of my sneakers was lost in the wail of a car alarm echoing off of the concrete.

Pressing the button for the elevator, I tried to shake off a growing sense of unease. This entire situation was just too strange. Nothing made sense. Emma would never believe it, but I'm actually a creature of order. I plan things practically to death, and then I double- and triple-check 'em. Because I want to control what I can. Invariably there are lots of things you *can't* control—completely unpredictable things that force you to improvise and think on your feet. But if you've got a handle on the other stuff, you have a better chance of success in dealing with the random crap. At least that's what I tell myself.

But in the words of my gran, this whole situation was "hinky" and "stank like week-old fish."

The bell rang, and the elevator doors slid open with a gentle whoosh. I stepped over the metal threshold onto white speckled linoleum waxed to a high gloss. Air-conditioning hit my wet clothes, making me shudder. In the distance I could hear the soft rush of water over stone. I froze. Running water—a big vampire no-no. Was it going to be a problem? The holy water hadn't been. I tried to think of a way of finding out without making a spectacle of myself and came up blank.

Screw it. Just suck it up, Graves. Squaring my shoulders, I marched toward the lobby. The piped-in stream that fed the moat of magical water surrounding the holding cells was surprisingly pretty. Not only was the waterfall supposed to inspire peaceful feelings in the prisoners, but it also nullified any spells that might try to break people out.

I passed it without so much as a flinch, which made me seriously happy. Thus far I was proving more human than bat, which was just fine by me. I just hoped the trend continued.

I stepped into the automated scanners set to detect weapons and offensive magic. Warmth swept over me, from head to toe and back up. When the light flashed green I walked over to admire the fountain that was part of a memorial to the department's injured and fallen officers. It's in plain view of the main building entrance, just past the main bank of scanners and about five yards to the right of the reception desk.

The fountain is a set of five long, narrow steps of polished black marble rising from a shallow pool filled with river rock to an eight-foot bronze statue of Blind Justice. Behind her, on a wall of black marble, are rows of gold and silver plates about an inch by two inches. Engraved on each are the name, rank, and dates of service of the honored officer: silver for those injured and disabled, gold for those who died in the line of duty. They didn't quite fill the entire section, but it was getting close. I recognized more than a few names, most of them on the shiniest plaques.

I'm not particularly religious, but I said a quiet prayer for the souls of the fallen to whoever might be listening. It's been a rough couple of years. The experts have been debating why. Maybe it's just a natural cycle. Maybe not. Nobody seems to have an answer, not even El Jefe and the rest of the experts. So the religious orders and the cops do the best they can fighting an increasingly losing battle against evil and destruction.

I heard the buzz of the security door opening and turned to see Alex standing in a discreetly recessed doorway, beckoning to me. Standing next to her was a middle-aged man with close-cropped graying blond hair. Everything about him was square and boxy. He wasn't tall, probably five eight or so, but he was built broad. Not fat, but broad and strong, like a former linebacker who, while he didn't precisely work out, hadn't let himself go to seed, either. He had a square jaw and big, blunt-fingered hands. His only jewelry was a plain gold watch. His suit was a medium gray that was almost the exact shade of the eyes staring out at me from behind a pair of rimless glasses. His fair skin had an almost greenish undertone and a flaccid quality that spoke of ill health. He was dying. I don't know how I knew this, but I did, just as I knew his blood would taste bitter from the toxins his failing kidneys were no longer processing. *He won't taste good.*

I shuddered a little in fear and revulsion. He was a man. He was *not* food. But as much as it terrified me, I couldn't take back that errant thought, the thought of a vampire. God help me.

6

"You can smell it on me, can't you?" Gibson spoke softly, each word measured.

I sat across the table in an interrogation room that looked pretty much exactly like the ones they show on the television cop shows. This one was clean, with a coat of paint fresh enough to still smell of chemicals. I sat across a scarred table from Gibson, facing a big bank of mirrored glass that probably gave another officer or two an unobstructed view of the proceedings. In the corner, near the ceiling, was a recorder—audio and video from the look of it. The lights weren't lit, but that was because Gibson hadn't hit the button on the remote.

We'd stopped by the commissary for a cup of coffee before coming up. It sat on the table in front of me. I couldn't drink it. I was too nauseous. Up close the scent of his decaying body was making me gag. Only keeping the coffee directly under my nose made it bearable. I shifted uncomfortably on the hard plastic seat and wished I were anywhere but here. My nose hadn't been this sensitive earlier. Would it get worse?

"I saw it in your eyes in the lobby." His lips twisted in what was supposed to be a wry smile. "If Alexander hadn't told me you'd been bitten by a vampire, I'd have assumed you were a werewolf. So far they've been the only ones who can tell." His expression turned into a grimace. "They act like I've got a really bad case of BO. The reaction outted a few people I'd never even suspected."

"Did you turn them in?"

His eyes met mine, his expression grave. "Technically, it's not against the law to be a werewolf—so long as you don't endanger the public."

Technically, no. But that doesn't stop the persecution. There are more than a few people who figure werewolves endanger the public just by breathing. The prevailing attitude is "cage 'em or kill 'em." In fact, that exact motto had been used by one of the more popular politicians.

I'm perfectly capable of killing monsters if they endanger me or the people I'm protecting. But for all but three days out of each lunar cycle werewolves were absolutely ordinary folks, with families and jobs. If they took appropriate precautions, there was no need for them to be made prisoners.

Evidently Gibson agreed with me, and it made me think better of him.

"Does Alex know about your condition?" I asked him.

"No. I haven't told anyone here at work. They'll find out soon enough. In the meantime, I don't want their pity." He gave me a dark look. "And I do *not* want to leave a big case open."

"And you think I can help?" I deliberately kept my voice neutral, my expression pleasant but noncommittal. "What sort of case is it?"

He didn't answer. "What do you remember from last night?"

"Not a damned thing. I've lost all of yesterday." I sighed. "It was bats, so I'm assuming the attack took place after dark. And I'm still alive, so I figure it took place just a few minutes before my rescuers showed up. But those are just guesses based on logic. I'm a complete blank from yesterday morning until I woke up strapped to the zombie table in the university lab."

He gave me a sharp look and I sighed. "I'm not lying. If only. I've been trying, struggling to find *anything*, but nope. Pisses me off, too." Because those few missing hours were some of the most important of my life.

The stare he gave me seemed to drill into my brain. Finally he nodded. "All right." He reached into his pocket and pulled out a little black microcassette recorder. I wasn't surprised he was using one. Recent rulings had caused evidence to be thrown out because digital recording devices were too easy to manipulate magically. So the cops were back to using old-fashioned tape. Flipping the switch, he set the recorder on the table between us before reaching for the remote and turning on the camera.

"All right, we'll start at the beginning. With your permission, I'll use a spell to prompt you on things that happened earlier in the day. We'll stop at sunset, so as not to risk triggering any traumatic memories. But sometimes going through the mundane stuff first helps people remember more of the details of what happened."

I nodded my agreement.

"This is Detective Karl Gibson, Badge Number 45236, Santa Maria de Luna Police Department. It is eleven A.M. on October 14." I only half-listened as he droned on, giving all the details necessary to make the statement official. I'd done this before. I knew the drill. In just a few seconds he'd ask me to state my name, address, and whether I was giving this statement of my own free will and volition and giving him permission to use a spell to elicit memories.

I gave the appropriate answers. Slowly, patiently, he led me back through the previous day. I remembered a lot of it with crystal clarity. It was Vicki's birthday and I had worked really hard to find her a superspecial present.

Good afternoon, Ms. Graves. If you'll pull over to the guardhouse we'll complete the inspection there."

I recognized the voice coming through the speaker. It was Gerry, the supervisor of day shift security at Birchwoods. It was an executive position, and I imagined the pay was impressive. It should be. The people who checked into the facility were willing and able to pay exorbitant sums to make damned sure that no one knew they were here or why. In all the years the place had been in business, not once had word leaked about a celebrity patient—much to the frustration of the press, who hovered at the required legal distance from a psychiatric facility.

I slid my visitor's card into my wallet and tucked the whole thing back into my bag. I heard the click of lock tumblers, followed by the buzzing of electronic equipment. A moment later the heavy outer gate rolled smoothly aside.

I stomped on the gas. The Miata positively leapt forward. I'd had it tuned up a couple of days earlier, and I still wasn't quite used to the upswing in power.

Still, it was better to move fast. I had forty-five seconds to get across the outer grid before the gate slammed shut. It took a manual override with a supervisor's key to get the gate back open. I knew this because I'd been caught once behind a ditz who'd decided to rummage in her purse for something rather than drive on in.

I pulled the car into one of four spots in front of a small white brick building with a red tile roof. As I turned off the engine, Gerry stepped out the front door. I was surprised to see him on gate duty. Since his promotion to management, it was way below his new pay grade to be checking IDs. Still, there he was, big as life and twice as ugly. He was wearing an electronic device clipped to the waistband of his suit trousers, with a cord connecting it to the wand he carried in his left hand. Behind him was a woman in the standard navy and white security uniform. She wasn't one of the regular crew. After all this time I know pretty much everyone who works at Birchwood, whatever the shift. And "Lydia" (according to her little brass name badge) wasn't familiar.

She was a mage of some sort. I'd have bet on it. Their talents may not be as versatile or as dangerous as some of the other "gifts" but are by far the most marketable and easy to control.

I took a good look at her. Probably in her mid-thirties, she had dark hair pulled tightly back from her face to reveal strong bone structure made even more harsh by the lack of makeup or jewelry. It was the kind of face that would look better in photographs than in person.

The woman strode up to the passenger side, ignoring me completely. Her eyes were only for the packages on the front seat. Yup. Definitely a mage. She'd sensed the power emanating from them.

"I've cleared those with the management. They're birthday gifts for Vicki. Since they're glass, the administrator required I have them put under at least a level-five charm to prevent breakage." She gave a slight nod but didn't take my word for it. Instead, she withdrew a palm-sized object from the pocket of her uniform trousers and began running it over the outside of the package as she murmured words I couldn't quite catch. Gerry, meanwhile, had been busy running the plates of my car and cross-checking them against the VIN number posted on the dash just inside the windshield on the driver's side. Next he'd run the wand over me to check for traditional weapons and have me sign the visitor's form with a silver pen—probably charmed to make sure I couldn't forge someone else's signature. The computer would then cross-check it not only against all of my other signatures but also against the file and the signature on my driver's license. Last, but not least, I'd be checked for illusion charms and sprinkled with holy water to make sure I wasn't a vampire playing mind tricks. This even though it was broad daylight and any normal vamps were still safely asnooze in their coffins, dead to the world.

We went through it every time. Well, most of it. Inspecting the presents was unusual but not unexpected.

Since I visit three to four times a week I've gotten pretty used to the whole rigamarole. Usually I even joke around with the guards. I know most of them by name and a little bit about them—from those times when I've been forced to wait on admission until after a group therapy session ended, or for whatever other reason. Today, however, everybody was acting grim and businesslike.

"What's up, Gerry?" I asked softly, while the female guard went over the outside of my trunk. I wasn't sure he'd answer, even if she couldn't hear, but he might.

"We've had an incident."

My eyebrows shot up in surprise. I mean, there are prisons and government installations that don't have the kind of personnel vetting programs they put people through to work here. And I've never, once, seen any hint of anyone bending the rules, which is pretty impressive all things considered.

"What kind of incident?"

Gerry's baby face hardened into harsh lines, his eyes darkening almost to black. I could see the sinews strain in his neck as he thought about it. For a moment, I thought he'd refuse to say, but he shocked me again.

"One of our guards was found murdered. His right hand had been cut off at the wrist. The body had been frozen, so we don't know how long he's been dead."

My stomach clenched in reaction. I hated to ask, but I had to. There was a good chance it was someone I knew. "Who?"

"Louis."

Shit. Louis, who had four kids under the age of ten, whose pictures he pulled out of his wallet every chance you gave him, so that he could brag about their latest report card, dance recital, or sporting event. Damn it.

"Julie had taken the kids to visit their grandparents in Idaho for a week. She says they talked on the phone every night until Thursday. That night she got an e-mail that he'd lost the cell phone, so he'd be sending e-mails instead."

"But I saw him . . ." I let the sentence drag off unfinished. It could've been him. Or not. He was night crew. But there aren't a lot of creatures that can use magic and illusion well enough to get by. The ones who can often do fingerprints. But they can't manufacture the oil in a human hand. Or DNA. Oh, shit. This was bad. And it certainly explained the extra searches and personnel shifts.

"Any idea why?"

He shook his head. "It could be anything. We're talking high-profile, high-money people here. There's plenty of folks who'd stop at nothing to get inside information."

"And now somebody has."

"Open the trunk please." The mage's voice cut across our conversation like a sharp knife. "I need to see inside."

I started to open the car door and Gerry stepped out of the way. Normally, I'd stay sitting, but something about her bugged me. I didn't like having her literally looking down on me. "I'm a professional bodyguard. My weapons are in the trunk. I lock them in there when I come to visit." Also locked in the car was the specially cut black suit jacket I wear on duty. There's magically charged Kevlar hidden beneath the silk lining. That jacket cost more than some of my guns, and I take very good care of it. I'd bet it was setting off all sorts of radar with her.

I stepped out of the car, standing with deliberate ease, leaving just enough room for rapid movement in any direction.

She noticed that, and she didn't like it. She turned to me, cold blue eyes the color of a December sky taking in every inch of me.

Her eyes lingered on the cut of my clothes, and the fitness of the body in them. Since I work out hard, I'm pretty damned fit. Early ballet training may have given me grace and good posture, but running, swimming, and exercise machines give me strength and muscle definition. It shows, even under clothing. She was no slouch, either, in the muscle department.

Her expression stayed neutral, except for the

eyes. Not for the first time I wished for just a bit of psychic talent.

"How *much* did you wish for it?" Detective Gibson's voice cut into the memory and I started. My eyes blinked several times, trying to focus on the here and now. When I did, the implication came home.

He was trying to trip me up. It probably works well when there's some guilt. But I didn't have any, so it didn't bother me. "Please. Get real. I'm not perfect, but I *like* who I am. A vamp turns you, you lose your identity, lose *everything*. Besides, if I'd asked for this, don't you think I would have stuck around to see it finished?"

He didn't rise to that bait. He just spun his finger in a circle. "Go on."

I tried to remember where I was. Oh yeah. Arguing with the bitchy mage about the trunk.

"I'm sorry, but we can't allow weapons of any kind to pass through the second gate. I need to see them. Then you can check them with Mr. Meyers here at the guard station and pick them up on the way back."

There was no hesitation in her voice and no sign of deference. He might be the one with the title, but she was definitely the person in charge. I gave Gerry an inquiring look and he flushed but didn't say anything.

"I'd rather not do that." I said it calmly. I wasn't

angry. But something about her set me off. I didn't want her going through my things. I didn't have any reason not to trust her, not to believe she was just doing her job. But I wasn't letting her get into that trunk.

She looked at me, her expression completely impassive. "Either I go through the trunk or you'll have to leave."

"Actually, there is a third option." I smiled when I said it, a bright, shiny smile that she was sensible enough not to trust.

"What?" Gerry's voice held equal parts suspicion and wary amusement. He knew me. And while he might respect Ms. Magicwielder, he didn't like her. Not one itty bit. He wouldn't help me sidetrack her, but he wouldn't mind watching while I did it.

"I don't check the weapons. I check the car."

She stared at me in stunned silence.

Gerry laughed and belatedly tried to cover it with a cough.

It was her turn to flush, but she held her temper admirably. Her voice was deceptively pleasant when she spoke. "Those packages appear quite heavy. Are you sure you want to carry them all the way to the main building?"

"Not a problem." I reached into my bag and flipped open my cell phone. I hit speed dial. The receptionist picked up on the first ring.

"Molly, it's Celia. I'm leaving the car at the outer

gate for security reasons, but I have birthday presents for Vicki. Could you have the bellhop bring down one of the carts for me? I'd be very grateful."

"Of course, ma'am, he'll be right down."

Gibson's snort of laughter brought me out of the spell-induced reverie again. He was good, damned good, to put me in and out of the memory spell like that. I hadn't felt a thing when he'd worked his magic. Oh, he didn't have Bruno's power, few do, but Gibson was smooth enough to make up for the difference.

"Clever, very clever." He grinned at me, and the impish expression on his face chased back the death's head for a moment.

"Thanks." I grinned back at him. "I thought so."

"Bet it pissed her off."

"Oh yeah." I didn't even try to keep the satisfaction from my voice. It made him shake his head and chuckle.

"So, you celebrated your friend's birthday, then what?"

"Dinner at La Cocina." The words popped out of my mouth of their own volition. I blinked in startlement. I didn't actually *remember* it, couldn't have told you what I'd ordered, but at the same time I was absolutely certain it was the truth. Weird.

"Anything else?"

I tried to relax, just let the information flow, but there was nothing. I shook my head. With the spell compelling me, I couldn't fake the lack of knowledge. Actually, I'd hoped the spell might pull something more out of my mind. No such luck.

"That's it?" He sounded disappointed. I didn't blame him. It was so damned frustrating.

Gibson stared at me for a long moment. I could see he was appraising me, judging me against some inner scale. Maybe he was trying to see if I was lying, despite the magic. Most people do. Some deliberately, because they want to misdirect the cops; some out of sheer habit, or from faulty memory. But the way he'd primed me, the memory *should* be there. *If* the freaking bat hadn't screwed with my head.

"How badly do you want to remember?"

I met the intensity of his gaze without flinching. "I don't *want* to remember," I snarled. "I *need* to."

He reached down to the tape recorder and abruptly hit the stop button. I watched the little wheels that moved the tape come to a halt, wondering what in the hell was going on. "How much money have you got on you?"

I blinked a little in shock. Alex is incredibly straightforward, honest, and honorable. I couldn't believe that a man she trusted as much as Gibson could be crooked, but he was certainly acting suspiciously. I picked my words carefully, trying to keep my voice utterly neutral. "Not much, but my office is only a couple blocks from here. I can get some. Why?"

He smiled a slow, wicked smile that didn't quite reach his eyes. "As a cop, I am not allowed to employ the services of a clairvoyant to look into the past, or hire a mage or hypnotist to make you remember. Particularly since recalling the attack might be traumatizing and could cause brain damage." He sounded both bitter and resigned. "But *if*"—he forced his face into neutral lines—"you, as a civilian, *choose* to employ one of those esteemed individuals, and if you should *choose* to have me present—"

"That's cutting the rules awfully fine, Detective Gibson."

I made sure I didn't sound judgmental. But I knew as well as he did that the courts frowned on this sort of thing. Magic is a fact of life, but it is too easily manipulated. For that matter, so is some of the newer and flashier technology—which was why Gibson was using a tape rather than a digital recorder. Somewhere along the way he'd turned off the camera as well. I could tell because there were no lights flashing on it at all.

"Ms. Graves." Gibson took off his glasses and rubbed the bridge of his nose with his thumb and index finger. "There are things we don't tell the press. Mainly because if the public knew, they'd panic and make things worse for everyone."

I nodded. It made sense. I didn't *like* it, but I'd seen a mob mentality in action once before. It had scared the shit out of me, and I didn't have to try to stop them. The cops were the ones who got to face that sort of thing head-on and get crucified afterward, no matter how they handled the situation. I could accept the need for . . . discretion.

"I need your help, so I'm going to tell you something—but you didn't hear it, and you sure as *hell* didn't get it from me."

"I can keep my mouth shut," I assured him.

"Good. Because we don't need this getting out, especially not right now. But you need to know why we're taking this so very seriously, and why I'm willing to bend a little to get the job done."

"Tell me."

Gibson leaned in and spoke even more softly. "There was a spell used on that alley to eliminate every trace of living or formerly living matter down to the pre-cellular level. Not even bacteria survived. The spell that was used is *anathema*. Do you know what that means?"

I forced my mind back to my history of magic classes in college and recited from memory, " 'The early Catholic church declared *anathema* all magic that was based on demonic power, magic that can be worked only by a demon or a half-human/half-demon spawn. Any human party to that type of magic is immediately excommunicated.' "

"Yep," he agreed. "And all spells that are *anathema* have been incorporated into the Nuremberg Accords. Their use is considered a crime against humanity and cause to be brought before the international tribunal. Demonic spells are war crimes . . . even when there's no war."

Demonic. Something must have shown in my expression, because he said, "*What?* You've thought of something."

It was so frustrating, I *almost* remembered something . . . a whistling sound, flashing lights . . . but out of context it didn't make sense.

Gibson gave me some space. We sat and sipped coffee and stared at nothing for a few minutes. When I had a little better grip on my emotions I broke the silence. "So we're dealing with at least the semi-demonic."

He let out a little growl and lowered his voice. "Don't say that too loud, and *never* in public. We've got the World Series coming up just a few short miles away in Anaheim."

Well, that certainly explained both why the police had decided to act dumb to Emma and why Alex had been careful about what she said to me. Assuming, of course, she actually knew anything. She might not.

Gibson slid his glasses back on and scooted back in his seat. He pulled a small notebook from his pocket and began reading from it. " 'The first officers on the scene were Conner and

Watson. They arrived within fifteen minutes of Ms. Landing-ham's call. The place was deserted, but they could see what looked like the remains of two adult males on the ground near the foot of a back staircase next to a Dumpster and a rather large pile of smoldering ash that they believed might be the burned remains of multiple vampires. They radioed for backup and proceeded toward the alley. Watson was in the lead. As he reached his left arm into the alley to shine his flash-light on the remains he felt . . .'" Gibson hesitated for a second before continuing with the same clinical detachment coroners use to stay sane. "'. . . a burning, tingling sensation in his arm. He told his partner to stay back and call for magical backup.'"

Gibson's jaw clenched, and I watched a slow flush creep up his neck. He kept it under control, but I could feel the rage beating off of him like heat from a furnace. "In less than two minutes, the bodies in the alley began to disintegrate, along with every other thing that had ever, at one time, been a living thing, up to and including the cotton of Watson's shirt and the arm beneath it."

Gibson's eyes locked with mine and I *couldn't* look away. His gaze compelled me to face him, face what he said next head-on. No hiding. No flinching. "It started at his fingertips and worked its way up, his arm *disintegrating* into powder-fine *dust* while he watched. It would have kept going if Conner hadn't thought to run back to the car for the vampire kit and the axe—" His jaw clenched, and the words cut off, choked off by his rage. He worked to steady his harsh breathing. It took a couple of minutes, but I waited silently. There was nothing to say. Just the thought of it was horrifying. I felt my stomach roll with revulsion that had nothing to do with the smell of his illness. "The Internal Affairs officer threw up watching the dash-board cam video. They brought in a priest to bless him and doused the tape with holy water—in case watching it activated another spell." Gibson paused again. "Watson and Conner are still alive. The doctors think they can magically alter their memories enough to let them out of the psych ward in a few weeks and send them home."

Gibson's eyes bored into me like lasers. "I want the bastards who did this. The priests can deal with the demons, but somebody human had to summon them—has to be working with them. I won't do anything that will risk a slick lawyer getting them off. But I *want* them."

I agreed wholeheartedly. The best part was, I must have been gone by then. Even if I recovered the rest of my memories, I wouldn't have to remember seeing one cop cut off another's arm with an axe. I even had an idea of how to get started on the right track. "Detective Gibson, my best friend is a level-nine clairvoyant. What say we pay her a visit?"

He shook his head. Alex must have suggested the same thing. "No dice. Vicki Cooper is an inpatient at a mental facility. Anything she got would be dismissed out of hand as being tainted."

Shit. He was right. Which sucked, because she was the best and I trusted her implicitly.

"So what do you suggest?"

"Not *what*, Ms. Graves. *Who*."

7

Dorothy Simmons was a sweet-looking little old lady with fluffy white hair and a round face. She met us at the door of one of a collection of tiny red-brick duplexes that formed the government-subsidized housing for the elderly in our fair city. She was wearing a lavender velour track suit with a white tank top and the kind of heavy sensible white shoes you see advertised in magazines for nurses and other folks who spend most of their time on their feet. At her invitation we followed her inside, moving slowly as she shuffled along using one of those aluminum walkers with bright green tennis balls attached to the front feet for traction.

We'd come here because Mrs. Simmons didn't have a history of mental instability. I was going to be paying her fifty dollars, because she was on a fixed income and needed the money. Seemed like a small enough price to pay if she could help me out.

At Gibson's suggestion I'd hung back a bit, in the shadows cast by a trellis of pink climbing roses. He wanted to make sure my appearance didn't startle her. After my experiences earlier, I didn't blame him.

"Dottie, I have someone with me who was attacked last night. She's a victim, and I swear to you she is not a danger to you."

"Don't be silly, Karl, I know you'd never put me at risk. Miss . . . come on in. There's no need to be skulking around in the shadows."

"Yes, ma'am. If you say so." I tried to show my appreciation with a smile. I shouldn't have. It flashed the fangs. She stepped back so abruptly she nearly fell, her face as white as a sheet, her blue eyes as wide as saucers.

"Dottie . . . Dot, it's all right," Gibson assured her. "Celia was ambushed last night. She was rescued before the process went too far, but we need your help to know exactly what went on in that alley. We need to catch the bat that did this to her."

"Oh, my." Dottie put her hand to her chest, her breath coming in short gasps. It took a couple of moments before she calmed enough to speak. "I'm so sorry, dear, but you *did* give me a turn." She shook her head. "So silly. I *know* better. A vampire couldn't be out this time of day. Still . . ." She shook her head again. "It is a shock. You poor thing. You'll be facing a hard time, I bet, with people reacting before they think, just like I did. How are you feeling?"

I shrugged. "Physically, I'm recovering. Mentally, I don't remember much and am still pretty much in denial." I made my voice as soothing as I could. "I know it's going to catch up with me eventually. But right now, I've got to find out what happened, before the bat that attacked me comes back to finish the job."

Again her eyes went wide, as she realized what I meant. "Oh dear. We can't have that. Absolutely not." Dottie appeared flustered. "No, of course not. Come in, come in. Have a seat on the couch while I go get my supplies. I won't be a minute."

Well, didn't I just feel like a heel, scaring the crap out of a nice little old lady. Not that I could help it. But still . . . I could only hope my gran didn't react the same way next time she saw me. She'd already had one heart attack. A bad enough shock might actually kill her.

I fidgeted on the overstuffed sofa and looked around to waste some time. It was a nice apartment. A little excessive, what with all the knickknacks, floral patterns, and doilies, but nice. The entire place smelled of air freshener and there wasn't a trace of dust on any of the ceramic and pewter statues, cups, and collector plates that filled the shelves attached to the wall: kittens and cats mostly, in all sorts of poses. Painted kittens romped around the base of the lamp sitting on the end table. But there wasn't a real cat in sight or any evidence of one. Then again, this was government housing. They probably had a "no pets" clause. Pity. She seemed like she would be good with pets.

Dottie reappeared in short order. A tray was hooked to the front of her walker. Balanced on the tray was an elaborately etched crystal bowl with a silver rim and a plastic half-gallon jug of One Shot brand holy water. With every step she took, the bowl clanked against the metal walker leg and the jug rocked back and forth.

I started to rise to help her, but Gibson beat me to it. He grabbed the bowl with both hands, moving it gently to the top of the coffee table. Next he took the bottle of holy water, uncorked it, and began pouring it into the bowl as Dottie carefully lowered herself into a worn but fluffy recliner.

"Do you have anything that was with you when you were

attacked?" she asked. "It can be anything small enough to fit in the bowl. Rings, car keys—" She left the sentence unfinished because I'd already started nodding. My clothes might be trashed. My keys hadn't been with me. But there were little garnet studs in my ears. Since I woke up with them, I must have been wearing them last night. Best of all, they were set in silver, which should make them even better for the purpose.

I reached up to take them from my ears as she placed one frail hand on each side of the bowl and began muttering a soft chant that I recognized as a basic focusing exercise. I dropped the earrings into the center of the bowl without being told.

Concentric circles of water raced toward the edge of the bowl. When they hit the glass, flames erupted, racing around the silver rim. Smoke gathered above the water's surface to form a black-and-white image of a sleazy bar. I watched myself from above, looking simultaneously bored and disgusted by the lewd scene just over my shoulder. There were too many nude, sweaty limbs and groping hands for my taste. I was keeping an eye on the prince—whom I recognized from the file in my car—and apparently I wasn't liking it. There are some things it's better not to remember. Then a pair of men rushed into the room and the situation took on an urgent feel. We raced out into a darkened alley. The image was so detailed that I could make out individual bricks and the long scaly tails of the rats feasting on a pile of garbage. I could actually hear their chittering and squeaks, along with the distant sounds of the city.

Vicki uses a mirror as her focus. It's impressive. But this was just . . . cool. I watched, mesmerized, as shadows shifted, then solidified to reveal vampires lying in wait. I held my breath as a rectangle of white light appeared as the back door of the building opened. The miniature image of Bob Johnson stepped into the alley with me following a few steps behind him.

Bob was there? But he's based out of New York now. What the hell? I shook my head, forcing myself to concentrate on what I was seeing. I watched myself look both ways down the alley.

One of the rats bolted, and I saw myself turn, my gun tracking its movement. The vampires struck.

As the fight played out in front of me in miniature, visceral flashes of memory hit me like punches to the gut—the smell of cordite mixed with the heavy scent of blood overwhelming the stench of the alley, the pounding of my heart as I dragged Bob toward the light and safety, only to have the escape route cut off behind us by the . . . *thing* pretending to be the crown prince.

Sweat beaded my forehead. Panting, I felt myself struggling as they ripped off my jacket to get at wrists and throat, felt arms like iron bands pinning me to the ground as sharp canines tore into my upper thigh. Though I knew I was sitting, safe and sound, on Dottie's comfortable sofa, I couldn't escape the sensations.

I heard myself screaming, a sound of hopelessness and rage, and though a part of me knew that Dottie had cut off the spell, I remained trapped in the memory. In my mind I saw a dark-haired vampire raise his head from my upper thigh, my blood smeared across his face, dripping from the silly little soul patch on his chin as he began chanting in a language I didn't know. Magic rose in a wave. I couldn't breathe, and I felt myself weakening as blood pumped from my wounds.

A female form rose in a liquid movement from where she'd been feasting on Johnson. "Are you insane? You'll get us all killed. She's supposed to *die* so they can blame it on Edgar."

She started to move forward, to interfere, but a melodic voice stopped her in her tracks.

"Really? How very interesting."

Every vamp in the alley turned at the sound of that voice. The chant above me stopped in mid-syllable. Soft as a sigh, three forms dropped to opposite ends of the alley from the rooftops. Only three, but even in miniature you could see the fear in the eyes of the bats who'd been feasting on me. I assumed the new bat was Edgar. He and two companions glided slowly forward. In the distance I heard the screech of tires and the slam of car doors followed by running feet. Edgar swore softly and gestured to his companions.

Edgar and the two vampires with him vanished, without so much as a puff of smoke, leaving the other bats to deal with the pair of snarling werewolves who tore through the mouth of the alley.

A harsh slap rocked my head back, and I blinked, trying to focus, as I found myself abruptly back in Dottie's sunny living room. My throat ached from screaming and the carpet was wet from where the crystal bowl had been knocked off the table.

I shivered, my teeth chattering, cold from physical and psychic shock.

I remembered.

Furious pounding at the front door made Dottie jump to her feet abruptly enough to stumble. Gibson managed to grab her before she could fall, then hurried over to deal with whoever. An alarmed neighbor probably. Not that I cared. I didn't. I couldn't even *think* past the roar of my own pulse, pumping adrenaline-laced blood through my body.

As if from a great distance I heard a worried male voice calling out, "Dottie, are you all right?"

"I'm fine, Robert." The old woman's voice was surprisingly unperturbed. She gave me a meaningful look before continuing. "Celia here just saw a mouse. It startled her."

I wasn't going to argue. I was too busy hyperventilating. Memory suppression is a psychological defense mechanism. The subconscious mind tries its damnedest to protect us from the things we're not equipped to deal with, and the vampire's spell had helped. It had been too soon to tear the lid off of these particular memories. Any time in the next millennium would have been too soon. "Trauma" is such a nice, sterile word for what was ripping through my brain and chest.

An elderly man shoved roughly past Gibson to stand in front of Dot, his eyes narrowing with suspicion. He turned to me, his mouth dropping open.

"I'm phobic." I managed to gasp out the lie, and saw real relief chase across my hostess's features.

"Really, Robert, we need to get an exterminator in here! What I wouldn't give for my dear Minnie. She was quite the mouser." Minnie the Mouser. That was just sick. But I liked it. I found myself choking on a hysterical laugh.

"Are you all right?" Gibson's eyes were on mine and were dark with concern.

"I'll be fine." It was a lie. Fine had gone for a long vacation somewhere along with my sanity. But I was alive, and here, and

I damned well needed to get my shit together if I was going to survive this. And I intended to.

Dottie stepped over my foot, splayed across her nice carpet. "Be a dear, Robert, there's a pitcher of lemonade in the refrigerator—"

"No." I shook my head and tried to collect myself. "Thank you, but no. I'm fine now, and we need to get going."

"Are you sure, dear?" Dottie might not want Robert to know what had happened, but she was obviously concerned about me.

I shook my head again. My brain was gathering the fabric of reality around itself again and I was happy to report the truth. "I'm okay. Just let me clean up the mess and we'll be out of your hair."

"Oh, you don't have to do that." But she wasn't hurrying to do it herself, either.

"Really. I insist. Are there paper towels in the kitchen?"

"Yes, dear. On a holder attached to the wall by the refrigerator. You can't miss them."

I got my feet under me and hurried out of the room. Yes, I'd clean up the mess. But more than that, I wanted a couple of minutes alone.

The prince was a fake. There hadn't been a raid. There had been no cops at either end of that alley. The entire job, from start to finish, had been a setup. I'd been supposed to die and have the whole thing be blamed on the vampire named Edgar. Why? Damn it . . . *why*? And who was behind it? I mean, the whole thing was being set up by someone with enough resources and money to make it all happen and have access to demons or half demons capable and willing to work spells that were anathema.

I'd come here for answers, and wound up with more, and scarier, questions.

8

Gibson slid his cell phone back into the pocket of his jacket. He'd called in and left a voice mail for his superiors as soon as we'd gotten into the privacy of his car. Now that the call was over, he glanced at me from the driver's seat. "You look like shit."

I didn't doubt him, but that didn't mean I liked hearing it said out loud. "Gee, thanks." I made the words as dry and sarcastic as I could, and it brought a tight smile to his face. "You try remembering your own murder sometime, see how you like it."

"Nah, I think I'll pass." He turned his full attention back to the road.

"Quick thinking, by the way—telling the neighbor I'd seen a mouse."

"Well, she had to say something. You were screaming bloody murder. And Dottie doesn't want anyone to know about her talent. The last time people found out, they hounded her constantly, wanting her to 'find out things.' She didn't get a minute's peace."

I shook my head. The lie had made me look like an idiot,

but I'd played along. "Did she really have a cat named Minnie the Mouser?"

"Right up until the landlord made her get rid of Minnie."

"Bastard."

He chuckled. "I take it you like animals?"

"Love 'em. But my schedule's weird."

He let out a heaving sigh as he took a left turn. "Too bad. I was hoping you might want a cat. She really is one hell of a mouser."

I started to laugh. It was a little bit hysterical, but I couldn't help myself. Sometimes either you laugh or you cry, and crying wouldn't do any good.

Unfortunately, I laughed hard enough that tears started. *Then* I cried. Gibson didn't say a word, just reached over when we hit a red light and popped open the glove box. Inside was a box of tissues.

I used a few to wipe my eyes and blow my nose. He pretended not to notice. It was a relief, really. I don't like crying. It makes me feel weak and out of control. I'm not weak, but out of control . . . today that was something of an understatement. Besides, Bob Johnson was a friend, and judging from what I'd seen in that vision, he was dead and gone. How the hell was I going to break the news to Vanessa?

I cried hard, but not for long. Still, even that small release was good for me. I was feeling a little bit better by the time Gibson pulled into the parking lot of my office building. My office isn't quite in central downtown. Even with office sharing I couldn't afford that. Instead, we're about four blocks off. It puts us closer to the county jail, which works well for the bail bondsmen. Being in the same building with the bail bondsmen (who do not and ethically cannot actually *refer* clients to a specific attorney) is good for the attorney. Because let's face it. Even without a referral, sheer placement means they're going to get noticed.

Left over from a bygone era and surrounded by squat office buildings, our three-story Victorian, once a mansion, has more charm and style than anyplace else within miles. The bulk of it is painted slate gray, but there's lots of gingerbread trim that is done up in white, burgundy, and black. A portion of the rents is pooled into a fund that pays for building maintenance, including lawn care, so David's son comes by once a week to keep the grounds picture perfect, including the huge trees that shade the front and back porches.

The place has its drawbacks. The parking lot is small, only holding six cars. And the high ceilings and choppy floor plan make it hard to keep it a reasonable temperature. In summer, the upper floors can be wretchedly hot. In winter . . . well, let's just say I'm glad it's California and it doesn't get *too* cold. Still, it's a gem of a building, with the original dark wood stain on trim and doors, a huge stained-glass window on the second-floor landing, and a turret where I can sit and eat my morning bagel and watch the world go by. I rent about half of the third floor, including said turret.

Gibson pulled his sedan into the spot marked with my name. It was one of only two in the shade. I watched him take a seemingly casual look around while taking in every detail. I didn't mind. The place looks good. Even the windows get washed on a regular basis.

He looked around and grinned. "Nice. You want to clean up before you go inside?" He unfastened his seat belt and got out of the car. He was moving slowly, with an unnatural stiff-ness that spoke of the pain he was trying to hide.

That made me frown. "No. Why?" I climbed out as well. As I shoved the door closed I caught a glimpse of my reflection in the car window. Gibson was right. I looked awful. Somewhere during the course of the morning I'd lost the ponytail holder, and my hair was hanging loose. Raking my hands through the tangled mass didn't help much, and nothing was going to make the dark circles under my reddened eyes any less obvious.

Ah well. There was nothing I could do to change things right now, so there was no point in dwelling on it.

Gibson waited patiently for me to join him on the steps onto the wide front porch. I touched my finger to the porch swing to set it moving. I do it every time I walk by, and have no idea why. Maybe just as a counterpoint to the other furniture. It wouldn't do any good to push the wicker chairs. They were permanently affixed to the floor.

He graciously held open the door for me, so I stepped into the muted shadows of the lobby. It took a minute for my eyes to adjust to the relative darkness, so I heard Dawna's gasp be-fore I saw her.

"Celia . . . Oh my *God*." Dawna's eyes are large and doelike under normal circumstances. Now they were the size of plates. Her jaw dropped open. "What's *happened* to you? I mean, Kevin said you'd been attacked last night, but ohmigod you have *fangs* and your *skin . . .*" The words tumbled out in a breathless rush. She was swaying on her feet enough that Gib-son rushed forward to help her into the nearest chair—the lit-tle rolling number behind the reception counter.

"I got attacked by bats. One of them was a master, and he

started to turn me, but the cavalry arrived before he could finish the job. I'm *not* a bat. I'm not going to *be* a bat."

"But you *look*—," she was whispering.

"Like something that should be staked and beheaded." It came out more bitter than I had intended it to, and she flinched, tears filling her eyes. *Crap.* "I'm sorry, Dawna. I didn't mean—"

She shook her head. "It's all right. Really. I mean, I can't even imagine—" She stopped, evidently at a loss for words, which was *so* not Dawna. I love her like a sister, but she can and will talk your ear off given half a chance. Which we didn't have time for right now.

"This is Detective Gibson." Gibson turned from where he was examining the elegant impressionist print hanging above a fireplace framed by built-in bookcases on the far side of the room. I continued, "He's investigating an incident from last night. He's going to need copies of some of the phone records. . . ." The sentence trickled to a halt as she shook her head.

"Hello, Detective." She rose, extending her hand as he approached, and I got a better look at her. She was wearing a classic silk suit in navy with a crimson blouse. The skirt was short enough to show an excellent pair of legs, made to look longer by a set of heels I wouldn't have attempted. Still, she looked good. Then again, she always does, and without resorting to any magic. Just good genetics and an eye for how to make the most of her assets.

She rallied enough to put on her best professional demeanor, but I could tell she'd had quite a shock. I was sorry about that, and wished to hell I'd taken the time to call ahead. Then again, Kevin had warned her and that hadn't done any good.

"I'm sorry Celia, I'd normally be happy to help the detective. But my computer crashed this morning. All the computer files; all the billing; everything . . . just *gone.*"

Oh, *crap.* Well, that sucked. Big-time. But while she obviously wasn't happy, she wasn't throwing a fit. Maybe seeing me put it into perspective.

"Oh, Lord. I hope you've backed up."

She sighed. "The backups are wiped, too. Must have been some sort of freak electric surge."

I cringed in sympathy. I keep hard copies of everything, in addition to my flash drive, but some of the others don't. It was going to be a monumental task to re-create all of the records from scratch. At least I could give her one bit of good news. "Well, if it makes you feel any better, I've got all my stuff backed up onto a memory stick and my laptop is in my safe. It'll save you having to re-create my stuff at least."

"That's something, I suppose." She sighed and turned to face me, her expression worried. "Are you sure you're okay? A pair of federal agents were in here earlier looking for you. They said you'd been hurt last night, made me check to make sure you weren't unconscious in your office. That's why I called Kevin. He usually knows where you are."

Federal agents? I glanced at Gibson, but if he was surprised, he didn't show it. He just continued to take in the decor with a seemingly innocent face. But what happened? I knew now, but I didn't want to talk about it. The memories were still too raw. So I brushed it off by turning to Gibson. "That was awfully quick. Think your people called them?"

"Possible." His voice held a trace of doubt, which I shared. The wheels of federal justice seldom roll that quickly. Thorough, yes. God, yes. But *quick*? Not so much. Then again, we were dealing with foreign royalty—the threat of a major diplomatic incident might have been just enough to light a fire under them. But who, before me, might have told them about the prince? That's the only reason I could think the Feds would be involved, and if they'd heard about it from Alex, they would have known I was at the station. I turned back to Dawna. "Are they still here?"

"No, but you only missed them by a couple of minutes. They left a card. You're supposed to call." She arched an elegant eyebrow. "And Birchwoods left an urgent message. But if I were you I'd call Kevin first. He's about to blow a gasket. Swear to God he's called at least ten times."

I sighed. He'd said to call and I'd flat forgotten. He was probably pissed beyond measure. I was sort of surprised he wasn't waiting in the next room. "Call him back. Tell him I'm helping the cops with their investigation and I'll get back with him as soon as I break free."

"He's not going to like that."

Of course he wasn't. But he'd have to live with it, because I needed to cooperate with the police to get the police to cooperate with me.

"Do you want me to call the agents, tell them you're here?"

I glanced over at Gibson, who was shaking his head no. I didn't blame him. A jurisdictional pissing contest would do nothing but slow him down. I'd give them whatever information they wanted. But I liked Gibson, so he'd get first dibs.

"Not yet. Let me finish with the detective first."

"All right. Is there anything I can get the two of you? I can start a fresh pot of coffee if you like."

"No need to go to any trouble." Gibson gave her a charming smile. "I don't intend to stay that long."

"Oh, it's no bother." She blushed. It looked good on her. Until that instant it hadn't occurred to me that she and Gibson had been eyeing each other. Leave it to Dawna. My world was going to hell, the office was in shambles, and yet somehow she'd managed to find an eligible man. I swear she's got radar. Or maybe her grandmother did some ancient Vietnamese magic on her that drew them like flies to honey. Whatever. As soon as Gibson was out of earshot I'd warn her off. He was dying. Getting involved with him would be an invitation to heartbreak.

I started up the stairs. Gibson followed. The staircase isn't wide and it's steep, with narrow treads. Most folks get breathless by the first-floor landing. By the time they reach my digs on the third floor, they're usually gasping and irritable. If the building hadn't been designated a historic landmark, we'd probably have been forced to install an elevator and make the whole thing handicapped accessible. Instead, we have a ramp leading up to the back porch and a shared, accessible conference room on the first floor.

The staircase ended in an open area on the third floor. It's a sunny space, lit by large east-facing windows. I usually like it, but today I hurried down the hall, past the door to Freedom Bail Bonds, to unlock the door to my office.

In some ways my office is very feminine. The walls are painted a deep, warm peach. The trim is painted off-white, as is the elegantly patterned tin ceiling. Heavy drapes printed with cabbage roses in white, peach, and russet cover the various windows. All of that femininity is nicely contrasted by the dark wood office furniture, black metal filing cabinets, and big, glossy black gun safe bolted to the floor. It's large enough to hold an arsenal. We had to reinforce the floor so it didn't crash down into the second-floor bathroom, which didn't make the landmark people very happy. I scrounged around old houses for nearly a month to find enough hardwood rafters from the right time period so we'd qualify for the brass plaque.

The safe is top-of-the-line, with not only heavy-duty locks but also level-eight magical wards protecting it. Anybody who tries to mess with it will wind up on their ass at least, and probably in the hospital for an extended stay. I'd have made the protections lethal—but the police frown on that sort of thing.

My mother whines to Gran about how I make so much money, where could I possibly spend it all? I was looking at a chunk of it. A lot goes into savings and investments, of course. No matter how good you are, you're going to get hurt in this job—if you don't get killed. Insurance companies won't give bodyguards a disability policy. So you have to prepare for the worst on your own. I have a tidy little nest egg, and anybody who signs my contract has to guarantee a lump sum payment of a quarter mil in case of death or permanent disability. I charge a rate that is significant enough to allow me to live quite nicely. What's left over gets either invested or spent on things like the safe and weapons.

And art. A couple of small high-quality framed prints are hung on the outer walls. The cherry frames match the wood of the coffee table and the arms of the visitors' chairs. The paintings were created by a magician several centuries before. I swear there's more to them than pretty seascapes. I just haven't figured out what yet.

The inside wall is all business—a large-scale, detailed map of the city and surrounding areas. It's been laminated and mounted on cork and takes up most of the wall. I use it to plan transport and emergency evacuation routes, among other things. I've marked ongoing construction projects and detours. Because if a map like that isn't accurate it's worthless.

Gibson wandered around the room, taking it all in. I stepped behind the desk and over to the safe. I stated my name very clearly, and a panel slid out. I set my left hand on it, palm downward, holding still as a soft blue light scanned from left to right, then top to bottom. Two of the lights on the display panel switched to green. The third, however, remained a sullen red.

"What the hell?" I glared at the machine. The technology part of the security was working just fine: My voice had passed, my palm and fingerprints accepted. But the magical wards, the ones keyed to my DNA, didn't accept my identity. I couldn't open the safe.

"Is there a problem?"

"The safe doesn't recognize me." I kept my voice pleasant, but I was swearing inwardly. This was bad. Really bad.

"How long before the wards wind down?" He said it as though he figured it would be a matter of hours. Little did he know.

"Probably a decade or so."

He stared at me with wide eyes. It probably took a full minute before he gathered his wits enough to say, "Isn't that a bit excessive?"

I turned, my eyes locking with his for a long moment. "There's no point in having a safe if it doesn't keep things *safe*."

He shook his head, obviously both annoyed and amused.

Glad he could find something funny about it. I didn't. Most of my weapons, and all of my computer files, were locked behind those wards. It had never occurred to me that *I* wouldn't be able to get to them. *Crap.*

I turned back to the desk and picked up the phone with my right hand as I thumbed through my old-fashioned Rolodex with my left.

I found the number quickly enough and was pleased when the tech support rep picked up on the third ring—without routing me through an annoying voice-mail system.

"Moore Lock and Safe, Justin here."

I blinked a couple times in surprise. Justin is the owner, and the man who most often comes by to refresh the warding. I couldn't imagine what was going on that he'd be stuck manning the phones.

"Justin, it's Celia. We have a problem." I settled into my desk chair as I explained to him what the safe was . . . or, more accurately, *wasn't* doing.

"Any chance you're preggers?" he asked. "That kind of a heavy-duty biological change can play havoc with the system."

I stared at the phone for a long moment in silence. I couldn't be. No. Not possible. But the question itself was unexpected. It would never have occurred to me that sort of thing could be a problem. I mean, yeah, you're carrying a baby, but you're still *you.*

I'd been quiet too long. He let out a soft chuckle that managed to mix wry amusement with sympathy. "Sorry or congratulations, whichever applies."

"No, it's not that." I shook my head, even though he

couldn't see it. "I mean, I'm not. But I got attacked by a bat last night, and he tried to change me."

The humor evaporated immediately, replaced by a flattering level of concern. "Oh, *crap*. Are you all right?"

"Apparently the safe doesn't think so." I tried to make it a joke, but I couldn't quite pull it off. There was just the hint of a tremolo in my voice. I plowed on anyway, hoping he wouldn't notice. "Any ideas as to how we can fix this?" Gibson was probably listening, but he didn't make a big deal out of it. He opened the door to the balcony and stepped out, then leaned against the railing and basked. Bright sunshine illuminated the harsh contours of his face.

"Well . . . um . . . wow," he muttered under his breath while he thought and I drummed my fingers impatiently on the desktop. "Theoretically the same procedure should work. I mean, I've never tried it, but the principle is sound." He sighed. "And let's hope it does, because if not you are *so* screwed."

"What do I do?"

"We need samples with your DNA from before you changed. Hair, fingernail clippings, something like that."

"I can get some hair from my brush in the bathroom."

"Good. Once you've got it, hit the reset button, do the voice recognition and the palm print, then say, 'Pregnancy override.' Two small drawers will open up beneath the palm reader. Drop the hairs in the left one. The right one has a sharp point in it. Jab your finger on it until it draws blood."

Ow.

"The drawers will close, and the machine will start cross-matching the DNA between the two samples. It'll take about twenty-four hours. When it finishes, if you're cleared, you'll get the green light and it will have reset to the 'new you.'"

"And if it doesn't?"

A long pause. "Call me back."

"Right."

He hung up without saying good-bye—probably to go find and study the tech manuals. I went down the hall to the bathroom I share with the guys from the bail-bonding company and retrieved my hairbrush. I followed Justin's directions carefully, with Gibson in fascinated attendance.

"Think it'll work?" he asked.

I sighed and steeled myself before stabbing myself on the finger prick. "Ow. It's never a good thing when the tech guys start saying things like 'theoretically' and 'in principle.'"

Gibson winced, but whether it was in sympathy or frustration at the fact that all my records were just out of reach I couldn't be sure.

"Even if it does, it's going to be twenty-four hours before I can give you any more information."

He put both hands on the back of the guest chair, leaning his weight on them. "You don't have *anything* that's not in the safe? Written notes? Message slips?"

I shook my head. "Not really. Everything's on the computer . . ." I wound up leaving the sentence dangling as my mind wandered. "Except . . . I remember the name and address of the place where I reported for duty. I can take you there."

He shook his head. "No way, Graves. This situation is a political nightmare, a freaking diplomatic 'incident' just waiting to happen. You're going to give me the name and address of the building and anything else you can remember about how you were hired, and then you're going to stay the hell away from that part of it. It's going to be hard enough finding out whether the prince you were guarding was the real deal or a body double and what happened. The State Department is going to have a fit, and they're going to want in. They're also going to want you *out* of it except as a witness."

"But—," I started to protest.

"I'll keep you advised. But stay away from it. Trust me, you'll have enough on your plate, dealing with the vampire end of things." He was probably right. That didn't mean I had to like it. I scowled at him but gave him the information without further argument.

Gibson reached into his pocket, withdrew a notebook and a silver Cross pen, and scribbled down the address of the hotel.

"I'll head right over. In the meantime, thank you for your cooperation. If you think of anything else before I get back"—he reached into the breast pocket of his suit for a business card—"give me a call. Otherwise, I'll meet you back here, this time tomorrow."

Crap. He was going to leave me stuck here without my car. I mean, yeah, he was in the middle of an important investigation and it was only a couple of blocks, but I had that whole sunlight allergy thing to consider. "Right."

He stopped so abruptly I wondered if he'd heard my thought. "Do you need me to take you back to your car?"

I could tell from the way he said it, he was hoping I'd say no. He was just that anxious to get on with the investigation.

"I can give her a lift." Dawna appeared in the hall, carrying a tray with coffee and creamers.

"Thanks." He took a Styrofoam cup from the tray and took a long pull. "I appreciate that." He took one more drink, then set the cup on the tray and started down the stairs.

"No problema." She gave him a smile that could've lit the entire West Coast.

She watched him for a full minute, until he disappeared from sight. When the door slammed, her face took on a calculating look I knew from long experience. She'd set her sights on the detective.

"Don't."

"But—"

"Seriously, Dawna. Bad idea."

She stuck her lip out in a pretty pout and huffed a bit, flinging her long black ponytail over her shoulder. "Damn. There you go, spoiling everything. Is he yours? Is that the problem?"

"No." I admitted. "He's sick. There's something wrong with him. I can smell it."

"You can *smell* it? Seriously?"

"Yeah."

"Ewwww. That is just . . . gross." She shook her head. "What do I smell like?"

I didn't even have to think about it. "Chanel Number Five, high-quality leather, and chicken salad on rye."

She blinked. "Well, all right then." Then, giving a gusty sigh, "Shame, though. He seemed nice. A little old. But nice."

I didn't answer. I'd grabbed a cup of coffee from the tray and was taking a long pull of liquid nirvana. Caffeine, nectar of the gods. I didn't gulp it down, it was too hot for that, but I savored each sip, letting the scent fill my nostrils and chase away the stench of illness.

"Thanks for that. Give me a few minutes more to myself, okay? I've got to make a couple calls." I'd start with my gran, which would be tough enough. But as soon as I'd finished with that I was going to have to call Bob's wife and break the news.

Gran still wasn't answering the phone. That was ominous all on its own. She's healthy as a horse, but she's not young. Of course it was much more likely that she was avoiding my calls. She does it every time my mother talks her into something they both know I'm not going to approve of—little things, like letting my mother, who has had her license revoked and is an uninsurable drunk, take the car.

Don't think about it. You don't know that's what's happening. She could be busy at the church.

I tried calling Kevin. I really did. But he didn't pick up. I left him a voice mail saying I was hanging in there and not to worry and thanking him, Emma, and Amy for saving my life.

My own voice mail was still *presently unavailable*, which was getting annoying. If I didn't have access in the next hour or so, I was going to be calling the main line and complaining to my carrier.

I hesitated before dialing the next number.

Gwendolyn Talbert had been one of the best therapists in the business until she retired two years ago due to health problems. She had specialized in trauma victims—particularly children. She saved my sanity and probably my life after the events that led to my sister's death and my own torture. It was Gwen's delicate use of magic that had blunted the memories of the trauma, making them bearable, enabling me to eventually have a normal, loving relationship with Bruno DeLuca. No, I hadn't dated anyone since we broke up, but that was by *choice*, not because I wasn't able to.

Now I needed help. I was hanging on to my sanity with my teeth and toenails, mostly by very deliberately not thinking about things. But that wouldn't last. The shock would wear off, and when it did I was going to need a damned good therapist. I wanted it to be Gwen.

The phone rang three times before going to voice mail. Apparently this was not my day to reach *anybody*. I listened to the calm, feminine voice saying, "You have reached Gwendolyn Talbert. If you have called on a professional matter, I regret that I am no longer seeing patients. If this is a personal call, please leave your name and number after the tone."

I waited for the beep. Taking a deep breath, I spoke as clearly and calmly as I could manage. "Gwen, it's me . . . um, Celia Graves. Um, something's happened. I need to talk to someone. I know you're retired, but I don't trust anyone else. If you can't see me, can you at least give me a name? Somebody *you* trust? Please?"

God I sounded pathetic. Desperate. Then again, I was. I left the office number and hung up. I would have left the new cell number, if only I'd written it down somewhere to remember it.

While I was making useless calls, I left a message for El Jefe. I needed to find out everything I could about abominations and brush up on any successful techniques hunters had used to find the daytime lairs of master vampires. I wasn't sure if he was back from Chicago, so I decided to start doing a little research on my own.

But first, I had one more call to make.

I had Dawna get me the number from the Internet. I hadn't been sure she'd be home. Still, I recognized Vanessa's voice when she picked up the phone on the third ring.

I tried to break it to her gently. I was rewarded by a stream of expletives screamed at top volume—loud enough that I had to move the receiver away from my ear the length of my arm. She followed this by blaming *me* for his death, then weeping hysterically and hanging up on me. Bob didn't have any other living relatives, so I didn't know who else to call. But it seemed *wrong*. He'd been a good man. Not perfect, but who is? He deserved to have somebody more than just me to mourn him. Maybe there was someone. I hadn't realized they'd gotten divorced until the screaming voice in my ear informed me of it in no uncertain terms. Did he have a new girlfriend? I had no way of knowing. I sure as hell wasn't going to call Vanessa again.

Maybe in a day or two, when things settled down, I'd put some effort into looking into it. But first, I wanted to take care of the crisis du jour.

I braced myself and sprinted from the curb to the front doors of the university library. Since most of the building's front facade is glass, I wasn't really safe until I'd gotten halfway down the stairs down to the basement.

I'd always considered it a nuisance that they'd put the

paranormal section down there, all by itself, behind every known kind of protection. Now I wasn't sorry. Being in the basement meant that I would be able to have a windowless study room to work in.

Halfway down the stairs I hit a magical barrier I couldn't see and nearly lost my footing. I had to grab onto the handrail and steady myself for a minute before I could move forward. When I did it felt . . . odd . . . like I was forcing my way through a wall of Jell-O. Tiny sparks exploded against my skin. None of them were strong, but there were a lot of them. The sensation was similar to that of being in a room with too much static electricity. I couldn't move backward at all and moving forward was slow. It didn't get better until I stepped off of the staircase. When I did, the change in pressure made my ears pop and my nostrils twitch.

I recognized the staff member behind the reserved desk. Anna had been in charge of the Paranormal and Metaphysical Desk for over a decade. She'd helped me with research for many a project, and could recite where every book or artifact was from memory. A soft-spoken woman of "a certain age," she had iron gray hair and warm brown eyes hidden behind thick-lensed glasses. I'd always admired her droll sense of humor, and knew she had enough mage talent to be able to handle any student-related accidents that might occur due to mishandling of the merchandise. I didn't doubt that it was her spell I'd passed through a moment before.

"Stop right there." Her voice rang with authority. She rose, leaning both hands on the counter. "You have no business coming here."

Anger rose up in a wave. How *dare* she? "It's full daylight,

Anna." I didn't bother to keep the scorn from my voice. "I'm *not* a bat."

"If you were a bat," she answered coldly, "you wouldn't have made it through the wards. But that doesn't mean you aren't dangerous. In fact, it makes you more so. Because you're still human enough to pass through unhindered."

I felt a surge of rage that sent the blood pounding through my veins. My vision narrowed, focusing on the pulse throbbing at the base of her stringy neck; the adrenaline-laced scent of her fear rose to my nostrils like the bouquet of a fine wine. I could almost taste—

I closed my eyes, shutting out the image of her pulse. Slowly, carefully, I fought to rein in my temper by controlling my breathing, panting through an open mouth so that the scents wouldn't overwhelm me. It didn't feel close to nightfall, but my brain was telling me, *Time to go hunting.*

I am not a vampire. I am not a fucking bat. I will not do this.

It took time. It wasn't easy and it probably wasn't pretty, but I fought down the beast within me. When I opened my eyes, I was myself again.

Silence dragged on for long moments as Anna stared at me. When she finally spoke, her voice was soft and careful. It was the same tone you use to talk to people standing on a ledge, or wild animals you don't want to spook. "I shouldn't have threatened you, Celia. That was stupid. But you don't belong here. You don't belong anywhere in public. It isn't safe. There are too many people. Too much temptation."

Her expression was so serious, so *pained*, that I knew there was personal history behind her reaction. I knew I should care.

But God help me, I didn't. Not really. All I cared about was getting away from her and finding out what I could do to fix this. There had to be something. When it comes to metaphysics, there are very few absolutes. There's almost always *something* you can do. It may be difficult to the point of being damned near impossible—but almost nothing was actually undoable, with enough power, time, and money.

"I *need* to know about abominations, Anna." I said it quietly, and while I couldn't quite manage not to lisp, I did my absolute best to stifle the part of me that wanted to rage at the injustice of the situation. "I need to know how to fix this."

"You can't." Her whispered words were just a bare breath of air. Normally I wouldn't have heard them.

I closed my eyes against her pain. I didn't want to see it. Didn't want to know. I had enough problems of my own. "Please. I have to try."

I heard her chair scrape back as she moved away from the desk. "I suppose you do." The words shook, just a little. But from the sound of it, her fear was being overcome by a combination of sorrow and determination. "But you don't have to do it here. And I will not allow you to endanger the other students and staff."

"So, what? What do I do?"

"Go to your office. I've already scanned and e-mailed copies of everything we've got to Dr. Reynolds, Professor Landingham, and a police detective." *Duh.* Why was I surprised that everyone had the same idea? "I'll send the documents to your student account. You can print out whatever you need. Now go!"

I felt the air between us harden into a solid wall of force. Slowly, inexorably, it began pushing me backward. It was actually kind of cool that she could do that. I was still annoyed. I could appreciate the technique without admiring the cause.

The drive back to the office didn't take long, but by the time I got there the place was locked up tight. It was lunchtime, and Dawna had hung up one of those little clock face signs saying she'd be back at 1:00.

I let myself in, grabbed my messages and faxes, and climbed the stairs to the copy room on the second floor. My laptop was locked in the safe, but we've got an old desktop hooked up in the copy room for people to use in an emergency. It's hooked directly to the big printer, so even if the network goes down, it's still possible to print. I had no idea if Dawna had managed to get the computers fixed, but even if she hadn't, I should be able to bring up Anna's e-mail and print it. While I was at it, I plugged the new cell phone in to charge.

It didn't take long to log on and find the right e-mail, but it took a while to print. There were a lot of pages. Good news for me. Maybe somewhere in there I'd find information to help me get through this. God I hoped so.

While I waited for the printer to finish, I started flipping through my messages. Kevin had called some more. Dawna had finally resorted to a sort of code—"K 29." *Twenty-nine? Wow.* I'd try him again as soon as I got up to the office.

None of the other messages were earth-shattering: some work stuff, a call from Gibson asking if I was *sure* about the address I'd given him, and Dr. Reynolds saying I'd left in such a hurry that he hadn't had a chance to give me my follow-up orders, so he'd be faxing them to my office.

I flipped pages until I got to his fax. His orders were hand-written and barely legible. I was exhausted. It wasn't long before the words on the pages began blurring in front of my eyes. I didn't intend to close them, had no intention of falling asleep. But there you go.

Come to me, Celia.

He was in a very ordinary motel room. I recognized the decor—or lack thereof. The drapes had been pulled tight. The only light came from one of those little wall-mounted lamps. He was sitting at a table on the opposite side of the room.

My sire looked like a kid of about seventeen or so. Dark hair, but with skin that had probably been as fair as mine even before someone had changed him. He was probably old as dirt, but he'd been young enough at his death that he couldn't grow a decent beard. All he had was a wispy little soul patch. It looked kind of silly, which made him just a fraction less frightening.

You must come to me.

The hell you say.

He frowned, as if he heard the thought. Maybe he had. I mean, if this was real and not just some funky dream, then he was a daywalker. He might not be able to endure sunlight, but he wasn't dead for the day, either. Even most master vamps can't manage that. Which meant that while he might *look* like a teenager and *dress* like a teenager, he'd been around long enough to get very, very good.

Of course, it could be a dream.

The frown deepened. He turned his head so that I was seeing him full-on. His expression changed, and while his body was still young, the look on his face was old, old and corrupt with power. His pupils expanded until his eyes were almost totally black. I could feel the power of them sucking at me as he willed me to meet his gaze. It was like fighting an undertow in the ocean, a pull that was irresistible, relentless.

As if in response to that thought I began to smell the tang of salt water and fish, hear the familiar sounds of the beach, the crash of waves, the call of gulls.

What the hell?

I woke with a start to the sound of a light tap on the door. "Celia?" The room was dark except for the flickering lights of electronic equipment. Apparently I'd dozed off. When I hadn't moved for more than ten minutes, the lights had shut off automatically, allowing me to sleep . . . like a dead thing. When I sat up they came back on. I blinked, trying to adjust to the glare and gather my muddled thoughts.

I wiped a bit of drool from the corner of my mouth and nicked the back of my knuckle on a fang. It stung for a second, then went numb. But the blood flowed freely—more freely than it should've. Swearing under my breath, I used the hem of my shirt to apply pressure on it, and called out, "Come in."

Dawna didn't come in, but she did crack open the door. All I could see through the opening was the tip of her golden brown nose and the reflection from her reading glasses.

"Celia, what are you doing in there?"

"Nothing. Printing, reading stuff the library sent me. Why?"

"Because about two minutes ago every speaker on every computer, cell phone, Bubba's TV—everything—began playing ocean sounds. Crashing surf, whales, and seagulls. It stopped when I knocked on the door. But the source was this room. So I'm asking again. What are you *doing* in there?"

"Is that even possible?"

She gave the door a gentle shove, so that it swung fully open, allowing her to give me a look, but she stayed outside. She'd closed in on herself, hugging her arms to her body as though she were cold. But she wasn't cold. Her body radiated heat . . . life that nearly vibrated around her. I felt drawn to that warmth, wanted to wrap it around me and ease the cold that was seeping into my fingers.

I watched her, standing in the doorway, her posture guarded as she took in every detail of the room . . . and me. I suppose she was looking for evidence of something weird or worrying. The only thing to find was the wet spot on the page where I'd drooled as I slept. Embarrassing, but hardly earth-shattering.

Of course she noticed. And for just a second her wary expression softened slightly. I almost believed I saw a flicker of amusement pass through her eyes. But if I did, it was gone in an instant, to be replaced by another worried look.

"Dawna, what's wrong?"

"We need to talk. I read those notes from Dr. Reynolds, and El Jefe faxed a bunch of research to you on the downstairs machine. This thing that's happened to you—it's really serious shit." Her voice sounded shaky, and I could see the pulse jumping at the base of her throat. I wasn't hungry, in fact I felt a little nauseous, but I couldn't not notice. I swallowed hard, dragging my eyes upward, making myself meet her worried almond-shaped eyes.

"Yeah. It is."

"What're you going to do?"

A part of me wanted to lie, wanted to give her the reassurance she so obviously needed. But Dawna's my friend, one of my best friends. You don't lie to friends. You just don't. "Longterm—I don't know. But if I want there to *be* a long term, I have to find the vamp that tried to bring me over and take him down. Preferably before dark." I looked around, trying to find a clock. There wasn't one. No windows, either. "What time is it, anyway?"

"It's almost four thirty. Did you find anything useful in what the library sent?"

"Not yet." Which was true as far as it went. "Lots of interesting stuff, but no answers."

"Maybe there isn't one."

I puffed up my chest and imitated El Jefe at his most pompous. "In magic, as in nature, there is balance. Where there is a spell, there is a counter."

She smiled, but not like she meant it. "Pretty to think so."

"Dr. Landingham knows his stuff."

"Absolutely. But this isn't just magic. It's anatomy. And *that* is a whole lot less . . . flexible."

Just like the pull of my sire's eyes was inflexible. He was still out there, still calling me. I just couldn't hear it over the sound of the ocean. My muscles started to flex, to pull me to my feet. I *wanted* to leave, even though I didn't know where I wanted to go. I could feel my will lessening with each moment, until— "Are you *sure* the ocean sounds originated from this room?"

"Like there was a boom box on full crank."

I shook my head. "That is so weird. I wasn't making any noise, but I could hear it in my dream."

Her carefully plucked brows lowered even as she reared back a little and looked around the room. "Weird. Very weird."

She was so right. Sadly, however, this was the least of my worries. I'd lost a lot of time snoozing. If I wanted to find and kill my sire I needed to find out where and how *now*.

It was time to visit Vicki.

9

One good thing about my nap—it had given my new phone time to charge. It didn't take long at all to load the minutes on it. I gave Dawna the new number so that she could contact me if there were any new emergencies and dashed out the door. I dialed Kevin. Again it went straight to voice mail. "Hi, Kev. It's me. I'm on the way to Birchwoods to see Vicki, to see if she can give me a lead on my sire's lair. Look, I know you've got to go out to the desert tonight, so I'll call you in the morning. Try not to worry." Useless request. He was already worrying. But hey, it was the best I could do. And at least he wouldn't be able to bitch at me about not returning his calls.

I also considered phoning ahead to Birchwoods to let Vicki know I was coming, but she has group from 3:00 to 5:00. By the time she got the message I'd be there. Besides, I was still a little shaken by my dream/vision. I needed a little time away from everything.

I did make a call to the phone number on the file I had on the prince. I got a recording telling me it wasn't in service—all three times I called. Not good. I needed to deal with the vampire sire thing first, but tomorrow I was going to be checking in with the royal family. If Gibson didn't like it, that was just too damned bad.

I set the cell phone on the passenger seat in easy reach and started the car. I took Ocean View rather than the expressway, telling myself that I didn't want to get caught in bumper-to-bumper rush-hour traffic, but I probably would've done it anyway, to be near the sea. I drove the Miata faster than I should've over the winding roads in the lengthening shadows cast in the fading daylight. The ancient trees and tall walls had been landscaped in such a way as to provide security and privacy without looking grim. I could taste the tang of salt on the air from the breeze blowing in from over the water. The racuous call of the gulls was louder than normal, but I'm one of those strange people who actually like the noise that gulls make. Most people around here consider them rats with wings, like pigeons are back east. But I like them . . . the way they swoop and dance on the currents around the shores. I couldn't ride with the top down, but nothing stopped me from opening the widows wide and watching and listening.

I was still feeling a little bit nauseous. Part of it was nerves. But I hadn't eaten since dinner last night. I can skip one meal without too much trouble, but if I let it go too long, I end up feeling sick, grumpy, and not at all hungry. I'd probably have to force myself to eat, but that would be later. First, I wanted to pick my best friend's brain for any memories she had of her two years of vampire studies. Then I'd have her take a peek in that mirror I'd bought her, see if we could find any useful information.

If all else failed, I'd see if she could wrangle me permission

to camp out overnight in the facility's chapel. Assuming I *could.*
Thus far I'd been doing pretty well against anti-vampire tools,
but I hadn't tested myself against holy ground. But hell, if I let
myself think too hard about it, the list of things that were liable
to be a problem would just overwhelm me. I needed to focus.
Take one step at a time. Visit Vicki. Find a safe place for the
night. Then, when daylight came and Kevin was back from
his hunt, we'd talk and plan.

Thinking about my friends made me feel a little better
about the whole mess. Not a *lot* better. But hey, I'd take what I
could get. They'd stick by me, no matter what. They already
had. And if there was an answer, we'd find it. All I had to do
was stay alive long enough for it to do me some good. I could
do that.

Maybe.

I took a deep breath, trying to convince myself that I was
capable of getting a handle on the situation. I almost started
to believe myself. Right up until the temperature in the car
began to drop.

Have I mentioned I'm haunted by ghosts? It was my one
weirdness when I was still vanilla human. My baby sister had
been a powerful medium. Whether the last name Graves came
from an ancestor with the same talent or was just a dose of irony
I don't know. I do know I'm grateful I wasn't born with the
"gift." The dead may try to contact me, but it ain't easy. They
can't use what isn't there. So only the most powerful spirits can
get through—those and the one spirit who attached herself to
me on her death . . . Ivy herself.

She doesn't manifest often, but it's generally memorable
when she does. If I had the talent, she could use my body to

talk to me with my own mouth. I don't. So she has to do things the hard way. Sometimes it makes her frustrated and I wind up with poltergeist-style behavior. Kids think they have the best temper tantrums, but *ghost* kids have them beat by a mile. Not what you need when you're at the wheel.

I pulled onto the nearest side street and up to the curb, my breath fogging the air inside the car, despite the open windows. One of the first manifestations of a spirit is a rapid, drastic temperature drop.

"I know you're here. It's all right. Just don't mess with the Miata, Ivy. You know how much I love this car." I kept my voice low, using soothing tones. Getting agitated creates a kind of energy that makes the ghost more likely to act out.

The dome light flashed on and off. If it was Ivy, we'd worked out a code over the years. Once was a yes. Twice was no.

"Ivy, is it you?"

Two flashes. *No?*

Well, shit. Not Ivy, but whoever it was knew the code? Did ghosts talk? I mean, if they cared enough to stay and latch onto someone, there was generally a reason, and they almost always tried to talk to the living, but do they communicate with *each other*? That I *didn't* know. *Damn it.* I wracked my brain. Ghosts attach to a person or thing that was important to them in their life, someone or something that they consider unfinished business. Until that business gets settled or the body gets cremated, they don't move on to the afterlife. Trouble was, I never have found out what Ivy wants from me.

True believers almost never ghost, so this was someone I knew who wasn't a churchgoer. Not many of those in my life, are there?

Um, just about everyone but my gran. But considering the level of violence in my life, there have actually been very few fatalities. Could it be Bob Johnson? The timing was right and he'd been with me once when Ivy had manifested. I couldn't think why he'd latch onto me, but stranger things had happened. The car was practically a meat locker at this point, and I shivered, my skin crawling with goose bumps.

"Bob, is it you?"

Two flashes. Wrong again. The spirit, whoever it was, was starting to get frustrated. I could feel an electric tension building in the air, enough to make my hair start to frizz.

"Easy. Take it easy. I know you're trying to communicate. We can work this out." A thought crossed my mind. It might work—or not, depending on how focused and powerful the ghost was. "See if you can focus the cold to use frost to write on the window." If it was an older ghost, they should be able to. I pointed to the rounded surface of the windshield. In response, the temperature dropped even further. My teeth started chattering as an arctic blast ruffled my hair to hit the glass with pinpoint precision. I watched in fascinated horror as familiar handwriting took shape and a name appeared.

Vicki.

My heart stopped for a moment and I felt dizzy. *No. NO!* Dammit, she wasn't . . . she couldn't be . . .

"Vicki?" My voice was a raw whisper. I stared at the frost on the window, tears freezing on my cheeks, a knot as hard as a rock in my throat. I could barely breathe.

The ghost reacted to my emotions. They always do. The Miata began to rock back and forth, the radio blasting to noisy life, static whining and crackling from the speakers, loud enough to make me cringe. The dome light and headlights were flashing.

I shuddered from the cold. Every breath I took burned going into my lungs. Every exhale was a visible mist in the air inside the car. "Stop. Vicki, you've got to stop. Please, you're hurting me."

It was as if I hit a switch. All the poltergeist-style activity just stopped. But the cold didn't diminish. She was still there.

"God, what happened? How? I mean, you were *fine*!" I picked up the pictures as though she could see them. "See? You were happy." Hot tears flowed down cheeks that felt chapped with cold. I couldn't believe it. It didn't make any sense.

Ever so slowly, I saw writing form in the frost on the window. Letter by letter, until I could read her full message.

Love you.

And then she was gone.

10

It was a long time before I could pull myself together enough to drive. My best friend was dead. The shock was horrible. On top of everything else, it was just too much. She *wasn't* dead. I didn't want to believe . . . *couldn't* believe —

I cried. I screamed. I cried some more. Eventually, I got myself under control enough to restart the car. Now I was definitely speeding, but I needed to get to Birchwoods, find out what the hell was going on. Yeah, I could've called. But I wanted to hear this in person. Discretion was *beyond* the grave there, so I was going to have to fight to get answers. I'd just get stonewalled on the phone and they'd have time to prepare a response . . . or a security team.

I pulled the car up to the outside gate and ran my card. I went through without problems and stopped before the second gate, rolling down my window. Gerry was on the gate again. He flinched when he saw me, and this time when he ran through the security protocol he did it like he meant it. I passed with flying colors, but that didn't seem to reassure him much. "Dr.

Scott has asked that you go to his office in the main administration building. He needs to speak with you urgently." Gerry's voice was its empty, professional best, giving nothing away. I shivered. His attitude wasn't helping my denial.

My stomach tightened into a knot, making the nausea worse. But I didn't ask any more questions, just handed back the clipboard along with my driver's license.

Gerry passed back my license. "Take the left fork of the road; the administration building is in the back."

"I know." Duh, I've been here how many times?

Gerry stepped back from the car and waved a signal to the gate operator. With the flick of a switch the heavy metal framework barring my way moved smoothly aside. I felt, rather than saw, magical protections I'd never known existed ease in response to the opening of the gate. I drove through and down the long, curving drive that led to the administrative part of the complex. The white brick buildings were gleaming and pristine, like pearls scattered decoratively across the vivid green of the manicured lawns.

I drove slowly. I hated this. Hated it so much. God, it was only *yesterday* that I'd had the bellhop haul stuff up that hill. What in the hell had happened?

She couldn't be gone. How many times had I driven up here in the past few years, bringing her news of the outside world? How many afternoons had we walked the path around the little freshwater pond behind the main complex, or fed stale bread to the ducks that congregated there?

I've had losses before. My father's abandonment, my sister's death, even, in a way, my mother's retreat into the bottle. You'd think I'd be used to it, that by now I'd have developed a hard shell that would protect me. I suppose that's exactly how it looks to people who don't know me. But it's a lie.

I pulled into one of half a dozen or so parking spaces with neatly printed signs proclaiming VISITOR PARKING and climbed out. The sun was low enough in the sky that the umbrella might not have been necessary, but I used it anyway.

I slammed the car door shut with more force than was really necessary and heard an ominous sound of metal fatigue that normal human muscles couldn't make happen. Another thing broken. I was broken, Vicki was broken . . . why not everything else? I hurried up the gentle slope of the handicapped-friendly entrance feeling both like an idiot and like a child who's been beaten one too many times. When I reached the shade of the small ivy-bedecked porch that protected the entrance, I collapsed the umbrella. The automatic doors whooshed open and I walked in.

"Good afternoon, Ms. Graves." The receptionist stood as I walked through the door. She had to notice the pallor and fangs but managed to hide her reaction admirably. I could not hide the fact that I was about to burst into tears. She was wearing one of those fitted suits that are tailored to emphasize every curve. It was tomato red and had been hemmed to a length that would show enough leg to be attractive without being improper. Her dark hair had been swept up in a twist. That, coupled with a sweetheart neckline, showed a lot of creamy neck and just a hint of cleavage, the effect emphasized discreetly by a pearl necklace and earrings. "If you'll have a seat, I'll let Dr. Scott know you've arrived." She gestured in the general direction of the expensive leather couches that graced the tastefully appointed waiting room.

"Thank you." My feet sank into the deep golden pile of the carpet as I crossed over to the cushy waiting chairs. There were magazines, of course. The latest copy of *People* sat on the polished mahogany coffee table. Vicki's parents were on the cover, under the headline "Hollywood's Top Power Couples." I shook my head sadly and reached for *US Weekly* instead. I'd probably have to see them at the funeral. I wasn't looking forward to it. Jerks. It made me wonder how they were going to deal with their daughter's death in a way that didn't reveal the embarrassing truth about Vicki to the world.

That was cynical of me, and I knew it. But it had been Vicki's greatest heartbreak—that her parents couldn't handle who and what she was.

I didn't read the magazine, not really. If you asked me what was on the page I was staring at, I wouldn't be able to tell you. But I was in a reception area. Reading magazines is what you do. So I pretended, flipping the pages while my mind was a million miles away. I could feel the stares of the other people in the waiting room but pretended not to notice.

The receptionist reappeared after only a minute or two. That she came to me instead of others who'd been waiting longer raised a few brows. I didn't care. I was too raw, the pain too fresh for me to bear being in public for too much longer.

"Dr. Scott will see you now."

I followed her down a long wood-paneled hallway lined with impressionist paintings in gilt frames until we reached a heavy set of mahogany doors. Despite their apparent weight, the receptionist pulled one of them open and held it for me with silent ease.

I stepped over the threshold and took a long look around.

To say Dr. Scott's office was spacious was an understatement. The house I grew up in probably would've fit inside. Although the house had a bathroom. Come to think of it, there probably was one behind one of the pair of doors on the north wall.

The entire west wall was windows, so that even through the thin film of cream-colored drapes I could see a wide expanse of ocean, a spectacular sunset coloring the clouds and water with shades of mauve, orange, crimson, and purple. It was just the sort of sunset that Vicki and I had watched only a few weeks before in her room, sipping on chilled iced tea with a hint of peach while breathing in the tangy ocean air.

The sunset expanded into this room, decorated to incorporate the view—the golden tans of sand with the blues and greens of the sea and sky. Dr. Scott sat behind a table made from glass and weathered driftwood. Instead of the traditional suit, he wore khakis and a melon-colored polo shirt that showed off his dark skin and the shining silver of his hair and beard. Loafers with no socks completed the outfit.

"Come in, come in." He gestured toward a conversation grouping in an area far from any stray patches of sunlight. "Pardon my appearance. I'd scheduled the day off—"

He gave me a penetrating glance, taking in the red eyes, the chapped nose that was already healing. "I don't need to tell you, do I?"

I shook my head, tears threatening again while my stomach wanted to relieve itself of contents, and mumbled, "No."

He moved behind the desk, settling into the enveloping leather of a high-end executive chair. "Has word leaked to the press?"

"Not from me." My voice sounded tight, not surprising. It was all I could do to force words past the lump in my throat. "I was on my way here for a visit when her ghost manifested in my car."

"Considering how close you were and the strength of her force of will, I'm not surprised." He shook his head sadly and modulated his voice. "I'm so very sorry for your loss. Please be assured we did everything we could. Unfortunately, based on her medical records, we always knew it was a possibility—"

I lowered myself into the enveloping chair without answering. I hadn't known it was a possibility. I'd never asked anything about Vicki's medical history. He could be telling the truth or lying through his teeth. I had no way of knowing.

"Which was why we had procedures in place to care for her in an emergency." He continued speaking without hesitation. If he sensed my mood, he ignored it. Leaning forward across the desk, he addressed me respectfully, his expression earnest. "As is the case with any death of one of our patients, we've reported the incident to the authorities, and they will launch their usual investigations. I don't expect them to find any negligence."

Neither did I. Even if there was a problem, there was enough money floating around this place that I was betting it would be handled *discreetly*. But I wasn't going to say that. It would be rude. And while I am more than capable of being rude when the occasion calls for it, I wanted information.

"I appreciate your concern. I know that Vicki chose Birchwoods because of its stellar reputation."

"Thank you." He gave me a gentle smile. "Can I get you a drink? I'd offer food, but the only guest we've ever had with your *condition* wasn't able to process solids, so I'm not sure it would be appropriate."

So, the closed drapes were no coincidence. Gerry must have called ahead, which also explained the receptionist's lack of reaction. I found it very interesting that they'd dealt with someone with my *condition* . . . especially since my condition was supposed to be pretty damned rare. I was curious, but he *wanted* me to ask, so I perversely avoided the question and got to the point of my visit.

"Can you tell me what happened?"

It was a deliberate question, because I'm not part of Vicki's family. He nodded, just the tiniest drop of his chin, and folded his hands on the tinted glass. "Ms. Cooper left the appropriate written permissions for us to speak with you frankly. You're probably aware that, as is the case with many high-level psychics, Vicki frequently suffered from both migraines and severe insomnia."

Okay, that I *did* know. Vicki was always trying the latest homeopathic treatments for headaches—from weird herbs to gadgets that would change the lighting in the room and even magic charms to change her "energy patterns." And she was forever calling me on the phone at weird hours. But I never really related those things to her psychic ability. Lots of people get migraines and can't sleep.

I got caught up in memories and nearly missed what he said next. "It was the late-shift nurse's duty to check on her when she came on duty at eleven and again at two. If Ms. Cooper was having trouble sleeping, at two A.M. she would be given the option of taking sleeping medication."

I nodded. This wasn't news.

"The file shows that when the nurse checked at eleven, Ms. Cooper was fine. She was using the mirror you gave her to channel her visions and seemed quite happy and pleased with the results. Nurse"—he flipped to a page in the file to check the name—"Phillips states that Vicki indicated it was her best birthday ever, and said that she would be going to bed after a bit." That made me smile. I'd worked hard to have that mirror made so it would respond perfectly.

He read from the notes on his desk, "'When she saw the light still on at one forty-five, Nurse Phillips knocked on the door. When there was no response, she entered and found Ms. Cooper unconscious and unresponsive on the floor. She called in a code blue and immediately began CPR.'"

I was trying to listen to what he was saying. I heard the words. But I couldn't seem to concentrate on their meaning. It seemed wrong, and I couldn't figure out why until it hit me between the eyes.

"Wait. She died *last night?*" *At nearly the same time as I did*—? "Then why did she only manifest in my car a few minutes ago? And why hasn't anyone contacted me until now?"

His brows rose just the slightest bit. "But we did try to contact you. Repeatedly. I presumed you were coming now because of my messages."

Crap. So I'd been dealing with my own piddly problems while my best friend had been lying here, *dead*? For long enough that she had to come get me to make me notice.

Another pain hit me in the chest and I felt my hands clutching the chair arms so hard the cloth began ripping under my grasp.

Dr. Scott kept talking. "Naturally, she's only now able to manifest because it takes time for the soul to leave the body, reject the natural transition to the afterlife, and return to Earth. Actually, the process normally takes longer, but Vicki was an extraordinarily gifted person. She was already on a higher plane of consciousness, so it's very clear why her return was faster."

Clear? It didn't seem clear to me. In fact, I was suddenly having trouble thinking clearly about anything. The final rays of sunlight behind Dr. Scott had turned that startling bloodred that spoke of clear sailing tomorrow. I found myself staring at the neck beneath that melon-colored collar, watching the pulse beat under his red-tinted skin. I could actually hear the blood pumping through his veins. My mouth started watering and my stomach rumbled audibly. I had to fight not to lunge across the distance between me and the doctor. I dug my fingers into the chair arms and felt them sink down, and down. An odd squeaking accompanied the sensation, making me twitchy.

Dr. Scott's eyes widened and he began sweating. The scent of his sudden fear tasted salty on my tongue. My stomach rumbled again, but I didn't move. That tiny part of my brain that was still *me* dug in with every ounce of stubborn will, refusing to give in to the overwhelming craving that had nothing to do with me, right here and right now. I moved my hands to my legs, forcibly holding them to the chair. I would *not* stand.

The last vestiges of glow settled into the ocean and the pale blue of the sky turned to new denim. Unexpectedly, things in the room grew brighter, as though each piece of furniture had an internal light. Brightest of all was Dr. Scott himself. He glowed and pulsed with healthy, vibrant life and I absolutely knew that he would taste as sweet and syrupy as the finest melted Swiss chocolate.

My eyes followed him with preternatural clarity as he moved with exquisite slowness to reach for the telephone extension on the end table next to him.

"Ms. Graves, can you hear me? Are you still in there?"

"Yesssss." My voice sounded odd and strained.

"When was the last time you ate anything?" He started punching numbers . . . misdialed, and had to try again. But his voice was steady and he was keeping his wits about him. So long as he didn't run, didn't *move*, I was almost sure I could hold on. Almost.

"Before the attack."

He swallowed convulsively. I watched his Adam's apple move, saw the pulse in his throat speed up. I forced myself to close my eyes, taking deep breaths through my mouth rather than my nose until I was almost panting. If I didn't see his pulse, didn't smell his fear, maybe it would be easier to stay in control. I needed to do something, because every second frayed that last thread of humanity I was clinging to.

"Heather, I need appropriate nourishment for Ms. Graves. NOW." He didn't sound panicked, but the tone of his voice left no doubt it was an emergency. I had to admire his self-control. As a bodyguard I've seen men who seemed far tougher than he was crumble in the face of this kind of stress.

I heard him set the phone carefully back in its cradle. "You need to hang on just a few more minutes. I'm going to stay very still."

"I'll try. Staying still would be good." Actually, still wasn't good, as far as my stomach was concerned. I wanted him to run. Wanted him to scream and fall and claw at the carpeting in a futile attempt to get away. My voice was thready, but oddly, the lisp was mostly gone. And my body wasn't moving. In fact, I could feel my fingernails digging through the fabric of my sweats, hard enough to draw blood from my quivering thighs. The pain centered me, made me feel a little more human.

"Ms. Graves, listen to me. You must eat every four hours *without fail*, and you will need to take particular care to eat just prior to sundown. Right now you're feeling your sire's hunger combined with your own. It makes controlling yourself considerably more . . . difficult. Do you understand?"

I didn't say anything. I wasn't sure I could. Coherent thought was fading in a haze of overwhelming *need* that throbbed in time to the sluggish beat of my abruptly undead heart.

"Ms. Graves, Celia. You need to answer me. Stay with me."

"*Hungry.*" The word was an almost-hissing growl, and I could feel the heat of magic filling the room. Still, I forced my body to stay utterly still, even though I couldn't seem to remember why it was so desperately important.

I heard the door creak open, felt the slight shift of air displaced.

"Don't come in! Leave the tray just inside the door."

My head snapped around and I locked the intruder in a stare. She was glowing so bright I couldn't see the color of her hair or skin. But her eyes . . . they were deep blue. And they were *mine*. Heather responded like she'd just come upon a cougar or wolf in the wild. I could watch each individual hair on her arms rise and her muscles twitch. "Sir—" There was fear in her voice. It resonated through my body like the ringing of a bell. I shuddered; my body jerked as I fought an instinct to lunge for the very human source of the terror. Her glow was strong, too, and her fear a vibrant thing that was nearly alive on its own.

"Close your eyes, Heather. Don't let her entrance you. Just put the tray on the ground and leave." She paused and he finally raised his voice. *"Do it!"*

The blue eyes closed, and my attachment to her faded. I heard the clatter of silverware against china as she nearly lost her grip. I followed her every motion as she set the tray on the carpeting. She backed out in a sudden movement, the door closing behind her with panicked finality.

I was panting in earnest now, breathing as hard as if I'd done a ten-mile run. I heard movement, knew the doctor was easing his way out of the enveloping chair. "I want you to stare at the plant in the corner, Celia. Look at the plant. Tall, lush . . . alive." I moved my eyes toward the towering ficus. It was tall and lush and alive, but it didn't have Dr. Scott's pulsing, glorious glow. The bright light of *blood*. It was starting to *hurt* not to move, to chase.

His voice came again, soft and soothing. "I'm going to leave the room now. The food is here. When you've finished, and you're yourself again, you can call out and I'll come back in. Do you understand?"

I made a noise that should have been assent. Instead, it was an animal moan. Still, I held on, feeling the wet blood on my pants as my nails dug even deeper so that I would *not chase*. I stared at the plant even as I heard him move, the scent of his fear like baking bread that I should follow to the source.

Only when I heard a door close and the sound of a dead bolt sliding home did I let go and move my eyes.

I could barely see through the blood vessels that had burst in my eyes. But I could smell. Food. There was food. I moved in a blur of speed, throwing myself across the room. I ignored the bowl and spoon and just grabbed the pitcher, pouring liquid heated exactly to body temperature down my throat so fast that some of it spilled out of my mouth and down the front of my shirt. Blood and juices from rare, nearly raw beef. No salt or seasoning. It should have made me gag.

It didn't.

11

I had been right about the bathroom. Not only did he have one, but it was as oversized and as luxuriously appointed as the rest of the office. Shining cream-colored marble with veins of gray, caramel, and gold covered 90 percent of the surfaces. The ceiling was painted the color of California sands. The throw rugs matched towels nearly the size of bedsheets, both a deep caramel gold that exactly matched the veins in the marble. The wall behind the counter and oversized double sinks was a single sheet mirror.

The reflection that stared back at me was the stuff of nightmares.

My skin glowed white. Not pure white, but pale grayish white with a greenish sepulchral undertone. Was this what Emma had seen? My eyes cast a reddish gold light that was the only color other than the stark stains that soaked my clothing. The cotton was stuck to me like a second skin and droplets of reddish brown left a dark trail where I passed over that pale, beautiful stone. I'd pulled my hair back when I cleaned up at the office, so there was nothing to soften or distract from the primal ferocity of a face that was both my face and not.

I stared at my reflection in horrified fascination, unable to look away.

I heard the creak of the door outside with unusual clarity, but it didn't make me react the way I had before. I could smell Dr. Scott on the other side, but now it was just his cologne and the lingering hint of Irish Spring soap, instead of the scent of his blood flowing under thin skin. "Ms. Graves, I'm leaving a stack of clothing and toiletries outside the door. When you're done cleaning up, we need to talk."

The sound of his voice brought me to my senses. I turned toward the door to answer him. "Thank you."

I was pretty sure there was a sigh of relief in his next words. "It's no trouble."

He sounded so . . . calm. It was uncanny. Of course, the danger was over. My belly was full, the bloodlust sated, if only for the moment.

What is happening to me?

Stupid, stupid question. I knew what was happening. I just didn't know what to do about it.

I stripped off my fouled clothes and let them fall in a pile on the floor, then padded, naked, to the door. Keeping my body hidden by the bulk of the door, I opened it and grabbed the promised stack. Setting the clothes onto the counter, I took the soap, shampoo, and conditioner with me and stepped into the shower.

A long, hot shower could scour my body clean of the gore, but it couldn't cleanse my mind of the image in the mirror. I wasn't human anymore. I might not be a vampire, but I wasn't human, either. Still, it felt good to be clean, and hiding in the shower wasn't going to accomplish anything. So I stepped out of the stall and began toweling myself dry.

The clothes he provided were sweats. High-quality plain gray sweats with a sports bra and underwear with the tags still on. He'd guessed fairly accurately on the size. The bra fit well. The panties were a little loose, but I wasn't about to argue.

I pulled on the sweatpants, over legs that had already healed the bloody punctures I'd inflicted on them. Using a drawstring, I tightened the waistband to fit.

I remembered Vicki talking about how, the first two weeks of their stay here, everyone was required to wear the same plain sweats. No jewelry. No sign of status or prestige. She said it was a great leveler, kept people from being distracted by trivialities and competitive attractiveness while they were supposed to be concentrating on getting well.

I felt another stab of loss at the memory. Dammit anyway.

"Ms. Graves?" The doctor's voice came through the door. "Are you almost ready? We need to talk."

Shit. "I'll be right there."

My shoes were splattered but not soaked, so I put them back on and returned to the main office.

He sat behind the desk, the lamp providing dramatic lighting that cast the fine bones of his face in harsh planes of light and shadow. He gestured wordlessly toward the seat across from him. I took it.

"I took the liberty of checking with Security. Our video from your visit yesterday shows you driving up with the convertible top on your car down and no sign of your current . . . condition. Were you actually attacked less than twenty-four hours ago?"

"Yes, last night sometime. We don't know exactly when."

His dark eyes grew very wide. For a long moment he didn't seem capable of speech. Still, he managed to collect himself, and when he spoke his voice was admiring. "I have to admit, you surprise me. I assumed that you'd had your condition for some time and were merely using illusion to cover the more obvious effects. Otherwise I would never have been so careless, particularly at sunset. I apologize."

"You couldn't have known. But why would you have thought that?"

"Because of the way you present yourself." He leaned back in the chair, steepling his long fingers in front of his face as he spoke. "In the course of my career I have met exactly one person with your condition and read of two others. Even after weeks or months of treatment, none of them were as . . . calm about it, or had a fraction of the control you've exhibited from the outset. Although . . ." He let the sentence drag off unfinished, his expression thoughtful. "Are you currently in therapy with anyone?"

"I saw Dr. Talbert for several years when I was a teenager. But she retired recently for health reasons. Since then, no."

He gave me a long stare over his steepled fingertips. "Dr. Gwendolyn Talbert? She specialized in childhood trauma, I believe?"

"Yes." My voice sounded flat, inflectionless. If Dr. Scott wanted more information, he'd have to work for it. And frankly, we didn't have time to go into my "childhood trauma"—not if I was going to hunt my sire or get to sanctuary.

A hint of a smile tugged at the corner of Dr. Scott's mouth. "Don't give away much, do you?"

"Not generally, no."

"Good. That kind of self-control may well be what pulls you through this." He set his arms on the table in front of him and reached for a notepad and pen. "I think you should consider checking yourself into a facility." He continued hurriedly, in response to the look I gave him, "It doesn't have to be this one. Although you are, of course, welcome here. You've gone through serious trauma before, so you know how difficult it can be to adjust. Combining that with the physiological changes—"

"No."

He held up a placating hand. "I'm not suggesting one of the state-run facilities." He shuddered. "I wouldn't consign a rabid dog to one of those. But—"

"No. Not there. Not here." I wouldn't go. I'd literally rather die than go to a "facility." If even half of what I've heard happened in those facilities is true, it would be far, far more merciful to just kill those committed. Other magically dangerous types get locked up, but vampires get staked and beheaded. An abomination? Who knew? At least there's a hope of getting out for some people. A minuscule hope, but a hope. Not for the furry, like Kevin. And, I suspected, not for me.

I couldn't do it. I couldn't voluntarily lock myself away and risk being officially labeled dangerous. That might put me in line to go to one of those places if anything went wrong in the future. Yes, Birchwoods could probably help me. And I make a good living, so it wasn't the money, although God knew a place like this would set me back. But unless I absolutely *knew* I was a menace to myself and the public, I wasn't checking in. Still, I needed to be careful. Because the good doctor *could* commit me. There wasn't a judge in the country who wouldn't back him up on it. The standard for commitment was "is he/she a danger to him/herself and others?" Based on my display a little bit ago, I quite obviously was. I kept my voice calm, not betraying even a hint of fear. "If possible, I would prefer outpatient treatment."

"Ms. Graves—"

"Dr. Scott, I'm not being deliberately difficult. Truly. But there are . . . practical considerations, things I need to deal with that can't be put off. I *didn't* attack you. You said I need to eat every four hours. I can do that as an outpatient. You say I'll need therapy. I can do that, too." I needed him to believe me. Needed him to work with me on this. As I focused my thoughts, I realized I could almost hear the sound of lapping waves through the window behind him. I smelled salt water on the air.

He stared at me through narrowed eyelids. I felt the weight of that gaze. He was testing me. Long minutes passed before he spoke. I sat silent, waiting. I didn't squirm. Didn't react much at all.

"The two people with your condition that I read about were killed by their sires within twenty-four hours after leaving a protected facility."

"And the one you treated?"

"Suicide—again after leaving the facility. She apparently couldn't live with the guilt of what she'd done."

I asked because he expected me to, not because I wanted to know. "What had she done?"

"She murdered her mother . . . tore her throat out, drank until she was full, and then left her to bleed to death. Even though she remembered who she was, the bloodlust was too much for her."

If he was hoping to shock me into submission, it didn't work. Oh, I'd be careful, damned careful. But the only way he was getting me to be an inpatient anywhere was by force. "I'm not easy to kill and I haven't murdered anyone. I can do outpatient treatment, Dr. Scott. I *can*."

The silence stretched long again. Now I could hear the rolling crash of waves against rocks . . . even though there were no cliffs outside. The harsh caw of seagulls seemed right outside the window. My eyes flicked up when I saw movement over Dr. Scott's shoulder. There *were* gulls right outside his window. Floating and dipping in a glimmering dance. Quite a few for some reason. A bit odd for nightfall, but I'm not an expert on shorebirds.

Dr. Scott's head cocked and he spun his seat toward the window. He watched the gulls swoop around in the glow of the lamp, for all the world like giant moths near a flame. He shook his head as if trying to clear it and blinked repeatedly. When he turned back and spoke, his voice was strained. "I will make you a deal, Ms. Graves. We'll try it your way—*if* you agree to follow the diet I am about to give you, take the supplements and medications I am prescribing, and come to this facility on an outpatient basis three times per week. But if I determine the situation has become too dangerous, you will agree to abide by my judgment and voluntarily commit yourself for two months of inpatient treatment."

It was the best offer I was going to get. I could tell from the set of his shoulders, the grim determination on his face. He didn't like bending even this far.

"I'll agree—as long as *you* agree to give it a fair shot. No cheating and ordering me in without cause."

"No *cheating*." He repeated the word drily. "Fine. We're agreed. Don't make me regret it."

I didn't answer, merely watched as he scribbled a long list of notes. Pausing briefly, he tapped the pen against his teeth a few times, then continued until most of the page was full. I decided to use the time to watch the birds outside, but when I looked out the window they were gone. Who knows why. So I stared at the twinkling lights down on the beach instead. Someone was having a party, if the flickering tiki lights were any indication.

When he finally looked up again, he met my eyes. "I'll have my assistant call these in to your pharmacy. That way they can have everything ready and waiting for you when you arrive. You should take a dose of the supplement immediately. While we have no way of knowing for sure, it seemed to help Rachel control her bloodlust."

I nodded my agreement. "I'll do that."

"Where should I have Heather call?"

I gave him the name and address of the place I usually use for my birth control and vitamins and he scribbled the information at the top of the page.

"I think we're done here for now." He rose and I did the same. "In answer to the concerns you didn't get the chance to express earlier, independent examiners will be on site to look into Vicki's death *thoroughly*. I should also mention that the reason I'm telling you any of this is because Vicki signed a written request that we explain the details of her death to all of the heirs and devisees in her Will. Naturally, we will abide by her wishes and keep you apprised of the results of any investigation. I imagine the investigators will want to speak with you as well."

His words confirmed what I'd suspected for some time now. He was a telepath, and a damned good one. He'd pulled the question about an investigation out of my head, plus God alone knew what else, without my even noticing. Dangerous man. *Of course, it will be easier to be in therapy with someone you don't actually have to talk to. There are a lot of things I'd rather not reach air.*

If, as he seemed to be hinting, I was inheriting money from Vicki, I'd have had one hell of a motive, and in the circles I ran in it would probably even be possible for me to arrange for a professional hit. I wouldn't. But that didn't mean I couldn't. Shit.

He led me to the door of the office, and was holding it open for me when I answered. "It doesn't matter if they investigate me. Let them know I'll cooperate fully. I loved Vicki very much. She was a genuinely good and gentle person." I smiled, knowing as I did that the smile didn't reach my eyes and showed more than a hint of fang. "For better or worse, I'm *not*. If she died of natural causes, fine. But if she didn't, I'm going to find out who did it and why. Then I intend to make them pay." I preceded him to the office doors. Since I got there first, I opened them for both of us. He paused at the edge of the wide hallway.

"Ms. Graves, may I ask you a blunt question?"

"I suppose."

"Do you know the contents of Victoria Cooper's Will?"

"No. She never told me, and it was none of my business. I assume she gave me a minor bequest—just like I'd do for her—

and that pretty much everything goes to either Alex or her parents. She didn't have any other family."

He gave me serious eyes. "I think you may be in for a shock. It's her *parents* who will be receiving the minor bequests. They do, after all, already have their own fortunes. And there has been an . . . estrangement between Vicki and her mother for some time."

A hard lump formed in my throat, making it difficult to swallow. *No. She wouldn't . . . would she?*

He noticed my expression and put a light hand on my shoulder. "Celia, do you really want to be out in public, enduring a media firestorm, in your current condition? Are you *certain* you wouldn't rather stay here for a time . . . learn some skills to keep you, and the public, safe?"

I took in a deep breath and let it out slow. Yes, this new information complicated things. Complicated them a *lot*. But— "Dr. Scott, a gilded cage is still a cage. And you know as well as anyone that hiding from your problems doesn't make them go away."

He gave a nod that was almost a bow. "My offer stands. If you find you can't cope, you are welcome here."

"Thank you. I do appreciate that." I did. But I wouldn't take him up on it unless there was no other choice. There were too many memories here. Good memories for the most part, but that wouldn't make it any easier. If anything, it would be harder. Everything would remind me of Vicki, of her loss.

Dr. Scott escorted me through the lobby to the glass doors leading to the parking lot. His body language was stiff, reluctant, almost as if he were being forced to let me go against his will. But he did it. And I was grateful as hell for it.

Because I needed to be away from here. Stupid, I suppose. This place was probably as safe as or safer for me than just about anywhere else right now. But I needed to leave. It wasn't smart, wasn't logical. But I needed to do it just the same.

The door closed behind me, and I heard the snick of the dead bolt being turned. I didn't turn around. Just stood on the concrete step, letting the warm breeze carry the scents of salt water and seaweed to my nostrils. The gulls were gone. But if I listened hard, I could still hear the ocean. For a long moment I just stood there, drinking it in, letting it calm me as much as anything could.

Mine was the last car in the lot, gleaming midnight blue under the street lamps. I crossed the wide expanse of asphalt, unlocked the door, and climbed inside.

Drawing a ragged breath, I forced myself back to the task at hand. I had calls to make. The news of Vicki's death might not have made it to the press yet, but it would soon. I didn't want Kevin, Bruno, or—oh, God—Alex to find out that way. They deserved a call. So, even though I knew he should be out hunting, I dialed the number for Kevin and Amy's apartment and was shocked when he answered on the first ring.

"Kevin?"

His voice was livid. Words spilled out of him in a flood of emotion that left me stunned. "Where the hell have you been, Celia?! We've been worried *sick*! Don't you ever answer your fucking phone?"

After everything, it was just too much. To have Kevin scream at me with such intensity . . . I came *this close* to hanging up on him. I don't like being shouted at. But I owed him, big-time. Besides, there was a full moon. He was probably having aggression issues. My being pissy wouldn't help. But how the hell was I supposed to answer? I mean, so much had happened in the past few hours.

"Don't *you*? I've been trying to call. I keep getting your voice mail. And frankly, I've had bigger things on my mind. Could you lower the volume, please? It's stressing me out even worse."

I heard him draw in a long, slow breath. "I'm sorry. I was worried. The last time, I called your office. Dawna said you left hours ago, something about going to Birchwoods. Did Vicki help you find out anything?"

I paused, not quite sure how to proceed. Then I just said it. "Vicki's dead, Kevin. She died last night, at nearly the same time as I was attacked." My throat tightened and I fought down a wave of tears.

There was stunned silence and then the sharp bang of the receiver hitting the table. I pulled the phone away from my ear in a rush. I miss my old hearing. He scrambled to pick up the phone again and I could hear him breathing for a few moments while he gathered his thoughts. "Oh, *shit*. Celie. Hon, I'm so sorry. Are you okay?"

Hell no, I wasn't okay. What kind of stupid question was that? And did he just call me *hon*? "I've been at Birchwoods meeting with Dr. Scott about it. They don't know the cause yet, but apparently it was sudden. I hope 'sudden' means 'painless.' But I need to talk to you about something else. While I was there . . ." I struggled to find the right words to describe what had happened but came up blank. Words just seemed totally inadequate for the situation. Besides, how was I supposed to tell a man who turns into a monster for three days of the month how terrified I'd been at my own bloodlust without insulting him? "The sun went down."

He figured out what I meant without any more prompting and started to swear. When he had himself under control he asked, his voice taut with strain, "Did you kill anyone?"

Wow. Okay then. Talk about thinking in terms of worst-case scenarios. But I'd probably ask the same thing of him, so who was I to judge? "No. I managed to control myself enough that I didn't even hurt anyone."

His sigh of relief echoed down the phone line. "Thank God for that. You have no idea how worried we've been. Everything we've been able to find says an abomination acts very much the same way as a newly turned werewolf or vampire. Their first feeding is almost always fatal to the victim." He sighed. "I swear I didn't know. Jones didn't tell me. If he had, I wouldn't have just let you run loose like that. God, you could've—"

"Well, I *didn't*," I snarled. He wouldn't have *let me run loose*? I didn't like the tone this conversation was taking. Yeah, he probably could've knocked me cold before I realized what was happening back in the lab. Having gone through it now, *I* probably wouldn't have even let me out of the restraints, or let me leave without a guard. But hearing it put that bluntly made me angry.

"Celia—" There was a warning in his voice, as if he'd sensed my irritation. Maybe he had. Subtle is not, after all, my best thing.

"Look, Vicki's death hasn't been made public yet, but it probably will be soon. Can you call Dawna, Emma, your dad, and the others?"

He sighed. "It'd be better if Dawna heard it from you. But I'll tell Emma and Dad."

I barely heard him and couldn't seem to stop talking. "I'd do it myself"—I took a shaky breath—"but I need to tell Alex. I really don't want to, but I don't know who else would—"

There was a stunned silence. "Oh fuck. Alex."

"Yeah."

"I'll make the calls." I could hear his hair brush across the speaker as he undoubtedly shook his head. "But Celia, you need to get somewhere . . . less public. And sooner rather than later."

"Thanks. I know. And I will. I promise." I'd do it, too. It was too late to hunt my sire tonight, and I was in no condition to do it. And while I have a lot of faith in myself, I'm really not reckless or stupid. So tonight I'd go to the estate and lock myself in tight, with lots of weapons to protect me. Tomorrow . . . well, I'd deal with tomorrow when it got here. "Look, there are things we need to discuss that we shouldn't talk about over the phone. If you're not going out to the desert, can you meet me at my place in two hours?"

"*Two hours?* I think this needs to be dealt with a lot quicker than that."

I had the distinct feeling we were talking about different things. I wasn't sure what his "this" was, but I was betting it wasn't the same as *my* "this." "Look, I have to stop by the pharmacy to pick up the stuff the doctor ordered. Besides, you need to get some dinner. You haven't eaten, have you?" I changed the subject as gracefully as I could, putting the ball squarely in his court. Yes, I was going to go to the pharmacy. But that would only take a few minutes. I wanted the extra time to be alone.

But first I needed to call Alex.

Just thinking about it made my eyes fill and my throat tighten. God, how was I going to tell her? She loves . . . loved Vicki so damned much. This was going to just kill her. But it would be worse, much worse, if she found out on the news, or from some jerk of a reporter. No. I had to do this. Had to.

Alex wasn't at work. I was glad about that. Nobody wants to get that kind of news at the office. She didn't answer at home at first, let the call go to her old-fashioned answering machine. Only after I'd started talking, giving my name and asking her to call me, did she pick up.

She sounded like hell. It was obvious she'd been crying. Her voice was raw and had that odd thick quality that comes when your nose is stuffed from crying.

"You're calling to tell me, aren't you?"

"You already know." It wasn't a question.

"She came to me in the car on my way home from work. I barely managed to pull over without getting in a wreck."

I wasn't surprised, after all, wasn't that exactly what Vicki had done with me? And while she loved me like a friend, Alex was her lover, the woman she might eventually have married, now that the law allowed it.

"I'm so sorry, Al. I know you loved each other very much."

"Yeah." The word was choked and rough, barely audible.

"Are you going to be okay?" I could barely say the words and tears were streaming down my face, dripping off my nose.

"No."

"Me either."

I hung up and the tears overcame me—as though a dam had burst. Deep, wracking sobs of grief and loss shook my body. I'd just start to get a grip on myself when another memory would hit, setting off another wave of grief. I cried until there were no more tears, my head ached, and my throat was raw.

For a long time after that I just sat there, numb and too exhausted to move. Eventually, I pulled myself together and started the engine with a roar. With a squeal of tires that was viscerally satisfying I took off into the night.

I could've turned right onto the expressway, taking the artificially bright, straight four-lane highway directly through town. Traffic would be light at this time of night. But I chose to turn left, back onto Ocean View. I didn't know how much time I'd wasted crying, and I didn't care. If I was late, Kevin would just have to wait. Too much had happened in the past twenty-four hours. I needed a few more minutes of peace and solitude to get a grip.

So I put the top down and sped along the winding road. The sky was perfectly clear, the moon riding high in the sky, bathing the ocean in silver light that fractured in ripples as the waves broke onto the shore. The salt-laden wind blew my hair back. I tuned the radio to the classical station, turning the volume up loud enough that I could hear it over the wind. All too soon I was back on the outskirts of civilization, where street lamps cast swaths of artificial daylight that only made the shadows seem that much darker and more menacing. Because make no mistake, the predators were out there. Say what they will about "taking back the night," most humans prefer to stay home, behind their thresholds. Those who do venture out do so mostly to attend big events where the police and the warrior priests are out in force to provide protection.

I switched off the radio as it started playing yet another commercial advertising job openings for "true believers" to work the graveyard shift. Sad to say, even with absolute proof of monsters and demons, true believers were still hard to come by. Hard enough that the convenience stores really couldn't afford to pay them what they were worth—any more than the stores could afford more lawsuits over slaughtered cashiers.

On that particularly cheery note I pulled into the driveway of my twenty-four-hour pharmacy. I felt the tingle of power as I passed the magical boundaries, but it wasn't painful. Not even close to the barriers they'd erected at the library or clinic. Then again, this was a chain store. They only put in enough money to do the minimum necessary to salve their consciences and mitigate any damages should there be a lawsuit.

A bell sounded as I pulled under the awning. A teenage boy with crooked teeth and a bright silver cross on a black leather choker around his neck slid back the window to greet me. "Welcome to PharMart. How can I help you?"

"I'm Celia Graves. Dr. Scott's office was supposed to have called ahead—"

"Oh wow." He stared at me, looking startled and afraid. "That's *you*? I'm sorry, but—"

"Look, I've been bit, but I'm only partially changed. You're in no danger from me."

"Yeah. Right." He wasn't being sarcastic, but he was still afraid. "The order's too big to fit through the window. You'll have to come inside."

Well, crap. If it was too big for the window I was probably going to have a hard time fitting it in the car. Damn it anyway.

"Are you sure it's going to be okay? People tend to freak when they get a good look at me."

"I can see why." He swallowed hard. "Look, park the car and give me a couple minutes to warn everybody before you come in."

Did I look that bad? A glance in the mirror said I did. The puffy, reddened eyes made them look larger and darker than normal and the red tinge had nearly overtaken the amber. "Right." I pulled around the building and took the closest parking spot that hadn't been marked for handicapped use only. It put me at the last bright edge before the shadows but well within the protections of the ward. So I shut down the engine and waited the requisite minutes before climbing out, making sure my credit card was in my wallet. I was betting this little trip would bring me right up to the credit limit, and it's a high-limit card.

The automatic doors whooshed smoothly open as I passed beneath the security cameras and into the bright fluorescent lights. One of them was flickering a little, and I could hear it buzzing, like a large, annoying insect.

The store was empty. Seriously. Completely empty except for the teenage boy who had talked to me through the drive-up window.

I blinked, looking around. There was a price gun on the counter in Cosmetics, a half-filled cart. But other than him, no people. *Weird.* "Where is everybody?"

"Everybody else went back into the pharmacy area where the wards are better. Just in case."

"What, you drew the short straw?" I didn't mean it to sound

bitter, but it did. This whole instilling fear in everyone was getting really old, really fast.

He shrugged. "Dr. Scott's office said you had been bitten and gone through a partial change but that we should be safe. I know him. He wouldn't lie about something like that. Besides, if anyone is going to get hurt, I'd rather it was me."

A hero in the making. I almost smiled . . . then remembered the fangs. "All right then, let's do this."

There was a huge stack of stuff waiting for me at the checkout counter, along with a shopping cart ready to take the load. There was a blender, cases of baby food (no formula, thank God), individual containers of flavored "shakes" from a popular liquid fast program, a jar containing a liquid form of a multivitamin and mineral supplement, jars of dehydrated beef and chicken broth, and more. None of it looked particularly appetizing. Of course, part of the problem was that somewhere I could smell fresh, hot pizza. The aroma reminded me forcibly of what I *wouldn't* be eating . . . possibly ever again.

I tried not to be surly about it as he rang up the order. Unfortunately, the total kept going higher, and the smell kept getting stronger. By the time he ran my credit card through I was more than a little bit grumpy.

"Do you want some help taking this out to the car?" Now that I hadn't shown any signs of aggression he was starting to relax. He smiled. Despite the crooked teeth, it was a nice smile, friendly, not phony, without that leering undertone I got a lot of the time. Since there was more stuff than the cart would hold, I accepted, with thanks. I wanted to get out of here and home.

It took some work to wedge all of my purchases into the trunk and the passenger side of the Miata, but we managed. The clerk had straightened up from the trunk and grabbed the cart, starting to turn away from me, when he just : . . froze. The cross at his neck flared white-hot as his face went limp and expressionless, green eyes dull and empty. One foot hovered in midair from the step he hadn't completed. Without the cart to balance him, he'd have keeled over and never even realized it.

I felt cold power like a snake brushing against me, sliding over my skin and moving on. I turned toward that power, turned toward the deepest shadows just past the magical barrier, to see three indistinct figures leaning casually against a midsized sedan.

I couldn't see their features, but I recognized the man in the center from Dottie's vision.

Edgar.

He struck a match and the light flared orange, casting his features in sharp relief as he puffed a cigarette to life. He killed the flame with a practiced flick of his wrist, letting the spent matchstick fall to the ground at his feet.

He was dressed much like Dr. Scott had been. Khakis and a polo shirt, standard casual wear for the upper middle class. No hint of blood on anything. Either Edgar was seriously good at illusion or he'd cleaned up from his earlier "meal." He looked more like an ordinary businessman than an undead monster.

My eyes adjusted and I was able to make out the second male figure. A black man, he had been killed in his late teens or early twenties and was dressed in the kind of clothes you'd expect to see on campus. He looked just like everybody else . . .

except for his eyes. Those dark brown orbs held the knowledge of someone much older. They were without warmth, pity, or any trace of humanity.

The third figure was a woman, but despite my best efforts, I couldn't see her clearly. It was her powerful mind magic that held the boy enthralled and kept me at bay. But, powerful as she was, she apparently couldn't get past the barriers surrounding the property. Because if she could have, she would have. I felt her hunger, her *malice* at being denied what she considered her rightful prey.

"Good evening." Edgar blew out a puff of tobacco-laden smoke as he greeted me, his tone pleasantly conversational.

"Hello."

He glanced at the contents of the overflowing passenger seat, his expression grimly amused. "You do realize it would be easier and cheaper to just take that last step?"

"No, thank you, I'd rather not." *No, thank you?* My words sounded odd even to my own ears. But Gran had hammered good manners into me and, for the most part, I revert back to them when I'm nervous. No matter what I'm thinking, I say the polite thing. She'd be so proud.

The black man snickered, his expression condescending. It pissed me off. Not enough to do anything stupid, but it took the tiniest edge off of my fear, made me able to think more clearly.

Edgar didn't say a word. He simply *looked* at the other man. Just looked. And the other bat instantly subsided.

"You're not my sire, Edgar. Stop it."

"You remember? I'm impressed." He sounded amused. "Then again, I suppose I shouldn't be surprised. You appear to be a remarkable woman. And, as much as it annoys my associates"—his casual hand gesture made the embers on the end of his cigarette glow briefly brighter—"I have decided that, for the moment, you're more useful to me alive than dead."

Good news for me. Because I believed, well and truly, that if they wanted me dead, I would be. There are people who are cocky because they think they're good. Others don't have to be cocky. They *are* that good. Professionalism is easy to spot but hard to define. I'm a professional. I'm not just decoration or mindless muscle. These three were professional monsters. I could tell. I know it sounds stupid. But that doesn't make it any less true.

"May I ask why?"

He took a long drag on his smoke while he considered it. He dropped it half-smoked, grinding it out with the toe of his shoe. When he spoke, his voice was measured, bland. "I need to get a message to Kevin Landingham—if you're willing."

"What's the message?"

"Tell him it was a setup. Plans within plans. The primary goal had nothing to do with you. You were supposed to be killed, and I was to be blamed for it. *They* want him back on the payroll, hunting the hard targets." He tried to meet my gaze, but I avoided looking at him. Maybe in my current condition I'd be safe, but I wouldn't bet my life on it. So I kept my eyes on his chin, which gave me a great view of the hint of a smile that tugged at his lips when he realized what I was doing.

"Who are *they*?"

"He'll know. Just tell him."

I let out a frustrated breath. "Why should I?"

His face lit up with honest amusement, his dead eyes

sparkling. "Clever and cautious. I'm beginning to understand what Kevin sees in you."

"She's just eye candy." The black man sneered.

"She killed Luther." The woman's musical alto, soft and compelling, drew my gaze to the blurred form. The other's rage drew it back. He glared at me. Hatred made his power rise in a burning rush that heated the air between us.

"That was just luck—and those damned knives. *I* won't be as easy."

"Enough." Edgar's word cracked like a whip, and the younger-looking vampire hissed. "Give Kevin my message."

Before I said a word in answer, they were gone. As they disappeared, the spell mesmerizing the clerk fell away. He blinked, shook his head, and looked around, but not like he suspected anything. Good thing. I really wasn't sure I wanted to explain what had just happened.

12

I **didn't** dawdle on my way home. A lot of the churches offer sanctuary. But they expect you to get there *before* dark. They certainly wouldn't invite in someone with fangs, no matter how easily I could walk through the door. Thanks to Bob and later Justin, Vicki's estate had fully maintained, state-of-the-art protections, even if she didn't currently live there. I'd be as safe as or safer there than anywhere else I could come up with on short notice. Besides, it was home. It was normal. I needed something normal to cling to—a psychic teddy bear if you will.

The estate covers ten acres. I stopped at the gate to lay my palm on the scanner, letting it read my print. The light flashed green, unlocking the computerized security system and rolling the gate open. I passed through quickly. It's set up similarly to the outer gate at Birchwoods, only staying open thirty seconds. Just long enough for you to get through and a little ways down the drive. I paused after I went through and watched the gates close, making sure nobody came in behind me. I didn't trust Edgar, and I trusted his "friends" even less. But the magical wards on the high fence were put in place by

Bruno, and he's one of the best in the business. They wouldn't get through once those gates locked.

I followed the wide, paved road that leads to a main house styled like an Italian *palazzo*. It's huge, with amenities like an actual ballroom, a movie screening room—you know, the everyday stuff. There's a servants' wing, where David and Inez live. It's twenty-five hundred square feet, renovated and decorated to their taste, with a separate outdoor entrance to ensure their privacy. There's a pool house to go with the Olympic-size pool. Vicki had had a weight room and exercise equipment put in there. My rent includes use of the pool and exercise facilities if I want to. I swim every day—in the pool or the ocean—and use the pool house to do my ballet stretches and martial arts kata. But I don't do weight training, so those machines would be gathering dust if David hadn't decided to drop that extra ten pounds he'd been carrying.

My place is the guest cottage. It sits a couple of hundred yards back from the main house, at the end of a winding brick path that passes through beautifully landscaped blooming plants and shade trees and over a tiny man-made brook that burbles in a rocky bed. The cottage isn't large, as those things go, probably eight hundred square feet, with one bedroom, one very ordinary bathroom . . . well, ordinary except for the big claw-footed tub . . . and a back deck that is only a few hundred yards from the little strip of sand and rocks that edge onto the ocean. It's too rough and rocky for good swimming, boating, or surfing. But it's beautiful. When I'm troubled I go there and sit on one particular rock, listening to the ocean as I watch the gulls dive-bomb each other as they compete for tasty tidbits. When I want to swim in salt water, all I have to do is go a little farther down the beach. All the residents here have unlimited access to the private beach.

This secluded spot has been my home for several years now, since before Vicki went into Birchwoods. When my lease ran out, we never got around to signing more paperwork. I pay month to month, direct to the attorney. What my status here would be once the Will got read I had no clue. I might inherit it. It might go to David and Inez, or charity. Most likely it would go to Vicki's folks.

I didn't want to think about things like "inheriting." It was too soon, and I would rather be as poor as I'd been growing up than have lost Vicki. I'd give just about anything to have her back. But all the money, all the power, in the world can't manage that. Magic or no, dead is still dead.

I dragged my mind away from the sucking hole of grief by thinking of practical things—primarily my ongoing survival. I got the feeling that so long as Edgar considered me useful he wouldn't kill me himself. I believed that. The same couldn't be said for his associates. And I wouldn't want to bet my life that he'd be able or willing to keep them in line. Then, of course, there was my sire—whoever he was—*and* the folks who'd set me up in the alley. I'd been supposed to die. Instead, I was alive and a witness to whatever the hell was going on. They wouldn't like that. Not one little bit.

Oh, and let's not forget the demon spawn. Nothing else could do that perfect of an imitation.

I pulled into the small parking area by the cottage and climbed out of the car, shaking my head. There was a line: a freaking *line* of people who wanted me dead. Worse, they weren't normal folks. No, I had monsters and professional killers hunting me.

Such were my cheery thoughts as I made my way up the sidewalk, burdened with bags of groceries. There was a note in Inez's handwriting pinned to the door with a strip of duct tape.

> *Dawna brought by a pot of her grandmother's pho for you. I put it in your fridge. I was afraid if I didn't bring it down here David would eat it all. Hope you are okay. We'll talk in the morning.*

Dawna's grandmother is Vietnamese. She married Al, a Marine, during the Vietnam War, coming back with him to the states. Tiny, exquisite, she is smart, tough, and one hell of a cook. Her *pho* is legendary. I might have to run it through the new blender, but by God I would eat it. In fact, I could smell it already, if ever so faintly.

I promised myself that it would be my reward as soon as I got my purchases put away. It took a couple of trips to get it all inside. The weapons bag came inside, too. I'd be putting on my knives momentarily—just in case. I mean, I *thought* the wards would hold. But better safe than sorry.

In the course of hauling everything out of the car I found the new cell phone. The light was flashing. I hadn't set up my voice mail yet, but I had a *lot* of missed calls and text messages. The texts were probably from Dawna. Unless she'd given the number out to everybody. Which she would.

I didn't really want to talk to anyone. But I could text. I sent a couple of quick messages out, letting everybody know I was safely home, thanking Dawna for the *pho*, sending condolences back and forth about losing Vicki. It didn't take long, and my friends really did need to hear from me if I wanted them not to worry.

The "cottage" isn't as large as David and Inez's place, but it's bigger than the house I grew up in, bigger than my gran's. It's also considerably nicer. The living room is airy and open, with French doors leading out onto a deck and skylights that let in sunlight or moonlight dappled with the shadows from the palm trees that surrounded the building. I plugged in the slow cooker with the *pho*, cranked the dial, then headed outside. I'd put everything away later. Right now I wanted the kind of solace I can only seem to find next to the ocean.

I made my way down the familiar path that led to that rocky little stretch of beach, my heart heavy and my mind too full to focus on any one thing. Just as well, I supposed. Any one of my thoughts was likely to send me over the edge.

Emerging from the path onto soft sand that glistened in the same moonlight that shone bright silver off the water's surface, I sighed in relief. Pale stars winked like diamonds from the velvet black sky. I clambered up onto a large rock, scraping my hand. Fast as a thought, the small wound began to heal. I watched the flesh knit itself together. It was eerie and deeply disturbing.

"What are you thinking?"

I jumped and whirled, silver knife drawn, to face the source. My skin began glowing with power. "Crap! Kevin, you scared me! Couldn't you make some noise or something?"

He waded out of the ocean, naked, water pouring along the

long muscled lines of his body in a way that drew the eye. My irritation evaporated as I watched him glide forward with inhuman grace. Normally he works to make himself seem human. Tonight, under the light of the full moon, he didn't bother. Under normal circumstances I'd have felt a wave of lust. But these weren't normal circumstances. Either stress or sorrow was keeping my libido in check. Pity.

He sensed my lack of interest, but it didn't bother him. Nor did the drawn knife. He came up to the foot of the rock and lowered himself onto the sand, sitting comfortably, facing me.

"It isn't safe for you here. You should be in sanctuary."

"The sun had gone down by the time I was done at the hospital," I explained. "And this place is warded nine ways to Sunday. I'm surprised you were able to get in."

"Moving water doesn't bother a werewolf the way it does a vampire, and even permanent wards aren't as powerful underwater. I swam. I got burned a little by the wards, but I've already healed. And if I can get in, you can bet Edgar could find a way."

I looked out over the ocean at the rising and falling surf. Would it burn to swim? I was born a water baby, a Pisces. I've never lived away from the ocean. If I couldn't *swim* . . . shit.

But there was no use talking about that. "I'm not worried about Edgar tonight." I slid the knife back into its sheath and settled into a comfortable sitting position.

"You should be. Celia—" Kevin's voice dropped almost a full octave and took on a rumbling edge that wasn't quite a growl. "You don't know him like I do. Believe me—"

I interrupted him before he could get more upset. "Oh,

he's a major badass all right. Scares the crap out of me, if you want to know the truth." I shuddered a little, thinking about the threesome I'd spoken with earlier. "But he wasn't my sire, and he wanted to make sure I let you know. In fact . . ." I paused for effect. "He gave me a message for you."

"What do you mean, he's *not* your sire? You *spoke* with him? When? Where?" Kevin's voice was cold and his eyes had gone dark. I could see the muscles in his jaw clenching as he fought to control his anger.

"He's not. Trust me. Edgar showed up with two of his people when I was at the drugstore. They couldn't cross the protections."

"Don't be so sure. If Edgar's your sire—"

"Hello? You're not listening. Edgar's *not* my sire." I ran my hand through hair damp with spray. "He and his friends showed up *after* I'd been bit, before you and Amy came charging to the rescue. And thank you again for that."

Kevin met my eyes, his own gone wide. "You remember?"

I looked away, at the stars, the ocean, anything but those demanding eyes. "A detective who's investigating what happened took me to a clairvoyant. It triggered the memories."

"Oh." The word fell into the air between us like a rock thrown down a very deep well. We sat in silence for a while before I answered the question he hadn't voiced but was waiting for me to answer.

"My sire was a thin guy who looked like a kid, with dark hair cut short. He died young enough not to be able to grow a decent beard, just this straggly little soul patch. I remember my blood dripping off of it as he started chanting the spell."

I turned my head, to watch Kevin's reaction. It was worth

seeing. Normally he has one hell of a poker face. Not now. He sat on the sand, his entire body vibrating with contained rage, his eyes glowing with the magic he held back by force of will.

"I figured you knew him. Care to share a name, maybe a daytime resting place?" When Kevin didn't respond, I continued. "He and the others in the alley were scared to death of Edgar and the vamps with him." I shook my head. "Can't say as I blame them. Edgar wanted me alive to give you a message, but the other guy would've killed me right there in the parking lot if he could've. And that woman was just . . ." I struggled to find the right words to describe what I'd sensed about her. I couldn't. "He couldn't have held them back. He might be their master, but he wouldn't have been able to hold them. They wanted me dead too badly."

"Did they say why?" Kevin's voice was bland. His expression wasn't. Not only could I see the muscle in his jaw jumping, but the hands gripping his knees had grown white-knuckled. If he hadn't been healing too fast, there'd be bruises forming under them.

"Something about my killing Luther."

He blinked slowly. Twice.

"You killed . . . *Luther*?" The lilt in his voice made it a question.

I shrugged, still not sure what it meant. "I killed a couple of bats in the alley. One with a gun, at least one other with my knives. One of them might have been Luther. I wouldn't know. It's not like they introduced themselves. Why is it important?"

Kevin gave a snort of combined aggravation and amusement, then shook his head and muttered something under his breath that I didn't quite catch. A day or so ago I might have been insulted by the reaction. I mean, I am a professional. But that was before I met Edgar and company. If *they* were impressed, well— Now I not only wasn't insulted, I was almost as surprised as Kevin. Of course I didn't *say* that. Instead, I tried to look aloof as I stared out at the incoming waves.

"Luther was very old and very smart. He was also ruthless as hell. *I* wouldn't have wanted to hunt him alone. I'm really surprised you were able to take him down." Kevin was staring at me as if he was really seeing me as a person for the first time instead of as one of his father's students or his sister's sometime friend. It was a little unnerving.

"What was Edgar's message?" Kevin asked.

I repeated what the vampire had told me, verbatim. Kevin sat as if frozen. He didn't answer. Didn't act as if he'd even heard. But I knew he had.

It was a long time before I broke the silence. "Can I ask you a question?"

He gave a curt nod.

"Who are these people?"

He shook his head. "I can't tell you. I wish I could, though, because you're in so far over your head that you may never see daylight again."

"What should I do?"

He rose to his feet in a single fluid movement. "Eat, then get some rest. But don't sleep too sound. I'm going to check a few things out. Try to put the pin back in this grenade."

"And if you can't?"

"That would be very, very bad."

I nodded glumly. I was afraid of that. He stood up and I

stood with him. We stared at the ocean for a long time before he said, "I'm sorry about Vicki, Celia."

Without warning, he pulled me into his arms and held me. Just held me. I pressed my cheek to his warm skin and let out a ragged breath. I would not cry again. I wouldn't. But it was tempting. He stroked my hair and just let me breathe and get control of myself. It had been a long time since I'd let a man just hold me. Since Bruno, really. There were a thousand things I'd always wanted to say to Kevin, and you'd think this would be the perfect time. But it wasn't. This was quiet time, the calm before the storm that would undoubtedly come. And while I realized his body was starting to react, rather strongly, to my presence, he didn't let the tension build. There was comfort in the knowledge that we could touch, skin on skin, without feeling the need to go further.

I was a little afraid of *further* with Kevin. Too, I wouldn't want to ruin what he had with Amy. That wouldn't be fair to any of us. And then there was the question of whether he wanted me. Maybe, sometimes. Maybe not. To him I might just be another "little sister" or forever a "good friend."

But I wouldn't worry about that tonight . For now I would take his comfort. There was little to be had elsewhere.

13

I'd had a long cry and a hug from a friend. I'd taken my drive. I'd walked on the beach. Nothing had helped get rid of the sorrow, the anger, and the sense of impending doom. That left a bath. Not just any bath, either . . . a long, hot bubble bath. I mixed a tall, stiff margarita to sip while I soaked. It's part of the ritual, lying in the water, sipping that lime-flavored nectar of the gods, carefully licking every single grain of kosher salt off the rim of my glass. I don't climb out until either the bubbles are gone or the drink is. A second drink gets me through a home pedicure and one of those mud pack facials everybody likes to make fun of.

Tonight I put a gun on the toilet seat and skipped the facial. My skin *looked* human, but I wasn't sure how it would react to magically imbued salt mud.

I stood in the bathroom, wrapped in a towel and trying really, really, hard not to think too much about anything—which is harder than it sounds, particularly when I could watch the nicks from the razor heal fast as a thought and see last night's injuries fade in fast-forward.

After the third margarita I figured I was as relaxed as I was going to get. I slipped into the most comfy "jammies" I own: a worn T-shirt I'd stolen from Bruno back in college and a pair of flannel boxers. I tucked the gun into the drawer of my nightstand and went to bed. Almost as soon as my head hit the pillows, I was asleep.

It was a dream. I knew it. But I couldn't make myself wake. I knew what was coming. It was always the same. The dream ended the same way the day had ended in real life. I didn't want to go there. I just didn't have a choice.

It was so clear, as if the sunshine from that long-ago morning were streaming through the windows warming my skin right now.

We were in the old minivan. My parents were in front. Ivy and I were in the backseat. My birthday presents were piled in the "way back," as my father called it. It was my eleventh birthday. I felt like such a big girl. And I was really excited because I was sure, almost positive, that I'd gotten exactly what I wanted.

We were driving past Woodgrove Cemetery. Normally we went the other way, but there was construction and the roads were closed and we were running late. So we drove past Woodgrove, for the first time since Ivy's talent had started manifesting.

The memory rolled inexorably forward, like a movie playing in my mind. I could hear my parents talking about whether or not we could afford for me to continue taking ballet. The teacher said I had real talent—like I could make a career out of it—so they really wanted me to keep going. But it was expensive, and Dad's company might be having layoffs soon.

Our happy little family drove past the cemetery, with its neatly manicured lawn, pretty brick and wrought-iron fencing, and row upon row of tombstones.

And the ground shuddered, rolling visibly beside us so that the pavement cracked. A maintenance truck rocked on its wheels on the gravel road behind the fence, and I saw the groundskeeper throw down his tools and sprint for the vehicle at a dead run as tombstones tipped over and skeletal hands began clawing their way free of the ground, decaying bodies following suit.

My mother started shrieking at the top of her lungs; my father swore and pressed the gas pedal to the floor, swerving between slower vehicles as if it were a Formula One race and we were headed for the checkered flag. Ghosts started whipping through the car and Ivy clapped her hands and squealed with delight.

But all of that was just so much background noise. Because I couldn't take my eyes off of the filthy, decomposing bodies that were shambling to the walls, climbing the fence, and flinging themselves at an invisible barrier over and over and over . . . trying to get at us.

We made it to Gran's without wrecking the car. Things got better the farther we got from the cemetery. By the time we stopped the car, even most of the ghosts were gone, with my baby sister waving bye-bye to them through the back window.

I got out first. Then Ivy. It was a long time before Mom climbed out, and I could see a huge wet spot on the back of her dress where she'd been sitting. She moved like she was a hundred years old, climbing out of that car. She closed the door gently, and stepped back with a sad expression.

My father drove away with a squeal of tires that left black marks on the concrete driveway. I watched him go, waving from the front step as though he were just going to park the car. But he never looked back. He kept driving down the road. And finally, my mother burst into tears.

I sat bolt upright in bed, shivering from a cold that had nothing to do with the temperature. My skin was covered in gooseflesh and felt as though it would crawl off of my body. My heart was pounding in my chest; my breath came in rapid gasps.

It was just a dream. Just a memory. It can't hurt you. Of course that was a lie. It had hurt me—hell, it still hurts me every time I let myself think about it, which is every time I have the dream.

I glanced at the clock on the bedside table: 3:15. I'd slept through the alarm and was overdue for a feeding. Never mind that I wasn't hungry—in fact, I was again a little bit nauseous. I wondered if maybe that was a warning sign. I didn't want a repeat of the incident with Dr. Scott, so I'd eat . . . or rather *drink.* . . . Oh, shit. I'd left the *pho* cooking. I'd gotten distracted, talking to Kevin, and forgot about it completely—

despite the fact that the smell of it was filling the house. Well, it was certainly hot enough to eat now. Besides, I wasn't going back to sleep.

When I'm stressed I have nightmares. Three particular nightmares. They're based on memories, and no matter what I do, I can't seem to keep them from playing out completely. The adult me is a helpless observer to the worst things that happened to me as a child.

It sucks.

If I went back to sleep now I'd drop right back in where I left off. So no. Throwing back the covers, I sat up on the edge of the bed. By the light of the moon I padded into the kitchen. I was reaching for the light switch when I saw a shadow moving outside. I froze. Listening hard, I could hear the rustle of leaves and what might have been a careful footfall on the wooden steps of the back deck.

Stealthily as I could manage, I slid over to where my bag was still sitting on the breakfast bar. Reaching in, I drew Bob's gun and checked it. Loaded. Good. Clicking off the safety, I rose and edged gently across the carpeted floor to the edge of the French doors leading out onto the back deck. By the silvered light of the nearly full moon, I could see a shadow squatted down near the base of the house, near the kitchen door.

My vision shifted as it had that morning, into a sort of hyperfocus. I could see every stitch in the black knitted ski mask the prowler wore, every mark in the gray and black camouflage pattern of his clothing. Quietly as I could, I turned the key in the lock of the door in front of me and reached down to lift the brace bar that served as a second lock, blocking the door's movement. I cringed at the soft metallic noises I couldn't help making. With the bar out of the way, I hit the latch and slid the glass door gently aside, never taking my eyes off the man, who had set a handgun onto the floor of the deck beside him and drawn a wrench from inside a black backpack. An unmistakable smell filled the air.

Oh, shit. He's messing with the gas line.

I needed out of here. Now.

I clicked the safety back on, thrusting the gun into the waistband of my boxers. A gun would be worse than useless right now. I could hear the hiss of gas escaping. I burst through the door and ran forward, kicking his gun off of the deck and out of reach before slamming into him, sending both of us tumbling down the wooden stairs to the hard concrete sidewalk below.

He started to swear, and we rolled together, struggling for supremacy. I was strong for a human, even before the bat got to me. Now I was stronger. But he was a match for me, not just in power but also in skill and pure, unrelieved viciousness. He went for my eyes, forcing me to rear back. I hissed, flashing fangs, and my power started to rise, making my skin glow a pale greenish white and cast an eerie light over the shadowed corner we'd rolled into. That made him pause for an instant. Less than a second, but it was enough. I put everything I had into a punch to his jaw, just as spotlights came on all over the grounds and David shouted from the main house that he'd called the police.

The man lay limply beneath me, his jaw at an angle that practically screamed "broken." His pulse, however, still beat strongly in his neck. He'd be coming back around soon. By then I wanted to be far away from the cottage and my assailant safely tied up.

David was coming toward us, holding a shotgun with the authority of a man who had hunted most of his life. He looked at me as though he'd never seen me before. And, in a way, he hadn't. I didn't doubt that Dawna had told David and Inez about my condition, but hearing about it and actually seeing the reality are two completely different things.

I spoke, and happily, it was my normal voice. "Don't shoot. We've got a gas leak."

He started swearing but backed away. Not just from the guesthouse, but from *me*. "Are you all right, Celia? The cops are on the way."

It was a loaded question. I knew it. But he needed some comfort now, too. "I'm fine." Actually, I wasn't. I hurt like hell where blows had landed. I'd lost Bob's gun somewhere along the way. But more than that, I couldn't tear my eyes off the pulse beating beneath a small mole on the man's throat, where the ski mask had pulled away to expose bare skin.

I could smell blood, fear, and sweat, and the glow around me grew brighter, casting harsh shadows. My stomach growled, and I felt actual pains from the hunger, as if a wild animal were trapped in my belly, trying to claw its way out.

I forced myself to my feet, stumbling a little.

My attacker must have been playing possum, because he chose that instant to strike. The movement was almost too quick to see. His leg moved with a blur of speed, aimed directly at the knee that held most of my weight.

I went down with a scream of pain, my head slamming against the concrete hard enough to make me see stars. He rolled, then lurched to a standing position, grabbing for his pack.

I made a clumsy lunge, unable to do much more with a dislocated knee that was in unrelieved agony.

I couldn't catch him. I did manage to grab the dangling padded strap of the canvas pack. He let it go, running full out in the direction of the beach. David started to take a shot, then thought better of it. Thank God. The last thing we needed was a gas explosion.

Sirens and lights were coming closer on both of the cross-streets. The cops would be here any second. I dropped the bag, then limped over to the gas hookup, thinking I could just tighten the valve again. Unfortunately, he'd done more than just loosen it. It was broken. We'd need to get the gas company out here.

"You should probably get out of here, Celia. If the cops see you . . ."

David was right. They'd see a monster and act accordingly. Later, they'd be very sorry about the mistake. But I'd still be dead or incarcerated.

"Right."

"I'll turn off the power until they get the gas fixed." He moved with smooth assurance toward the breaker box, shotgun at his side.

"Call my office when we get the all clear," I called out as I limped through the French doors as quickly as I could. The smell of gas was intense. I didn't dare stay more than a minute or two. Even so, I took a second to stash the Crock-Pot back in the fridge before grabbing my keys, phone, weapons, and wallet and rushing to the car.

14

I went to the office. It was the wee hours of the morning. Normally one of the bail bondsmen would be in, but there were no cars in the lot. Still, the place was well lit, the carefully placed security lights ensuring that there were no deep shadows where monsters or bad guys could hide.

I pulled into my usual parking place and cut the engine. My leg hurt. It was healing. I could feel that. But it *hurt*, dammit, and using the manual transmission hadn't helped.

I didn't like the fact that I'd had to avoid the police. It made sense. But I didn't like it. Then again, there weren't too many things about my current situation that I *did* like. Maybe the healing. If it weren't for the vampire healing abilities I'd be looking at surgery on the knee. But even that was weird. Some things were healing practically instantly. Other injuries, ones that really didn't seem any worse, were taking longer.

I hobbled over to the front door, let myself in, and punched the buttons to reset the alarm while trying to remember whether I'd left the faxes and paperwork in the copy room or taken them up to my office.

Upstairs.

Oh, hell. That was going to hurt. A lot.

It did. And it was slow going. I had to stop every third step or so to rest my knee. I was on the fifth stair when the grandfather clock struck four. I wasn't even at the top when it hit four fifteen.

I was swearing pretty steadily under my breath by the time I reached the third floor. I walked past the locked offices of Freedom Bail Bonds and the empty office that we all used to store spare junk and let myself into my space. Most of the places I needed to reach wouldn't open until nine or ten. My gran gets up about seven, and I really needed to talk to her, to reassure us both. That gave me a couple of hours to eat and go through the research.

At which time I realized that all I had in my office microfridge was a soda. There would be food downstairs—if nothing else one of those wretched diet shakes Dawna favored. But they were *downstairs.* Just the thought of it was daunting. I was so freaking *exhausted.*

I was having my own personal pity party when I heard someone opening the downstairs door. "Graves, it's me," Bubba's voice called out. "Don't shoot." There was a swift series of beeps as he keyed in the alarm code. Heavy footfalls started up the stairs.

I yelled out through the closed door, "Bubba, do me a favor?"

"What?" He sounded grouchy. Not good. My bet was he'd had to hunt down a jumper. As a bail bondsman, Bubba worked very hard to make sure his clients showed up for their hearings. When they don't, he hunted them down. He's good at it.

He might be a "good ole boy," but he's smart and tough. But tracking and hauling in a bail jumper is a lot of work, a lot of bother, and it always, always, makes him irritable.

I raised my voice to just short of a shout. "Go into the kitchen and see if Dawna has any of those Ensure things or maybe a diet shake?"

"Do it yourself," he grumbled.

"Can't. I've screwed up my knee and I need to have something nutritious to drink."

"Well, hell." He gave a gusty sigh. "Give me a minute."

He stomped back downstairs and I heard him banging around in the kitchen, muttering under his breath the whole time.

Eventually he started climbing up again. He called out, "Got it. Hope you like banana."

I loathe banana in all its many forms. But beggers/choosers and all that.

"Thanks, Bubba. Leave it outside the door."

He snorted. "Whatever."

I waited until I heard his footsteps go down the hall to his own office before I levered myself out of the office chair and limped over to the door. My knee wasn't happy about it. Healing abilities aside, three flights of stairs had been a mistake. Opening the door, I found a four-pack of twelve-ounce cans. Bending awkwardly from the waist, I picked it up, using the holes in the cardboard carrier.

"Dawna told us what happened, but I didn't really believe it."

I looked up, meeting Bubba's gaze. He was standing in the doorway of his office, staring at me. His eyes were wider than they should've been, with whites showing all around the blue of his pupils. He didn't look afraid, precisely, but more startled. "You look like . . ."

"A bat. I look like a freakin' vampire."

"Yeah. But you're still you?" He made it a question.

"I'm still me," I answered him, "and I intend to stay that way."

"Attagirl! You decide you need help hunting, you let me know."

"Thanks, Bubba."

He nodded, then shut his office door as I opened the first shake and chugged it down fast enough that I managed not to gag on the taste. I heard the snick of the dead bolt sliding into place, smelled gun oil. I could just imagine him pulling the .38 from his drawer and setting it on the desktop in easy reach. Just in case. I couldn't blame him. I'd have done the same thing.

I fell asleep studying . . . again. I woke up to the sounds of phones ringing and the smell of brewing coffee. The swelling in my knee had gone down some, but my neck and back were stiff from sleeping in an unnatural position and my mouth tasted like something had crawled in it and died.

The grandfather clock struck eight. I sat up, blinked a couple of times, and tried to stretch out some of the kinks. As I ambled down the hall to use the facilities I noticed that Bubba was gone. Not only was his door closed and locked, but there was no smell of gun oil, and I couldn't smell him or hear anyone moving around in his office.

"Celia?" Dawna called up the stairs. "You up? Want any coffee?"

"Coffee would be wonderful!" I hollered back. "Oh, and I drank a couple of your shakes."

"Yeah, Bubba told me. Hang on a minute, I'll be right up."

I washed my hands and went back to the office. It was time to try calling my gran again. If I didn't reach her this time, I'd go by the house. I was starting to worry. I hear from her once or twice almost every day. Yesterday I hadn't been able to reach her at all. It could be nothing, but she's not a young woman. . . . I punched the buttons and waited.

She answered on the first ring. "Celia! Where have you been? I've been calling and calling ever since the news about Vicki broke on the TV. Are you all right? I'm so sorry, punkin. I know how much you cared about her." The words tumbled over each other in a rush.

So. The press had got hold of the story. "I'm sorry, Gran. I tried to call a couple times yesterday, but there was no answer at the house."

"Oh, you must have called when I was out."

Her voice changed abruptly, taking on an evasive tone that I didn't like, mainly because I knew it too well. She only sounded like that when she'd done something she knew I'd be upset about, usually something involving my mother.

"Gran—"

"Really, Celia—" She got defensive, the second surefire sign. "You're so suspicious! What I do with my time is none of your business."

Absolutely true. And normally I didn't pry. But the last time she sounded like this, Mom had just "borrowed" ten thousand dollars, leaving Gran with no savings and not enough money to pay her property taxes for the year.

I didn't say a word. There was no point in starting another argument. Not now. She wasn't going to change. Taking a deep breath, I changed the subject.

"There's something I need to tell you, Gran. The other night, when I was on a job, I got hurt."

"Oh, Celie!"

I plowed on, ignoring the interruption. "A vampire bit me, tried to turn me. Kevin and Amy rescued me. I'm not a bat. But I'm not completely human anymore, either. I'm pale, and I have fangs. . . ." The words trailed off uncertainly.

There was no hesitation in her voice, no fear, and a huge weight lifted from my chest. If my gran had thought of me as *evil*— "Oh, honey. I'm so sorry."

"I look like a bat, Gran. I do. It's awful." Tears filled my eyes, but I blinked them back. I would not cry, dammit. Not again.

I think she was stunned. The silence on the other end of the phone was profound.

"I wanted to let you know, to prepare you so you wouldn't get scared when you see me."

"You could never scare me, punkin. Have you told your mother?"

"No." It came out cold and harsh.

"Celia, she's your mother. She loves you. She deserves to know."

I didn't want to argue, so I didn't. Besides, she had a point. Lana is my mother. "Fine. I'll call her."

There was an awkward moment. "You'll need to wait until tomorrow. Sometime in the afternoon."

"Why?"

The silence stretched between us. She didn't want to answer, that was obvious. I waited. Eventually she couldn't stand it any longer. "Your mother got picked up again for driving without a license—"

"What? Whose car was she driving?" My mother didn't have a car. It had been impounded when she got picked up for her *second* DUI with no insurance. She hadn't had the money to get it back and I wouldn't lend it to her. After all, she didn't have a license, so she didn't really need a car.

"Now Celia, you know your mother has her doctor's appointments—" My grandma started making excuses, but I cut her off.

"She can take a cab. Or a busss. Or you could drive her." My lisp grew as I spoke even though I knew what I was saying was useless. My gran has been enabling my mother since before I was born. It's not like she was likely to stop anytime soon. But that didn't keep it from driving me crazy. "And ssshe wasn't picked up near the doctor's office, was ssshe?" I fought to get my tongue under control.

She didn't say a word, which meant I'd hit a nerve. If we were running true to form, she'd get angry now, use my full name, and refuse to talk about it.

"Celia Kalino Graves, I've had just about enough of your lip. I know your mother isn't perfect. But she does the best she can."

The sad part was, Gran was probably right. It's just that my mother's best was so damned pathetic. But there was no point in saying that. Instead, I said the only thing I could that would end the argument: "I love you, Gran. I really do."

"I love you too, punkin. Don't worry too much about the car. I don't like to drive much anymore anyway. There's too much traffic, and I don't see as well at night as I used to."

I let out a deep sigh. "We can talk about it at Sunday dinner." I always had Sunday dinner with Gran. Although, come to think on it, dinner was liable to be problematic. Maybe I could have soup?

"I was hoping maybe you could take me to church on Sunday morning?"

Of course she was. Hope springs eternal, and Gran is an optimist. A cross hadn't bothered me, but what about a full-blown church? Would I burst into flames and force the priest into a change of sermon?

"Someone just came into the office, Gran. I've got to go."

The first part was true and no doubt she'd heard the squeak of the door hinges. Dawna had come in, carrying two steaming mugs of fresh-brewed coffee that smelled like heaven.

"Celia—"

"Bye, Gran. Love you." I hung up before we got into another argument. Dawna was shaking her head and snickering under her breath.

"Your grandmother never gives up, does she?" Dawna passed me the mug. She looked tired, with dark circles under eyes puffy from crying. But her makeup was perfect and unsmeared, her dark hair styled, and she was wearing a tomato red suit and matching heels that looked absolutely stunning on her.

She sank into one of the wing-backed chairs, crossing her legs with easy grace. I knew she didn't make a lot of money as the receptionist here, but you'd never tell it by looking at her.

She has a gift for making even inexpensive clothes look like designer originals.

I inhaled deeply, savoring the aroma of fresh-brewed java before taking my first sip. "Nope."

Dawna gave me a very direct look over the rim of her coffee mug. I could actually watch her go through the process of forming the questions she was about to ask me.

"How are you holding up?"

"About as well as can be expected. You?"

She sighed. "I can't believe she's dead. I mean, it's just unreal. I just called and talked to her on her birthday—she thanked me for the purse I got her and was going on and on about the mirror and her presents from Alex. It just doesn't make *sense*."

No. It didn't. Then again, nothing else did, either. We sat in shared, miserable silence for a long moment, sipping our coffee.

"Just how much trouble are you in?"

It wasn't a question I'd been expecting, and I raised an eyebrow.

"Don't give me that innocent look, Celia Graves. I'm not an idiot. You're half vampire—you have *fangs*, you're being hounded by cops and federal agents, and this morning you're barefoot and in bloodstained pajamas. You've got a stack of messages an inch high from reporters and lawyers, and I don't know if that's because of Vicki or the fangs or something you haven't told me yet! You're my friend, and you know I'll stand by you. But you're going to need my help, and if I'm going to be able to do anything useful I need to know just how bad it's going to get."

I winced. Put that way, it sounded pretty awful. "It's already bad. I'm honestly not sure how much worse it's going to get."

Notice that I didn't say it *couldn't* get worse. It can *always* get worse. I know this. And thus I refuse to tempt fate. Superstitious—probably. But magic exists. So does karma, and karma can be a bitch.

"What can I do?"

"Um, don't you have a computer system to rebuild?"

She rolled her eyes. "I'm not on the clock until nine. I usually come in early to get out of the house and have a quiet cup of coffee without listening to my sister's screaming kids. So, what do you need?"

"In that case—" I rolled my chair backward and checked the lights on the safe. It hadn't quite been the full twenty-four hours, but the lights were flashing green. Green was good, but I wasn't sure what flashing was. I hoped that meant I could get past the wards on the safe and not that the whole thing was fucked up beyond all relief . . . otherwise known as FUBAR.

"I *really* need some fresh clothes: jeans, medium T-shirts, underwear, and a sports bra. You know my sizes. Also, a men's large denim jacket and some running shoes in a seven wide." I thought for a moment, then continued. "And you'd probably better buy me a case of those diet shakes to keep here at the office. Chocolate, please. Oh, and replace the ones I drank earlier."

"I'm not worried about that. But shouldn't you have something a little more . . . I dunno, substantial?"

"There's a bunch of stuff the doctor ordered on the counter at home. This is just to get me through in a pinch."

She made a *hmph* sound and pursed her lips. "Like last night?"

"Exactly."

"And just what happened to bring you here in your jammies? You haven't said."

I used the process of opening the safe to buy me time to figure out how to answer her. Taking a deep breath, I ran through the steps to disarm the wards and punched in the combination with a little more vigor than was strictly necessary. Closing my eyes and saying a quick prayer, I pulled the door lever. Dawna was carefully crouched behind my desk in case the whole thing blew. When the door opened, we both let out a little whoop of joy.

I drew out the old-fashioned cash box I keep on hand for emergencies. I only kept a couple hundred dollars in there, but if Dawna didn't go nuts, that should be enough to cover the basics.

"Last night we caught somebody messing with the gas line to the cottage. Before you ask, he got away. And I didn't think it was a good idea for me to meet with the cops after dark in my current . . . condition. So I bugged out before they got there."

She blinked rapidly several times, her expression one of complete shock. "Oh. But why—"

"Would somebody want to blow me up? No clue. And if I could've thought of somewhere else to go that would be safe and unoccupied, I would've done it. I don't want to put anybody here in danger."

She sat up straighter, her face flushing, her breath speeding up. I noted the pulse on her neck without meaning to but was able to tear my gaze away before she noticed. "Do you think we're in danger?"

"Honestly, I don't know. It would help if I had a clue what was going on, but I just don't." I gave her a slow smile. "But I intend to find out."

She shivered. "You scare me sometimes, you know that?"

"It's the fangs."

"No," she said firmly, "it's not."

I didn't know how to answer that, so I changed the subject. "Are you sure you're okay with this?" I asked as I opened the box and forked over the cash, which was actually three hundred. *Yay.* "I know it's a bother."

She glared up at me from the pen and Post-it note she was using to make a list. "Don't be an ass," she scolded. "I wouldn't have offered if I didn't want to help. I'll lock the door behind me on the way out and you should have the whole place to yourself until I get back. Ron and the others aren't exactly known for getting here early, and Bubba just left." She took the cash from my hand, tucking it into the pocket of her suit jacket along with the note and pen.

I put the cash box and duffel into the safe, then closed it and put up the wards. I was going to be down the hall for a bit, and I do *not* leave weapons unattended. Ever.

"Thanks, Dawna. Really."

"No problema."

I grinned. It was her standard answer to everything—unless she was annoyed. Irritate her and she got all formal, with a "yes, *ma'am*" or "no, *sir.*" In five years, I've only earned two "ma'ams." Ron, on the other hand, gets about half a dozen "sirs" a day and doesn't even catch the sarcasm.

Some people are just so dense.

I limped out of the office and down the hall to the bathroom. Hitting the light, I took a look around.

It's a fairly good-sized room. Not big by modern standards, it would've been considered positively luxurious back when the house was built. In those days, the standard was to have one bath for an entire house. But this building had started life as a mansion. Along with real parquet floors and an honest-to-God stained-glass window on the landing between the first and second floors, it had been built with a bathroom on every floor. The original tub had probably been a big old claw-footed monstrosity, but somewhere around the sixties an ambitious owner had decided to do an update of the bathrooms. There was a shower, with ceramic tile squares and a matching oversized tub in flamingo pink. They exactly matched the pedestal sink and toilet. The wallpaper was candy-cane striped in pink, silver, black, and white. It was loud but undeniably eye-catching. A plain white shower curtain hung on the metal rod, the only *plain* thing in the room.

I rummaged around in the built-in linen closet and the medicine chest, lining up toiletries on the edge of the tub. Nobody in the building used the showers much, but the plumbing worked just fine, and I always kept supplies on hand, just in case.

I decided to brush my teeth first.

I glanced into the mirror as I squeezed toothpaste onto the brush. Good news, I had a reflection; bad news, I looked like crap. My skin was normally pale, but not like this. There was an inch-long gash healing on my right cheek and nasty green and purple bruising along my jaw, none of which I remembered getting. They had to have come from this morning's scuffle, but they looked days old. My hair was a wreck, standing out in all directions, decorated with leaves and twigs. Jeez. No wonder Dawna had stared.

My T-shirt had started out white but was now liberally decorated with blood- and grass stains, and it was really too thin to wear in public. Only my plaid flannel boxers seemed to have survived the attack unscathed.

But it was the weariness and strain around the eyes that was the most telling. It had been a hard couple of days, and that was taking its toll. My body might be healing better than the average human—not as well as a vampire, but then, who did? But the healing, while welcome, couldn't erase the signs of exhaustion and pain that had nothing to do with physical damage. I had dark bags under my eyes that looked like I'd been punched . . . repeatedly.

I looked down at the toothbrush, trying to escape my reflection, and was trying to master the specialized technique of brushing fangs when I heard a commotion downstairs.

"Dawna? Dawna!!" Ron's bass bellow carried easily up the stairs. "Don't worry. Our receptionist is here somewhere."

Of *course*. Of all the days for Ron to meet clients early. I stepped out of the bathroom, intending to yell down that she'd be right back, but he was talking to someone, using a tone that was ever so accommodating. I knew it must be a big client to earn that level of brownnosing. Mere mortals were never treated so well.

"You can have a seat in the lobby if you like. I can get you some coffee."

"No, thank you."

I recognized that voice. Hell, anyone who'd been to the movies in the past decade would recognize that voice. It was Cassandra Meadows, star of stage and screen, "America's Darling," and . . . Vicki's mother.

I stepped back into the bathroom, looked up, and addressed my reflection. *Well, fuck a duck.* Spitting out the toothpaste, I slid the brush into the little chrome holder mounted on the wall and grabbed rather desperately for a comb.

It wasn't that I expected to make myself look good. Only God does miracles. Hell, in Cassandra's company I'd look like a toad no matter what I did. But there's a certain *tension* between most attractive women. If I went out looking like this, I'd lose points and she'd use it to her advantage. I couldn't do a damned thing about the clothes. But my hair would be combed, my face clean, and my breath, by God, would be minty fresh.

"Where are Ms. Graves's offices?"

"She takes up most of the third floor. You can't miss it." I could hear the puzzlement in his voice, could almost imagine him looking at the very beefy professional bodyguards she always had with her and wondering why on earth she'd want to hire me.

She wouldn't. Cassandra and Jason were an industry unto themselves. They earned salaries in the multiple millions for every picture even before the points and incentives; their income rivaled the economies of some small countries. They hired a team of security experts—one of the best teams, actually. Miller & Creede were top-notch. Most of their staff were former military or government operatives. All of them had magical or psychic ability of one sort or another, and Miller & Creede required ongoing certification and continuing education. To hire on with them you had to be the best. I'd never applied. First, I wouldn't have met the magical/psychic requirements. More important, I didn't have the right attitude. The staff at M&C work as a team. They are used to following orders without question, complaint, or comment. I wouldn't last a week. Hell, I probably wouldn't last a *day*.

I heard footsteps on the stairs. Two men in dress shoes followed by a woman in heels, then, much more softly, a third man. I could smell gun oil and expensive perfume, feel the frisson of magical power moving ahead of them, scanning for threats. *Damn*, they were good.

I'd combed out my hair and scrubbed my face by the time they reached the top of the stairs, so I was as presentable as I could be when I stepped out to greet them in the hall.

"Hello, Mrs. Cooper." I watched eyes the violet of morning glories narrow slightly at my use of her actual name rather than her stage moniker. "I'm surprised to see you here. You must have come straight from the airport."

That last was a guess, but a good one. Her royal purple silk suit had deep creases across the lap, as if she'd been sitting in it for a long time, and even the perfectly applied makeup couldn't completely hide the evidence of tears. I was glad of that last. Vicki deserved more than a few tears.

Cassandra gasped at my appearance, flinching backward. One of a pair of large bodyguards stepped between us, his hand automatically going beneath his jacket.

Well, hell. *I hadn't said more than hello and already things were going badly. Of course, it could be the pale skin, bruised eyes, and fangs. Nah.*

"Celia?" Just my name, spoken in a tone that was more

cautious than friendly. It occurred to me that I'd surprised her by not reacting with outright hostility. She knew I didn't like her, mainly because I thought she'd treated her daughter shabbily. But Cassandra was Vicki's mother, and her daughter had loved her deeply. So I swallowed my resentment and forced myself to play nice and provide a basic explanation. "I was attacked by a vampire the other night. I'm not a bat—but there have been some changes. Go on into my office. Make yourself comfortable." I gestured in the direction of the open door.

As I expected, the two heavier guards went first, but only after they made sure Cassandra was out of reach and protected by the third man. They were big—impressively so. They probably stood six four and six six, with the kind of muscles that come from serious weight work, but without any of the muscle-bound stiffness you see in folks who neglect flexibility training. They wore expensive, well-tailored suits in navy, with crisply starched white shirts. The only bit of color on either of them was their ties. The first wore one of knotted silk in pale yellow; the second, a more traditional red. I watched them step cautiously into the room, their eyes immediately seeking the source of the magic they'd felt downstairs, and finding it in the safe.

"What's in the safe, Ms. Graves?" The man standing between Cassandra and me smiled when he spoke. It was a good professional smile, charming, showing straight white teeth in a face that was handsome but not excessively so. Like me, he hadn't won the genetic lotto, but he hadn't lost his shirt, either. He had a strong jaw and good cheekbones, but his nose was a little bit large and hooked, almost, but not quite, a beak. Eyes the color of honey met my gaze easily, and I felt him sizing me up in ways that had nothing to do with sex but weren't ignoring the possibility. His hair was his best feature, or would have been if he hadn't cut it so short. It was a warm light brown with golden highlights that would've fallen in soft, unruly curls if he'd given it the chance. Instead, it was cropped short enough to be kept under complete control.

I recognized him from their television ads. John Creede. Second billing on the letterhead, he was rumored to be the real power behind one of the biggest personal protection agencies in the business. *When you care enough to hire the very best.*

"It's a weapons safe," I pointed out drily. "What do you think is in it?"

"Impressive." This time when he smiled he meant it, and it changed his whole appearance. Just that small change, but I felt my heart speed up just a little, my body suddenly becoming aware of him. The small hairs on my neck tingled, as did my fingers. I'd say it was his magic testing what I was, and that might have been part of it. But there was more to it. A deep shudder coursed through me as he pressed power against me more strongly. He noticed the reaction, of course, and his eyes started sparkling with mischief. Damned if he wasn't *intentionally* teasing me. I'd never felt anything like what he was doing. It was primal, wild, yet absolutely controlled. His eyes started to glow lightly, liquid honey that forced me to stare while his magic made my skin ache. The worst part was I was pretty sure he wasn't even trying.

Still, he kept his voice even and professional when he spoke. "I don't know what you have in there, but I could feel the power almost a block away, through the building's shielding. It takes something very ... special to capture my attention. Makes me want to check it out personally, Ms. Graves."

I wasn't sure how to answer that, but I was saved the trouble by the timely return of one of the guards, finished assessing my office for threats.

"You can come in, Ms. Meadows," red tie announced. "It's clear."

Cassandra strode into the office, taking the visitor's chair opposite the desk. She crossed her legs with lazy grace, showing a long expanse of silk-stockinged limb. I suppose they were good legs—I'm no judge of such things. But Lloyd's of London had insured them for some outrageous amount during her last picture. Whatever.

Creede gestured for me to precede him. It was a polite gesture, so I did it, but my shoulders were tight and twitchy until I was in my chair with a wall at my back. I could tell he knew it and was quietly amused.

"To what do I owe this visit?" I kept my voice pleasantly neutral. So far, things had gone pretty well. If I was lucky, we would politely detest each other for a few minutes, get whatever business done, and I could get on with my day.

She looked at me across the desk as if miles separated us rather than a few inches of polished wood. I stayed impassive as those amazing eyes took in the bloodstains and the injuries. I caught her staring at my legs and tried to convince myself she was looking at my tattoo. Unfortunately, it was far more likely she was staring at the very old, very nasty scars that I tried not to think about but knew were just visible beneath the hem of my boxer shorts.

I watched her search for the right words and not find them.

"Were you and my daughter lovers?" I could tell it wasn't the question she'd intended to ask, but it was the one that made it past her lips.

I burst out laughing, which startled her. "No. We were just friends. She was seeing someone the past few months. It was starting to get serious."

"Friends." She shook her head. It was a gesture of unconscious grace that made her shining dark hair move like a living thing around her shoulders. Her eyes met mine and I saw them shining with unshed tears. "Do you know that in my entire adult life I have never had a female *friend*?"

I wasn't surprised. Friendships are usually based on give-and-take between equals. Not many women would be secure enough to consider themselves her equal, and I wasn't sure she'd accept it if they did. But saying that wouldn't be polite, so I settled for something a little more neutral but no less sincere: "I'm sorry to hear that."

She gave a rueful grimace. "I came here intending to raise hell—accuse you of seducing my daughter to get her money and not even giving enough of a damn about her to arrange for a decent cremation."

"Why aren't you?"

"Because"—she looked around her—"because of this office. Because looking at you right now, I find that I *can't*." She sounded exasperated, frustrated. "My husband told me you weren't using Vicki, that you never had. He said that you were the one who saved her from the fire, that you visited her several times a week at the hospital, that you *cared*."

Unexpected sorrow lanced through me. "Yeah. I do . . . did."

A single glittering tear tracked down her perfect cheek. She sat up straighter in the chair and uncrossed her legs. "I'm told that Vicki told you her wishes with regard to her funeral arrangements?"

I chuckled. I couldn't help it. Yes, she'd told me—and Alex and Dawna, after we'd finished our second pitcher of margaritas at the little Mexican restaurant not a block from here. Fortunately, I still had the cocktail napkin I'd made Vicki write it all down on. Just a little square of paper covered in tiny, smudged handwriting. I'd filed it in the same folder with the receipt for my pre-paid arrangements because Vicki had made me promise not to lose it.

"What's funny?"

"Just remembering." It had been a good night, one of the best, with good friends, good food, and bad karaoke. I scooted the chair back from my desk and got up. It was the work of a moment to find the file. I pulled out the cocktail napkin.

Cassandra laughed, then gave a startled, guilty look as if it was too soon. She was grieving, and nothing should be funny.

"I'll go downstairs and make you a copy."

"You're going to keep the original." She stated it as a fact.

I nodded. She was right. It was silly and sentimental, but I'd do it. Because every time I ran across that little piece of paper it would remind me of that night and the fun we'd had. I wanted to be reminded. Because in the press of day-to-day life it was too easy to get caught up in the bad things, let the small joys slip away.

"You're sentimental. I wouldn't have expected that."

I shrugged, my hand on the doorknob. "You don't know me."

Her eyes seemed to dim, the last of the humor draining away, leaving sorrow in its wake. "No. I don't."

I wasn't sure what to say to that. She could've gotten to know me at any time over the past several years—if she'd cared enough to bother. She hadn't. Any more than she'd bothered visiting her daughter at Birchwoods. Saying that, however, would be cruel. I try not to be cruel—unless I'm really, *seriously* provoked. "You'll need to talk to her attorney about the funeral arrangements. He already has a copy of this and is probably getting started. I think she made him the executor." That was so obviously a slap at both of her parents that all Cassandra could do was open her mouth in shock. I used the excuse of someone coming in the front door to duck out the door before she could say anything unfortunate.

I ran into Dawna in the hall. She was back from her errands. Her face was flushed with anger, her eyes flashing. She had several shopping bags hooked over her wrist. "If I throttle that bastard, will you help me to hide the body?"

"Dawna!" Ron bellowed. I watched her eyes narrow, saw her take a deep breath as if to answer.

I took the packages from her hands. "I'll deal with him," I interrupted before she could say something she'd regret. Ron was being a jerk, but she needed the job. And if he pushed, he could probably get the others to agree to fire her even if I fought it. "Can you make me a couple of copies of this?"

She took the cocktail napkin curiously, opening it fully to make sure there was writing only on the one side. "No problema." She went down a few steps and stopped. Turning to look over her shoulder, she grinned at me. "But if you kick his ass, I get to watch."

I laughed and followed slowly behind her down as far as the second floor. My knee was still twinging. She peeled off toward the copy room. I continued down to the landing. Ron was taking a deep breath to shout again when I came down those last few steps. I stopped one step up from him. It was close enough to invade his personal space and high enough to put me at exactly eye level. I smiled and started speaking to him, keeping my voice, soft, gentle, and all the more scary for it.

"Ronald, what time is it?"

He didn't bother to look at me. That's not unusual for him. I sometimes think he doesn't actually *see* anybody else. Ron's world revolves around Ron. He stepped back, intending to walk around me. I stepped forward, taking back the space he'd just given himself. "I *asked*, 'What time is it?'"

He puffed himself up, taking in as much air as his chest would allow, trying to loom over me. He expected me to back down. Nearly everyone does. He's not a small man, and he's loud and obnoxious. Most people don't want to antagonize him. They seem to sense that he lives to dominate others. But I'm not most people. I'd had a *really* rough couple of days. And I was well and truly tired of Ron's bullshit.

"Eight fifteen. Why?" He spit the words at me like a curse, and started to lean around me, drawing in another huge lungful of air, preparatory to screaming.

I stepped directly in front of him. "Dawna's hours are nine to five. It's not nine. She's not on duty."

He opened his mouth to argue, but I silenced him with a look and a gesture upward, reminding him that we had important clients on site. "Bellowing like that does not make you look important, Ron. It makes you look like an ass. Hogging the facilities and the secretary's time does not make you more important than the rest of the tenants, who pay just as

much for the privilege as you do. It makes you a selfish, obnoxious prick." I hadn't raised my voice once. In fact, my
tone was gentle enough to be conversational. But that didn't
fool him. Because I wasn't backing down. My body language
was aggressive. And my skin had, yet again, started to glow.
He flinched, taking a half step back. This time I let him
keep it.

"I have had two attempts made on my life in as many days.
I am tired and out of patience. As a personal favor to me,
Dawna went on her own time to the store so that I would not
have to meet with potential clients looking like this. Unfortunately, the clients arrived early. But you will *not* berate her for
not being here at your beck and call. You will not, in fact, berate her for anything."

"Is that a threat?" he blustered, but I could smell the fear on
him. Fortunately, I'd already eaten. My stomach didn't even
rumble.

"Ronald." I smiled, making sure to flash plenty of fang. "If I
decide to threaten you, you'll know it. In the meantime let's just
call this a *friendly sssuggestion*." The lisp was back, but oddly, I
didn't mind. Not even a little.

And *that* was when he finally took a good look at me. He
backed away, his eyes huge at the sight of the fangs. But despite
his obvious fear, he continued to bluster. "How *dare* you!"

I was saved a response. The front door opened and Bubba
stepped in with my mother at his heels. Right behind them
were Kevin Landingham and Bruno DeLuca.

For a full ten seconds the world stopped. I swear. Right on
its axis. I stood there, staring at Bruno, the man I'd thought
was the love of my life back in college.

My mouth went dry, my heart racing. For just a minute the rest of the world disappeared and it was just me and him.

Bruno had changed. He was still five feet, eleven inches, of pure Italian studliness. But there were touches of gray at his temples, and worry lines had appeared between his brows and at the corners of his mouth. A smile was twitching at his lips and there was laughter sparking in his dark brown eyes. Then again, there nearly always was, when he saw me.

It was my mother who broke the spell, drawing me back to the present with more speed than grace. "Celie?" My mother's voice rose nearly an octave between the first and second syllables of my name. "Oh my *God*, honey, what's *happened* to you? You look like *hell*."

Everyone turned to stare—including Ron. He seemed to see past his anger, fear, and the fangs for the first time, looking me over from head to toe.

"She's right, Graves. You look . . . terrible. Are those your *pajamas?*"

Oh, hell. I decided to take charge of the situation before things got any worse. It didn't seem likely and the mere thought was horrifying, but you never could tell. "Yes, Ron. I came here in my pj's because the gas company wouldn't let me back in the house." I turned to my mother. "Hi, Mom. It's been a rough couple of days. Come by the office when you're done with Bubba and I'll drive you home. Kevin, Bruno, why don't you go join everybody else up in my office? It's a regular party in there." Okay, the sarcasm was a little overdone, but I couldn't help myself.

I stepped aside so they could trudge past. Bruno gave my shoulder a quick squeeze on the way. It was a small gesture, but it really did make me feel better. When they were past the landing, I turned back to Ron. He was still staring, his eyes too wide. "Are you telling me the truth? Did somebody really try to kill you?"

"Yessss." I pointed at my mouth "Notice the teeth? I didn't have them last week."

"Twice?"

"Yup."

"Why?" He seemed truly puzzled. Apparently, he didn't *not* like me enough to even consider elimination. That was sort of flattering.

I shrugged. "Damned if I know. But I intend to find out."

15

I had Dawna deliver the photocopy of the cocktail napkin to Cassandra and make my excuses to everyone. I needed a shower, and I wanted to put on some clothes fit for wearing in front of people. Selfish, probably. Chicken, definitely. But screw it. The fact that I'd gone downstairs for a confrontation with Ron showed me more clearly than any words that I was reaching the end of my rope.

So I locked the bathroom door, stripped, and turned the water on as hot as I could stand. I scrubbed until I was as clean as I was going to get, checking my injuries as I went. The knee was the worst. Joint injuries suck. Even with the boost to my healing, it was swollen and hurting. I'd been an idiot to go downstairs, and now I was paying for it.

If I'd had any sense I'd have put an Ace bandage on the list I'd given Dawna. But I hadn't thought about it, which meant that I was probably going to be taking another trip to Phar-Mart. I'd read enough of the research before I fell asleep to get a fair guess of how fast I could heal—roughly a day's worth of healing each hour. At that rate, my knee would be a problem for a few more days—*if* I took proper care of it.

I climbed out of the shower and toweled myself off. I used a second towel to rub most of the moisture from my hair before combing it out. It'd have to air-dry. I hadn't thought to bring a blow-dryer to the office. But that was all right. It was clean. *I* was clean. I opened the bag and found myself grinning. Leave it to Dawna. She'd bought me underclothes all right. *Lingerie-*type underclothes. Lacy and pretty, in silk. And the top wasn't just an ordinary tee. Nope, she'd supplied me with a matching tank and overblouse in black, probably the only color that would actually look good with my new complexion. The jeans were black, too, and my favorite brand. She'd even sprung for jewelry—small hoop earrings and a delicate pendant. White gold, not silver. I hadn't given her enough money to pay for half of this. But I was really, really glad she'd done it. Because Bruno was here and Kevin and . . . well, strangely, Creede. And in this outfit I wouldn't have to feel completely outclassed by Cassandra.

The socks were just as pretty but were nylon rather than cotton. I detest nylon ones because they make me sweat, so I pulled the tennis shoes on over my bare feet. I left the denim jacket in the bag. It was too warm to wear it inside. It was *probably* too warm to wear it outside, too. But I had to cover as much skin as I could.

I reflected sourly that while covering up would keep me from burning, dying of heatstroke was a distinct possibility. But wearing the jacket would enable me to carry my weapons.

The whole process probably didn't take more than fifteen to twenty minutes. When I was as ready as I was going to get, I took a deep breath, grabbed the door handle, and stepped out into the hall, expecting to hear voices and see a crowd in my office. Instead, I was met with blessed silence except for the gentle clicking of the keys on a laptop computer.

"Where'd everybody go?" I muttered.

Bruno DeLuca's disembodied voice answered me, coming from my office. "Mrs. Cooper and her entourage left with her copy of the funeral information. Fair warning, she doesn't like the 'no cremation' thing."

"Terrific. Just ducky." I walked back down the hall to my office. I felt an odd tingle as I stepped over the threshold. Sort of a pins-and-needles sensation that prickled against my whole body. It was unnerving. I would've said something, but Bruno was already talking.

"Kevin is taking your mother home. After the scene with the attorney downstairs, I think he was afraid what you might do to her if the two of you left here alone."

I blushed. I probably shouldn't have threatened Ron. Yes, he was being an ass, but it's not like he can help it. It's his *nature*. You might as well blame a dog for barking. And they were right about my mother, too. Because while Ron is annoying, my mother takes me to a completely irrational level as easily as breathing.

"Relax." Bruno looked up at me and smiled, and it warmed me to my toes. We were both older. Maybe we were even wiser. But looking at that smile, I felt the familiar tug on the old heartstrings and had to remind myself why we hadn't worked as a couple.

"You didn't hurt him, and from what I heard, he deserved an ass chewing." Bruno looked me over, from head to toe. "Like the outfit. It almost makes the coloring look normal."

"Thanks." I draped myself sideways in one of the visitor's

chairs and ignored the sudden twinge in my leg. "And yeah, Ron deserved that and more. But I don't like the fact that I keep almost losing control."

Bruno turned away from the laptop he'd been working on to give me a long, level look.

"You're going to need to be careful about that, Celia. I've been reading up, and while the effects of becoming an abomination are very individualized, uncontrolled rage seems to be pretty universal. It also seems to kick in any latent magical abilities that hadn't manifested in human form."

"I don't *have* any magical abilities. Thank God for small favors." In fact, I'd failed the standard tests I'd taken in grade school so completely I'd have gotten a negative score if it were possible. But the anger control thing was going to be a problem.

"It's not all bad news." He turned the laptop so I could see the screen. He'd been researching on an internal website for the company he worked with. I could tell because the company logo was prominently displayed at the top of every page.

"You get improved healing, strength, and speed. Depending on how far the process went, you might be able to eat some solid food eventually. You might start with soft foods and see if you can work your way up."

I found myself grinning until my face hurt. I love food. *Really* love food. Especially the ethnic stuff like real Mexican, Thai, and good-old-fashioned Italian, heavy on the garlic. Oh, crap—*garlic*. Was it going to be a problem? I hoped not. But even if it was, I could cope. I mean, garlic or no, I might be able to eat real food. Solid stuff. Like a normal person. I could start with scrambled eggs. And maybe a nibble of bacon. *Yum.*

Bruno was shaking his head in amused disbelief.

"What? I'm not supposed to worry about eating?"

That earned me a look. "Solid food should be the last thing you're thinking about. You need to concentrate on finding your sire, before he—"

I waved that away. "Yeah, yeah, I know. But honestly, I'm more worried about the guys who set up the ambush than about the specific bat that bit me. And I don't think that Kevin bugged out with Mom just to keep the peace."

"You think he's hiding something?" Bruno sounded tired enough that I took a closer look at him—without the glow of nostalgia and sexual attraction.

He *was* tired. There were worry lines and wrinkles I hadn't noticed before. And while I could feel a steady stream of energy emanating from him—deep, strong, and more powerful even than what I'd sensed from the M&C boys, he looked strained. His body practically sang with tension, even sitting still.

"Are you okay?"

"It's been a rough few months," he admitted. "I'll be fine."

A little white lie. And just like that I knew. It wasn't mind reading, well, not of the psychic sort. More the sort of connection you have with someone when you've been close to them for a very long time. I started swearing. "Damn it, DeLuca. You *know* better."

He glared at me, dark eyes flashing dangerously. He answered the accusation I hadn't bothered to voice. "It's not like I've had a lot of choice. You don't know what's been going on."

"Maybe not," I snarled. "But I know that draining your power without rest is going to cause it to get out of control, maybe even *fail*. I know that it'll cut more years off your life than a two-pack-a-day cigarette habit." My knee spasms had finally gotten to me, so I had risen to my feet and was leaning on my arms on the desk. I'd invaded his personal space, but unlike Ron, Bruno wasn't backing away.

"Yeah, well, right now I know that there's a lesser demon wandering around loose in the metro area and my brother's hunting it even though he's injured, one of my best friends just died by magic, and another one barely survived a vampire attack. Things are a little *tense*. So, bitch at me all you want, I think maybe my resting will just have to wait."

I rocked back on my heels as if he'd slapped me. It would've been better if he had. I wasn't the only person who counted a certain clairvoyant as my best friend. "You're sure about Vicki?"

"I'm sure." He rubbed the bridge of his nose with his left hand. It was a familiar gesture from nights when he'd stayed up too late studying and was tired. "They called our company to perform the independent investigation. I had enough pull to insist on coming along."

"Tell me."

"I can't. It's confidential, and I've taken oaths." He rolled up his right sleeve, showing me a mark like a brand on the inside of his forearm. It was bright red and probably hadn't been there a minute earlier. He shook his head. "If I wasn't so damned tired, I wouldn't have let even that much slip."

I backed off, because I knew he was right. Binding oaths were . . . well, binding. Breaking them isn't supposed to be fatal, but there are worse things than dying. I didn't like that he'd allowed himself to be bound, but he was a grown-up. And since the deed was definitely done, well, the best thing I could do for him was back off. "It's all right. The mark is just

228 • CAT ADAMS

a warning that you're on thin ice, not that you've fallen through." I lowered myself back into the chair. I wasn't about to do anything that would harm Bruno. But I could ask other people questions: people like Dr. Scott at Birchwoods, who would get a full copy of the report.

"Can you tell me about the demon?"

"That's not a secret, as far as I know. I'll tell you about it on the way to the hotel. Get your weapons." He nodded in the direction of the safe. "I need to check them before we go any-where."

"They're fine." I didn't want him checking them. Because I knew Bruno. If the knives were at even a hair less than full power, he'd refill them. And he needed rest, not more work.

He gave me a sad smile, as if he'd read my mind. Maybe he had. It wouldn't surprise me if he had a smidgen of a psychic gift along with the mage talent, and it *really* wouldn't surprise me if he hadn't told anyone.

"Fine. But don't push yourself." I went to the safe.

"Yes, *Mother.*" Even though they were the same words, he said them entirely differently than Kevin had.

"Oh, shut up," I muttered, but I was smiling. I'd missed Bruno. I love Kevin Landingham dearly. He's big, he's brood-ing, he's oh so sexy. But he's *serious.* And secretive. Bruno has always been a breath of fresh air. He's got . . . pizzazz. If you get him in a tux, he'll quote James Bond movies all night. He not only sings in the shower, it's a medley of Barry Manilow songs and show tunes. No situation has ever been so serious that Bruno DeLuca wouldn't crack wise about it.

A lot of people find him annoying. They assume there's no

substance under the flash. They're wrong. Bruno has his fun, but underneath that camouflage is a fine mind and the kind of ruthless determination that got him to the top and keeps him there.

Having him sitting in my office, serious and worried, got to me. A lot. I could feel him behind me, a close, warm presence at my back. My pulse sped, my body intensely aware of his. It distracted me enough that I fumbled the controls and had to start over. That earned me a low, wicked chuckle. Which I ignored . . . mostly.

Eventually I managed to lower the wards and enter the combination to the safe. Pulling it open, I drew out the duffel containing the box with the knives. I set the box on the desk in front of him. Bruno waved his hand over it in a casual gesture. Wherever his hand passed, traces of sparkling rainbow colors moved over the lid.

"That is so cool." I hadn't meant to say it out loud. It just popped out.

He laughed, and for a minute a little of the "old" Bruno shone in his face. "Yeah, it is." He grinned over at me. "I will have you know, young lady, that not *every* mage can do that."

"Of course not." I agreed. "You 'da *man.*'"

He laughed again, a sound of real delight. "Damned right. And don't you forget it."

"Why can I see that? And why can I feel magic? I couldn't before." I knew he'd know the answer. Of all of our crowd, he'd been the best student. He wasn't the smartest. But he'd had talent to burn and he always worked the hardest. He read every assignment, took detailed notes, listened and participated in class. His research papers had always been top-notch. Even in college he'd subscribed to all the trade magazines. If anybody could tell me what was going on, it'd be him.

"Magic is harmful to vampires—to most of the monsters really, but especially the bats. At a guess, I'd say that the ability to sense it is a trait that passed to you from your sire when you got drained. Sensing magic would be one of the abilities that would keep a bat alive long enough to become a sire."

He opened the box. The knives gleamed. The wooden handles were polished to a warm glow, but the blades gleamed with a cold fire. When he passed his hand over them there were no rainbows. Instead white light, blinding as a magnesium flare, burst to life. I flinched back, shielding my watering eyes with my arm. I couldn't see a thing, but I could hear the pride and satisfaction in Bruno's voice.

"Oh yeah. Best thing I've ever done. Maybe the best thing I'll ever do. I hope not, but you never know."

The light died. I had to blink a few times. Tears were running from my eyes and my retinas were still overloaded. I wiped my eyes with the back of my hand.

"Those knives saved my life the other night, bought me enough time for Kevin and Amy to come charging to the rescue."

"That's why I made 'em." Bruno rolled back his left sleeve to expose a forearm laced with fine white scars.

Before I could ask what he was going to do, he had picked up the first knife. With a practiced movement he sliced into his flesh. Blood welled up from the wound and traced the silver and steel of the knife blade. He muttered words in a language I didn't recognize. There was a hiss of power and the air seemed to thicken and heat. I watched the blade absorb the blood and the wound on his arm scab over, then heal, until all that was left was another delicate scar line.

He set the knife back into its case and reached for the second blade. "I have to tell you, Celia, if it had been anybody else . . . but Vicki swore to me back in college that if you didn't have the right weapons in that alley, you'd die of that vampire attack and your body would never be found. If she'd known the exact day, she'd have stopped you from taking the job. I know it."

She *knew*? Even back in college? "She never told me."

"She didn't tell Kevin, either. She only told me that she knew I *could* make the knives, and that it would make all the difference if I would." He gave me a droll look. "She did *not* tell me that I would have to bleed myself every damned day for five flipping *years* to get them finished." He grimaced. "There were some days I really wanted to give up and say 'screw it.' Especially after we broke up. But if anything had happened to you, I'd never have forgiven myself. Not even when I was angry enough at you to strangle you myself."

I winced. Slicing yourself open every single day for five *years*? *Ow.* I didn't even know what to say in the face of that kind of dedication and effort. "Thank you" didn't seem to be enough, but it was all I had. So I said it. "Thank you."

He smiled, and it softened his expression, bringing the usual warmth back into his dark brown eyes. He leaned in close, giving me a quick kiss on the forehead. "You're welcome."

The level of emotional intensity had risen to the point where I was getting uncomfortable, so I changed the subject. "You said the hotel. Does this mean you're actually going to *rest*?"

"Only a catnap. I'm going to try to meet up with my brother Matteo before sunset—see if he's gotten any leads on that demon I was telling you about. But I need a ride. Kevin drove me here."

"I'll grab my keys." I shook my head in halfhearted disapproval and made a decision. I was *not* going to tell him that the demonic was involved in my mess. Not *yet*. He might not be my lover anymore, but he was and always would be my friend. I was worried about him. The days when we were close enough for me to have any say or influence as to what he did were long gone—if they'd ever existed in the first place. But if I could delay telling him a few hours until he was in better shape, I would. "Hope you don't mind my stopping by the drugstore on the way? I need to wrap my knee."

There was a tap on the door. We turned in unison to find Dawna standing in the doorway, looking distinctly uncomfortable.

"What's wrong?"

"I'm sorry, Celia, but you're not going anywhere for a while. Detective Gibson is downstairs with a pair of men who keep scowling and muttering to each other in some foreign language. And the three of them are staring daggers across the coffee table at the FBI guys from yesterday. They all want to ask you questions. Now. In fact, they're being pretty insistent about it."

Crap. "Well, doesn't this just suck?"

"You shouldn't talk to them without an attorney present," Bruno advised.

"I've already met with Gibson. But you're right about the Feds." I doubted an attorney would help much with the other two. Unless I missed my guess, they'd probably been sent here by Rusland's king. I was actually kind of glad they were here with the police. Otherwise I might just have been taken off somewhere for a very *private* interrogation. Maybe even one that involved a certain level of . . . unpleasantness and ultimately my untimely permanent disappearance. Lucky for me, I had absolutely nothing to hide. It was unlikely any of my visitors would believe that. But if I disappeared there'd be lots and lots of uncomfortable questions and bad publicity. Bruno would see to it, even if Gibson didn't. The king didn't need bad press, even if his retainers did have diplomatic immunity.

And of course I said I'd cooperate fully. Hell. Don't think about it, Graves. At this point if they want to kill you, they're going to have to take a number. Just get through the meeting.

I pasted a smile on my face that I hoped would fool Dawna. I couldn't fool Bruno. He knew me too well. "Dawna, do me a favor, put them in the conference room and order us up some coffee and rolls. I'm going to call my lawyer."

"Ron's got the conference room."

"Of course he does." I felt my smile wilt around the edges but tried to sound unfazed. God, why did this feel like every other weekday? "Fine. Give them coffee and tell them it'll be a few minutes, we're waiting for my attorney. Then order rolls. We'll meet here in my office once the attorney arrives." I turned to Bruno and tried to keep the frustration in my voice to a minimum. After all, none of this was his fault. Mine either, if it came to that. "Looks like you'll be taking a cab."

"I'm not leaving."

I started to protest, but he silenced me with a look. "Consider me your *supernatural* advisor. Federal law dictates you can have one when you're not fully human." There was no arguing with him when he was wearing that expression, so I didn't bother to try. Mollified, he closed his laptop, put it in the case, then got up and moved to the other side of the desk, settling into a chair in the far corner.

Dawna was shaking her head in amusement as she ducked out the door. Let her laugh. She'd never tried to budge Bruno when he was in one of his moods. Besides, considering what he'd gone through to make those knives, I owed him.

"You realize they're not going to let you stay. *Supernatural advisor* or not."

He gave me a smile that was more a baring of teeth. "Unless they are very, *very* good, they'll never even suspect I'm here."

I blinked stupidly. "You can *do* that? I mean—I thought it wasn't possible for people to disappear." Then again, wasn't that exactly what Jones had done?

"You'd be amazed at what I can do." Bruno gave me a genuine smile this time. "But no, I'm not disappearing. It's a kind of illusion spell. It makes me very, very, unnoticeable—a part of the furniture. Don't get me wrong. There are telepaths who can use mental manipulation to make you and everyone in the area *think* they're seeing someone else. But I'm not a telepath. So I make do with a little magic."

More than a little magic, unless I missed my guess. But I wasn't going to start an argument I couldn't win. Besides, I was curious. I'd studied the paranormal for four years and *none* of this stuff had come up. "So you get a good enough telepath and they really could go up in front of the crowd and pretend to be the president and everybody would think it was him?"

"If he had enough oompf, yes. *But* he'd have to be damned careful. Because while folks with the gift can influence what people think, they *can't* manipulate reality. So a mirror, window, whatever, is going to reflect what is actually there."

I sat there for a few seconds, trying to absorb that. I mean, telepaths had always kind of scared me—they're mind benders after all. And it's one of the skills the government and the schools keep the tightest rein on. But Jones had done it. Had to have. I was just starting to ponder the implications of that when Bruno's voice brought me back to the present.

"You'd better call that attorney. Your guests won't wait forever."

I looked up, intending to make a snappy comeback, and he wasn't there. Oh, he was. And if I looked *really* hard, I could see him. But at first glance, hell, even *second* glance, I would've sworn he was a rubber tree. Except I don't *own* a rubber tree.

"Show-off."

"Yeah, well, it's a spell, not psychic manipulation, so I can't move and keep up the illusion. And don't stare or they'll know something's up."

Not staring was harder than it sounded. I tried to practice, looking everywhere *but* at the rubber tree in the corner as I dialed the number for my attorney.

It took a couple of minutes to get through but considerably less time than it should have. I found my attorneys through Vicki's referral. To the esteemed professionals at Pratt, Arons, Ziegler, Santos, and Cortez I was just a teeny little fish in a great big pond. It's a big firm, with specialists in various areas of law. They're the best, but you pay for it. There was no doubt in my mind that the only reason they dealt with me at all was as a favor to Vicki. That I wasn't left on hold for ten minutes with the answering service meant something. I just wasn't sure what.

Roberto Santos is the senior attorney in criminal defense matters. If you haven't heard of him, I assume you've been living in a Carmelite convent or hiding somewhere under a rock. He represents the famous and infamous—provided they pay their bills. He's a bottom-line kind of guy. I can respect that. I'm the same way. I've never been a big enough client to merit an introduction. My stuff has always been handled by very, very junior associates. So the last thing I expected was for the man himself to pick up the line.

"Roberto Santos, Ms. Graves. I understand you have a problem?" His voice was smooth, cultured, flowing like molten chocolate down the line. Impressive as it was over the telephone, I could only imagine the reaction of a jury in person.

It took me a second to gather my wits, but I managed. As succinctly as I could, I caught him up to speed.

He let me talk. I could hear a pen scratching across paper as he took notes, but he didn't interrupt once as I ran through the facts. Once I finished, however, he had questions. Probing, intelligent questions. He voiced them with brisk efficiency—and actually listened to the answers. The whole conversation took maybe twenty minutes.

"I can be at your office in a half hour. In the meantime, I want you to print hard copies and make a CD for me of everything you've got. We'll probably not want to share it all, but it'll save us all time and effort if you have it all ready when I get there."

"Right. How much am I going to owe you for this?" I didn't really want to know, but I needed to. I just hoped it wouldn't bankrupt me.

I managed not to gasp at the amount he quoted. I kept the firm on retainer, but the hourly fees for actual work—well, I could afford it . . . barely. Provided, of course, that things didn't drag on. "I'll have a check ready for you when you arrive."

"Thank you. I'll see you soon."

I hung up the phone and started getting everything ready for him. There wasn't much. Telephone messages, some hand-written notes. I scanned those into the computer, which thank-fully Dawna had gotten working. The signed contract was already on file.

Not too many minutes later I heard footfalls on the stairs and smelled fresh coffee mingled with the sweet cinnamon aroma of baked goods. Thank the good lord for Cinnabon. My stomach rumbled audibly in response.

Dawna was chatting amiably with the deliveryman from the bakery and I could hear Roberto grumbling that with this kind of workout he wouldn't need the StairMaster. *Good.* I'd rather we didn't have to wait much longer. In fact, I wanted to get this over with as quickly and painlessly as possible.

I flipped open the laptop and was in the process of cabling it to the printer when the three of them walked in. Dawna and the deliveryman started bustling around in the corner, setting up the baked goods. Roberto moved one of the chairs over so that he was sitting next to the desk.

I shook Roberto's hand before he sat down. He barely glanced at my fangs. Who knows? Maybe he'd seen worse. Dawna kept casting covert glances at the rubber tree, looking confused.

238 I CAT ADAMS

But she didn't say anything, just kept helping the deliveryman. When they'd finished with the food, she began rearranging the chairs, even bringing in the patio chairs from the balcony so there'd be enough seating for everybody. Only when she'd finished and left the room did Roberto speak.

"I told the people downstairs that I needed ten minutes alone with you before they came up. We've already lost nearly half of it. So we'd better hurry. Give me what you've got."

I passed over the copies and plugged a jump drive into one of the computer ports to transfer files for him as he was scanning the printed pages. It didn't take him long.

"Is there anything you haven't told me? Anything else I need to know?" He sounded suspicious. I suppose it's only natural. He's a criminal defense attorney. People lie to their attorneys all the time.

So I told him the *rest* of the information. Sadly, there was no way for Bruno not to overhear.

16

I have a reasonably large office. But it was fairly crowded with everybody crammed in there. Gibson had taken a seat in the patio chair nearest the balcony doors. He was quiet, subdued, and acting very much as if we hadn't spent a good chunk of yesterday together. So either he *had* told them already or he *hadn't* and didn't want to. Either way was fine with me.

The Feds were both alike and opposites. Their names were Erikson and Rizzoli. The former was very Nordic and handsome in the same way as the models in those Tommy Hilfiger ads. Rizzoli was about average height, built blocky, and as Italian as pasta, even more Italian looking than Bruno—something I wouldn't have believed possible if I hadn't seen it for myself. Both agents were dressed in identical conservative suits and carried themselves in a way that just *screamed* Fed. I don't know what they do at the federal training center, but the men and women who make it through the program all wind up with a certain way of moving and dressing that is easy to spot once you've seen it.

The king's retainers had long names that I couldn't hope to pronounce. They were impeccably dressed, their suits hand tailored, top-of-the-line, and up-to-the-minute in European fashion. I could also feel a frisson of power that told me they'd been spelled, probably with the same concealing magics I'd had on my jacket. If I'd thought they'd answer I might even ask if theirs came with a garrote. But I decided against it. They didn't look like they'd have a sense of humor about that sort of thing. In fact, despite the window dressing, they looked like they were just the sort of people to *use* that kind of weapon. They were big and intimidating looking, with heavily eastern European features. Maybe the plan had been to scare me into revealing all my secrets? Their English was almost perfect, except for a bit of stilted formality and the occasional odd turn of phrase. In my head I labeled them Tweedledee and Tweedledum. Dee was the senior; Dum, the more powerful.

They asked questions.

I answered.

The Feds asked questions.

I answered.

Then back to the retainers.

It grew tiresome. Then tedious. The time for breakfast passed. Then lunch. I knew I was supposed to drink something, but I didn't think it wise to ask for a break. So I crossed my fingers and concentrated on answering the questions.

We'd all had coffee, but while the men apparently had cast-iron bladders, I didn't. Maybe it was some sort of non-pissing pissing contest. Whatever. Eventually, I gave in and told everyone I needed a bathroom break. I'd planned to drink a shake when I got in there, but the box was missing. Were they in the refrigerator? It didn't really matter, because I didn't think my audience would appreciate me taking ten minutes to hobble downstairs to the kitchen to get one. When I came back, they were chatting amiably and munching down on the cinnamon rolls. The smell started to drive me crazy, so I decided to join them.

Bad mistake.

I took a bite. I chewed (which, by the way, is a seriously tricky proposition when you have fangs). And I choked. Badly.

I couldn't swallow it.

I tried washing it down with coffee.

No luck.

A single small bite, well chewed, and it wouldn't go down. It was stuck. Well and truly stuck, right in the middle of my neck. I coughed and hacked and even stuck a finger down my throat, hoping to push it down.

I sat at my desk, turning slightly blue, my guests looking more and more alarmed. Even the rubber tree was shaking.

Finally I just gave up and excused myself again, went into the bathroom, and stuck my finger fully down my throat until I threw up. Hauling out the toothbrush again, I brushed until my breath was minty fresh. I stared at my reflection in the mirror and cried. I had fangs. I couldn't eat solid food. It was real. It was permanent. I wasn't human anymore.

I didn't cry long. Despite the past day or two, I'm not the weepy type. Besides, I had agents and an attorney waiting for me. So I grabbed a washcloth from the built-in linen cabinet and scrubbed down my face with cold water. Since I still looked a little blotchy, I reached for the small silk bag that held my makeup and started putting it on. A few drops of Visine helped with the eyes but not the face.

I looked like a clown.

I'd always been pale, but my skin was now pure white and colors that had been subtle before were just plain garish.

Swearing under my breath, I washed it all off. While I was at it I took down my hair and brushed it out. I stared at my reflection. Better. I looked better. Not good. There was still a hint of panic in my eyes. But there wasn't much I could do about that. Life goes on, whether you're ready for it or not. Since I was as ready as I was going to be, I stepped out into the hall. Taking a deep breath, I went back into the lion's den.

They'd been arguing, loudly, while I was gone. But there was instant silence as I stepped back into the room.

"This is getting us nowhere. You are wasting our time." The hint of an accent was slipping into Dee's voice, probably because he was angry. "We would see for ourselves what has happened." His face was still flushed from arguing. "I believe you have already submitted to magical memory enhancement and a visit to a psychic, have you not?" He glared at Gibson, who remained utterly impassive except for a muscle that was twitching in his jaw from where he was clenching his teeth.

I felt my eyebrows crawling up my forehead. How the hell had they learned about my visit to Dottie? I didn't like that. And I *really* didn't like the idea of these two terrorizing that nice little old lady. Judging from Gibson's expression, he didn't care for it much, either.

"You *will* do it again. For us. Now." It wasn't a request. All around the room people were bristling. My attorney started to argue, but the Ruslander continued, speaking over him. "We would prefer my companion assist you in this. But if not, perhaps your friend in the corner"—he waved in the direction of Bruno the rubber tree—"can do more than just hide himself. Hmn?"

Well, shit. Wasn't this just awkward. Everyone in the room turned to stare at the corner until, with a sigh, Bruno gave it up and dropped the illusion.

"And just *who* the hell are *you*?" Erikson's voice dripped icicles.

"His name is Bruno DeLuca," Rizzoli answered. When his partner turned to give him a look he answered the unasked question with a curt, "We've met." He turned to Bruno. "What are you doing here?"

Bruno opened his mouth to speak, but it was Dee who answered. "He has been involved with Ms. Graves for many years. They were once affianced. He is no doubt here to protect her from any . . ." He seemed to search for the right phrase. "Funny business?"

Bruno's eyes narrowed as he nodded.

Roberto shot a chilly glance at me. Okay, so I hadn't told him *all* my secrets. I hoped that wouldn't lose me the services of the firm.

"Fine," Dum said coldly. "We have no problem with Mr. DeLuca being present. We simply need to know exactly what has occurred. And time is fleeting. So, Ms. Graves, if you would be so kind?"

He phrased it as a request, but it wasn't one. And while the

Feds raised objections, it really didn't matter to them, and we all knew it.

"What *exactly* do you plan to do?" The look Bruno gave the other mage made it clear that he was just as much of a tough guy, and magician, as anyone present.

Dee started to explain, but he only got a couple of sentences out before the arguments started. Bruno was starting to get pretty heated about concepts I wasn't close to understanding. Apparently, it wasn't the fact that there would be a bespelling but what it would entail. Then Erikson coughed softly, drawing everyone's attention. "We all have enough information to start our various investigations. I suggest we let Ms. Graves get some rest. You can always resort to more drastic measures if the investigation dead-ends."

"Assuming she lives that long." Tweedledum's smile didn't reach his eyes. Then again, neither did mine.

"I'll do my best." I was tired of the posturing, tired of them. So I gestured to the open door. It was a dismissal, and they didn't like it one bit. Even so, everyone but Bruno took the hint. I waited by the door for a moment, listening. I could hear their footfalls and muted conversation even when they reached the ground floor.

Dawna's voice came through the clearest. "Excuse me, Agent Erikson, don't forget your pen. You left it on my desk this morning."

Someone mumbled something that was probably thanks. I heard the front door squeak open, then the slam of the screen, and they were gone.

"Thank God that's over." I meant it as gratitude, not blasphemy. Although since my relationship with the almighty is a little sketchy, I suppose it could be taken either way. I went into my office. Pulling the door closed behind me, I sank gratefully into my chair. I was exhausted, but wired and twitchy rather than sleepy. The scent of the cinnamon rolls that had been so appetizing earlier now made me nauseous. I thought about taking them downstairs to the kitchen, but it just seemed like too much bother.

"I wouldn't count on that." Bruno's voice came from the chair across from mine. "Those foreign guys aren't the type to give up. They had to behave because of everyone else who was here. But that doesn't mean they won't try to catch you alone later."

"I know that." I didn't hide my exasperation. "I'm not an idiot, you know." I opened my eyes to glare at him. I was tired and irritable. But more worrisome, my gaze kept straying to pulse points . . . the base of his throat . . . his wrists. "What time is it?"

He told me and I flinched. *Crap.* I was *way* overdue for a feeding. Stretching out my arm, I punched the intercom button. "Dawna, could you bring me up one of those shakes?"

"On my way."

I closed my eyes. If I didn't look and didn't move it should be easier to ignore the fact that I'd been wondering what Bruno would taste like.

"Are you okay?"

"Hell, no." I admitted it freely. Fortunately, Dawna's tap on the door saved me from having to elaborate. She came in and handed me a pair of cans filled with the dark chocolate nutrition that should get me through another four hours without incident. I hoped.

I flipped the tab and downed the first drink in one long

chug. It hit my empty stomach hard, and I had to fight to keep it down where it belonged. I decided to sip the second can while I ignored the cramping that made me want to curl into a fetal position.

Dawna left, pulling the door closed behind her. When she was out of earshot, Bruno said, "I'm sorry, Celia. I know you can take care of yourself. I do. But this . . ." His voice trailed off. Apparently he was at a loss for words.

I set the drink can on top of my desk, dragged myself out of the chair and over to open the weapons safe. Staring at the contents of my safe, I debated what weaponry I wanted on hand. The chances were good I wouldn't make it back here or to the house before dark, so I wanted to be prepared. Besides, I was feeling just a touch paranoid. Of course there was a growing list of people who were out to get me, so maybe "paranoid" wasn't the right word. Let's call it *proactive*.

"If I hadn't stayed, would you have told me about the demon spawn? Or would you have just left me in the dark?" Bruno's tone was perfectly conversational, but I knew better than to believe his questions were casual.

I didn't look him in the eye as I spread the denim jacket out flat on the desktop and inspected it. It wasn't the same brand as the one I usually wore, but the pockets were lined with cotton and tacked down the same way, creating a pair of nice little slots that were just the right size to hold one of the little One Shot squirt guns or a sharpened stake. I grabbed one of each from the safe. I considered a couple of the little ceramic disks that held "boomers," a spell similar to the flash-bangs used by the military, or maybe one of the immobilization curses but decided against it. They are handy as hell in certain circumstances, but I didn't really think I'd be needing them and there was only so much I could carry in this jacket. "I absolutely would have told you." I glanced over and gave him a wry grin. "*After* your nap."

He gave a snort that might have passed for laughter.

"You're wearing yourself out. You've got power to burn, but it won't do you any good if you're too tired to use it properly." I expected him to argue, but he didn't. He just gave one of those guy grunts. Knowing I wasn't going to get anywhere pursuing it, I changed the subject.

"How do you know Rizzoli anyway? He doesn't seem to like you." I grabbed the pair of wrist sheaths I'd bought for the knives. It was the work of a moment to strap them on. Bruno passed the knives to me one at a time, hilt first, without comment. I slid them into place, feeling the power hum through my fingers as I did. *Damn, he's good. Better than back in college, and he was no slouch then.* But I was still worried about him. He'd pushed himself too hard, too long. He wasn't just tired, it was more a bone-deep weariness. One little "catnap" wasn't going to cut it. I shook my head, brushing the thought away with a gesture. There was no point fretting about it. I couldn't *make* the man rest. And he did have a point. Hell, in his shoes I'd be doing the same damned thing.

"I came out this direction a few weeks ago to recruit his former partner." He gave me an amused glance. "I don't know if he's more pissed that I recruited Manny or that I didn't recruit *him*."

I chuckled. Ah, wounded pride. That'd do it. And it also explained something I'd been wondering about—why Rizzoli and Erikson didn't seem comfortable with each other. The partnership was too new.

I reached into the safe to retrieve a shoulder holster. It was a custom piece, tailored to fit me by the same man who'd tailored my lost, lamented suit jacket. Isaac Levy worked out of a tiny shop tucked between a dry cleaners and a men's suit shop. The modest place belies the very nice income he takes home and spends on his wife and children. Gilda Levy was, in fact, so "gilded" that most of the time she practically clanked. Her rings—one on every finger—could put your eyes out from the glare. To say Gilda likes jewelry is like saying the Pope is Catholic. I'd had Isaac's number programmed into my cell phone, so I hadn't bothered to memorize it. I would have to stop by the shop or call soon. I wanted to replace that jacket as soon as possible and maybe get a second one, too— assuming the price wasn't too high.

The holster wasn't completely comfortable over the thin fabric of my new top, but then, they rarely are. You get used to it when you wear them often enough. I checked the Colt, making sure it was fully loaded with silver, clicked on the safety, and holstered it. I put some extra ammo into both jacket pockets.

"Got anything in there for me? I was flying, so I didn't bring my own."

I gave him an inquiring look. I knew Bruno knew how to shoot. But I'd never known him to carry a gun. Ever. "Do you have a concealed-carry permit?"

"It's required for the job. Have to be recertified for accuracy every six months, too." He gave me a wicked grin. "Bet I can clean your clock at the range."

"In your dreams, DeLuca. In your dreams."

17

The ads say: *If you want it, you can find it . . . at Phar-Mart.* Thus far I'd found quite a bit of what I wanted: an Ace bandage for my knee, heavy-duty sunscreen, a gardening hat that, while silly looking, had a wide enough brim that I could lose the umbrella and not risk crisping. Oh, and one each of a big, conspicuous gold-tone cross with lots of rhinestones, a Star of David, and a Buddha necklace, all from One Shot's special line of "Certified Blessed Holy Items for True Believers." While I am not a true believer, the looks I was getting in broad daylight made me decide that I needed something distinctly unsubtle if I wanted to go out and about without people trying to stake me or spraying me down again with holy water. Subtle it wasn't, but I was beginning to learn that most humans don't think in terms of subtle when dealing with vampires. The fear comes more from that basal, animal part of the brain—fight or flight. The thing was, an actual vampire might go unnoticed, whereas I, who wasn't completely turned, couldn't. Must have missed out on some of the camouflaging magic or something.

I'd downed another pair of shakes, just for good measure,

and set the alarm on my cell phone to ring in four hours. I'd had coffee earlier, but I wanted something cold to drink, so I picked up an extra-large Pepsi, sipping it cautiously at first. Do vampires get gas? Could I digest it? But to my delight I'd discovered that *yes, I could* drink soda. *Hallelujah!*

Bruno had called his brother Matty from the car while we were on the way to the store. Matteo had been delighted to have a lead on the demon but had been royally pissed that the lead was me. Which was why I was glad to have an excuse to be staying right where I was, for however long it took.

I had, inevitably, chosen the one checkout line in the store where a little old lady wanted to do an exchange without the receipt, wanted the manager to look and see if they had something in the back room that they were out of on the shelves, *and* was now proceeding to count out her payment in small change. Bruno had gone through the express lane with his purchase of incense and holy water. I could see him outside, arguing with his brother.

Father Matteo DeLuca is a Catholic priest of the Order of St. Michael. It's a militant order. They actively seek out vampires, demons, and monsters and either slay them or send them back to their eternal damnation, whichever applies. While I was not technically either of the former, I got the definite impression that Father Matteo wouldn't mind doing a little slayage right about now. Oh, don't get me wrong. He wouldn't do it. But he was human enough that the temptation was there. I had, after all, broken his baby brother's heart. Never mind that he'd broken mine, too. So, while I waited in my own personal version of purgatory, Bruno was trying to explain away my now unearthly pallor and fancy new teeth.

Better him than me.

A bored clerk was setting the brand-new shipment of tabloids and magazines into the wire display racks near the checkouts. One proudly proclaimed that Abraham Lincoln not only had been a woman but also was actually the mother of the Bat Boy. *Wow.* That set me back on my heels long enough for the woman in front of me to finish counting her change—and discover she didn't have enough, so was going to have to put a few things back. Was Elvis a father after death, thanks to alien abduction? Sheer perversity was almost enough to make me reach for the publication in question. I actually might have bought a copy for Bruno, but the cover of a less entertaining, much more mainstream magazine caught my eye.

Holy crap, it was the prince and the rest of the royal family posed in front of a row of beefy, heavily armed men who looked more like military than bodyguards, with the prince's new fiancée.

I stood there blinking stupidly for at least a full minute, long enough that the cashier had to actually say something to get my attention. I grabbed the magazine, tossing it onto the stack of stuff I was buying. I'd read it in the car while Bruno and Matty reinforced the wards around PharMart. They refused to leave the night shift defenseless, particularly after I'd told Bruno about Edgar's female companion and how she'd been able to bespell the kid last night—through the line of protection and with his cross glowing—without so much as breaking a sweat. In fact, that little tidbit, combined with her ability to fog my brain, made both men very nervous.

Either she was an übervamp, a thousand years old or better,

or she was that lesser demon Matty and his fellow priests had been hunting. Of course, thus far they'd been so busy doing the sibling arguing thing that I didn't think they'd even gotten around to investigating. I'd had a chance to meet the entire DeLuca clan one Christmas when Bruno and I were still engaged. They'd argue long and loud, but it never kept them from getting the job done, and it wouldn't keep them from uniting against anything or anyone that went after another family member. It was a perfect example of the classic "nobody picks on my brother but me" attitude you find in so many big families, and it had made me wistful for my own sister.

I paid for my purchases, but my mind was elsewhere. Something about the magazine picture was nagging at me. Actually several things, but whether it was stress, lack of sleep, or something else entirely, I couldn't seem to bludgeon my brain into coughing up the answer.

Scowling, my hat pulled down to my ears, I stepped out of the air-conditioned comfort of the store into the heat of a full-blown argument that ground to an abrupt and awkward halt when they saw me. *Gee, think they were talking about me?*

I decided to pretend I hadn't noticed. Smiling, I turned to the elder of the two. "Hey, Matty. Long time no see. So, is she the demon and do you think she'll come back here?"

Matty turned, glaring with enough heat that I expected to burst into flames at any second. His chocolate brown eyes had darkened to black, and there was a dangerous flush creeping up his neck. Still, Mama DeLuca raised her boys to be gentlemen. He responded politely—through gritted teeth. "Hello, Celia. We were discussing that very thing."

Didn't anyone ever tell you lying's a sin, Father?

"Really? What did you come up with?"

Matty started to say something negative, but Bruno talked over him, earning an even blacker look than the one I'd been given. Brave man that he is, he ignored it. "She's not a demon. Just a very old and dangerous bat. But why do you think she'll come back?"

It was a good question. Logically, she shouldn't. There was an entire world of victims out there, a veritable buffet. But I'd bet money she'd be back here tonight, waiting for those protections to fail.

"*Celia?*" No, the DeLuca boys weren't impatient. Not at all.

I tried to explain what I'd been thinking. "She *hated* that she couldn't get to him. Almost as if it were a personal affront. And she didn't like that Edgar ordered her back. I can't swear to it, but I'd bet she'll be back, if for no other reason than to prove he doesn't control her." Petty, maybe even stupid. But while vamps may not keep their memories, they do keep their basic personality traits. I was betting Ms. Übervamp had been quite the bitch back in the day.

"You sure about the demon thing?"

"Positive." Matteo smiled, a baring of teeth. Reaching into the pocket of his black uniform trousers, he pulled out a little car that was very similar to the one I'd lost, except this one had a crucifix emblazoned on its tiny little hood.

I whistled, impressed. I'd looked at one of those the other day. It had been so far out of my price range.

"So what's the plan? She's not what you're after, but she is a serious threat. Even if we put the barrier back up, she bespelled the kid last night as if there was no barrier. She might do it again."

Bruno looked at his brother "Matty?"

Matty sighed. "We can't afford to take anyone off of the main hunt. But if she got her hooks into the kid deep enough, she'll be able to call him. I can't take that risk. I'll stay and deal with this."

"Not alone you won't." That wasn't diplomatic. Yes, he'd hunted bats professionally. But he hadn't met her. I had. One person was so not going to take this one down.

"*Excuse me?*" Matty puffed himself up to his full height and would gladly have launched into me, but Bruno stepped between us.

"She didn't mean it like that, Matt. And it's an *old* bat. You yourself have said that any bat over two hundred needs at least a two-person team."

Matty glared at me over his brother's shoulder, but he didn't argue, so Bruno continued. "Besides, it's been a while since we worked together."

Oh, Lord. Male bonding. Male *family* bonding. I had to put a stop to this before I drowned in testosterone. "Is Matty a mage, too?"

"Yessss." Bruno drew the word out slowly. It was a subtle way of telling me that while Matty was a mage, he wasn't in Bruno's league. No surprise there, few are.

"I'm only ranked at a six." Matty spoke calmly, but the flush was still there and his jaw was thrust out just a little more aggressively than I would've liked.

"Six is enough to do a trip wire, isn't it?" I turned to Bruno for confirmation. I *thought* I remembered my lessons correctly, but my last class in the paranormal had been a long damned time ago.

He grinned, flashing deep dimples and showing a lot of white teeth. "Yes it is, you clever girl."

Matty looked from one to the other of us. He was bright enough to know that he'd missed something, but he didn't share enough of the same background and education to know exactly what. I could tell it irritated him, but beneath the frustrated anger there was a glimmer of comprehension. Until that moment I think he'd figured I was just arm candy that his brother had been infatuated with. Our being able to finish each other's thoughts, however, meant there was more to our relationship than Matty had originally thought. And while his figuring that out didn't change a damned thing, it did make me feel a little bit better. Because dammit, I'm *not* eye candy.

"Care to enlighten me?" He looked from Bruno to me, impatient for either of us to elaborate.

Bruno gave me the nod, so I started to explain.

"Either one of you could just put up the barrier. But if you do, she'll sense it. And she'll go somewhere else for tonight's kill, and we might lose her."

"I *know* that." He scowled.

"But we don't dare leave them unprotected knowing that she's singled this place out, and that kid in particular."

He was losing patience, but I wanted to make sure that we all were on the same page about the plan. If he wanted to be pissy, fine, but better safe than sorry. There was no room for error here. Not with lives at stake.

"So, we set up an invisible boundary line, a magical trip

wire as it were. When she crosses over, it signals both of you and you each raise a perimeter—one in front of her, one behind. Trapped between them, she'll be pinned down enough that we can take her out with minimal risk."

I watched him rolling the plan over in his mind, looking for flaws. Honestly, I was surprised it wasn't one of the standard plans used by the order, but then again, maybe they didn't get a lot of mages. It wouldn't surprise me. The church doesn't pay nearly as well as the private sector, and while the militant orders only ask for a five-year stint, they still require abstinence for the duration. Not too many people are interested in *that* lifestyle anymore.

The plan wasn't perfect by any means. First, it assumed she would come here, tonight. I thought she would. But I wasn't a clairvoyant. I was basing the whole idea on a hunch and my personal experience of human nature. I'd bet money the vamp would strike here tonight—but not a *lot* of money.

Too, it would take a coordinated effort. And with both Bruno and Matty tied up working the spell, I'd have to to take her out. Not that I couldn't do it. I've done for more than a few bats in my time, after all. Silver bullets and holy water to wound her enough to move in for a kill, then a stake, and beheading with an axe. Messy and gross, but effective. Of course, now that I had my spiffy new knives, it might be easier to use them for the kill. I'd still do the staking and beheading, after, and I'd still make sure the authorities took the body and the head to separate crematoria and spread the ashes over running water. Paranoid? Maybe. But I didn't like taking chances. I particularly wasn't going to take chances with a creature as old and powerful as this one.

"It could actually work." There was an unflattering amount of surprise in Matty's voice. Being a grown-up, I ignored it.

"Can you think of anything better?" Bruno challenged him.

Matty sighed. "No." He made the concession with ill grace, but I appreciated his honesty.

"Between the three of us, we can handle one vampire." Bruno sounded supremely confident.

Talk about your famous last words.

18

I should've been exhausted. God knows it had been a rough couple of days and I'd had too little sleep. But I was wired and jumpy, too tired to sleep. So I dropped Bruno off at his hotel, promising to pick him up well before sunset. The rest of the afternoon I spent running errands: visiting the attorney about Vicki's funeral arrangements, seeing Isaac about making a replacement jacket and having it delivered ASAP. Dawna had texted me several times—about Bruno mostly, although she did send word that Gwendolyn Talbert had called me back.

That was one call I needed to return. I pulled off into a shady parking lot to dial.

"Hello."

"Gwen? It's me."

"Celia! It's good to hear your voice." She paused. "I was so sorry to hear about Vicki. How are you holding up?"

"Not well," I admitted. "Did you get my message?"

"Yes, and I can't say how sorry I am that I can't help you. When I retired I let my certification lapse. But I've got a few

names for you. They're really excellent. And if you'd be willing to try an inpatient stay—"

"No."

She sighed. "I know you don't like the idea. But admitting
you need help is not a failure."

"I'm not locking myself up, Gwen. Particularly not now.
Not if I can help it."

"Why particularly not now?"

I forced myself to stay calm and answer her question ra-
tionally. "Because I look like a monster—a vampire. It fright-
ens people. If they lock me up, they just might throw away
the key." The next words came tumbling out as if of their own
volition. "And when the money is gone, they'll send me to the
state."

She didn't argue the point. She was too honest for that. In
fact, she was honest enough to admit I had reason to be afraid.
"But can you be sure they won't lock you up anyway? If you're
really as frightening as you claim, what's to keep the authorities from treating you like any other monster?"

Nothing. Absolutely nothing. And that was freaking terri-
fying.

When I didn't answer, she let it go, not pushing further.
"It's your choice. But I worry for you, Celia."

"You and me both."

She sighed. "Just think about it, okay? In the meantime, try
one of these."

I wrote the names and phone numbers she gave me on
the back of an envelope. We didn't talk too much after that.
There was an awkwardness between us that hadn't been there
before, as if the wall of professionalism had gotten taller and

thicker after she retired. It made me a little bit sad. Still, I thanked her, and promised I'd set an appointment with somebody.

I kept checking my mirror as I drove around town doing my errands. I'd half-expected to find Dee and Dum following me, but there was no sign of them—or they were good enough that I couldn't catch them. Unsettling thought, that. Still, I pretended it didn't bother me and went about my business. By the time I let myself into Bruno's hotel suite I had accomplished quite a lot, but none of it was earth-shattering.

As I opened the door, I could faintly hear the sound of running water and Bruno's spirited rendition of "Copacabana." I shook my head, smiling. Some things never change. At one point or another all six of Mama DeLuca's boys had been called on to sing at their uncle Sal's lounge. But only Bruno really took to it. He has a great voice and an honest love of songs I consider just too cheesy.

"It's me," I called out, even though I was pretty sure he already knew. "And I brought Chinese." I'd called in the order and used the drive-up so as not to scare anyone.

I heard the water shut off. "Bless you, woman, I'm starving."

He was always "starving." Only the fact that he had the metabolism of a chipmunk on speed kept him from becoming as wide as he was tall. I'd chosen Chinese because it's the one type of ethnic food I don't like. Something about the smell, I think. Or maybe the look of it just turns me off. But I could bring him Chinese food and not get aggravated at having to suck down yet another shake.

I glanced around the room. It was nice but nothing fancy. Standard pair of double beds, one recently used, a large window with blackout curtains, nice dark wood table and chairs, with a matching armoire to house the television and store clothing. I pulled a chair away from the table and sat down just as Bruno ducked out of the bathroom wearing nothing but a towel and a smile.

I stared.

Hell, I'd dare any red-blooded heterosexual woman *not* to.

I mean, the man looked *fine*. Oh, there were a few more scars and gray hairs, but there wasn't an ounce of excess fat on that body. In fact, he was in better shape than when we'd been together. Broad shoulders, narrow waist, and muscled legs all said he still ran stairs, like he used to run bleachers in school.

He laughed and his smile widened to the wicked grin I remembered so well. "We don't have time," he teased.

"No, we don't," I agreed, but I couldn't help feeling that it was a damned shame, and I didn't look away. Still, there was real regret in my voice when I said, "And we probably wouldn't do it even if there was."

"Don't bet on that." He grabbed the sack of food from my hand and reached into it to pull out an egg roll. This, of course, left the towel held together with only a loose little half-knot. One little tug . . . He gave me a wink. "I mean, I've only *just* recovered from the last time."

I blushed. I couldn't help it. With him standing there, like that, the memory of *last time* was just too fresh.

He laughed again, a sound of pure delight. "God, I've missed you, Celia." He leaned over, giving me a gentle kiss that tasted like egg roll and *him*. Combined with the gentle caress of his hand down the side of my face, it set things in motion all over my body. "I know all the reasons it didn't work. But I do miss you."

"I miss you, too." I felt a little pang of sorrow admitting it out loud. I'd loved him so much, wanted it to work so badly. Even though we'd both tried, it just hadn't. But even at our worst the sex had been spectacular, and athletic enough that we'd actually broken the frame of his bed.

He leaned forward and kissed me again, this time with more . . . enthusiasm. He even managed to French-kiss me without stabbing himself on my fangs. He pulled me to my feet and I let him. Smooth muscles pulled me tight against him until I groaned. Then his mouth was on my neck, nipping and kissing until I felt tension in places I hadn't felt in a long time. His hands moved up and down my body with practiced ease, remembering the curves and hot spots that made my knees weak without even trying. I couldn't help but glide my fingers over his still-damp back. I was sorely tempted to pull away the towel and pull him onto the floor on top of me. To hell with the vampire or the Feds or anything else. I *missed* feeling like this. Missed *him*.

He moaned then, apparently thinking the same thing, because his hands found their way under my shirt and began to tingle my breasts and parts lower with that old, familiar magic. Even before, he'd been able to use magic during sex to make things feel . . . better. Now it wasn't just better, it was *amazing*. My muscles began to ache with need, and the flush of early embarrassment had turned to heat of a whole different kind.

The sensations were scary amazing, and he realized it, too. Gentle caresses turned desperate and demanding, our hands clutching at any hint of bare skin. It happened so fast I couldn't catch my breath and I realized we were a ticking time bomb. If we didn't stop soon, a lot of things were going to happen— some we'd probably regret. But only some.

He pulled back from the kiss, his pupils fully dilated and his breathing harsh. A full-out shudder wracked his body and his hands clenched into fists, as though struggling against his better judgment to reach for me again.

I knew the feeling.

"I'd better go get dressed." As he stepped back, out of reach, I noticed that the towel was tenting out from his body.

"Either that or take a cold shower," I called after his rapidly retreating form. I didn't hear his response, but I was willing to bet it was profane. Frankly, I could use a cold shower myself. My lips were still tingling from both residual magic and sheer body heat. Damn, he was going to be a tough man to ignore while he was in town.

I was still shivering when I crossed the room to sit at the table by the balcony. The late-afternoon sun glimmered through the metallic fabric of the full-length sheers. I pulled out the nearest chair, setting it in the shadows just past the edge of the light, and settled myself in comfortably to wait. The same magazine I'd purchased earlier was sitting on the polished wood surface of the table. I stared at the cover, trying to figure out exactly what was bothering me about the picture.

Obviously I felt sorry for the fiancée. I mean, if the real prince was anything at all like the fake, he was a complete scumbag. But there she sat, at a long table in an elaborately decorated room, facing the throng of press. She was seated between the prince and a sour-looking old man in traditional garb who could only be her father.

Arrayed at an angle behind them on either side of a pair of national flags were what appeared to be military-issue bodyguards, all large, all male. There was nary a smile to be seen in the group. Damn it, what *was* it about this picture? I tried to bludgeon my brain into giving up the information, but it just wouldn't. Maybe if I read the article.

I started to flip through the magazine and had just reached the page I wanted when Bruno stepped into the room, fully dressed. "Okay, let's go. Daylight's burning."

We got back to PharMart as the sun was sinking in the western sky.

Bruno and I had run through one of the chain roast beef restaurants. He had the French — I had the dip. It wasn't a perfect solution, but we'd had to do something. The sun was starting to sink toward the western horizon and I could feel my body starting to tense. Everything was so *intense*. I could hear heartbeats. Scent sweat and fear in ways that I would never have believed possible.

"Are you going to be able to do this?" Bruno's voice was gentle, but he wouldn't look at me, deliberately pretending that pulling the rental car into a parking spot in the nearly empty PharMart lot took every bit of his attention.

"I'm fine." I was . . . mostly. My skin wasn't glowing and my vision hadn't gone into hyperfocus. But I did wonder if I would've had a repeat of last night if I hadn't eaten. Would every sunset be a battle? Scary thought, and one I refused to dwell on. For now, there were vampires to slay. Matteo was already there, had done his meditation and was ready to go. We didn't know when, or if, the bat would show up. So we needed to be ready.

Matteo tapped on the window. If he was nervous, I couldn't tell. His expression was serious, even grim, but that was it.

"I called the order. They confirmed I won't get any backup from my fellow priests." He sighed. "They admit the vampire is a serious threat, but our resources are stretched very thin here on the West Coast." He made it sound matter-of-fact, but I was shocked. It's a big order, with a lot of resources. They couldn't even spare one monk? That made no sense. Unless . . . "It isn't just one minor demon anymore, is it?" I spoke softly, mainly because I was scared. I might not remember everything from college, but the chapters on demonology were gruesome enough to be unforgettably etched in my mind.

"I did *not* say that." Matteo had paled and started trembling. "And don't you say it, either. We can't afford for word to get out. It'd start a panic."

"Oh, *shit*. Should you even *be* here?" Bruno's voice was a little breathy. Evidently I wasn't the only one who remembered my studies.

Matteo closed his eyes and sighed. "I'm *supposed* to be on medical leave. I'm not allowed to help with the other problem, so I might as well be here."

I hadn't seen any injuries, but if he was hurt enough that they weren't letting him on the demon hunt, he was probably too hurt to be doing this. I opened my mouth to say just that, but a look from Bruno silenced me.

Ah, male pride—or maybe just DeLuca pride. Matteo couldn't be in on the big demon hunt, but he needed to do *something*. So we were giving him the next best thing, an über-vamp. If things went according to plan, we should be able to take her down without anyone getting hurt. Of course, how often do things actually go according to plan?

I squashed that thought like a roach. It was as good a plan as we could make. We were well armed. Matteo was the weaker of the two brothers when it came to magic, so he reactivated the outer ring of defenses. It takes less power to recharge something that's already established than to set up something new. Bruno would have the harder job, but I didn't doubt he was up to it. I was just there to play trigger woman.

If the authorities showed up they'd do the dirty work for me, but I didn't think they'd be here. I'd done my civic duty and called in to get the kill sanctioned, but the police forces were stretched pretty damned thin this week. Anaheim was hosting the World Series for at least two games—night games. All hands had to be on deck, particularly with the militant priestly orders otherwise occupied. Then again, maybe that was *why* the demons and bats were moving now. They might be evil, but they weren't stupid.

Matty walked the ring using holy water. I felt the hum of magic vibrate through the ground at my feet. It raised the hairs all over my body, and I wondered if it was too much. If I could sense it, maybe she would, too. If she did, she wouldn't cross the line and get caught in our trap. I opened my mouth to say as much, but the magic eased back down before I could get a word out.

Shaking my head, I went back to examining my weapons.

Nothing had changed since I'd checked them earlier, but I needed reassurance. I find the razor's edge of a knife and the smell of gun oil comforting. So sue me.

An old beater of a Chevy pulled into the parking lot and the teenage clerk climbed out. He was in his uniform, ready to go on shift. He noticed me and gave me a smile and wave as he hurried into the building.

That was creepy. I mean, I knew he didn't remember being bespelled. But I did.

The sun sank farther in the west and the automatic lights flicked on, illuminating everything with flat orange light that made the shadows seem all the darker. Day transitioned into night with little fanfare. Cars drove by on the main road, radios blasting. When the light turned red, mariachi horns competed with the thumping bass of hip-hop. I was hunched down in the seat of Matty's rental sedan, waiting out of sight, alternately hoping and worrying that I had been wrong, that she wouldn't show up. I didn't know where Matty and Bruno were hiding.

Time dragged. My back started spasming in protest at the unnatural position I was in. The discomfort was such that I was almost tempted to get out of the car and stretch. I might have, if I hadn't heard the purr of a car engine pulling slowly into the shadowed parking lot a short distance away. I heard the soft whump of a car door closing and the unmistakable crunch and click of high heels on rock-strewn asphalt.

And then I felt her, like the faintest hint of a breeze across sweat-soaked skin: power, soft as a lover's whisper, calling. It was seductive, irresistible. Right then and there I thanked God that she wasn't calling me. Because I would've gone, gone with a smile on my face and a song in my heart. I'd have gone rushing headlong, gladly, to the arms of death. She was that good.

I heard the automatic door of the store whoosh open, heard voices calling out in protest. And still I waited. *Hurry up, guys. We're running out of time here.*

Almost as if they heard my thoughts I felt the surge of energy as strong walls of power snapped into place.

Time to roll.

I rose and climbed from the car, pulling my gun and flipping off the safety as I did. I wasn't moving fast. I didn't want to take any chances.

She heard me coming and turned, hissing, flashing ivory fangs; the skin of her face was stretched taut over her skull in a way that bore no resemblance to humanity. Her skin glowed, creating its own light, so that I could see my target with utter clarity.

I heard the kid shout and run for the door of the store, her spell over him broken by her distraction. Setting myself into a classic shooter's stance, I very deliberately fired two shots at her chest. After the first shot, blood and skin exploded backward to run down the thickened air that formed the wall behind her.

The second shot missed the vampire, embedding itself in a newspaper rack. By then she was moving, racing between the two rings of power, trailing gouts of blood as the arteries pumping into her shattered heart hosed their contents into the night. She was searching for a weakness in either wall, an escape, but Matteo and Bruno had done their jobs too well.

She screamed, an unearthly sound of rage combined with raw magical power that nearly deafened me.

In my peripheral vision I saw the boys step out of their hiding spots. Bruno aimed the gun I'd loaned him. Matteo was armed with something just as deadly to a bat—one of the oversized water guns, filled with what had to be holy water.

He opened fire, aiming not at her neck or heart but across her legs in a steady stream. It wasn't enough to cut off her legs, but it dropped her to the ground in screeching agony, giving me a chance to fire again into a chest that had already almost healed.

I was nearly deaf at this point, and felt fluid running down my neck. Whether it was sweat or my ears were bleeding I didn't know or care. I dropped to one knee, braced my elbow against the concrete base of a light pole, and aimed for her neck, hoping to sever her spine and cut off her head, putting an end to this. I was concentrating hard, looking for the right opening, which is my only excuse.

I didn't hear it coming, didn't see the car until it slammed into Matteo, sending him flying across the line of protection to lie, crumpled and bloody, beside the vampire. She howled in triumphant rage, grabbing him and pulling him into her lap to use his body as a shield. Despite what had to be hideous injuries, he struggled until she forced his gaze to meet hers. I watched furious resolve melt into a passive smile that was horribly, disturbingly, vacant.

I aimed for the eye that peeked over the top of Matty's head but was distracted by a blur of movement in my peripheral vision. It was moving too fast to be anything human, so I pulled the trigger as I turned. Blood and worse blossomed from the vampire's back as the bullets tore into his chest. He grunted with pain, but momentum carried him into me, slamming me against the concrete with a vicious impact that sent the gun spinning from my hand.

That he was stunned was the only thing that saved me. Fighting with abnormal strength and utter desperation, I managed to get out from under him. As I crab-crawled awkwardly away, Bruno fired one shot after another. The shots tore through the creature's neck, severing the head. It was messy but effective. Blood splattered and pooled around him, but his chest stopped moving and his eyes stared vacantly upward.

My ears were still ringing, my right arm was numb. But I grabbed the gun with my left hand and scooted over until my back was braced by the base of the streetlight. I felt blood soaking into my trousers, but it didn't matter. What mattered was killing her. I raised my knees, propping my arms on them so that my aim was nice and steady.

She spoke.

I didn't so much hear it as feel it vibrating through me, as if my body were a tuning fork struck by her words.

"I could take him now, make him one of us." She stroked a manicured finger along Matteo's neck. He settled against her with a sigh of contentment. Apparently he was beyond pain, beyond thought. I shuddered. She saw it and laughed, a cold, bitter sound that scraped across my raw nerves. "His memory of his family, his *God*, everything he was, gone, just like that." She snapped her fingers.

She was toying with us. Trapped and injured, she still acted like she had the upper hand. I glanced at Bruno and realized she did. Matteo would have told us to kill her, would've sacrificed himself. But he was Bruno's brother. Bruno would rather die himself than let Matty die, and if she made him a vamp, we'd have to kill him. The bitch knew it.

"I offer you a deal." She looked at me when she said it, as if Bruno were beneath her notice. "You let me go—I let him go. For *now*." She glanced over at the corpse of her companion and glared back at me. I could almost feel the heat of her hatred burning my skin. "But it isn't over between us."

"No. It isn't," Bruno answered her. She turned her gaze to him, watching avidly as with a word and gesture he lowered the outer wall of power that kept her trapped. She flung Matteo away from her, his body hitting the pavement with a wet thud. In a blur of speed, she was gone.

I crawled to the fallen priest as fast as I could manage. I didn't holster my gun. I hadn't missed the "for now" part of the deal, and I wouldn't put it past her to come straight back. Yes, she was injured, but to my mind that only made her more deadly. Because she was *pissed*. Too, there was always Edgar. He'd been with the two of them before. Was he hanging around in the shadows, waiting for his chance? I didn't feel him out there, but that didn't seem to mean a thing. Bruno held Matteo's body draped over his lap. Tears were streaming down his face. I knew Matty wasn't dead. I could hear the breath rasping in and out of his chest. There were red bubbles at the corner of his lips. He had a punctured lung and God alone knew what else. I fumbled in my jacket pocket and pulled out my replacement cell phone. I dialed 9-1-1 with trembling fingers, explaining to the dispatcher what we needed as I propped the little phone between my ear and shoulder and set the gun on the ground within reach so that my hands would be free.

I reached inside my jacket again, fumbling the phone a little, but not so much that I couldn't still give directions. My fingers grasped the hard plastic handle of the one-shot I'd packed earlier. I said a silent prayer upward, hoping that my grandmother was right, that there is a God up there who listens to those in need. I pulled the little squirt gun from its concealment and yanked out the tiny plug.

I leaned toward the two of them, but Bruno pulled his brother back, out of my reach.

"Let me see his neck, Bruno. I need to make sure she didn't bite him while we were dealing with her partner."

Bruno stared back at me, his eyes nearly as blank as Matteo's had been earlier. Shock. He was in shock. *Shit, shit, shit!* "Bruno! I need you, buddy. Stay with me. We've got to check Matteo's neck."

Bruno nodded, but the motion was jerky, and the hands he used to pull off the clerical collar and unbutton his brother's shirt were shaking so badly it took longer than it should. But he got it done, and with the shirt collar open we could see the delicate half-healed punctures.

"Oh fuck. *Matty!*" Bruno's words weren't quite a sob.

"Hold him still," I ordered. "This is going to hurt and he's liable to fight."

Bruno shifted his weight, getting a better grip. When he was ready, I upended the little gun, pouring holy water over the tiny bite mark.

And Father Matteo began to scream.

19

The police were gone. The ambulance had taken Matty and Bruno to St. Joseph's Hospital—holy ground. Matty was badly hurt, but we'd done the best we could for him. Tough as he was, he might make it. Maybe.

I was resting, sitting on the slight curb next to the newspaper dispenser in my blood-soaked clothing and gaudy holy items, sipping a strawberry diet shake and reading a magazine, when the traditional long black limo pulled into the parking lot, cruising smoothly to a stop a mere six feet from me.

A pair of large suited men who looked like older, larger versions of Dee and Dum climbed out, standing in perfect bodyguard formation on either side of the rear door of the vehicle. The one on my left bent and opened the door for the man inside.

I rose as King Dahlmar exited the vehicle.

I might not have recognized him if I hadn't been reading about him just a few seconds before. He was average height and build. He was handsome, with sharp features, olive skin, and penetrating gray eyes. His silver hair and beard were perfectly trimmed, his dark gray suit impeccably tailored to fit a man who wasn't carrying even one extra pound.

"Good morning, Ms. Graves."

"Is it already?" I glanced at my watch. *Yep, sure enough. Just after one.* "Then good morning, Your Majesty." I bent ever so slightly at the waist, using the opportunity to check his reflection in the tinted windows. It was him. Or maybe a spawn. But I was betting it was him. It was too weird for the ruler of a small nation to hunt me down in the predawn hours in the parking lot of a twenty-four-hour pharmacy. Nobody setting up a fake would do something that hokey. Too unbelievable.

"I would speak with you for a moment."

"Of course you would. The question is whether I would speak with you."

He gave me a long look, the corner of his mouth twitching slightly with amusement, before using his hand to brush off the curb next to where I'd been sitting and lowering himself comfortably onto the concrete. His retainers were too well trained to show their shock by more than a slight widening of the eyes.

"Have a seat." He gestured to the spot I'd vacated on his arrival. "I'd offer to have you join me in the limo, but I doubt you'd be willing to."

I sat. "You'd be right. I'd get blood all over the upholstery. You wouldn't get back the deposit."

"They don't make royalty give deposits. But I'd hate to ruin the fabric." This time the smile was broader and more genuine. He had a nice smile. It lit up his face, making his gray eyes sparkle. The change in expression changed his entire look, making him handsome. I was betting he'd been quite the heart-breaker in his youth. Maybe he still was.

The smile faded, like the sun disappearing behind clouds. He gestured to the magazine beside me, with his son's picture on the cover. "You've read the article?"

I nodded.

"My elder son, Rezza, has quite recently rediscovered his religion. He has turned away from drinking, drugs, and wom-anizing. Whether it is sincere or a ploy to gain the support of the fundamentalists who have growing influence in my coun-try remains to be seen." He continued, "There are those who would see me dead, and Rezza on the throne, thinking they could control him."

"One of the perils of being king." I was surprised Dahlmar was being this open, but considering the circumstances, who else did he really have to talk to except a commoner from an-other country whom nobody would believe even if she told someone?

He smiled, but it was wry acknowledgment, not the happy expression I'd seen earlier. "It is. They'd be wrong about con-trolling him, though. He is his own man. Not the man I'd choose, but his own nonetheless." He shifted his weight, trying to make himself more comfortable on the unforgiving con-crete before he continued. "My younger son, Kristoff, is . . ." He paused, seeming to look for the right word. He finally settled on one I wouldn't have expected. "Weak. He is weak. And there are those who would discredit my elder son so as to see *him* on my throne in my stead."

That explained the pictures. "They think they could control *him*."

"Oh, they could. Easily," Dahlmar said drily.

I didn't know what to say to that, so I kept my mouth shut. Eventually, he continued.

"It wasn't such an issue before we found the natural gas deposits. Now, however, we have wealth and, with it, power. The European Union courts us, our enemies fear us. It's a dangerous combination."

And power draws plots like a corpse draws flies.

"Both groups want me dead." His smile was a baring of teeth. "I'm not inclined to oblige them."

"I can relate to that."

He laughed. "I am sure you can. Your file is quite impressive." He paused, then, "You are caught in the middle of our power struggle. One of these groups has already tried to use you. The questions I want answered are"—he ticked off items on his fingers—"Who in my retinue has betrayed me? And which, if either of my sons, is complicit?"

I nodded, not sure what that had to do with me.

"The situation is made more difficult by the fact that there are demons and spawn involved."

I acknowledged that with a dip of my head. "Still, I'd think that the religious extremists wouldn't want to be involved with the demonic. Pretty much every religion frowns on that sort of thing."

His expression soured. "Yes, but sadly, there are always those who believe the end justifies the means; and the offer of enough money can frequently make a man forget his loyalties and his beliefs." He reached into the inner pocket of his suit coat and pulled out a heavy white envelope. "My men have questioned the retainer who they saw in your memories."

My memories? That comment made me frown, since we'd never actually made it to that stage in the office. Had someone been prying into my brain while we'd been negotiating terms? That would not make me happy.

He paused, his eyes darkening, his expression steely, but his voice was utterly emotionless. "They were quite . . . thorough."

I couldn't decide whether to shudder or growl. I hadn't particularly liked the man who'd hired me, but I was starting to wonder about Dee and Dum's ethics.

"He had become involved with an organization that hired professionals to execute a plot against me. We learned enough of the details to make reasonable preparations."

"I'm glad."

"But I am left with questions." He sighed and shook his head. "As a king, that is neither uncommon nor unexpected." At his gesture, the driver of the limo popped open the trunk and walked to the rear of the car, where he retrieved a black and white bag that might have passed for a bowling bag but wasn't. Matty had carried a similar bag. It had two completely separate inner compartments, each of which was impervious to blood, and the whole thing had been blessed. The king continued, "We will, eventually, get to the bottom of this."

He sounded absolutely certain. Then again, he might well be. With enough time, money, and effort, most conspiracies can be unraveled, particularly if you're not too particular about whether or how much blood will be spilled in the process. "As a father, I find it unacceptable that I carry suspicions about my children for even one moment longer than is absolutely necessary."

He extended the envelope to me. It was of heavy, high-quality paper in a rich cream color, without writing of any kind on it. I took it but didn't open it. I was waiting for the other shoe to drop.

"Neither of my sons has ever been good at maintaining a deception when confronted by the truth. I am hoping that you will assist me in confronting them."

"Assist you how?" I tried to keep my voice neutral but didn't quite manage to keep a note of suspicion from creeping in.

"In that envelope are two tickets to the World Series game on Friday night. I have purchased a section of tickets and will be attending with my sons and our retinue."

A *section* of tickets? For Game One of the World Series? I didn't even want to think how much that had to have cost. And oh, wouldn't his security people be having fits.

"Ivan"—he gestured to the driver—"will meet you next to the giant cap to the left of the main entrance. He will escort you and your guest to my section between the singing of your national anthem and the throwing of the first pitch. And I will see which of my sons or my retainers reacts to seeing you join me."

It didn't sound like much of a plan to me. But he was a king, and even I knew better than to point that out. So I held on to the envelope and kept my mouth shut.

"And in case I am a fool, and my sons are better liars than I believe them to be, I will also have with me skilled telepaths to read their thoughts as you arrive."

Now *that* was more like it.

"In exchange for this, I will pay you the money that was

promised when you thought you were guarding my son, and the amount your insurance would have paid for your injuries." He gestured to the driver, who came to stand in front of us. The king stood in a single fluid movement, and I stood with him. "To ensure that you will be alive on Friday, I have taken some . . . additional precautions."

On cue, the servant unzipped the front of the bag, revealing the bloody severed head of my sire.

Um, wow. Okay then.

And while he didn't show it to me, I was betting the heart was in the second compartment. How they'd found him I had no idea. But it was him. No doubt about it. *Wow.* That went way beyond the pale as far as payment in advance.

I was more than mildly surprised that I hadn't noticed when it happened. Shouldn't I have had some sort of attack or felt pain or something?

I looked at the pleasant, debonair man standing calmly beside me. Everything he'd said had been excruciatingly polite, but I wasn't being given a choice about this and I knew it. I could assist him willingly, or not. But I *would* assist him. Or it would be *my* head in the bowling bag.

I took a deep breath, and it came out in a sigh. I was incredibly tired of being corralled, but I would like this to be over. "I'll be there."

20

Dawn took its own sweet time coming but eventually arrived. When it did, I got into the rental sedan and drove my sire's head to the nearest crematorium. It was one of the big chains, so the minute they saw the head they knew what had to be done. I was told it would be given priority treatment and that I could pick the ashes up anytime after two. The look the clerk gave me said that he'd probably like to shove me into the furnace after the bag. Fortunately, I was standing in a broad ray of sunlight, so he couldn't quite decide what to make of me and just took the head and walked away.

That done, I drove back to the expensive hotel where Bruno had been staying.

There was no way I wanted to brave the lobby, what with the bloodstains and my vampy appearance, so I parked around back. Using his guest key card, I let myself in through one of the secondary entrances. I could have gone home. The gas company had made their repairs. But David had called and left a voice mail telling me how the intruder had gotten through our security. He'd killed our pool boy and taken his right hand.

Exactly what had happened to Louis at Birchwoods. Home might not be safe, which made a nice, anonymous hotel room seem pretty damned attractive.

I trudged wearily up a set of concrete fire stairs until I reached the appropriate floor. Pushing open the door, I came face-to-face with a pair of men in almost identical navy suits with crisp white shirts and dark ties. Each also wore a barely perceptible little ear-radio and a gold cross and each discreetly held a single-shot pistol filled with holy water. They stood in front of the doorway looking stern and alert. *Well, crap.*

"Good morning, ma'am. We're with hotel security. We'd like to ask you a few questions." Of course they would. Who *wouldn't* at this point? I smiled pleasantly. I'd seen the security cameras downstairs. I wasn't surprised that security had spotted me. My appearance was somewhat . . . irregular. "Of course. My name is Celia Graves. I am Mr. DeLuca's former fiancée and I've just gotten back from a police-sanctioned vampire hunt of the bat that tried to turn me dead. Mr. DeLuca and his brother, Father Matteo DeLuca, will verify it. I'll be perfectly happy to wait here in the hall while you check with the police."

The larger man grimaced at the thought of us standing here, in the hall, in full sight of any guests who might pass by. But I was too paranoid right then to go anywhere with someone I didn't know. Hell, I was having a hard enough time with people I already knew.

Yes, they *looked* like hotel security, but no, I wasn't taking any chances. Besides, the odds of anyone actually being up and wandering the halls at this time of day were minimal. So long as we stayed quiet and didn't wake anyone, everything should be just ducky.

The shorter man reached to the small black box affixed to his belt and began speaking very quietly to the dispatcher downstairs. It only took a few minutes for someone to call the police, confirm my story, and get a detailed description of my appearance.

"A *sanctioned* vampire hunt, huh?" The big man looked down at me with some surprise. Apparently he wasn't used to the idea of women being hunters. It also isn't easy to get the authorities to give you the nod. They're jaded about that sort of thing. I suppose it comes from all of the idiots and teenagers who go out and get drunk, then think they can take on the bats.

"Looks like you got him." His voice was low and respectful as he gestured at my bloodstained jeans.

"Got one, anyway."

"There was more than one?" The shorter man sounded surprised. Obviously he'd never had to deal with vampires. His partner, however, was more savvy.

"Aren't there always?" The big guy shook his head sadly. "It's why I stopped hunting. If you don't get them all the first time, it just pisses the survivors off. You do not want to deal with a pissed-off bat."

"Think they'll be coming here?" The boy sounded both nervous and eager. He was so damned young. Or maybe I was just getting old. There's more to age than chronology.

The big man shook his head. "It's daylight, John. The bats are all dead in their coffins for now. But we'll call Maintenance, have the wards upped just in case." He glanced down at the pale tan carpet that was now stained with a trail of drying blood in the shape of my shoes. *Oops.* "And Housekeeping. They'll want to get the carpet cleaned before the rest of the guests get up and moving."

He gave me a curt nod as I slid the plastic room key into its slot. "Good luck, Ms. Graves." His expression grew very serious. "I hope you get the rest of them before they get you."

"Thanks. So do I."

I tried not to think too hard about his words as I stepped into the room and immediately slapped the DO NOT DISTURB sign onto the doorknob. That done, I ducked into the bathroom and stripped off my clothing. I didn't want to think. I wanted a hot shower, a stiff drink, and sleep. Oh, God, how I wanted sleep. Yes, I was worried about Matteo and Bruno, but my body was on the verge of collapse. Only sheer stubbornness and fear of what might jump me unawares was keeping me upright. I needed rest; I was practically useless. But I was afraid of what might happen if I gave in and closed my eyes. I stepped into the shower. The clothes were trashed. I had no idea what I was going to wear when I left this room, but I'd worry about that later. Right now I was cold and shaky from exhaustion and nerves. No big surprise. I'm one of those folks who do great during the crisis, then fall apart afterward, when the adrenaline drains off. I'd managed to hold it together long enough to get behind a locked door, but I was done. Stick a fork in me, not only done but also burned to a crackly, crunchy done. I turned the shower on full blast, hot as I could stand it on full-body massage, and stepped in, letting the water sluice over me in torrents, washing away blood, sweat, and, yes, tears.

I don't know how long I was in there. Long enough that my skin turned wrinkly. My water heater at home would've given out from the strain. But when I stepped out and dried off I felt better. Not good. That would've been expecting too much. But definitely better. I wrapped myself in a towel and stepped into the dim confines of the main room.

I sank onto the edge of the bed and grabbed the telephone. Hitting the button for an outside line, I dialed Bruno's cell number. It was answered on the first ring.

"'Lo."

"Bruno?" It didn't sound like Bruno. The voice was too low, with a basso rumble to it that seemed vaguely familiar but that I couldn't quite place.

"Who is this?"

"Celia."

"Ah, Graves. I shoulda known. Hang on a sec. Sal wants to talk to ya."

Sal—as in Uncle Sal. Oh, crap. I'd been talking to Bruno's cousin, Little Joey. No wonder the voice had sounded familiar. I'd only met him once, but he's the kind of guy who leaves an indelible impression.

A smooth baritone came onto the line. His voice was pleasant and cultured. Almost exactly like King Dahlmar. A part of me was absolutely positive Uncle Sal would sound pleasant and cultured ordering someone to break your kneecaps. Not that he would ever *do* such a terrible, wicked thing. The Italian Mafia was an invention of the media. Total fabrication.

Right.

Still, whatever else you may say or believe about him, Uncle Sal never loses his cool. "Hello, Celia."

"Hello, Mr. DeGarmo."

"I assume you called to check on my nephews?"

"Yes, sir."

"Matteo came through the surgery just fine. He's stable. The next few hours will make all the difference." He paused, and I waited, twitchy with nerves, for him to continue.

"They'd drugged him pretty heavy, but he woke up about a half hour before dawn. Said *she* was calling him. Even drugged and on holy ground, he could hear her. He says her name is Lilith."

Oh, shit. She had enough control of his mind to *introduce* herself? That was so not good.

"But he didn't try to go. Said he could hear her, but he didn't feel a pull, even though he remembered getting bit."

I let out the breath I'd been holding in a rush.

"Bruno tells me it was you who thought to look for the bite and clean it with holy water?"

"Yes, sir."

"That was smart." He paused, like he wasn't really surprised. "Thank you."

I wasn't quite sure how to respond. I mean, I would've done it for anybody. But he was thanking me, and I had to say something. "You're welcome. It wasn't a big deal."

"Maybe not at the time, but it wound up being important. So I'm going to give you some advice."

All right then. Advice from Uncle Sal is like hearing from E. F. Hutton. He talks. You listen.

"Don't be coming down to the hospital. Bruno'd be glad to see you. Hell, Matty would, too, after that. But my sister . . . not so much. I'll tell the boys you called."

"They admitted *Bruno*?" I was surprised. He hadn't been hurt. A little shocky, but I hadn't thought he'd been that bad off.

"Exhaustion, overstraining his magic." Sal chuckled. "I told him to stay put. He didn't like it much. First time he's ever really argued with me. He wants to go after the bat that did this, but he's not up to it. Not right now." He gave a meaningful pause. "Neither are you. Daylight or no."

I wasn't going to argue. He was right. Some of the really old vamps don't need much rest at all. A couple hours and they were as fresh as a daisy. They might not go out in daylight, but you couldn't count on them being down for the count, either. Since she was old enough to be an übervamp, she was probably up and about by now. Of course, come nightfall, she'd be looking for me. She as much as said so.

"I don't plan on going hunting." I was honest with him. "But she threatened me. We hurt her and killed her partner, and she blames me for that."

"So I heard."

I'd bet he had. I could just imagine Bruno saying it. Loudly. And it wouldn't have made a damned bit of difference to Sal. Because, ultimately, Bruno is family. I'm not. Keeping him alive is more important to them than I am. More important to me, too, come to think of it.

Sal kept talking. "So I made a call; told Archbishop Fuentes about this bat, how she could call a priest on holy ground. He didn't like the sound of that. Decided that maybe they should send some reinforcements in from Mexico and South America. A few dozen or so. You manage to lay low for a day or two, this could all be taken care of. "

Whoa. When he said it like that, I realized he was right. A vamp calling an ordained priest on *holy ground?* That probably raised a few eyebrows at the Vatican. "Thank you." I meant it. I mean, not everybody would've been able or willing to do something like that, particularly not for their nephew's ex-girlfriend.

"You're welcome." He quoted my own words back at me with just a hint of amusement. "It wasn't a big deal. Take care of yourself."

"I'll try."

He said good-bye and hung up and I followed suit. For a couple of minutes I just sat on the edge of the bed, staring blankly at the opposite wall. *Wow. Um . . . Wow. Okay, then.*

I decided I was going to strain myself if I thought too hard about it, and I was too tired to think coherently anyway. So without further ado I dropped the towel on the floor and climbed under the blankets. I was asleep almost as soon as my head hit the pillow.

21

Dawna said, "You are the only thing standing in her way now. She'll kill you if she can."

I choked. "That's the message?" I'd called the office while waiting for Room Service to bring up my double order of tomato soup.

"Not all of it, but yes. A little old lady came by and dropped it off, along with a pair of diamond earrings. She said her name was Dottie and I needed to make sure you got the message right away, that it was very important."

No kidding. Ya think? "When did she give it to you?"

"About a half hour ago."

Well, it wasn't as if the vamp hadn't told me as much. But *dammit* anyway.

"She also said to tell you she was very sorry, she hoped you didn't mind, but she showed those men your vision. They were *most* insistent. And they took your earrings. She couldn't stop them. So she brought you these to replace them." Dawna paused. "It looked like she had been crying."

Aww. They made a sweet old lady like her *cry*? It had to have been Dee and Dum. So that's how they got hold of my

290 • CAT ADAMS

memories. Jerks. No, more than jerks. Assholes. "She didn't have to replace the earrings. They weren't that valuable."

"I said you'd feel that way, but she insisted. And you should see these things. They're like a carat each."

That didn't make me feel any better. Worse, actually. "Jeez. Yeah, well, she shouldn't have. She's on a fixed income, for crying out loud."

"Well, judging from the wear and tear on the box they're in, they may be ones she already had. But if you don't want them—"

"Not a chance. I'm giving them back." Poor Dottie. It really ticked me off to think of Dee and Dum intimidating that sweet little old lady. I say again, Assholes. "Did she leave a number?"

"No. She said she'd decided to go away for a while. She didn't want to be around if anyone else came looking for her. But I was supposed to tell you it can still work out all right, but you need to be very *observant* and remember your schooling. Oh, and she said, 'Thank you.'"

"For what?"

"She didn't say."

Since I hadn't done anything nice yet, I had to assume it was typical clairvoyant stuff. Vicki had always been commenting on or thanking me in advance of things I was going to do. It was confusing and sometimes frustrating but part of the package. And while I would've liked to talk to Dottie again, if only to reassure her about the earrings, I was kind of glad she'd decided to go into hiding. I'd have felt worse than I already did if anything were to happen to her.

Dawna broke the silence that had grown while I was lost in thought. "So, spill. What's with you and Bruno? I could feel the tension between you. Hell, even Ron commented on it."

I didn't see how Ron could've noticed anything. I mean he'd only seen Bruno and me together for maybe a minute and a half while the guys trooped upstairs.

"There's nothing going on. He's here for work."

"Yeah, right."

"Dawna." My voice held a warning.

"Fine, fine. Whatever you say. He's still smokin' hot. Feel free to bring him by anytime so I can drool on him, if you're not interested. Are you going to be in today?"

I shook my head, even though she wouldn't see it. "Not today. It's already after one. I've got to go spread some ashes, and then I have a doctor's appointment. And I'm going to my gran's church right after. I want to be in sanctuary before dark." I didn't tell Dawna that I wasn't planning on going to the office unless it was absolutely necessary until this mess cleared up. The office and the estate were the first places the bad guys would look for me. Ergo, they were the last places I wanted to be. As long as I wasn't there, Dawna and the others should be safe. There were wards. And Bubba and the other bail bondsmen in the building were real hard cases. Nobody'd want to bother them if they didn't have to. Staying away was the best I could do for them. Not nearly enough, considering the company I'd been forced to keep over the past couple of days. I cringed at the thought of the severed hand of our murdered pool boy.

"Celia . . . are you okay?"

Apparently I'd let the silence drag on too long again. I forced a smile that I hoped she'd hear in my voice. "Just tired. It's been a long couple of days."

"Amen to that."

"I'll call in for messages."

She sighed and I knew she realized I wasn't coming in. "Okay. Let me know if you need anything. And be sure to eat."

"I am, I am." I was, too. Maybe not every four hours, but as often as I could manage. Hence the tomato soup.

We hung up on that note, and I dialed the next number on my list. Bruno answered his own phone this time, on the first ring. His "Hello" sounded irritable. Not the world's best patient, eh? I fought down a snicker, even though I actually had some sympathy for the nurses. Dealing with the DeLuca clan was *so* going beyond the normal call of duty. Particularly Mama Rose. That woman is *scary*.

"I called 'cause I'm going to need to borrow some of your clothes. My stuff got ruined in the vampire hunt."

"*Which* clothes?"

"Well, I need some trousers, a clean shirt, and a hat."

"A *hat*." He said it like he'd bit into something sour. I wasn't surprised. In fact, I found myself grinning for the first time this morning.

"Welll . . ." I dragged the word out. His response was worth it. Pure Bruno DeLuca. It made me smile.

"Dammit, Celia! The only hat I've got there is my Mets cap. Don't you be touching my Mets cap."

I tried being reasonable, glad that he couldn't see me laughing at his expense. "I don't have any sunscreen here, Bruno. I can check down in the gift shop . . ." I paused for a long moment, letting my grin build. I knew the gift shop didn't sell them. I'd already checked when I called for the soup.

He growled, but I could hear that he wasn't serious. He was teasing, too . . . *mostly.* "I'm going to want that back before the game tomorrow night."

"You're going to the game?" I'd been going to ask him to come with me. I don't trust people easily, and I probably trust Bruno more than anyone else in the world. If I was meeting the king, I wanted somebody solid by my side. But if Bruno already had plans, I didn't want to ruin them. Trust him to get tickets that were all but impossible for anyone else to come by. Yeah, the locals were rooting for the Angels, but the *world* was rooting for the Cubs. I mean, come on, they hadn't won a championship since God was a baby and dirt was new. Even the scalpers were having a hard time getting tickets.

"Bonus from the boss. Four seats, in the stands by first base. I'm bringing Sal and Joey. I was gonna take Matty, but since he's laid up, Kevin's coming instead."

I couldn't decide if I was upset that Bruno hadn't thought to invite me. I mean, I don't really like baseball that much and he really *was* here on business, but—

Plus, there went my second choice for a backup—Kevin. But I kept my tone cheerful. "You don't need the cap, the Mets aren't playing."

"It's my *cap.*" He said it like it should be self-evident. It wasn't, but I wasn't going to argue. This must be one of those guy things.

"Fine, fine. I won't wear it. I'll pick something up at the store and then bring your cap by the hospital tomorrow morning."

"Don't bother. I'm checking out."

"Bruno—," I started to protest.

"Don't say a word. Just don't. I've already heard about it from my mother, my brother, *and* my uncle. I can rest just as well at a five-star hotel with all the amenities as in the freaking hospital, and I am *not* missing the game."

He probably could rest at the hotel. If only he would.

"Celia? Are you there?"

I'd been silent too long . . . again. I was having a hard time focusing this morning. Then again, I hadn't had any caffeine yet. *Hurry up, Room Service!*

"Yeah, I'm here. Just a little tired. And worried."

"You're the one who should get some more rest. You didn't get back until after sunrise and you're already up. *And* you've had a helluva time the past couple of days." His voice was gentle, and it made me smile. Bruno is an original tough-guy Italian. But he is also a sweetheart, *my* sweetheart. Well, my former sweetheart. But I'll always love him. No matter what. And while he was right about resting, I wasn't going to do it. I still had a life-threatening emergency going on.

"In that case I won't deliver the hat back to the hotel. Because if I do neither one of us will rest." I was only partly teasing. I remembered yesterday's kiss so clearly it made me shiver.

"How 'bout you bring it by the hotel pool? Say tomorrow, one thirty?" He suggested this with a hint of laughter in his voice. "It's nice and public. We should be safe."

"I'll do that. You can buy me a margarita."

"Make it a pitcher and you've got a deal."

"Are you planning to get me drunk and take advantage of me?"

"Would I do such a thing?" He spoke in an exaggerated drawl that made me laugh. We were still laughing when we hung up.

I thought about who to take to the game most of the day—while I dumped half the vampire's ashes into the ocean and the other half at a designated dump spot on the river—and was still thinking on it as I drove out to Birchwoods for my doctor's appointment.

Yes, doctor's appointment. One of the names Gwen had given me was for a doctor at Birchwoods. She'd said Dr. Scott had specifically asked her to make time to fit me in.

Peachy. And while I knew it was important, that I really *needed* to talk to somebody, I didn't want it to be a stranger. Besides, I hate shrink appointments. Yes, I did them. For years. Then I was done, and glad for it. You can only get out of psychiatric treatment what you're willing to put in. I know that. I also knew that I'd needed the treatment then, and now. I'd been a patient of one of the best shrinks in the business, and she'd gone pretty damned deep into some seriously painful and dark places with me. I was grateful. But it hadn't been easy on either of us. Who could blame me if I wasn't anxious to repeat the process?

On top of that, I looked utterly ridiculous. Dawna would have a stroke if she could see me. The only things of Bruno's that even came close to fitting me were a red T-shirt and a pair of oversized black nylon basketball shorts with a drawstring waist.

The shirt wasn't so bad, but the shorts hung past my knees and looked damned silly, particularly with the added touches of the denim jacket, ball cap, and sneakers without socks.

I'd been too upset to notice before, but the outpatient treatment area shared an entrance with the administration building. I hauled my oh-so-elegantly clad ass up the sunlit sidewalk as quick as I could manage, huddling under the umbrella I'd borrowed from the lab and feeling surly. I'd bought sunscreen from the hotel gift shop, but it'd been a small bottle and only SPF 15, which didn't really cut it with my new pallor. If there was time before sundown, I was definitely going shopping for something decent to wear, a replacement hat, and heavy-duty sunscreen. Until then, I decided to feign blithe indifference.

There was a different receptionist this morning. This one was just as attractive as the previous model but younger. Her blond hair was darker than mine, exactly the color of honey, but with well-applied highlights. Her clothes were stunning and fit her well. I didn't want to know how much those designer shoes had set her back.

She was also too polite to gawk at my appearance. She did blink rapidly, several times, looking at the umbrella as I collapsed it, as if she wasn't quite sure what she was seeing was actually in front of her.

"I'm here to see . . ." I dug in my jacket pocket, pulling out the note I'd scribbled on hotel stationery. "Dr. Greene."

"Ah." She smiled, her eyes lighting up with understanding. "Ms. Graves." She reached beneath the counter and pulled out a clipboard and a thick stack of forms. "If you could please take a seat and fill out these forms for us, Dr. Greene will be with you soon."

"Soon" is a relative term.

I'd been there long enough to get through the maze of paperwork and was scanning my second magazine when a familiar voice brought my head snapping up.

"You *bitch*!" Cassandra Meadows charged at me, past her husband and bodyguards and heedless of the other patients in the lobby. *"How dare you!"*

It was a big lobby, but I had barely enough time to stand before she was in front of me. She swung her hand back, intending to slap me, but I caught her arm and blocked the blow before she could make contact. If I hadn't had control of my senses, I would have snapped it in two. As it was, she let out a little wince.

"What the hell, Cassandra!"

The bodyguards stepped between us, and Jason pulled his wife against him. She didn't stop struggling. She was just too furious. I only wished I knew why.

"What the hell is the matter with you?" I tried to talk to her between the twin walls of muscle that had interposed themselves between us. Creede and two others were fanned out around Jason.

"How *dare* you!" she repeated, her voice a venomous hiss.

I shivered, from both the look on her face and a blast of frigid air I hoped was coming from the air conditioner. The last thing we needed was for Ivy to start acting out.

"What *exactly* is it you think I did?" I asked Jason. He was rigid with fury, but he was being quiet about it, because we had company. Pretty much everyone in the building had come running to see what had Cassandra Meadows screaming like a shrew. She'd be damned lucky if there weren't cell phone photos up on the Internet before sundown.

Creede answered, his voice calm but cold. "Someone leaked a story to the press about Vicki's stay here. It was very specific about the number of visits her parents have made, and it was illustrated with an assortment of pictures of her with you." There was a look on his face that I didn't like. It was both disappointed and disgusted . . . like he'd thought better of me and I'd let him down.

Obviously, I hadn't done it, but as I stared at him, a hideous thought formed in my mind. I didn't want to, but I had to ask. "Were they taken at a family dinner?"

He nodded and my heart sank. I'd always thought my mother had *some* limits. Apparently, I was wrong. I wasn't sure how she could have found out about the number of visits, but money crossing palms was probably involved.

"I could *kill* you." Cassandra had lowered her voice, but it was intense. At that moment, she meant every word. It wouldn't do any good to protest my innocence. And in a way, it *was* my fault. Leaving those photos at my gran's was the equivalent of leaving a diamond necklace in front of a kleptomaniac.

The temperature dropped even more, and at least one of the big brutes in front of me knew what it meant. His expression grew wary . . . right before it was wiped clean like a slate. He turned to face Jason and Cassandra, but the movement wasn't his. Before, he'd moved with the speed and grace of a predator. This move was softer, more feminine. It takes a hell of a lot of ghost to do something like that. We're talking serious mojo. I felt a shiver of primal terror run down my spine like ice water. I shuddered but forced the fear down, slamming the door on it.

"She didn't do it, Mother." It was Vicki's voice, but cold, hard, unlike anything I'd ever heard from her. Objects began levitating, slowly at first, then with building momentum. The stereo that had been playing soft music in the background burst into sudden earsplitting static. I knew what that meant, knew that I had to stop her before someone got hurt.

"Vicki, stop it! Stop!" I shouted at the top of my lungs to be heard over the din. Everything stopped as abruptly as if I'd hit a switch. Flying objects dropped to the floor. The stereo shut off.

"You're crying." Vicki's voice softened, sounding more like the woman I knew. Objects started rising again. "She made you cry."

I interrupted Vicki before things could get even further out of hand. "It's been a rough couple of days. See, I lost my best friend the other day—" I tried to make it light, sarcastic, but my voice cracked. Not only was I scared, I *hurt*. This was Vicki, or a part of her. And I *missed* her. So much had happened in such a short time that this loss hadn't really had time to sink in. She was dead. Gone. Forever. This might very well be the last time I ever got to hear her voice.

I closed my eyes against the pain, tears pouring down my cheeks.

Usually ghosts feel cold, but this one didn't. The air moving around me in a gentle breeze was warm and scented lightly with a familiar perfume. I felt a finger trace the curve of my cheek.

I took a ragged breath, fighting to get myself under control. It took a couple of false starts before I could speak, forcing words past the hard lump that had formed in my throat. I kept my eyes closed, preserving the illusion of the Vicki I remembered. "Your mom loves you, Vicki. That's why she tried to slap me. She thought I'd betrayed you, and them."

"You wouldn't." Anger was seeping back into the voice, it was getting hollow, deeper.

"No. But she didn't know that. She's never *had* a woman friend. There's no way she could understand."

I heard movement, smelled a different, heavier scent, and knew Cassandra was there. She spoke to the ghost, her voice rough with emotion. "I'm sorry, baby. I'm so sorry. I was wrong, about her, about *everything*. I'd do anything to take it back, to fix things."

"You can't. I'm dead."

Ouch. Ghosts can't lie, but that was cold, and harsh as hell. I opened my eyes, staring at the man whose body she was using. "Vicki. She said she's sorry, that she was wrong. What else can she do?" I felt the air go still around me. I was close, so close. If I said the right words, Vicki would let go, cross over, and be free. But she'd also be lost to me forever. It took more effort than was pretty for me to make myself say the words I uttered next, but sometimes you have to do the hard thing. "I love you, Vick, I do. And I don't want you stuck here forever because you refuse to forgive her. You deserve better than that. You *are* better than that. You have to let it go."

The ensuing silence was profound. I think we all were holding our breath, waiting. And then the bodyguard spoke again.

"I'm not here because of *her*, Celie." Just that. Then the air pressure in the room changed enough that my ears popped. And the hulking bodyguard I'd been talking to collapsed bonelessly to the floor.

22

Well, that was certainly . . ." Dr. Greene struggled to find the right word. She eventually settled on, "interesting."

I smiled a little wryly, and she smiled, too. It was a good, professional smile, showing straight teeth and general good humor, but without any particular meaning. I wasn't surprised. She looked every inch a professional, from the tips of her sensible-but-stylish pumps to the no-nonsense-but-flattering cut of her short, dark hair. Her makeup was understated, her jewelry tasteful. Her suit was nice and fit well but was a mid-range gray, worn with a plain white blouse. Her whole appearance was meant to be professional, comforting, and non-threatening. Which, I supposed, made perfect sense.

We had adjourned to her office, leaving Dr. Scott to deal with Cassandra, Jason, and everyone else in the lobby. I was glad to be away from them. The whole scene had been too much. An emotional ambush. I closed my eyes, feeling exhausted and old. A part of me wanted to strangle my mother. This *had* to be her doing. She'd be more than happy to sell

Jason and Cassandra out for whatever the tabloids would pay. And Gran certainly wouldn't stop her. She might not even discourage her much. Gran didn't approve of the way the Meadowses had treated their daughter and was big on humiliation as a teaching tool.

"Do you need something to eat or drink?"

"Water would be lovely," I admitted. Actually, a pizza would be lovely, but it would only depress me more when I had to throw it up.

"I'll be right back."

I opened my eyes, taking a look around. It was a nice office: not as nice as Dr. Scott's, but he was the head administrator. She was just one of the psychiatrists on staff. Still, the room was spacious, the walls painted a gentle robin's egg blue with off-white trim. There was only one window, but it was a large one. Heavy satin drapes in a rich shade of royal blue matched both the upholstery of the chairs and the print in the plush Oriental rug beneath my feet. The furniture had a polished cherry finish that picked up the burgundy in the rug and the shade of the lamp on her uncluttered desk. A grouping of black-framed family photos were arranged on the credenza behind her seat, showing the doctor, two handsome children, and a huge Old English sheepdog in various combinations.

The doctor reappeared, carrying a crystal glass and a bottle of water. "Here you go." She passed them to me before resuming her place in the chair behind her desk. "We can sit in the conversation area if you prefer," she suggested as she reached over to set the timer on her BlackBerry for thirty minutes.

"No, this is fine. Where do you want to start?"

"Well, I suppose we should start with introductions. I'm Evelyn Greene." She held out her hand for me to shake. I took it and answered, "Celia Graves."

"It's a pleasure." She smiled again. "Do you know why Dr. Scott recommended me to Dr. Talbert?"

"Because you're good?" I suggested.

"Yes, in general," she answered without even a hint of false modesty. "But he could have suggested any of our therapists. He chose me for a specific reason."

I felt my eyebrows raise. I knew she wanted me to ask, so I did. "Why?"

She watched me intently as she spoke, her expression guarded. "He was very disturbed by the fact that you were able to use vampire powers to manipulate him psychically to the point where he agreed to your 'deal.'"

I felt my eyes go wide. *What the hell?* "I didn't."

She steepled her fingers. "Oh, you did. He did tell me he didn't believe you did it *intentionally*. But in order to make sure nothing like that happens again, accidentally or otherwise, he asked me to work with you."

I held back my irritation, keeping my expression as neutral as I could. I realized suddenly that she was one of those therapists who made you do all the work, never actually *telling* you anything, just leading you around by the nose until you got where they wanted you to go and drew the conclusions they wanted you to draw. A large part of me wanted to act dense, just to see how long it would be before she told me what she was getting at. But it could be years. And I was paying for this out of my own pocket. I *hate* wasting money.

"You're a null?" I guessed.

This time her smile actually reached her eyes. "Yes."

Well, that was kind of interesting. Before the bite I'd been plain vanilla human. I couldn't use magic and didn't have any psychic gifts. But magic and psychic stuff had worked on me. A true null was different, and much, much rarer. A psychic has a mental radio that plays in their head non-stop. In most people, that mental radio is turned off unless specifically turned on. Dr. Greene didn't even *have* a radio. Magic didn't work on nulls. Psychically they were unreachable. Clairvoyants couldn't "see" them; telepaths couldn't read or influence them. They can walk through magic power circles without anyone even knowing they are there. It was considered by most to be a rare birth defect, but I'd always thought that in work like mine it'd be damned handy. Vampires could use their physical strength on a null, but they couldn't bespell one, would never be able to turn one. A null bitten by a werewolf might die, but they'd never turn furry.

"I wanted you to know, so that there wouldn't be any mis-understandings between us."

"Thank you."

"Dr. Scott also wanted me to ask you to seriously reconsider becoming an inpatient for the next few weeks, until you've had a chance to determine the full extent of your physiologi-cal changes and adapt to them. What has happened to you is extremely traumatic physically as well as mentally and emo-tionally. It is dangerous for you—"

I interrupted her, "I know that. But right now I have things I have to do. In a few days—"

It was her turn to interrupt. "You may not have a few days. We are talking about your physical and mental survival. Surely whatever it is can wait."

Her disapproving tone made it more of a statement, but I answered as if it had been a question. "No, it really can't." I sighed. "Other than the incident with Dr. Scott, I've been able to keep things under control."

She opened her mouth, but I waved her to silence.

"I'm following his directions to the letter." Well, maybe not exactly to the letter, but close. And it wasn't easy, either. "But in the past few days I've had multiple attempts on my life. I can't be stuck in one place where they can find me and get to me easily."

"I assure you—"

I interrupted again. "They got to Vicki. They had to kill Louis to do it. But they got in, and they killed her. And you know it. *And* they got in through protections that were just as good at Vicki's estate. They killed a sweet kid who just liked to clean pools, because he had a useful body part. No, thank you. I'm not going to be a sitting duck, and I'm not putting your patients and staff at risk."

"I could force the issue." She said it coolly.

"That would be a mistake," I replied, just as coolly. Except I wasn't cool. I was pissed. As I looked into her deep blue eyes it occurred to me that she was provoking me deliberately, trying to get me to lose it, so she'd have the excuse. *Bitch.* I kept calm and didn't take the bait.

We sat in a silent battle of wills for long moments, neither of us willing to give an inch. Each tick of the wall clock fell into the silence, and the sound of the air conditioner kicking in was almost startlingly loud. I leaned forward, opening the water bottle, pouring the fluid into the glass. I sipped it quietly, comfortably, crossing my legs with deliberate casualness. I was not giving in to her bullshit. If this was her way of doing things, I was not going to be her patient much past the first meeting. Dr. Scott would just have to refer me to someone else. Of course the doctor might have to do my counseling while sitting inside a sacred circle.

"This is getting us nowhere," she announced.

I couldn't argue with that, so I didn't. Instead, I raised my brows and took another sip of water, being ever so careful not to show any hint of pleasure at her being the one to break the silence.

"It's going to be very difficult to make any progress if you refuse to cooperate." She sounded a little waspish. Her professional demeanor was slipping just a tad.

"I am not refusing to cooperate. I am merely choosing outpatient treatment, which was an option offered to me."

She let out an irritated little huff of air, her eyes narrowing. She glanced at the elegant gold watch on her wrist and shook her head. "We don't have much time left."

"Where do you want to start?" I asked.

"I suppose that would be up to you. Where do *you* think we should begin?"

I leaned back, thinking about it. There were so many possibilities. But the one that was top of my list at the moment had to do with the scene in the lobby.

"Let's stick with tradition and start with my mother." I'd intended it to sound more humorous than it came out.

"Your mother?"

"Have you talked to Dr. Talbert about my past?"

"I like to start fresh." She smiled, but it didn't reach her eyes. "What do you want to tell me about your mother?"

Wow. Where to start? I mean, there was just so *much* and none of it particularly good. I didn't even know if I loved her anymore. But I sure as hell didn't *like* her.

I was still trying to come up with the right words when the bell rang, indicating the end of the session. Typical.

Dr. Greene picked up her BlackBerry with a sigh. "Why don't we set you up for Monday at eleven fifteen? That will give you the weekend to decide how to begin." She looked up, meeting my eyes directly, "Although I really feel I must try one more time to convince you that it would be in your best interest at this point to pursue inpatient treatment. . . ." She let the end of the sentence drag on hopefully. She needn't have bothered. I shook my head no.

She let out a little sniff of displeasure but didn't raise any further objection. "Fine. Monday at eleven fifteen." She entered the appointment into her BlackBerry.

I was still thinking about my mother as I drove the Miata down the main highway back to the city. Traffic wasn't good, which meant I wasn't going to have time to stop and buy decent clothes. Not if I wanted to get some nourishment into me and arrive at the church before sundown.

Part of me wanted to throttle my mother for what she'd done. Oh, I didn't have proof. But I knew. It was just so . . . *her*. Damn it anyway.

I knew I shouldn't let it bother me. I mean, God knew it wasn't the first time she'd betrayed me. I should be used to it and not expect any better from her. And yet there was that little part of me that just wouldn't give up hope: hope that she'd change, dry out, become the mother I remembered from before.

Hurt and anger formed a hard knot in my throat that made it hard to swallow. "Grow up, Graves," I told myself sternly as I took the Thirty-eighth Avenue exit that was the quickest route to Old Town. "She is what she is. She isn't going to change." And maybe she'd always been that way and I was just remembering her through rose-colored glasses. Maybe it had only been my father who kept her in any sort of check.

I went through a drive-through pharmacy and bought some more nutrient drinks and the liquid version of a popular multi-vitamin. I chugged two of the former and took a dose of the latter before I even left the parking lot. I was going to a church, my *gran's* church, for sanctuary. I needed to make damned sure I wasn't going to lose it when the sun went down.

I forced myself to pay close attention to where I was going. I didn't want to get lost, not in this neighborhood. When my gramps had been alive, Old Town had been a working area. Very blue-collar. Back then, there were no gangs to speak of and the bats and monsters weren't nearly the problem they were now. Things change.

Christ Our Savior Chapel is a little white clapboard and brick building in one of the more run-down sections of the Town. The parking lot is bare dirt, but there isn't a spot of trash on it. The windows are clean and the wooden doors gleam with polish. The last time anyone tried to graffiti the place, Reverend Al caught him at it. With the approval of the kid's mother, the good reverend set the kid to scrubbing the sanctuary floor — with a toothbrush — while Al read to him from the scriptures.

My gran swears the kid still comes to services every Sunday and alternate Wednesday nights.

I pulled my little sports car into the empty parking spot between Reverend Al's ancient Chevy and my gran's Oldsmobile, fresh back from impound, just as the sun's last rays were sinking below the western horizon. I hoped the Miata would be all right. The last thing I needed was for something to happen to the car. But the sun was sinking fast, and I needed to be on holy ground.

Just as soon as I was safe I was going to take it for a nice long drive along the coast. It'd have to be at night if I wanted the top down, but I like moonlight.

It was a goal to shoot for.

But for tonight, I was going to take Uncle Sal's advice and lay low. And just in case the überbat got any ideas, about coming after my nearest and dearest, Gran was going to be right there with me.

I hurried up the cracked concrete sidewalk that led to the glass front doors just as the orange glow of halogen lights came on up and down the streets. Pulling on the handle, I stepped over the threshold into safe haven and wound up standing less than six inches away from my mother.

I felt a rush of emotions the minute I set eyes on her. Anger, lots of anger, but frustration and pity were in there, too, and a deep, aching sadness that I didn't like to think about.

She was arguing with Gran, her voice raised, her words just a little bit slurred. If she wasn't completely drunk yet, she was certainly well on her way. Nothing unusual about that. She was dressed for a night on the town, in a nylon leopard-print top that was cut low enough to display ample cleavage and a pair of black jeans that clung like a second skin. Four-inch stiletto heels with a matching bag completed the outfit. She didn't look *quite* like a hooker, but with her figure and peroxide hair she had definitely gone over the line into the realm of white trash.

I mean, four-inch heels? Damn, I wouldn't attempt those *sober*. But then, that was my mother, all over.

"I can't shtay, Mama. Celiash comin' and you know how she'll be."

"Too late. She's already here."

My mother turned on a dime, her eyes wide with honest-to-God panic. If I'd had any doubt as to whether she was the culprit behind the photos and the story, that look took care of it.

My grandmother spoke up. "You can't leave, Lana. There's a vampire out there hunting Celia and the people she cares about. You need to stay here tonight." Her voice was unyielding. She stood solid as a rock, all of four foot eleven in her sensible shoes and hand-knitted cardigan, refusing to budge.

"Then I should be jusht fine. Because we all know my little girl doesn't give a tinker's damn about *me*." Crocodile tears filled her eyes.

Oh, for the love of — "Cut the crap, Mom," I snarled. Anger was driving the other emotions off. I love my mother, but sometimes I almost *hate* her. "Nobody here's buying your little pity party. Besides which, even if you had a valid license, you're too drunk to be driving."

She straightened to her full height to glare down at me. "I am *not* drunk."

"Of course not." My voice dripped enough sarcasm to earn me a filthy look from both the reverend and my grandmother.

"I don't have to stand here and take thish." My mother turned to face Gran. "If you won't loan me your car, I'll just call myshelf a cab." She stalked unsteadily past me, slamming the glass door open.

I turned to follow, emerging just in time to see her freeze in mid-step about six feet from the property line, her eyes glazing over.

Oh, *shit*.

23

had my knives out. They glowed pure silver white in the moonlight. The streetlights had gone out. So had the church light. The only illumination came from the moon, my knives, and the gleam of greenish light shining from my skin. It wasn't the best way to introduce my gran to my condition, but I had little choice.

I saw movement, a deeper shadow moving in the velvet darkness. It was her. Had to be. The question was, was she alone? Knowing my luck, probably not.

"Mom." I tugged at her arm without letting go of my knife. She was stiff as a board. She'd stopped just inches from the boundary. If she didn't take that last step, the vamp wouldn't get her. But with the beast fighting for control of her mind, I couldn't be sure she wouldn't take that last fateful step.

I couldn't let that happen.

I loved her.

I might want to throttle her more than half the time, but I still loved her. And I wanted her here, alive, and in full possession of her faculties. Because if she died or became undead, we'd never be able to fix what was wrong between us. And I wanted that. Until this moment I hadn't realized just how badly I wanted it.

I decided to take the vamp by the fangs. "Hello, Lilith."

The darkest shadow responded, "Celia."

She stepped out of the blackness—lithe, feral, and hungry. I didn't look at her face. I didn't dare. One look in those eyes and she'd have me for sure, just the way she'd caught my mother.

"There's a bit of a resemblance"—she looked Lana up and down—"but not much."

"Yeah, well, she's had a hard life." I stepped between my mother and the vampire, hoping I wasn't being an idiot. Because if Lilith had enough control of my mother's mind, she'd be able to force her to attack me. But if I could break Lilith's line of sight, my mother *might* be able to slip her mental bonds. I didn't think she was strong enough, but I wanted her to be. I mean, this was the woman who had stuck around when our life had gone to hell. She'd started drinking to cope, but she'd stayed, which was a damned sight more than Dad had done.

"So I can see."

I felt Lilith's power slither around and past me, slick and sinuous as a snake. *Hang on, Mom. Fight it.* "What will you do if I call her to me? Will you try to save her? Sacrifice yourself? Or will you stand there behind your line of protection and watch as I drink her down, then use my magic to replace Luther with your dear mommy?"

"You don't have her yet."

"Don't I?" I heard the crunch of heels on concrete, felt a body press against mine as my mother shifted her weight in response to the call.

"Hang on, Mom. Hang *on*."

I didn't dare look back, even though I could hear movement from the direction of the church.

"Lana, *no!*" my gran shouted behind me, and suddenly the darkness was bisected by a spear of white as blinding as a magnesium flare. Reverend Al strode forward, holding the cross from the altar in front of him. It was glowing with the blinding white light of pure faith. He's a big man, six two, probably a good 250 to 275 pounds of former fullback. He was impressive at any time. Tonight, he was awe inspiring. The scent of incense, heavy with myrrh, floated to me on the chill night air.

"Begone, demon!" His voice rang with authority as he shouted the prayer of banishment in its original Latin. I recognized it from my readings in college, but I'd never actually heard it used. Lilith wasn't a demon, just a very old bat, but it seemed to work. She screamed in frustrated rage, her power lashing out at him like a living darkness. It struck the wall of his belief with a sound like the clash of swords, but the light of the cross in his hands never wavered. Reverend Al was a wall of solid muscle standing beside me, between the bat and her prey, armed only with the cross and his belief.

The vampire raised her head, howling in agony.

It was the only opening I might ever have. Sending a silent prayer upward, I shifted the knife in my right hand to a throwing position and hurled it into the bulk of her body.

It wasn't a throwing knife. There was a good chance it might not strike point first. But it was a well-balanced weapon, and with the magic Bruno had imbued in it all I needed was a scratch. It struck home, the blessed blade sinking hilt deep into the soft flesh of Lilith's abdomen.

She opened her mouth, but no sound came out. Instead, I

saw flames eating at her from the *inside*. *Cool*. Don't know what magic made it work, but it was very impressive.

With a whoosh of air her body imploded, until it was nothing more than coarse gray ash, with my blackened knife smoldering on top.

Vampires do not die like that. They just don't. Killing a vampire is bloody and messy and involves beheading and taking the heart. They do not simply burst into blinding flame and burn down to a knee-high pile of dust—well, not without the help of copious amounts of sunlight. So what the hell had happened? I wanted to call Bruno or Matteo, but I couldn't seem to move.

I don't know how long we stood there. Long enough that the light from Reverend Al's cross faded and my eyes adjusted to the velvet darkness of a night filled with clouds. One by one the streetlights came back on. As if from a distance, I heard my grandmother crooning a lullaby to my sobbing mother.

"We need to gather up the ashes and spread them over a natural source of moving water." Reverend Al sounded even wearier than I felt, which was quite a trick. Because I felt as though I'd gone twelve rounds with Mike Tyson.

"Yeah, we definitely want to dispose of her properly. And I need to clean my knife."

I wanted rest in the worst way. But I couldn't until I was absolutely sure we'd eliminated any possible chance of Lilith coming back.

The reverend's voice was a little unsteady when he spoke next. "I'll go get a broom and a dustpan, although what we'll put the ashes in I don't know. I don't have anything ready." I managed to move my head enough to look at him. His normally ruddy face was gray with fatigue. He looked old, a bit frail, and more than a little afraid.

I said, "I have a bag you can use in the car. Although how we're supposed to tell the head from the heart I have no clue. And you did great—as well as any of the priests from the order."

"I didn't kill her. Didn't even wound her, really." He shuddered, his whole body shaking in reaction. "Saints preserve me, but she was powerful. I've never felt *anything* like that."

"She had to be over a thousand years old. There aren't many vamps who live that long, and the ones who do are powerful as hell. And if you hadn't wounded her with the cross, I would never have been able to get her. You saved us all."

He ran a hand over his thinning hair. "I think you can claim as much credit for that as I can," he said shakily. "If you hadn't stepped between them, I would never have made it out here in time." He stared at me for a long moment. "That was the bravest thing I've seen in my life. I know you don't get along with your mother, Celia. Your grandmother has us pray about it all the time. But you do still love her. Of that there is no doubt."

"Yeah. I do." I didn't sound happy about it, even to me.

"Then when we're done with cleanup I want you to come in. *Talk* to her. Sort out your differences."

Oh fucking goodie.

24

The reverend ordered pizza and pop to celebrate. It took longer than it was supposed to to arrive. I would've complained to the driver, but Gran intercepted me before I could get to the door.

Still, we reheated the pies in the church oven and the reverend even went to the trouble to dig through the cabinets until he found a blender.

It was my first attempt at "real" food. Yeah, we watered it down and ground it up, but it was pizza. It should have tasted just the same as when it was eaten normally.

It didn't. It tasted really weird. Maybe it was because everything was all mushed together, so I didn't taste the individual parts—the crust, the tomato sauce, the cheese, and the toppings. There was this weird twang to it that I couldn't quite place. Still, I was grateful enough that I wasn't going to complain. I did manage to get *some* of it down, and it was certainly better than some of what I'd been "eating." And it gave me hope. Real food might be possible. Maybe.

I was sitting in the reverend's study, drinking my watered-down pizza shake and a glass of milk as I wiped down my knife with an oiled cloth. I'd been using considerable elbow grease with no luck at all thus far. It was as if the metal itself had blackened. The wooden handle was fine, but the metal of the blade, while still hard and sharp, was absolutely black. Weird. Very, very weird.

As soon as I got the shake down and the knife cleaned I was going over to Karl Gibson's. I'd called to tell him about the visit from the king and offer Karl the chance to be there. He'd jumped at it. Turned out he was an avid baseball fan as well as a detective on a mission.

My grandmother stepped into the room. She gave Reverend Al a meaningful look before asking, "Would you mind giving Celia and me a few minutes alone? We need to talk."

I closed my eyes but didn't say a word. My mind, however, was racing. *No. Oh, please, no. Not a "talk." I don't deserve this. I'm* tired, *damn it. Don't make me talk to my gran.*

"Of course, Emily." The look he cast over his shoulder as he left had a hint of sympathy directed my way. Gran waited until the door was firmly closed behind him before lowering herself primly onto the chair opposite mine, setting her coffee cup onto the little cork coaster on the table in front of her.

"I was very proud of you tonight. That was a courageous thing you did, standing up for your mother like that."

"Thanks, Gran." I fought not to yawn. I was really sleepy. Probably just everything catching up with me.

She gave me a long look. "I've always been proud of you, Celia. You know that." Her eyes met mine and for just a moment she looked *old*. I mean, she's my gran, and over eighty. Of course she's old. But she never looks it. She's got this energy about her, like a miniature whirlwind. Always on the go, always

320 | CAT ADAMS

doing something. But tonight she looked old and sad and more than a little bit worried.

"Gran, what's wrong? The bat's dead. She didn't get Mom."

"No"—Gran gave me a tired smile—"she didn't."

"Look, you're exhausted, why don't you get some rest?"

"No, Celia. There's something I need to tell you, and after what happened tonight I know it can't wait. I *should* have told you when you hit puberty. But you were in therapy because of what happened to you and Ivy, and I didn't think you were ready to cope with it. Besides, it didn't affect your mother—or not much anyway. I didn't really believe it would bother you." She shifted uncomfortably in her seat, her gaze suddenly absorbed by the contents of her coffee cup. She sounded both suspiciously guilty and simultaneously as if she'd been trying very hard to rationalize something away.

"What are you talking about?" The words came out more harshly than I'd intended, and she flinched. I apologized immediately. "Sorry. I didn't mean to snap. I'm just tired."

"No, no. It's all right." She reached over and patted my hand. Her hand was gnarled and age spotted, the veins and sinews standing out harshly beneath the tissue-paper skin. "You've always referred to yourself as an 'ordinary vanilla human.'"

"Yeah."

"Well . . . you're not."

"Well, no, not since the vampire—"

She squeezed my hand hard, and I looked up, meeting eyes that had gone solemn. "You weren't completely human before the vampire bite, Celia. My husband, your grandfather, was only *half* human."

I blinked. I hadn't known that. He'd *looked* human. And

really, there aren't many magical creatures that can inter-
breed with us. Werewolves, of course, but that's because they
generally start out human in the first place. And Gramps
hadn't been a wolf. No way.

"What . . . what was he?"

"His father was a human sailor. His mother was a siren.
Which means *you* are part siren."

A *siren*? No way. Not me. I mean, she was talking to the
woman who got kicked *out* of eighth-grade choir, whose dorm
mates threatened to call the cops when she sang in the shower.
And sirens were *beautiful*—I mean drop-dead gorgeous creatures who have men panting after them.

"Um, Gran . . ." I struggled for words, but all I could come
up with was, "I can't sing. I mean, I *really* can't sing."

She laughed, hard, her head flung back, eyes dancing. Part
of it was the stress, but part was pure humor. When she finally
calmed down enough to catch her breath she said, "No, baby,
you really can't sing." She wiped tears from the corners of her
eyes. "But while some sirens focus their call through music,
the call itself is psychic. A female siren calls males to her to
fulfill her needs, even to their doom."

"But—"

She continued as if I hadn't spoken. It was as if the words
and emotions had been building up inside her and, now that
they'd been loosed, there was no stopping them. "The vampire that bit you tried to change you instead of killing you because he was *male*. The werewolf who found you in that alley,
out of all the alleys in the city, did it because you called him to
you." She gave a sad smile. "And you don't get along with other
women because you've come into your power."

"That's not true. I get along with women," I protested. Actually, it was a lie. I've never gotten along with most women. I have a few good friends, Dawna, Vicki. . . .

Gran didn't say a word, just raised an eloquent eyebrow.

"Vicki was my best friend."

"Vicki was a lesbian, Celia."

"Well, yeah, but she was a woman."

Gran nodded once, then raised those formidable silver brows again. "Fine. Anyone else?"

"Dawna. I get along really well with Dawna. Really, really well, and she *doesn't* like women in . . . that way."

Gran smiled, but there was a tinge of pity along with the humor. "Is she, by any chance, postmenopausal?"

"Well, she had some plumbing problems and had a hysterectomy a while back, but what's that got to do with anything?"

Gran gave me a level look. "Name one close female friend you have who is both heterosexual and fertile. Just one."

I thought about it. Hard.

Silence stretched between us for probably two minutes. Two of the *longest* minutes of my life.

"You can't, can you?" She smiled gently. "In fact, most women you interact with get almost completely neurotic, almost to the point of insanity, around you, *particularly* if men or other women they love are around."

I thought about it. There had been incidents in college, at parties. Men always rush forward to open doors for me, or hold out my chair, and tick off their girls. Hell, not two weeks ago there'd been a scene at El Jefe's between me and Kevin's live-in girlfriend, Amy, when he brought me a drink before he delivered hers. There were other things, too. I didn't like to think about them. It's always just confused me. Yet if I was a siren, it all made sense. But *was* I? Was I *really*? "How could I know for sure? Is there a test kit in the pharmacy or something?"

"Whenever you're in real need, you call men to you, and they do whatever it takes, at whatever cost, to help you."

Now *that* I had an answer for.

"Then why didn't I call someone to help me when Ivy and I were kidnapped? God knows we needed help."

Tears filled her eyes, her grip on my hand tightening until it was actually painful. "Oh, honey. If only you had come into your power. But you hadn't hit puberty. If you had—"

If I had, my sister might still be alive. I might not have been tortured. Everything . . . my entire life . . . would have been completely and totally different. If only I'd been a few years older?

I sat there, stunned. My mind was racing, but it refused to pull anything into any semblance of coherent thought. It was as if my whole world had turned upside down. Nothing made sense and at the same time everything suddenly did.

"It's one of the reasons your mother had such a hard time adjusting to your father's abandonment. Men simply do *not* leave sirens. She knew about her father's side of the family. Had met them, integrated somewhat. Losing your father didn't just hurt her, it *damaged* her. I think she would've killed herself if it hadn't been for you girls. And then, when Ivy . . ."

She let her voice trail off, her gaze shifting to the door as if she could see through it to where my mother slept on the other side. She sighed.

"I know it'll take some time to get used to the idea." Gran's reassuring voice came to me as if from a distance. "And eventually you'll need to get in touch with your great-grandmother or one of her sisters. But not now. Right now you need to rest."

As if I could.

25

I hadn't expected to be able to sleep. After all, Gran's news had been quite a shock, and a sleeping bag on a concrete floor isn't exactly my idea of comfort. But I must have been more tired than I expected, because I was out the minute I zipped myself into the bag.

I knew I was dreaming, recognized the dream, but couldn't drag myself out of it.

I was twelve years old again. It was noon on a bright midsummer day, and hot. I wore cutoff jeans that were a little too short and tight to be comfortable, not to show off my legs, but because I'd outgrown them and there wasn't any money to buy more.

There was never enough money. Mom was working as a bartender, but most of what she made went up in smoke—cigarette smoke, pot smoke, and liquor. She always came home late, seldom sober or alone. Ivy slept through most of it. She never heard the sound of the headboard hitting the wall, or the moans that accompanied it. I did.

326 I CAT ADAMS

There were no more ballet lessons. The only reason Ivy was getting lessons training her "gift" was
because Gran insisted, paid for them, and drove her.
That's why I was alone now. Gran had taken Ivy to
lessons and Mom was off "working."

Finding him had been easy. I'd gotten on the computer at the library. It was right there in the telephone listings. The address was less than four blocks
from our house.

Four blocks. It might as well have been a thousand
miles. But I didn't know that. Not then.

I rounded the corner on foot, my thongs slapping
against the cracked concrete. Sweat slid between my
shoulder blades beneath the cheap pink tank top I'd
taken from my mother's closet.

The part of me that knew I was dreaming tried to stop right
here, to pull out or change the dream before it went any further. I knew what came next. I'd lived it once, dreamed of it
often, and had no desire to see it again. But I was sleeping too
deeply, so the images moved inexorably forward, my younger
self pausing beneath the corner street lamp, looking for the
right house number.

It was the fourth on the right. A tidy little one-story
white wood frame building with red trim and a
picket fence in front. I saw him. He was playing catch
in the front yard with a boy a year or so younger than
me. A girl of five or so with blond curls and a pink
jumper was playing dolls on the front stoop. She

looked enough like Ivy that it was startling. He was laughing until he looked up and saw me.

Daddy.

The joy slid from his face. He turned to the boy and said something. I couldn't hear it, but I could see the urgency in his eyes. The boy seemed startled but obediently bent to gather up his things. Not fast enough, apparently. My father hurried forward, chivvying him and his baby sister into the house.

I froze, right hand extended, my mouth open to call out.

My father's eyes met mine for one endless moment.

He closed the door.

"How very tragic." I recognized the voice that slid into my dream as smooth as silk. Jones was back and he was being sarcastic. "Poor little thing."

"Get the hell out of my head."

"No. I don't think so. We need to talk and I don't have a lot of time."

The dream shifted and I could see him. He was in a gymnasium, standing in the center of a pentagram drawn within the circle at center court. Both the circle and pentagram shone red and wet by the light of the black candles placed at each point of the star. He'd had to use his own blood to draw those symbols, and I felt their power, and the pain in his forearms, even through the filtering dream.

"I need you to get a message to Kevin Landingham."

"What, you can't use a phone?"

"Not safely. And while I'm not sure how he did it, he's managed to cut me off from hearing his thoughts." Jones sounded pissed. "Somebody's gone off the reservation. It's got to be one of the telepaths, otherwise I'd have been able to pick up on it—or somebody at the main office would've tipped me off to it. Whoever it is, they've eliminated the few clairvoyants we had on the payroll."

"So, what's the message?"

"We're in the middle of a high-profile assignment. It's too important to let it fail over a rogue. So they're offering Kevin a deal. A one-year limited contract, hunting hard targets, starting with the rogue. He can write his own ticket. And they'll guarantee your safety. No one associated with the firm will ever use you or harm you in any way. They'll take whatever binding oaths he wants on it."

"Why would he care about my safety?" I wouldn't have said it out loud, but we were operating in a dream, in my thoughts, so he heard it just the same.

"You don't know?" He chuckled and it was creepy as hell. "Oh, my. Well, if he hasn't told you, I certainly won't. But be sure to give him my message. Word for word."

He stepped forward, very deliberately rubbing out the edge of the circle with his foot. The image in my mind went to black. Apparently our conversation was over.

I opened my eyes, no longer able to sleep. As I did, I became simultaneously aware of several things: I wasn't in a sleeping bag on the floor of the study of Reverend Al's church; my head was pounding; and I had a terrible, metallic taste in my mouth. I was in a straitjacket, on the floor of a padded room, and Dr. Greene was watching me from behind the safety window.

26

You are a damned nuisance." Greene's voice was only slightly distorted coming through the speakers into the room. "The drugs in the pizza were supposed to keep you out for twenty-four hours."

I'd been drugged. That explained the taste and the bindings. I'd never have let myself get in this situation otherwise. The pizza was delayed, cold, and tasted like crap. You'd think I would have been suspicious. *Sheesh.* And while I was still a little thickheaded, I was starting to be able to think through the sedative-induced fog. Let's hear it for the vampire metabolism. Or maybe siren. Or both. Whatever, I was awake. But I couldn't *do* anything. Yet.

"They haven't even had time to get to the church yet, let alone link it to you and declare you a danger. I haven't had time to meet with Dr. Scott." She gave an exaggerated sigh. She stood behind the window in her sensible gray suit, arms crossed over her chest, fingers drumming absently against her arm. "Personally, I'd rather just kill you outright. But that would bring your werewolf into things and my employer has been *very* clear about not wanting him involved until after sunrise tomorrow."

My werewolf? Kevin wasn't anywhere close to *mine*. Her fingers drummed faster. "We'll try another shot. Perhaps a higher dose—" She turned and walked from the observation room.

I didn't have long, perhaps only a minute or two. "Ivy, Vicki, are you here?" I tried to keep my voice a bare whisper so that it wouldn't get picked up by the room's monitoring equipment. Of course Greene had talked freely, so she had probably turned it off. But I decided to be quiet, just in case.

The temperature of the room dropped until I could see my breath fogging in the air. I wasn't surprised. Ghosts are more likely to manifest when the person they're attached to is in a strong emotional state. Can't get much stronger than life-threatening terror. I could almost feel the adrenaline bubbling through my veins. "Find Dr. Scott. Tell him what's happening. Then warn Reverend Al. Get Gran and Mom out of there."

I rolled onto my back and began pulling against the confining straitjacket with all of my might. I'd had enough strength to strain the metal of the table back in the lab. It should be easy to Hulk my way out of a contraption of mere canvas and leather. Assuming, of course, it wasn't bespelled. Which it probably was. But it wasn't like I had a glut of options. So I struggled, and I pulled, and succeeded in just about pulling my own arms from their sockets. But spelled or not, the fabric was starting to give. I strained harder. To hell with it. My shoulders would heal. I wanted, *needed*, this damned thing *off*.

As if from a distance I heard the crash of waves, the call of gulls. And suddenly I knew. I had called power when I fell asleep at the office, had influenced Dr. Scott. And *I could do it again*. I concentrated as I pulled, thinking of Dr. Scott, of Gerry and every other male I knew who worked at Birchwoods.

I didn't know what time it was, didn't really know what I was doing, but I had to try. Because here came Dr. Greene, carrying a needle, her sensible heels clicking briskly against the linoleum.

I pulled harder against the bindings, adrenaline roaring through my system, giving my senses the hyperfocus they'd had the other morning. Her breathing, harsh and loud. And, fainter, in the distance, but closing fast, running footsteps.

She lunged at me, syringe at the ready, but I was too quick for her. Moving with unnatural speed, I rolled, kicking at her knee with both feet. The blow connected hard, and with the extra strength behind it her knee didn't just give, it tore, the bone breaking through the skin with a spray of blood.

Screaming, she fell to the floor, her lower leg nearly severed. Blood was everywhere, the scent nearly overpowering. She grabbed her leg, trying to apply pressure, but it wasn't working.

My stomach growled, my eyes started to bleed red. I could see the needle, far from her reach. Hear the sound of her racing pulse as she stared at me in horror and growing fear. My arms were free, the straitjacket torn apart, but I couldn't remember doing it. Couldn't think past the roaring in my ears and the hunger that had drool running from the corner of my mouth.

She tried to back away, shoving herself with her good leg, a trail of smudged blood shocking red against the stark white linoleum.

I fought not to follow, fought every instinct with the one remaining shred of humanity left to me.

The door to the observation room slammed open. Gerry

and Dr. Scott burst into the room, both panting hard from exertion. They took in the scene on the other side of the window with a single horrified glance.

"Thank God!" Greene shouted. "Save me. She's gone feral!"

"*Liar.*" My voice sounded not the least bit human.

"Dr. Greene, please. Don't antagonize her." Dr. Scott's voice was still a little breathy, but calm, and I could feel him using his talent to try to reach the part of me that was still human, to soothe and calm me. "Celia, you must stay calm. Vicki told me everything. The police are on the way here and to the church. You've done nothing wrong, and we'll find proof of that. But you *must* hold on."

I turned to look at him, the movement difficult and disjointed, as if my body were unwilling to follow the orders my brain was giving it. My skin was glowing.

"I'm going to send Gerry to get you some food, and then I'm coming in to treat Dr. Greene's injury. I can't let her die. Can you let me do that?"

"Yes." I forced the word through clenched jaws.

"Good. Now if you'll back up to the far corner, please." He moved past Gerry, who was standing, pale and shaking, in front of the door. He'd switched off the intercom before turning to leave, but with my heightened senses I could still hear them as clearly as if we were in the same room.

"Are you insane? You can't mean to go in there with that . . . *thing.*"

"I would remind you that *Ms. Graves* could easily have killed and eaten the doctor. She hasn't. In fact, she's shown admirable self-control. But it would be foolish to push the issue by leaving her in there with a bleeding woman. So go to the kitchen and get her some food. Now."

Gerry left. I heard his footfalls going down the hall at a jog that was not quite a run. And I heard Dr. Scott's gentle knock on the door.

I managed to make it through the next few minutes without killing anyone, but I don't know how. It was one of the hardest things I'd done in my life. I *wanted* to kill Greene. Not just the beast in me, but the human part as well. Because a part of me felt she'd deserved it. Reverend Al was dead—the cops arrived in time to protect the people in the church from the bad guys, but the drugs in the pizza had reacted with the pain meds he was on for an old football injury. I knew all this because Vicki had Alex make some calls.

I'd been kidnapped and set up for a perfect frame. Even if I was proven not guilty in a court of law, I was a monster. I'd be locked up in one of the state institutions, probably never to see the light of day again.

But it didn't happen.

Everything worked out exactly the way I *needed* it to. To the sound of ocean waves and the call of gulls. It wasn't subtle, and there'd be a price to pay. But I did what I had to do.

Was it wrong to manipulate everyone I dealt with? *Hell, yeah.* Did I care? *No.* Because I was running out of time. Everything, from start to finish, was tied to the plots against King Dahlmar. Good people were dead, I'd been turned into a monster, and demons were loose in the city. While it seemed to

me to be a lot of trouble just for a pool of natural gas under Rusland, there could well be things I wasn't aware of yet.

Tonight the king would go to the World Series game. Tomorrow, first thing, he was scheduled to fly back home with
his sons and entourage. Security before and after would be
incredibly tight, but there's only so much you can do in a
crowded public venue. It was all going down at the game. I'd
have bet my life on it. Greene's comment about Kevin had
just confirmed what I already suspected.

Gibson pulled up to the door of Birchwoods administration
building in the same midsized Buick sedan I'd ridden with
him in earlier. I was climbing into the front seat almost before
the vehicle had come to a complete stop. I didn't dare dawdle
in case the mojo wore off. That was entirely possible, since I
didn't really know what in the hell I was doing.

I pulled the seat belt tight over my oh-so-chic gray
Birchwoods sweats. At least they were clean, and better than
the stuff I'd borrowed from Bruno, even if I was liable to die
from heat prostration. "Did you get everything?" I reached
into the bag on the seat next to me and began rifling through
its contents.

"Yeah." Gibson pulled the car around the circle drive, heading toward the gate. Gerry was there, but he didn't smile or
wave. No surprise.

"I've got to tell you, that little toy of yours is worth damned
near as much as this car." He didn't bother to keep the disgust
from his voice.

"Yeah, well, I'm the one paying for it. And if we need it, it
will be worth twice the price." I pulled out an assortment of
gaudy holy items and a pair of mirrored sunglasses that I slipped

on. Next were an Angels cap and a new denim jacket. I pulled the former onto my head and yanked the price tags off the latter, unbuttoning it to reveal the lining. Sure enough, tacked pockets. Perfect.

I slid a pair of single-shot squirt guns into the slots made by the stitching and began unwrapping the replacement sensor car. This time I'd splurged on the deluxe model. It looked exactly like the one Matty used. Taking it from the hinged jewel case it came in, I tucked it into my pocket and began skimming the directions. It worked basically the same way as my previous one, but with a few added features. Good to know.

Last, but not least, I grabbed the small blue water bottle with a sponge on the end that you can buy at any office supply store to seal envelopes. Twisting off the cap, I filled the bottle with holy water. Sealing it closed, I tucked it into the right side pocket of my jacket, the opposite side from where I'd put the gizmo. Taking a deep breath, I told myself I was ready.

I lied.

Gibson had slowed the car nearly to a stop. Not that he had much choice. It was already 4:15 and traffic to the ballpark had things jammed up back onto the highway. "The king's driver, Ivan, will meet us at the giant cap on the right with the replacement tickets."

"Good." I didn't look up, I was too busy checking the water pistols one last time, making sure that they'd function if I had to fire them. I've always had better luck with the actual One Shot brand than with the imitations, but Gibson had been doing the buying.

"I wish he'd have called it off," Gibson said. "It's stupid to deliberately walk into a trap."

"No chance. He wants to find the traitor and to know whether or not his sons are involved. He figures his people can handle whatever comes up. They've had plenty of warning." I grinned. "Of course, he may decide to hire a double. If a spawn does a shapechange, it actually becomes a double of the target's body. Fools fingerprints, voice analysis, lab work. Everything down to DNA."

"I know," Gibson said bitterly. "Makes life hard for us cops. Fortunately, there aren't too many spawn out there."

"Yeah, but what do you wager the king's got at least one on the payroll? We *know* the bad guys do."

Gibson grunted and turned the car onto Gene Autry Parkway. We were nearly there. From where we sat I could see fans in Angels red and Cubs blue hiking toward the stadium across the packed parking lot as outdoor vendors hawked their wares. Four fifteen in the afternoon and already there were plenty of people who acted as if they were trashed. I shook my head. Call me a prude, but I can't imagine paying a small fortune for a ticket to a game like this and then getting so wasted I wouldn't remember the game.

Traffic was moving at a crawl. Just ahead, a man in a neon orange vest signaled with a flashlight that there were openings in that row. Gibson followed the line leading toward him.

"Did you get hold of your boyfriend and the werewolf?"

"I tried. Neither one of them answered his phone. I think Bruno's pissed at me for standing him up. Of course he may have just not recognized the number. But I doubt it. He knows I had to get a new phone the other day and I imagine he got the number from Dawna."

Gibson had to stop to let the driver ahead of us pull into a parking space, so he had the chance to give me a shocked look. "You stood him up?"

"It's not like I had a choice. As you'll recall, I was unconscious at the time. But he doesn't know that, and he's pissed and won't answer his phone because I was supposed to return his Mets cap and I didn't."

"He should know you better than that."

"Yeah, he should. And he'll realize that about the fifth or sixth inning and start worrying. He'll call me back during the seventh-inning stretch."

Gibson laughed as he pulled the car into one of the last few vacant spots. "You know him pretty well."

"We were together through most of college." I didn't quite manage to keep the wistfulness from my voice.

"Sorry."

"Don't be. It's things like today that made me so crazy. If he'd just *pick up the damned phone*. But nope. He's too hard-headed."

"And I bet it's things like today that made him crazy, too. Knowing that you're going off into danger and there's nothing he can do about it."

I managed not to flinch, but ouch. That was a little too close to the mark. I climbed out of the car so that I wouldn't have to answer. Not that Gibson didn't notice. Still, he didn't press. I was glad. I didn't want to think about Bruno. I didn't need the distraction.

We moved across the parking lot with the rest of the herd, making our way past the huge "A" with its lit display. Peppered throughout the crowd were plenty of uniformed security and warrior priests of the various militant religious orders in full regalia and armament. Even from this distance the noise of the crowd beat against my sensitive hearing. Competing scents vied for my attention. Unwashed bodies, cologne, buttered popcorn, hot dogs, and beer were the most prevalent, but by no means the only, smells floating in the air.

The announcer was doing the usual pregame nonsense that most of the spectators were happy to ignore. The first pitch was set for 8:00 EDT. It wouldn't be too much longer before they announced the starting lineups and played the national anthem.

Ivan was waiting right where he was supposed to be. He stood there, unmovable as a mountain, dressed in jeans and a polo shirt under a Cubs jacket. The clothes were supposed to help him blend in with the crowd but didn't. For one thing, they were pressed. His jeans had a *crease*. And then there was his posture. The regular fans were excited but relaxed. He wasn't. He held himself in absolute readiness, his eyes constantly moving, taking in everything. I wondered if I looked like that when I was on duty, and figured yeah, I probably did.

I paused, letting Gibson take the lead. I took off my sunglasses, turned slightly, and, pretending to clean them, took a good look at old Ivan in the mirrored surface. He passed test one. He wasn't an illusion.

Sliding the glasses back on, I reached my right hand into my pocket, pressing it against the little sponge until I felt wetness on my palm. Test two was something Matty had suggested when I called the hospital. Spawn and demons can change form until they look just like the real thing. But that uses demonic magic—which can be shorted out by the judicious use of holy items. If Ivan was a spawn this little dab of water wouldn't make him change back, but it would sting like hell (literally) and give me a glimpse of his true form.

I walked up to Ivan, my arm extended in the classic "shake hands" gesture. I could tell he hated it. But there were witnesses, and refusing would be obvious. So he grimly shook my extended hand as quickly as he could manage, discreetly drying his damp palm on the leg of his jeans when he thought I wasn't looking. "Follow me."

He led us to the gates and into a line that was rapidly thinning as game time approached. One at a time we passed through curse and then metal detectors, pausing briefly as the security agent admired my little gadget. Then we were off, moving briskly through dim, wide halls lined with vendors and shops. Ivan was setting a quick pace, but we didn't seem out of place. The announcer was reading off the lineups. Almost everybody was hurrying, hoping not to miss the first pitch.

I stopped when I saw something . . . odd. In the corner of my vision I saw a pair of spectators heading toward the elevators. The woman looked vaguely familiar, like I'd seen her before, and recently. The drunken companion she was helping walk looked, to my eyes, like a petite blond woman. But the reflection in my glasses was of a dark-haired young man, looking ill and only semiconscious.

I did a double take and the woman noticed. She glared at me as she stabbed her finger against the elevator button, and I recognized her from the expression. It was the guard . . . Lydia. The woman from Birchwoods on Vicki's birthday. And that . . . *oh*, crap, that was the younger prince, Kristoff, Rezza's little brother. I shouted a warning to Ivan and took off at a dead run.

The elevator dinged and Lydia shoved Kristoff in ahead of

her, moving before the doors were even completely open. I was close enough to see her jabbing at the button panel when the doors slid closed in my face.

Shit, shit, shit!

Ivan and Gibson slid to a stop next to me as I watched the lights on the elevator winking to a stop at every floor.

"She's got Kristoff. The guy with your people is a fake."

"We don't know that. *This* one could be the fake. Or you could be lying to distract us."

Paranoia, thy name is bodyguard. "Fine, have your people spray him with holy water. If it's him, he'll be annoyed but fine."

Ivan's expression grew distracted and I knew he was talking mind to mind. A telepath then. No wonder he hadn't bothered to check out Gibson and me the way I had him. He could look in our minds and see who we were.

Then he could also see that I was serious. And I hoped he'd understand what I was about to do.

I went dashing down the nearest stairs, taking them three at a time, dodging last-minute arrivals. Gibson was at my heels. "I hope you know what you're doing," he gasped out.

I heard Ivan's voice inside my head. *They have unmasked and are detaining the impostor. We are to pursue while our mage attempts a tracking spell.* Sounded like a plan to me. But just in case they'd taken precautions against things like tracking spells and telepaths, I needed to think.

Kristoff wasn't big, but he was practically deadweight. Lydia—or whatever her name was—wouldn't want to lug him far, not alone. And they'd need a vehicle to transport him in. Probably a van or a camper, so that he'd be out of sight in case he tried to raise a fuss. Not that he'd seemed coherent enough to do so. But they'd want to be careful.

A catering truck? *Nah.* They'd be long gone by now, their work completed. As the soaring notes of the national anthem began to play for the crowd and the television audience, a new thought occurred to me. *The press area. There'd be plenty of vans and trucks to choose from. It would be close to the stadium, too.* Unfortunately, I hadn't had time to do any research. I had no idea where the news vans would be. In the distance I heard the voice on the P.A. system order everyone to rise.

Good thought. I will find out.

It didn't take Ivan long. Seconds later he was giving me directions. It wasn't far. Just around the next corner.

Gibson and I took the corner at a sprint. He looked like death, but he kept up, just a step or two to my left. He gave a cry that was more a cough than a shout, and I saw them.

They were a third of the way across the crowded lot, heading toward a white van with the Channel 9 logo emblazoned on it in bold red letters. *Erikson* crouched inside the open doorway. He called out a warning to our quarry and reached inside the van to grab a long weapon. *What the* hell?

Kristoff seemed to gain focus a little, managing to struggle weakly against his captor. But I barely noticed. My eyes were only on Erikson, who had dropped into position and was preparing to fire.

"Look out!" I shouted to Gibson as I dodged between vehicles. I couldn't see the shooter anymore, but I heard the crack of a shot even over the sound of blaring guitars, and the window just inches behind me shattered. He was good, scary good. I ducked my head and kept running, making myself as

much of a moving target as I could, using the vehicles for cover, doing my best to close on the woman and her captive.

A second crack, barely distinguishable from the pyrotechnics playing over the sound system, and I heard the thud of a body hitting the ground. Glancing back, I saw a crumpled form in a slowly spreading pool of blood on the pavement a few feet away.

The last words of the anthem trailed off, and the distant roar of jets flying in formation overhead took their place.

Risking a look around the edge of the portable radar dish I was hiding behind, I saw Lydia less than twenty feet from me. Though injured, she was rushing toward the spot where the prince lay on the ground. The door to the van was empty, but its motor was running. Ivan lay collapsed in the open ground between his prince and the van, the vehicle behind where he'd been standing splattered with meat and blood.

I charged, shouting in rage and defiance, throwing myself into the woman with a jarring full-body tackle that sent us sprawling onto the pavement.

She was tough, and good. She rolled with the impact, using my own momentum against me and breaking free. I rolled, too, gaining my feet, taking a defensive posture that put me directly between her and her quarry.

The van was moving, heading for us. She glanced at it and seemed to make a decision. I readied for an attack, but she did something I didn't expect and couldn't have prepared for. Reaching inside her jacket, she pulled out a ceramic disk not much bigger than a half-dollar. It looked almost exactly like one of the "boomers" I use, its spell released when the disk is smashed. As the van swung up beside her, the side door open and beckoning, she threw the disk to the ground, shattering it. Her smile, as she turned to jump into the vehicle, was pure predatory malice.

27

At first nothing happened. I didn't feel any spell. I figured it must have been a dud, so I turned to help the fallen prince. I was hefting him upward when I heard a hiss much like aerosol spraying from a can, followed by soft male laughter that was purely sexual. It was the kind of laughter meant for dark nights spent between silken sheets and just the sound of it tugged at things low in my body. I turned; I couldn't not.

He was *beautiful.* Not the twisted, frightening monster of my grandmother's illustrated Bible but a perfect, heart-wrenchingly beautiful angel, with only the cant of his expression and the red tint in his irises giving any hint of the corruption beneath.

A demon. I knew it, and the knowledge brought with it a fear that dried my mouth to cotton and had me trembling with both terror and desire.

He gave a delicate sniff and laughed again. "Oh, my. A *siren.* I haven't tasted siren in *far* too long. And not a bit of faith to preserve you." He smiled, taking a slow step forward, and my heart lurched in my chest. "I'm going to enjoy this. I'll have to come up with a suitable reward for Lydia."

I couldn't take my eyes off him, but I could still move my hands. Reaching into my jacket pocket, I fumbled blindly for the switch to turn on my little sensor car, and was rewarded by it coming to screeching, almost deafening life, red light from the alarm showing clearly even through the thick denim fabric.

He scowled, and even that expression was as beautiful as a cloud passing across the sun. "I'm disappointed in you. Do you *really* want us to be interrupted?"

"Hell, yeah." I'd meant to sound defiant, but I could barely get a breath of sound past my lips. My hands, though, were still busy. This time I reached into the inside of my jacket, searching for the single-shot water pistol I knew was hidden there. I didn't have much time. I knew that. His *presence* was starting to overwhelm my will. I couldn't hurt him. Even if I'd wanted to. And God help me, I *didn't* want to.

He laughed again, and it sighed against my body, bringing a low moan from my lips and an ache to my loins. Where *was* everybody? There had to be crews in the trucks and vans. Security should be all over this.

"Oh, they're coming," he answered my thoughts. "But I've slowed time. I want to *savor* this. Savor *you*."

Oh, shit.

I started trembling in earnest, and almost fumbled the little squirt gun I'd been drawing. Still, I managed to hang on to it, pulling it out in a jerky motion, pulling awkwardly at the refill plug with my left hand.

"Stop that!" he snarled, and it wasn't beautiful. His voice and power lashed out at me, strong enough to make me stumble, spilling drops of the precious holy water onto the ground. But that was okay. I wanted it on the ground. The whole idea was to draw a protective circle around the prince and me. I did just that. As the demon blurred forward across that last bit of distance between us, he slammed hard against an invisible barrier.

Hissing in frustrated pain and rage, he began pacing around the edge of the circle. "You shouldn't have done that, little one. It only bought you a minute or two at best. And when it comes down, I'm going to make you *suffer.*"

"You'd have done that anyway." Now that the barrier was up I could think clearly, although that was a mixed blessing. Because while I desperately needed to come up with some sort of a plan, knowing exactly what I was facing had me just about wetting myself in terror.

"Yes," he admitted, "but I would've let you enjoy it. At least at first. Now I'm not feeling so generous."

I focused, trying to call on my newly discovered talent. *I really do need a rescue here. The cavalry, an exorcist, a few militant priests, maybe accompanied by the National Guard?*

An exorcist. *Oh, crap.* I tried to marshal my thoughts, to remember the words Reverend Al had used successfully just last night. I couldn't do it. I felt the power of my circle starting to fade and flicker. Saw the anticipation in the demon's eyes as he gathered himself to strike the moment it fell.

Pushing my thoughts as hard as I could, I sent out a mental plea, not knowing who, if anyone, would hear. *If there are any telepaths out there, anybody at all who knows the high church exorcism prayer, please,* please *tell me now.*

And in my mind I heard Kevin's voice, joined by Bruno's, Matteo's, and others', weak but still clear, chanting in perfect unison. I felt a surge of hope, powerful beyond reason. I repeated the words, not even stumbling over the pronunciation.

The demon began to throw himself bodily against the barrier and the force threw me against the opposite side to land in a heap. I grunted and missed one of the words being chanted. I opened my mind to them and felt the words come again—whether by spell or some sort of psychic attachment. My voice was deeper this time when I chanted, a solid alto.

Again the demon attacked and this time I felt searing pain in my cheek as a claw slipped through a break in the circle. The wound began to smoke and burn, as though my skin was on fire. Even the vampire part of me was having a hard time healing a demonic attack. The scent of frying flesh made my stomach roil and my eyes water. He started to hammer at the weak point with a force that could probably shatter brick. I pressed myself as tight against the far side as I could, hoping against hope that this was not a *long* spell.

I saw a circle of figures began to converge on us across the parking lot. All of them were chanting the same words I was using. Each carried a symbol of their faith that shone with a blindingly pure white light that hurt the eyes. Crosses and stars and crescents and bells, all glowing brighter with each word.

The demon threw back his head, letting out a harsh bellow of pain and frustration that was both sound and more—the power of it washed over me and slammed into the vehicles around us, rocking them on their wheels, shattering windows, and setting off alarms.

The demon let out a scream that caused fire to spray in a wide arc. The priests scattered, their concentration broken by the nearly sentient hellfire that began to chase them across the pavement. He screamed again and I found myself racing around the inside of the barrier, trying to escape the tiny line of fire that chased me, putting out the flaming bits of brimstone that were landing on my hair and clothing. Who knew demons could breathe fire? Either that never came up in class or I played hooky that day. Either way, I was getting an education. I hoped I'd live to share it with El Jefe.

I kept chanting as the demon laughed and began to hammer again at the opening, which was now large enough to fit his muscular arm through. I was running out of options and the spell didn't seem to be working. Soon all I could do was curl up in a fetal position at the very bottom of the barrier, doing my best to protect Kristoff's unconscious form, just out of reach of claws that crept closer with each second that passed. I snapped my jaw at the demon when I could between words. My fangs seemed longer than I remembered and actually made him pause. He wasn't sure what to make of me—but that didn't mean he wasn't going to kill me.

I was so tired. My voice was getting hoarse, cracking over some of the stranger Latin words. The fire was growing, too, licking at my clothing and skin. If I didn't pass out from pain, I was going to lose my voice. His arm was fully inside now, reaching . . . pressing . . . grasping. He caught my hair and yanked me toward the hole. I screamed the next word, knowing it was going to be my last.

"Amen!" The word startled both of us. The demon's eyes went wide and he froze—his hand clutched around my throat. There was a sudden change in pressure inside the circle . . . a nauseating, disorienting sucking sensation. My ears popped painfully, and I had to close my eyes to keep my balance. I threw up. The claws burning into my neck spasmed and then the demon screamed again. It was a sound I'd hear in my nightmares, worse than the screams of my sister as she died, worse than anything I'd ever heard. It seemed to last forever, but it was probably only a moment. When it ended, I opened my eyes.

The demon was gone.

Unfortunately, his claws, with no hand attached, were still embedded in my neck and were still on fire.

I finally was able to scream with all the agony I'd been ignoring. As I gathered what might be my last breath, I spotted the others running my way, Kevin and Bruno battling for the lead.

That was the last sight I remember.

28

I **can't** believe they let you out of the hospital to come to a wake." Bruno shook his head and handed me a frozen margarita. I licked some of the salt off the wide rim to blend with the sweet, powerful drink as it slipped down my throat.

"Well, I was nearly healed anyway, and they had to let me out tomorrow by court order. I have to report to Birchwoods." The authorities have no sense of humor. They tried to prove telepathic manipulation in connection with my release prior to the ball game. On Roberto's advice I agreed to take a battery of tests, all of which I failed spectacularly. I'm not a telepath. I'm a siren. But they didn't ask that *specific* question, and my attorney felt no need to offer the information. Said it "wasn't pertinent."

"You should have appealed," Emma added. "You know the law school faculty would have helped you fight it. You're admittedly a little nuts, but a *dangerous animal*? Just because of the abomination thing?"

I shook my head and took another sip of drink before answering. "There were a lot of witnesses to the Birchwoods incident. But they couldn't push too hard. Not after somebody leaked it to the press. Besides, there must have been twenty ordained priests, pastors, rabbis, and monks lined up to testify at the hearing that I was fighting the demon, not helping him." Still, it was touch-and-go, and I'd been forced into agreeing to an inpatient stay until the *extent of my disability is known*.

Bruno nodded at Emma. "The Feds pushed to put her in a state facility."

That made me spit out a harsh laugh. "Fat chance. I can afford Birchwoods. Sixty days, with day passes for Vicki's and Gibson's funerals, and I get to stay in Vicki's old room that looks out over the ocean. I can do that." I hadn't asked for the view, Dr. Scott had insisted. Partially because of my siren blood, no doubt. But also I think as an apology. After all, he's the one who'd pushed for Dr. Greene to be my therapist.

They laughed just as another poor soul stepped up onstage to assault our ears with bad karaoke. This time it was Alex, which made me smile. She began to sing "Wind Beneath My Wings" and the air chilled again and confetti began to spin and rain down on the hardwood floor. It was nice that Vicki had decided to attend her own wake.

Her parents weren't too happy with this particular aspect of her last wishes. I think they'd expected a more somber affair, a tasteful memorial service that the press could attend, rather than a wild wake at La Cocina y Cantina, with cheesy sombreros and piñatas for decorations. The piñatas were filled with both confetti and little pouches of Pop Rocks—Vicki's favorite guilty pleasure when she got drunk. The place sounded like there were firecrackers going off after we broke open the first papier-mâché burro, and the cops had come in more than once, only to leave with annoyed shakes of their heads when they saw the cause of the commotion. The police are my *special escort*. The court deemed me a security risk because too many people felt I shouldn't be committed. The judge was afraid someone would slip me out of the country before the hearing. Since I report for my confinement tomorrow, the judge insisted on guards at the door of the wake and Dr. Scott attending to be sure I wasn't *endangering* anyone. He seemed to be having an okay time — if the pickup game of darts in the corner with El Jefe was any indication.

"This was their song." I said it to nobody in particular as Alex began to cry and raised one hand to touch the cold breeze swirling around her head, still singing into the mic while sobbing. Emma nodded and smiled, too. Yeah, this party really was what Vicki wanted and there was no denying that Jason and Cassandra's daughter was having the time of her undead existence. Everybody who'd ever known her was there. I'd had to really dig into online records to find everyone she'd listed on the back of the napkin.

When the song was done, I looked up to see that Bruno was staring hard at something across the room. I followed his gaze to see John Creede sitting on the other side of the bar, next to Cassandra. They were really glaring daggers at each other and I nudged Bruno to get his attention. But he was lost in his own world, so I just shrugged and started to talk to Emma again. It was nice to be able to talk to her.

I tried to touch on the subject delicately. "Have you heard from Kevin?"

Emma shook her head, her face both concerned and sad.

"Not since he resigned from the university. But"—she reached into her pocket and pulled something out—"he left this on my desk. I completely forgot to give it to you."

It was a plain white envelope with my name printed on the front. I slit it open and looked inside. It held a yellow sticky note with two sentences written on it.

> *Lydia is first, then Erikson. I'll be back for you.*
> *Kevin*

I passed it to Emma to see, because she was twitching so much to know what was going on that she was about to climb over the table and grab the note anyway. She frowned, but then again, she didn't know about Jones's offer. I was a little worried about the *I'll be back for you* part. Was I the third "hard target" on the list and he was giving me advance warning? Or was it a warm and fuzzy confirmation that we'd see each other again?

"That's like Kevin. He thinks he's telling you the whole situation and it's only in his head." Emma shrugged, so I did, too, and then she changed the subject. "So, Matty really stood up for you in the hearing? I thought he couldn't stand you."

I nodded. "You and me both. He might not *like* me, but I think he respects me now. That's something."

She raised her glass and clinked it with mine. "To respect." I dipped my head in thanks and thought about Matteo at the courthouse. He'd seemed genuinely pleased to see me when I showed up, which surprised me. I doubt it made much impression on their mom, but she's a tough nut to crack. The hearts of her babies aren't to be trifled with. Like I consider either of her boys a *trifle*.

As if on cue, Bruno touched my arm. "C'mon. We need to talk." My brows rose at his very serious expression. Unfortunately, there weren't many places to go where we could be alone. After hurriedly telling Emma to watch our drinks, I stumbled away with Bruno pulling me forward by the elbow. We wound up in the ladies' room, because it was bigger than the men's.

"So what was all that about? What do you and John Creede have against each other? You were glaring at each other so hard, I was afraid I was going to have to stand between you like with preschoolers on the playground."

He reared back in surprise. "Glaring? We weren't glaring at each other. He was offering me a job." At my confused expression, Bruno tapped his temple. "He's a telepath, remember?"

Oh. Duh. "But you *have* a job. Didn't you submit to a binding oath to them?" Like the confidentiality oath, the noncompete oath prevented employees from moonlighting or being double agents. Nothing worse for a firm's reputation than an employee killing the client because he got a better offer from the bad guys. "Didn't you tell me once that your fingers would start to burn off before you could finish signing your name on another deal before the contract term was up?"

He tipped his head ruefully and crossed his arms over his chest, unconsciously hiding his hands from sight. "That is a point. But my current job is on the East Coast and the term is up at the end of the quarter. Creede's offering to make me the head of the L.A. office. It's less money, but—" He raised his brows significantly. "It's just down the road from here. What do you think?"

My jaw dropped far enough to feel cool air on my fangs. "Are you asking my opinion? On your career?"

He shrugged and started to fiddle with the button on the wall-mounted hand dryer, tracing the edge of the square over and over before he answered. "I don't really know. It just came up and I thought . . . I really didn't like you facing that demon alone. You were lucky and you know it. And it's not the only one out there—"

I took a deep breath and let it out slow. We both knew something big was happening, which was why the Vatican had been beefing up on warrior priests.

The door opened before I could reply. Dottie walked in and reared back in surprise to see a man in the bathroom. He blushed as she let out a little squeak. I grabbed Bruno's arm to push him out of the room and had started to follow, thinking about what to say to his offer, when Dottie tapped me on the shoulder. Her face showed that she was eager to talk to me, so I said, "Be right out, Bruno. Keep my drink cold."

"I'll ask Vicki to spin by the table again. Sure is saving on ice having her here."

When the door closed and the music faded somewhat, Dottie smiled. "I'm so glad you survived, my dear. I was *very* worried when I saw the demon in your future. But I just couldn't tell you." She seemed both embarrassed and afraid.

I gave her a small smile. "It's okay, Dottie. I understand. I was friends with Vicki long enough to know how hard it is for clair-voyants to live with what they see. It doesn't always come—"

"—true. Precisely. If I told you *everything* I saw, either you'd not believe me or you'd want to rush it . . . or, worse, ignore the signs. But that's not what I'm here to ask you about."

I raised my brows and leaned back against the sink. I should have looked first, because I felt cool water from the last hand washer wet the back of my shirt.

"You know that Mr. Gibson died."

I nodded. "He was a good man. I'm glad he died in the line of duty. He would've wanted it that way."

She sighed. "There was nothing to be done. I think he probably didn't move fast enough . . . intentionally. But he was taking care of Minnie for me, and now that I'm back in the housing project I was hoping—"

Minnie the Mouser. I'd forgotten about the cat. Birchwoods allows pets. I'd even thought about buying a pup for Vicki at one point but never got around to it.

"I've read that cats don't seem to have the same problems with vampires that dogs do. In fact, I saw her sitting on your lap in a vision, and you were petting her just the way she likes. Since you haven't met her yet, I thought that perhaps—"

A cat. I've never considered a cat, but they do purr and I like things that purr. I don't know why the words came out of my mouth, but, "I'd be happy to keep her. Provided you visit her from time to time if I have to go out of town."

She beamed and promised to call, then pranced to a stall. I walked out of the room to the happy yells of another piñata being beaten to a pulp. Every half hour or so one would start to spin and dance in the air. Vicki was choosing the victims and then someone would grab a stick and start to pound away.

I noticed Dawna sitting in the corner and started to go over to talk—but she saw me coming and got up, hurrying off in the opposite direction. That hurt. A lot. I hate that she's avoiding me. Bubba says she feels guilty. Lilith got the information on where to find me from her. I don't blame her. Nobody could stand up to that level of mental manipulation. Hell, I'm just grateful she's still alive.

I glanced over at the corner of the bar. Seems the good doctor is quite a darts player—if the grin and the green pieces of paper crossing his palm were any indication. I made a decision and headed that way, with a wave of my hand to tell Bruno I was going to be another minute.

"Dr. Scott? Can I talk to you for a second?"

He clapped a man I didn't know on the shoulder and nodded. He sat down at the only free table in the place and looked me over carefully. "Is everything okay? The stress getting to you?"

I let out a harsh laugh. "I'm fine. After the past few days this is hardly what I'd call *stressful*. But thanks for asking. No." I carefully pointed my thumb toward where Dawna was sitting at a different table chatting with Emma. "See that woman over there? Her name is Dawna Long. She's a friend of mine and the receptionist at my office building. Remember I told you about the vampire, Lilith?" He nodded and I took a deep breath. "Lilith tracked me down by attacking Dawna on her way out of the parking lot at work. She didn't kill her, but the bite and the psychic trauma have been devastating. I don't know if she'll ever be able to come back to the office. Is there any way you could talk to her a little? I know you're not really here for *business*, but—"

His face grew concerned and he looked at her the same

way he'd looked at me. Then he frowned. "Actually, business is *exactly* why I'm here. And you're correct. She's not dealing with things very well. Very close to suicidal, actually. I appreciate your bringing it to my attention."

Suicidal? Crap. I hadn't realized it was that bad. I felt sick to my stomach and wanted to race over to her to try to make it better. But the fact that she hadn't already sought me out . . . no, it was best if this was dealt with by a professional. "I don't know if she has the money to afford you, though. We pay her pretty well, but you guys *are* sort of pricey."

"I'm sure we can work something out." He added, quickly, "Now, if you'll excuse me." I looked across the room. Dawna stood up, looking dejected, terrified, and nearly angry. Dr. Scott rose smoothly and touched my hand. "We'll talk more later. Right now, I think I need to speak to your friend before she does something she'll regret."

I stared after them until I saw that he'd caught up with her and offered his arm with a kind smile. She hesitated, then accepted, and they stepped outside into the cool night. I caught a glimpse of the entrance that told me that the police department had added another two uniformed officers to the contingent at the door. Probably not the best advertisement for the business, but I . . . or, rather, *Vicki* was paying through the nose to rent the whole place for the night, so it was really nobody's business.

I slid back into my chair after a few dodges around the newest piñata to fall. "Did I miss anything?" Emma and Bruno shook their heads, each lost in their own thoughts as another round of firecracker mouth candy exploded in unison. This batch appeared to be glowing in the dark, because green and pink sparkles began to fill the air as people walked around the room. I would rather not know what ingredient would cause glowing sparkles, and I certainly didn't want to put it in my mouth.

A little chirping sound caught my ear from my wristwatch. It was 1:00 A.M.—last call. La Cocina had always shut down in plenty of time for the 2:00 liquor cutoff. They do a first-last call and a last-last call, so that all cups were off the tables by 1:30. It was time for the toast.

I stood up and shouted over the laughing, yelling crowd, "Hey! Hey, everybody. Listen up!"

Nobody responded.

After two more attempts with my still-hoarse throat, Bruno stood up. He put his two baby fingers between his lips and let out a blast of noise that stopped all sound in the place and caused the front doors to open—revealing officers with guns drawn. Bruno ignored them and shouted, "Celia wants to talk. It's time for the toast."

Everybody nodded and gathered round our table. I thought about going up onstage and getting the microphone, but with everyone quiet, it should be fine.

"First, thank you all for—" I coughed, cleared my throat, and took another sip of margarita. "Thank you all for coming. As you know, this is a triple wake. Some of you are here to offer fond farewells to Vicki Cooper, some for Bob Johnson, and some for Karl Gibson. They were all great people, and I was proud to know them."

There were a few "Hear, hear!" comments from the back of the crowd.

"We're honored to have Vicki attend her own wake." Confetti

and cool air began to swirl around my head and I smiled. "Few people ever get the chance to hear how people feel about them after they're dead. So, I'm going to open the floor to let you all tell her directly how you felt, how she made a difference in your life, and why you'll miss her."

A woman's voice I didn't recognize came from the farthest row of people. "You could always drink me under the table, Vic! Only person to ever have done it! You rocked!"

General laughter erupted and then Larry Davers, an old friend from our freshman year, spoke up, his voice serious and cracking with emotion. "You saved my life, Vicki, and I never thanked you. You insisted I not ditch chemistry to go skiing because you saw that something bad was going to happen. I was pissed that you kept following me, pulling my arm. I finally got mad when you threatened to turn me in and went to class with you. And then the avalanche hit, on the very slope I was going to use, and killed those rangers. I would have been out there, too. I would have died if you hadn't made me listen. Thank you . . . on behalf of myself, my wife, and the children I never would have had." Confetti rained down on him and he laughed through his tears as he pulled a dark-haired woman close and kissed her.

More people started to talk, one on top of the other—telling stories of Vicki saving them, or setting them up with the person they'd wind up marrying, or just hanging out and having fun. There was a little piece of me that was surprised by how many people she'd affected. There's always a part of you that thinks you know your best friend better than anyone . . . and yet there were dozens of people here whom I'd never known she knew.

A woman named Laura was just explaining how Vicki had

saved her when the music started to play again. We looked up
to see if it was Vicki doing it, but instead, we saw a drop-dead
gorgeous woman in a slinky black dress pick up the microphone. She began to sing, and every person in the place turned
as one. It was the theme song from *The Phantom of the Opera*
and she was not only singing on-key but also quite possibly
singing it better than the Broadway version.

As everyone stared at her, completely entranced, the only
thing I could think was how indescribably *rude* it was to interrupt the eulogies. Even Vicki was annoyed and began to pick
up larger objects, not just confetti but candles from the tables
and sharp cutlery. But although the ghostly wind tried to heave
them at the singer, Vicki never connected. It was as though the
singer was immune to the missiles.

When she finished her song minutes later, the place erupted
into applause, with the exception of me, Bruno, Alex, and a few
others, who glared at the intruder with righteous indignation.
She had to be an intruder, because I hadn't remembered seeing her as I passed around the room earlier. And I *would* have
noticed her.

She slunk down from the stage, the spotlight turning her
luxurious red mane of hair into something fluid and shimmery
as she walked. The crowd parted as she passed and she did it
with the air of a goddess—as though she fully expected people
to part for her.

Of course, maybe she *was* royalty and I just didn't know it.
The king and his retinue had returned home to Rusland to
get ready for Prince Rezza's wedding. I'd been told to expect
an invitation, but the court refused to let me out of the country. I have it on good authority that the king has been putting

discreet pressure on our government to make sure I don't
wind up jailed or permanently institutionalized. I appreciate
that even more than the sizable deposit that was wired into my
bank account. Rezza's been rethinking his allegiance to a
group who'd hire a demon and kidnap his brother, which is
probably for the best. He might not be as big on the American
ideal as his father, but at least Rezza won't be a sworn enemy
if he winds up on the throne.

This woman had that same air—more like Rezza than his
father. Rezza's father felt more like a commoner than a king,
but Rezza had that *otherness* that made you want to bow or
grovel.

"You must be the abomination." The woman held out her
hand when she reached me.

I didn't take the offered limp fingers. "And *you* must be
rude." She reared back in surprise, like I'd intended. "I'm
sorry," I said with narrowed eyes and just a hint of fang showing (I'm learning how to do that better), "but didn't you hear
that people were trying to talk over here—trying to *honor* the
people we came here to celebrate? Just who do you think you
are?"

Now the eyes grew stormy. They looked a little like mine,
gray with swirls of blue and green. I felt pressure against my
head, as if someone were squeezing it with both hands. She
glared harder and the pressure grew. Bruno realized what was
happening but wasn't sure what to do about it. It didn't seem to
be any sort of spell, although she did have that *evil witch* look
about her. Sort of Jessica Rabbit meets Snow White's step-
mother.

"I *think* I am Princess Adriana Kalino, heir apparent of

the Pacific sirens. And I think *you* have just insulted me, abomination. What body part do you wish to lose to make reparations?"

Oh, fuck a duck. This was *not* how I imagined I was going to meet Granddad's side of the family. Most of the crowd started to move backward to get out of fallout range. Bruno stepped forward, being the nice guy he is, but I reached an arm back to stop him. Interestingly, John Creede also stepped forward, as did Emma and Alex. But I shook my head.

Two could play this game. "No . . . I didn't insult you. You stormed into a solemn occasion and decided to show off your body and voice for no good reason. I think that's rude in pretty much any culture. How do you plan to make reparations to *me*?"

She seemed taken aback at that, as though nobody had ever really stood up to her before. I was willing to be the first. "We have an impasse. Very well. Then we agree to battle to satisfy our grievances. At the stroke of ten, after you have appeared at your hearing before the Pacific lords on the Isle of Serenity to defend your right to exist, *and* if you survive, then we will fight to settle this."

Whoa, whoa! "Back up, Your Royal Siren-ness. What the hell are you talking about? What hearing, and who are the 'Pacific lords'? And where is the Isle of Serenity?"

She smiled, and while it was beautiful, it was also mocking. "Had you greeted me as a siren princess is entitled, I would feel inclined to answer your questions. As it is—" She shrugged. "I can be every bit as stubborn as you appear to be. When you complete your court-ordered stay in the treatment facility, you will be *collected* to appear for the hearing."

She turned on her heel and started to walk back through the crowd, slinking and twitching those perfectly formed hips. As hard as I tried to follow so I could kick that perfect ass into next Tuesday, I couldn't. My feet flat wouldn't move. Bruno either couldn't move, either, or chose not to, since he was squeezing my arm in a signal not to follow her. Maybe he was stopping me.

Or maybe *she* was.

Not good.

Just before she walked out the double doors, which two officers in tan were holding for her with the rapt expression of starving puppies, she turned and raised one brow. "If I were you, I'd use my time in the treatment facility to study siren culture and heritage. Perhaps once you understand why you have to die, you'll do the honorable thing and commit suicide. Otherwise, we'll simply kill you." She smiled pleasantly to the rest of the crowd—most of whom smiled back. "Please, the rest of you enjoy the remainder of the party. You might include the hostess in your remembrances. This may be the last time you'll see her alive."

Another smile that was a chilly baring of teeth was directed to me. "The next time we meet, dear cousin, will be the last."

Dear *cousin*?

Well . . . shit. Didn't *my* life just suck moss-covered swamp rocks?